Michael Scott Rohan was born in Edinburgh in 1951, of a French father and Scottish mother, and educated at the Edinburgh Academy and St Edmund Hall, Oxford. He is the author of eleven fantasy and science fiction novels, including the award-winning Winter of the World trilogy, and co-author of three more, as well as several non-fiction books. His books are published in the USA, Japan, Israel, Russia and throughout Europe. Besides writing novels he has been a *Times* columnist, edits reference books, reviews CDs, videos and opera for *Classic CD* and other magazines, plays with longbows and computers, drinks beer, eats Oriental food, keeps up with hobbies including archaeology and palaeontology, sings, argues and travels a lot. After many years in Oxford and Yorkshire, he and his American wife Deborah now live in a small village near Cambridge, next to the pub.

The Singer and the Sea

A Winter of the World Novel

Michael Scott Rohan

ORBIT

First published in Great Britain by Orbit 1999

Copyright © Michael Scott Rohan 1999

The moral right of the author has been asserted.

A CIP catalogue record for this book is available from the British Library.

ISBN 1 85723 741 2

Typeset by Solidus (Bristol) Limited
Printed and bound in Great Britain by
Mackays of Chatham PLC

Orbit
A Division of
Little, Brown and Company (UK)
Brettenham House
Lancaster Place
London WC2E 7EN

For Len and Minna Scott

Acknowledgements

As ever, to esteemed editors Tim, Colin and Lisa, for all manner of arcane things. To Allan Scott and Mark Funnell, for much corner-fighting on my behalf. To Olga Nikiforovna, for infectious Russian enthusiasm. And once again to my wife Deb, without whom …

The songs on pages 81 and 300-1 are, respectively, freely inspired by Swedish verses by Bo Bojesson, and my translation of a Finnish folksong.

Contents

N

THE ICE

NORDENEY

Harthaby
The
Starkenfells
Asenby
Nordenbergen

Athalby

TAOUNE 'LA-AN-ARATHANS

Rasby

Saldenborg

Thuneborg

MENETH SCAHAS

River Gathriel
R. Kestrllenei

THE GREAT FOREST

Tensborg
Randeby

Dunmarhas

Debatable Lands
Corsair's Fortress

The
Marshlands

Kermorvan's Tower
Ker an Aruel

MENETH AITHEN

(TAPIAU 'LA-AN-AITHEN)

Iylan
Irmelet

Armen

Forest
(Aithennec)

The Shield Range

Ker Bryhaine

Cogh 'An Orhy

Anlaithann

Bryhannec

THE WASTES

BRYHAINE

THE ISLANDS

Marshlands
Forest
--- High Roads

Miles
0   500

CHAPTER ONE
Ancient Music

IT was the stirring of the warm body at his side that woke him, and the shifting of the furs that covered them. She had flung her arm over her eyes, leaving one breast bare above the covers, the nipple firm in the chill air. He reached out sleepily to caress it where the growing light suffused it, cupping the warm skin against the cold. She stretched and mumbled with drowsy pleasure. Then she sat bolt upright, the covers falling, her long brown hair flying. 'You've got to get up!' she gasped. 'To go! My brothers will be up and about.'

Gille laughed, though softly. 'Those slugabeds? And what would send them barging in here? They'll be out counting the fowls and milking the bull - whilst you and I cuddle up snug and silent and loving…'

She squirmed lazily under his hands, then pushed him away. 'Go on, I said! You don't know what they might do!'

Gille did not; but he could guess, and let himself be pushed. His resistance had been mostly for form's sake, and he suspected she knew it. 'Till three nights hence, then! While they're off to market. Or would you come to town some day sooner?'

She shivered. 'No! That'd be too risky. Folk would see!'

He rubbed her naked back. 'There's the Icebreath in this breeze. Let them see! We're to be married one day, aren't we?'

'Yes!' She gave in to the rubbing, with a little breathless laugh. 'Yes, surely. But they'd still talk! Three days, dearest—' She smiled, her plump cheeks dimpling wildly, and reached out to cup him in her turn. 'It'll give you time to revive.'

He landed a smacking kiss. 'For you, Utte my honeycake, no need!' he said ardently; but he was already hauling his shirt over his head, and wriggling it into his breeches. A cock crowed, and he reached hastily for his sword-belt and short tunic, laid across the chest that was all the room's furnishings, save the carven bedstead and chair. Cautiously he opened the shutters, and, blowing the girl a kiss, hopped nimbly out on to the sill and caught hold of the eaves.

Gille was not an especially brave man, but swinging his way hand over hand along the ends of the beams caused him no concern. He was used to it by now. This was the kind of derring-do the bold lovers of the romances took in their stride, and he gave no thought to the drop of three times his height. The tall poles in the vegetable patch below became sentries' spears, the pig sty beyond a deadly swamp. It pleased his humour, and added a spice to the affair that he felt it otherwise rather lacked.

So the Chronicles speak of him, a man of some thirty-two years, darkly handsome, bright-eyed, small in stature, still young by the reckoning of his time, younger still in looks, and, as so often follows, in his thoughts and actions. He reached the end of the wall, swung himself down, dropped lightly on to the stable roof and padded easily along the steep gable, freed of frost by the warmth that rose from the gathered beasts below. He jumped down on to the surrounding wall of coarse stone and ran across to the old steading where he had tethered his own mount, with the blankets, hay and water Utte had left. They were needed, even in this burgeoning spring; for in the North no night was warm, amid the unending Winter of the World.

He led the horse briskly some way along the wall before mounting, out of sight of the tall shutters. Outlying farms, beyond town walls, needed walls of their own, even in peaceful times, and this was the largest manor hereabouts, a rich estate with four or five tenant farms. Nothing to what he had seen in the South, of course; but Utte's brothers were not lords, and their tenants were free men. He liked the place; he liked them, for that matter, in their stolid ways. He liked Utte - well, more than any woman else in a long while. There would always be other girls, was his usual thought; but now he was increasingly inclined to wonder about one other, one different from all the rest, a soulmate, an ideal. Not Utte, of course. Bouncy, bright little thing, altogether too ordinary. He felt at home with her, certainly. He could feel at home here; it was like his father's steading, only here he would not be the middling and least valued of many sons. So why was he so eager to get away?

Perhaps he was just beginning to feel shut in. The memories of his prentice days drifted back to him, and his great journey, hauled the length of two lands by his former master, in and out of scrape and skirmish, of corsair lair and sothran citadel... He sighed. Half the time he had been scared and half starved, but this was not one of his more realistic moments. He thought back to the warm and wealthy Southlands, with their tall red-haired women - not at all like these little local butterballs, delightful though they were - and heady wines. His grand constant dream of going back there, of leading a trading trip and making his fortune, came flooding back to him; but so did the unlikeliness of its ever coming true.

He sent the horse cantering easily across the

half-ploughed fields, keeping to the margins and the windbreak trees, still out of sight. A thought came to him as he reached the wide meadows fringing the Wold, and he unhitched the crossbow at his saddle. He feared no pursuit; but there might be rabbits out breakfasting, and he had a use for a free breakfast of his own. So it was that, once away from the house, he rode more slowly, and scouted the grey-green slopes for movement, watching carefully the line where they stood out against the slaty sea and sky beyond, so clear in the low pale light that every tuft and tussock showed, and every twitch of a leaf or grass blade. It was thus that the chase caught his eye.

A sail billowed there, a common sight so near the port of Saldenborg. Gille was no great seaman, but he had been aboard ships often enough to realise that this one was running fast with the rolling iron-grey waves, careless of their buffets, kicking up great fans of spray as it smashed their crests. Then, as the waves dipped a moment, the reason became obvious, a long, low dark streak lancing through the troughs astern, its single mast bare. A galley; and one that would not raise a sail in this brisk breeze. Therefore, most likely, a corsair galley. A desperate one, to pursue a prey so near a port; but they had been starved of late, with the Marchwarden Kunrad, Gille's old master, harrying them in their marshland lairs. He shaded his eyes, trying to judge. They were not such fools, either, the sea-wolves; they would overhaul that wallowing great merchantman long before it came in hail of the town, and the watch was probably asleep. No boat could get out to the prey in time, not against the wind. But if it were coming from astern ...

He looked down the coast, to the little fishing village that nestled in the crook of the cliff. He could be there in minutes, though the road was

steep. He wasted no more time thinking. The village
Headman would surely have a good boat, if nobody
else. The horse skidded and slipped on the stony
path, but Gille held him to his fast trot, grimacing
at the drop that opened alongside. He had been
aboard a ship taken by corsairs; he hated the memory. The wood-tiled rooftops rose below his feet like
the backs of scaly sea-creatures beached in the cove,
faint wisps of smoke curling up from night-damped
fires. There was a wooden palisade at the narrow
foot of the path, the watchman nodding on his
perch above the gate; but when he heard the
hooves, and Gille shouting about corsairs, he sprang
up so fast he almost fell over it. The gate opened,
and Gille cantered into the little square beyond.
Without dismounting, his horse panting steam, he
seized the bar from the heavy steel triangle that
hung there and rattled it frantically.

The metal was old and rusty, but there was
a virtue in it he could see, that commanded awakening and heeding. The jangle echoed between the cliff
walls as if twenty alarms were sounding, and within
a moment a tall grizzled man in a fur-trimmed robe
came rushing out on to the gallery of the largest
and most freshly painted house. 'What's this?' he
rasped. 'Be you piss-headed, boy?' Then, seeing Gille's
black tunic, and the gold trimmings at the neck, he
ducked his head. 'Sorry there, Mastersmith! We have
problems now and again, y'see…'

'I can guess!' wheezed Gille, waving towards
the sea. He kicked his leg over the pommel and slid
down on to the stony earth. 'But we've got another
now!'

It took only a moment for the Headman to
grasp the situation; and by then others could see it
too. Within minutes there was a general rush down
to the shore, with the Headman still hitching up his
oilcloth trousers. 'Can you do anything?' coughed

Gille, wishing he had shouted a little less.

'Maybe! Good that you came to us, Master, and not to the town. That was in your mind, was't? You'll have some sea lore, then. We stand best chance of overhaulin 'em ere they reach the middle o' the bay, in my little *Sea Mare*.'

Gille gaped as he saw the long, low craft lying alongside the rickety jetty. But for its cheerful green paint and lack of mast, it could have been a smaller cousin of the sleek predator out there. 'Like her, do you?' grinned the Headman, displaying a graveyard of stained teeth. 'Bought her as a prize, after an encounter five summers back, damaged somewhat. We could set her aright without costly shipwrights, see?'

'What in Hella's name d'you fish for in *that?*'

'Oh, you'd be surprised, Mastersmith. Mortal fast some fishies are – ever see a marlin, to be sure?'

Gille never had, and didn't want to. The most likely use for such a craft was casual smuggling, probably to avoid road tolls and town tithes; the green paint would be concealment in a light summer sea. Not that it was any of his business, anyhow. The Headman swung aboard, and offered him a hand. Gille hesitated, as fishy-smelling bodies barged past him.

'Nay, come, sir, and welcome, you all hot for the scrap with that bow o' yours!' Gille grimaced, but let himself be swung aboard. He had feared to leave the valuable bow on his saddle, that was all. But there was no way to back out of this without shaming himself.

'I'll take an oar!' he said, lingering in the safer stern. 'I've rowed in attack before!' He winced at the memory.

'Nay, nay, sir!' beamed the Headman. 'Making a master row, what'd folk say? Up you come to the bow with me! Hurry aboard there, lads, come on, and Sarre, there, do you give the master some bolts for his bow now. All aboard? Got the helm there, Erke? Then cast off, forrard!' He seized a huge boathook and pushed off from the jetty. 'Heave now! And heave!'

The narrow boat was well laden, with fisherfolk crouching between the rowers and on the cargo platforms, waving a fiendish array of weapons from bows like Gille's to boarding pikes and steel-toothed rakes. The lean craft wallowed and flexed alarmingly in the swell, but the oars bit, the carved bow dipped and rose, and suddenly the waves were not smashing against it but lifting it and hurling it along at a drastic speed. The rowers broke into a hoarse chant, and almost at once they were passing the point and out into the bay. Gille, kneeling beside the Headman on boards glistening with dried scales, kept his grip firm on the gunwale and fought down his empty stomach. Spray slopped in and puddled, soaking his knees. The white sail seemed invisible at first, and he had a momentary twinge of alarm - had it already been taken and hauled down? Or capsized, in a wild manoeuvre? But then, as the *Sea Mare* climbed one high crest, he saw it again, taut and strained as the merchant ship sought for speed. Against it, very close now as it seemed, the thin black mast whipped and rocked.

'If they could only get off on a tack,' shouted the Headman over the noise of the rowers and the creaking of rowlock and timber, 'they'd outrun the bastards for sure. But that'd be out to sea, and then the bastards could hoist sail too, and cut 'em off ...'

'Of course!' agreed Gille, as confidently as he could. 'How long—'

'Not long,' grinned the Headman tautly. 'Maybe half an hour, less. And they won't be expecting us, with no masthead to make out.'

'And what then? What's our best plan?'

'Plan? Bless you, Master, we need no plan! We up and tear straight into 'em! We ram!'

Gulping, Gille looked down over the bow. There it was, breaching the black water on the end of the main keel timber, a shining steel staff tipped with a cluster of spikes like a chicken's claw, flinging spray in all directions. Shining indeed to the eyes of a true smith, for the metal coursed and ran with the strange virtues one such could set within it, like rippling sheets of lightning ensnared, cold as the Northlights over the distant Ice. 'Looks well made,' he ventured.

'Glad t' have your word on that, Master, for what it cost! See there, they're closing! Heave now! Heave!'

Gille could only cling on through that wild ride, jamming himself with knees and elbows to avoid being flung out as the bows plunged, desperately wishing himself snugly back in Utte's bed. He clutched his bow close, though, and thrust the bolts firmly into his belt. Face this armed, if he had to, was all his thought. The longboat lanced across the waves, and time seemed to lose all meaning with the sea-roar in his ears.

Then, all too suddenly, the bulk of the merchantman was before him, with the sail no longer taut but billowing and flapping in panic; and alongside it the black shark shape, and figures swarming off it up the curving planks and boiling on to the deck. The Headman shouted something, and the rowers gave a single gasping grunt as they leant still heavier upon their oars. Gille remembered the crossbow, and struggled frantically to draw it as the *Sea Mare* sprang forward under the quickening pace. The Headman was roaring directions, and the wind carried the sound of their coming to the corsairs. Those still in the boat looked around in surprise and panic, and shouted to those attacking.

Some went on climbing unheeded, others, looking back, dropped down into their craft in disorder. Oars were unshipped as they sought to escape the longboat bearing down on them, but it was too late. Gille struggled to aim, then gave up and threw himself down. The *Sea Mare*'s bow lanced into the corsair's stern, and the ram sang like a striking arrow as it bit into the planking and carried away the rudder in a shower of splinters.

The corsair craft heeled wildly with the impact, flinging men into the sea, and there was screaming turmoil. A wild-looking figure sprang up on to their bow, aiming a spear. Gille, sprawling below, could hardly miss. The bolt vanished into the man's body, and he was hurled sideways out of sight. The fishermen cheered wildly, and sent a small shower of bolts past Gille as he sat up, some so ill-aimed that they thudded into the wood around him. He flung himself forward to get out of the line of shot, a wave surged up and slapped him icily in the face, and he found himself half sprawling over the gunwales of both boats as they bobbed together. Another wave, and he fell headlong into the stern of the corsair craft, in a tangle of smelly bodies. The villagers, assuming he was leading an attack, surged after him with uncouth cries, loosing off bolts and striking out at any head that showed itself. A snarling face rose over Gille, a blade flashed, then fell limply as somebody's spear butt crashed into the back of the corsair's neck. The other corsairs Gille had fallen among lay sprawled and twitching now. The fight had rolled on, and nobody was bothering him. He scrambled up, drew his bow again and shot at the most obvious corsair in sight, a tall copper-skinned Northerner shouting by the mast. Gille was a good shot; the man sagged, pinned to the timber.

There had been few corsairs left in the boat,

after the impact fewer still; but now those on the merchantman's deck saw the new danger, and came swarming back. Too late: the villagers' rush had carried them to the side, and they were striking at the reivers even as they leaped, casting them into the water that churned between the hulls. Gille loosed, caught one, who fell like a sack, then missed two more as their landing made the boat heel again. The remaining corsairs tried to counterattack, but the *Sea Mare's* rowers, having got their breath, were quitting their benches and charging aboard to join the fun, as they seemed to find it.

Gille could no longer get a clear shot, and his fingers were tired. He drew his short sword, nervously; he had not used one in anger for years, and had never been very adept. A corsair with an axe swung at him, Gille parried, they both missed and fell heavily into one another in stinking bilgewater. Gille hit him with the crossbow, the corsair howled and kicked Gille's thigh, lashed out with the axe, missed again, and Gille punched him ineffectually in the nose, then bit his filthy ear. It tasted horrible. The corsair jumped up with a scream and fell backwards over the gunwale. Perhaps somebody had hit him with something; it made little difference, with the hulls grinding against one another as they were.

Spitting and shaking, Gille scrambled up and retrieved his sword and bow. There seemed to be no more corsairs about, and a lot of water around his ankles; the rammed boat was beginning to founder. A few fisherfolk were having wounds bound up, but there looked to be nothing too serious. The Headman was busy in the stern, organising makeshift repairs lest this new prize slip through his fingers. On the merchantman's deck above, the row had died down to a few snarling voices, captured corsairs by the sound of it. Gille sat down unsteadily on the heaving gunwale, slightly faint with the sensation of having once again survived some horrible tangle. Sickness, relief, a little giddy; he tittered slightly, then caught hold of himself.

'Ahoy below!' boomed a voice. Gille jerked to his feet. A burly-looking man was leaning over the merchantman's rail. A sothran, by the accent, and the dark red streaks in the dishevelled grey hair, caught back in a tail behind. He spoke the Northern tongue with a rolling burr. 'You the skipper o' that little beauty? My thanks!'

'No, I!' called the Headman cheerfully, then, because it was always a good idea to be fair to a smith, 'Twas the Master there as raised the alarm, though. And led the boarding.'

Gille bowed. If that was how it looked, he was not one to argue.

'Then I'm deeply obliged to the both of you, sirs. Tanle Athlannyn of Bryhannec, Master of the Mariners' Guild, owner and skipper of the *Ker Dorfyn*, for to serve you.'

'Gille Kilmarsson, Master of the Smiths' Guild, desires your further acquaintance.'

He and Gille saluted one another, as was proper for masters even from different countries, while the Headman looked on wryly at the antics of educated men. 'Best we make straight for harbour, I think,' said Tanle. 'I'll be honoured to entertain you gentlemen aboard.'

'I thank you, sir, but we need to make this shark seaworthy again,' said the Headman. 'And get our wounded home.'

'Take your time,' said Tanle. 'There's a few things we may attend to meantime. And you, Master?'

Gille, thinking of breakfast, scrambled for the rope ladder that was cast down to him. But something else fell with a rattling thud further along. It was a body, on a rope, and its boots scrabbled briefly against the hull. Gille swallowed. From the other side came more shouts and thuds, and bodies rose kicking to dangle from the mainyard in the morning sun. Tanle was clearly a man who wasted no time attending to things. Gille's appetite vanished.

'Best I reclaim my horse,' said Gille. 'We'll ride over and see you docked.'

'We'll open a choice bottle or three,' called Tanle. 'Till then, sirs!'

Gille bowed and turned, to find the Headman cheerfully unsticking the body of the corsair he had shot from the mast. 'A Northern man!' he growled, waggling the lolling face at Gille. He deftly relieved the body of its jewellery and a purse. 'Never like to see one of ours among these sea-scavengers, let alone leading 'em! Funny thing, though – these earrings and a necklace, not like I've ever seen anyone wear. And he's all over scars – deliberate ones, like. Patterns.'

'An offcomer, maybe,' shuddered Gille. That was the not unkindly name Northerners gave to the copper-skinned refugees who sometimes appeared from a far land across the ocean, fugitives from the Ice and its murderous votaries. 'Newly arrived from over sea, fell in with a bad crowd. I've heard there have been some new ones coming over of late – another conquest for the Ice, maybe.'

'Well,' said the Headman decisively, 'this one could have saved himself the trip.' He heaved the corpse over the side with a splash.

By the time they came to town the harbour was already bustling, and most of all around the new arrival. The fight and rescue had been seen from the shore, and an idling crowd had gathered around the wharf where the *Ker Dorfyn* was tied up, young men pointing at the ugly black shapes swinging from its yardarm, and children staring open-mouthed. Executions were rare in the close-knit Northern communities, and were never public. Gille and the Headman had to push their horses through.

Tanle was waiting for them by the gangplank, grinning widely all over his freckled face. 'Our gallant rescuers!' he boomed, and the idlers cheered. 'Come, sirs, have you broken fast? Only a bite, surely.' He led them to a table on the open deck, now clear and sunlit. 'While we have fine sothran meats and pickles, and fresh bread hot from your market, and rare fruits of the deep South, and wines – by the hot Sun that Raven stole for us, such wines!'

He was a generous host, and Gille, who for some time past had been living on plain, afford-able fare, managed to ignore the swinging shadows above, and take full advantage. 'Fighting gives a man an appetite!' he declaimed, feeling it sounded like the sort of thing he ought to say. He was feeling absurdly pleased with himself.

'Well,' laughed Tanle, drinking deep, 'eat your fill and more, sir, for without you we'd have been feeding the sharks, surely. Whence came those bastards, anyhow? I'd heard this Marchwarden Conreid, or whatever his name is, had cleared the Norrard Way of them.'

Gille smiled easily, stroking the elegant wisp of beard on his chin. 'Kunrad. He has indeed, as I can say, for I was once his prentice, and helped him to his high place.' The others looked suitably impressed, and the onlookers, hanging on their every word, murmured. 'There's always a few vul-tures, though, lurking here or there. No threat, save to ships lone or lost, and never yet as bold as today. You were unlucky, that's all.'

'Lucky, rather, that we had you on hand. His prentice, you say? Then I can believe what's said of your master! I knew he was a Northerner born, but a mastersmith, eh?' He shook his head. 'So, then. You've saved my ship, my stock, and all our lives, bar a couple. Tanle's known throughout Ker Bryhaine as a man who pays his debts! You, Headman, you have that slick demon's skiff of theirs, and well earned, but I give you some ballast to it!' He fished out a purse that hung heavy, and put it into the delighted Headman's hands. 'But you, sir – how shall I reward you? I doubt that a mastersmith lacks for much here, if all they say is true.'

Gille shrugged modestly, but was careful to say nothing. 'I must give you something, sir!' pressed Tanle. 'Why, the pick of my stock—'

'That's very generous of you, Captain Tanle!' said Gille, loudly enough to be heard, and wrung his hand. 'More than I deserve, I'm sure!'

Tanle's genial expression stiffened ever so slightly, the look of a man who might just have made a very expensive mistake. Gille could almost read his thoughts. He was far from home, and had to deal with people here to make his profits. It would not do to let the word go round that he had failed to reward his rescuer. His foot traced the shadows as they swung. And there was honour. He did have much to be grateful for ...

'Then do you pick any piece as takes your fancy!' he boomed, and could not help adding, 'Any one piece ...'

He clearly resolved to make the best of it, and added, 'Sit you at your ease here, and we'll parade the best of it for your pleasure.' And, incidentally, for the watchers. Word would get around, and customers.

Gille bowed, and murmured something suitable, while Tanle gave his orders. The first items up were fabrics, stored well above the water line, bales of fine sothran linen that dazzled in the sun, strong hemp cloth, soft wools of Northern growth, but subtly spun and woven, dyed with richly glowing colours, silks and satins that seemed to flow like liquid, stiff embroidered brocades. Gille was politely loud in their praise, but he made no choice. Then came foodstuffs, spices and sugars in great quantities, long-lived cakes and sweetmeats made from them, sothran wines of the mellow vintages that were making his head spin, stronger burnt liquors, sweet and potent. 'High prices they'll command, too,' murmured Tanle happily. 'Some of your merchants' and Guildsmen's wives'll pay a small fortune to put what's hard to come by on their boards! Perhaps your good lady – no? Ah, well. Next, now, next we have glass – well packed, to be sure, well nigh a hundred cases—'

Goblets and pitchers winked in the sun, stained in deep shades, cut in facets like glittering gems. The Headman was dazzled by these bright gauds, so unlike the rough utensils of his village life, and Tanle gave him a tankard – an especially robust one, noted Gille, suitable for such uses. An honourable man, clearly, and his conscience plucked at him a little for taking advantage, but he guessed the most valuable stuff would be left till last. So it proved, for Tanle was carrying a load of furniture, new and antique. For woodwork, carving, inlays, rare woods and finishes, graceful mouldings and shapes that gratified the eye, sothran craftsmen were renowned; and this stuff was unusually fine. Gille caressed the chests they brought out on deck, fingered the fine chairs with their scrolled arms, traced the gold inlay on long dining tables polished to a glassy shine, and came close to breaking Tanle's heart as he paused to admire a huge and ornate dresser. But it was only to peer at a wide box, a flattened triangle of rich red-hued wood, strapped inside the top, so as to protect it.

'Captain, what's this?'

'*That?* Why, Master, let me show you—' The merchant captain was trembling with so much relief he could hardly undo the knots. 'Very old, so I'm told, and well crafted; but very fine still. Something you folk in the North call – what is it?'

'A *kantel*,' murmured Gille, cradling the lustrous wood in his arms, admiring the sheen of the thick lacquer and the silver inlays, the carven fingerboards and silvered steel endpieces, in which the ornate bridges were set. Built to last and to travel, evidently. He ran his fingers idly across the strings, and nodded. 'A kind of dulcimer, in the South. Fine tone, as you say.' He plucked a string or two, hastily tuned them by ear, tuned a couple more, then picked out a short measure or two with the abalone-shell plectrum dangling from a scrap of wire. The broad fingerboard at the left gave suddenly under his grip, and he panicked for an instant as the string tension changed and the sound with it, fearing the shell had broken. Then he laughed; the strings had changed their pitch, that was all. The fingerboard was some sort of ingenious device that shifted one bridge, and with it the tension of all the strings equally, so you could change key as you played. It had been stuck at first, that was all; probably not used for years, but it moved smoothly enough now. This was the sort of instrument he would have liked to make. He peered through the fretted hole into the wide soundbox. It was finished as beautifully within, with a liner of aged parchment. There seemed to be something written there, but he could not read it. These things were made in both Northland and South; but if he was not mistaken...

Light flashed on the metal endpieces, threads of light like caged lightning; but neither the Headman nor Tanle seemed to see it. Northern, then; and strong, strong and complex virtues. Strange to find such things in a mere musical instrument. He turned it over, looking for a maker's mark. Then his own voice suddenly sounded unnatural in his ears, as if from a great distance. 'Captain, whence came this?'

'That? Oh well, that I had from a merchant who bought up an old house,' began Tanle eagerly. 'One that all the heirs of had died off, see? Last one of some mucky distemper on his country estate, see? Name of Keraldein. Hadn't been to town for maybe thirty years, his house falling into decay, nobody to claim it save some connection by marriage who has a better one, and sells off all save a few bits and bobs to this merchant. And he knows I'm seeking out good solid stuff for the North, so sells me a job lot and throws that in with it. Fond of music, are you then, Master?' he added tautly.

'Oh yes,' said Gille calmly. 'Very… Well, Master Tanle?'

'*That?* You want that? That's all? I mean, it's very fine, very old piece, very valuable … for a musical instrument.'

Gille nodded. 'That's all, Master.'

Tanle gave an almost hysterical little cackle, ridiculous in such a robust voice. 'And you'll have nothing else? Nothing more?' He gave a great swallow, and tugged at his long ponytail. 'Well, bugger me. Bugger me backwards through the bilges! I'll have no man say that Northmen are grasping, not in my hearing, never again!'

'Nor sothrans stingy?' grinned Gille. They roared with relieved laughter.

'Well, well,' wheezed Tanle. 'We must have another drink or two on that. And you, Headman? Put your tankard to the trial, eh? Northmen? Finest fellows alive, and I'll drink to that, don't care who hears it—'

When Gille reeled off the *Ker Dorfyn*, an hour

or two later, he wondered why the dock was going up and down. But he had the kantel hanging very carefully across his back, by a strap of the merchant's finest strong leather; and as he rode, swaying slightly, he felt its curved flank bump against him, gently, like a woman's, and thrilled to the faint reverberation.

When he came to his smithy, set high on the slope in the less expensive end of town, he dismounted carefully, and led his horse into the unkempt yard. Then he saw the other horse munching quietly at the manger there, and almost forgot himself as he dashed indoors.

'Olvar!' he shouted, to the huge dark man who was sitting by the hearth. 'How long have you been back?'

Olvar, draining a mug of thin ale, looked at him disapprovingly. 'About half an hour. Long enough to see your bed hadn't been slept in, unload the ore by myself, hear some strange gossip about you, and find out there wasn't a thing to eat in the house.'

Gille subsided. 'Yes. Sorry.'

'Run through the money I left?'

'Not quite. Almost.'

Olvar's heavy features lifted. He could almost have been smiling. 'Well, that's some achievement, anyhow. I didn't think it would last you half the month.' Gille snorted in outrage. 'You must have been going very short. Or, wait a minute, has little Utte been helping you out? Or Laris? Or what's-her-name the flesher's wife? Thought so. And the takings?'

'The trade hasn't been good. How'd you fare?'

'A bit better. The farmers along the road still need their ploughshares and axes and eating knives, kettles mended and so on. Tinker's work, but it mounts up. And I got the ore, with no adventures to speak of. Which I gather can't be said of you. What's this about chasing corsairs, anyhow? You hate boats. Trying to be like old Kunrad?'

Gille made some explanations, without trying to decorate them overmuch. Olvar knew him too well, from their prentice days together. The brown man nodded soberly. 'Kept your head for once. Not bad, laddie. And what reward did you wangle yourself from the grateful Master Tanle?'

This time Olvar blinked rapidly, and then seemed close to bursting. 'A bloody kantel? Are you mad, boy? Those sothran pedlars are rich as kings, and you saved it all for him! Could've picked yourself up a tidy little sum there, maybe a step on the way to that trading trip southward you're always on about. Drop in on Master Kunrad, maybe even get as far as sunny Ker Bryhaine again. And you tossed that away for a box of strings?'

For answer Gille swung the instrument around and ran his fingers over the strings, then followed up with the plectrum; and the smithy seemed to fill with the warmth of a Southland sun, rippling around the sooty walls like a breeze stirring leaves of vine and scented eucalyptus.

'I did,' said Gille. 'Picked myself up something, as you said.'

He upended the carcass, and held it out for Olvar. The big man hefted it gingerly, nodded in surprise, sniffed at the laquered wood that was much the same shade as his cheek. 'Well crafted, wood and metal both. No, beautifully, with those endpieces. Not a style I recognise; more sothran than northern, maybe. And old. All right, it's a nice piece, maybe worth a penny or two – for a jingle-kist.'

'That's pretty much what Tanle said,' Gille answered, relishing his moment. 'The style's much like the old late Morvan pattern, rich and subtle, like you've seen on those old eating-knives. Haven't looked at the maker's mark, have you?'

Olvar held the instrument in his huge paws and squinted. 'Mark? A master's piece, then, or a good journeyman's – hard to read, this! Worn with polishing, the style's odd; must be really old, then. Looks like – one character, an *ash* – or is it a *vay*...' Suddenly he was holding the instrument as if it might explode, or bite him. He looked up, stricken. 'Wait a minute. *Vayde?*'

Gille nodded brightly. 'Lord Vayde of Kerys his cantankerous, necromantic, sorcerous self. Over two hundred years gone, unless what the sothrans say about that creepy old tower of his is right. And that's not his master's seal, you'll note, it's his personal one. So the chances are this was his own instrument; they say he played beautifully. Uncannily beautiful. Might be fun to go down there and strum it on the tower battlements one night, eh?'

Olvar's narrowed eyes flickered. Such matters made him very unhappy. Gille took pity and retrieved the precious instrument, and the big man breathed more easily. '*Brrh!* Anvils of Ilmarinen, *Vayde*! Only once handled anything the old bugger made, and that those goblets of Lady Alais's – and them with his master's mark only. How could this Captain Tanle come by such a thing? Keraldein the family name? Doesn't sound properly sothran ...' He thought for a moment. 'Ker Alvedan, could once have been – and Alvedan's a northern name. One of the stay-behinds, maybe, who had sothran kin to shield them. Vayde might have given one of his friends such a gift, to remember him by. Maybe foreseeing his death, as the tales say. We can look into that!' He rubbed his big hands. 'I take it back, friend. There's great men north and south who'd pay a small fortune to own Vayde's own kantel, though they could never play a note. Master Kunrad'd give you a small estate for it, maybe. And Tanle has only himself to blame for not investigating—'

'True, Olvar. I'm sure it's genuine; although…' He stroked the strings. 'A nice enough tone, but I might have expected something more … well, exciting. But genuine or not, I'm not selling it. I've always wanted a good one, and never been able to make one to suit me.'

Olvar, an unexcitable man from a stolid race, sprang up so fast he nearly fell into the forge. 'Man, are you daft? Could you not maybe buy a thousand kantels for what that'd fetch, with tone as fine as you like? Kit us out for that little trading trip indeed, and make our fortunes at last? Or are you so happy with our rich living that you're afraid to wallow in luxury?'

'No. But this is the only thing so rare I'm ever likely to have. And I earned it hard, Olvar - all the harder for not wanting to. And besides … it speaks to me, somehow.'

Olvar turned away. 'Wouldn't listen, if I were you.'

'Why? Vayde wasn't evil, just … uncanny. But I don't get that feeling from this. Or any other sense of anything; only strong virtues in the metal, flows and fluxes that don't seem to make sense. Yet I'm sure it was his right enough, and nothing he touched was ordinary. There's a secret in this, great or small; and I want to know what it is.'

Olvar sighed. 'Well then, until you find out, I suppose the coffers can stand a good homecoming dinner in some tavern. The Longbow? Or the Emerald Fountain?'

'The Fountain. I've had enough of bows today. Crossbows, shipbows… Let me tell you, comrade, when those fisher bumpkins let loose that bloody spray of bolts - and don't order fish, by the way. I've had the smell up to here!'

The Fountain was an unpretentious, comfortable inn, but known to craftmasters and merchants of the better sort for its excellent food, priced high enough to command respect, yet reasonable enough to let such canny men of affairs feel they were getting a bargain. Its spicy Southern sauces suited Gille, its large portions Olvar. The young mastersmiths pushed away their empty plates, sat back in their cushioned settles, Olvar's creaking loudly, and let the cares of the world slide off their shoulders awhile. Gille, who had been unable to leave his new plaything behind, took up the plectrum, and flicked the strings gently, stopping them with the fingertips of his flattened left hand. The landlord had been careful to admire the instrument, aware there was no music in the house tonight. He nodded approvingly now, and the regulars with him; they knew Gille as a decent player, for a casual song, anyhow. 'How's about a turn, then, Master? Sing us a ballad of your derring-do's today.'

Gille took him seriously, and preened a little. 'Powers, no! You don't want me going on about that! Besides, I'm not so good at making things up as I go along. Something a whit easier, maybe, like *The Norrard Reiver*.'

Olvar belched, which was a comment. Since this was a ballad of piracy and bloodthirsty swashbuckling, it was a choice less modest than Gille pretended; but the merchants were ready enough to let the young smith have his way. Gille tuned the strings a little, found the key with his left hand and began to play rippling, bouncing chords, while the melody he plucked with his right glanced across them like light on a racing wave.

> *Let her free! Out to sea!*
> *Sailing swiftly to the reiving*

Tacking fast, straining mast,
On the wind a hawk is riding!
Men now sleeping
Safe abed
Will instead
Leave widows weeping,
Ships at sea
Towns ashore
Safe no more
From stooping talon!
At the helm, with streaming hair
Stands the Buccaneer Orcanan,
Dispossessed, young and fair,
Fighting for his rightful fortune.

Orcanan had been a hero of the wars with the South, a century ago, or a villain, depending on one's side of the border. His claim to some minor estate in Ker Bryhaine might or might not have been just, but he had used it as a licence to harry the South by sea, at one time commanding a Northern fleet until he threw it away in reckless savagery and was betrayed to a glorious end in the bows of his blazing vessel. The rights and wrongs were lost to the listeners, as the rippling thrust of the music caught them up. They were there with the dashing lordling, and also with Gille as they believed he had been that morning, standing proud and valiant in the bows of a racing ship, daring all for justice and vengeance. Gille was beginning to believe it himself. Even Olvar joined in as they chanted the chorus with a force that rattled the shutters, and raised eyebrows in the street outside.

Sail you free, to sothran sea,
Sweep the waters of their burden!
Safe return, as rooftrees burn,
To lands of light and shores of laughter!

Gille strummed the melody to a swift con-
cluding chord, and they rattled the tables with their
mugs and roared in lusty approval. Gille grinned as
a brimming ale mug was slid before him. 'Well, that
didn't go too badly!' he grinned, wiping foam off the
end of his nose.

'You sang it better than usual, was why,'
rumbled Olvar. 'More spirit. Maybe your adventure
this morning did you good!'

'It got me out of myself, I'll allow. My vital
forces have been low of late.'

Olvar grinned. 'And that couldn't have anything to do with keeping three girlies on the go? We
could economise. Sell your bed. You're never bloody
well in it!'

'Ach, there's only Utte, really. The others are
just … there. When she isn't, or rather her brothers
are, bless their block heads.'

'You should wed the girl, Gille. Why not? A
man of your age …'

Gille glared. 'What about you, then? You've a
year or two on me. You want to settle. Why aren't
you chasing some poor woman?'

Olvar frowned. 'Would if I could. Way things
are now, how can I afford to marry? Who'd want
me?'

Gille shrugged. 'I'm no better off, am I?'

'Not your problem,' Olvar grumbled. 'Utte'd
have you on that farm of theirs, you could earn
your keep as a smith there. Her brothers'd like that.
You just want to go on as you are, hopping from
bed to bed like a bright little bug, dangling marriage
and leaping free at the last moment. How many is it
you've promised, this last year or two? Six? Seven?
Better hope they none of them find out, or they'll
maybe take a bit each!'

Gille stirred uncomfortably. 'It's what they
expect. It just smooths the way; like a, a password, a

courtesy! Satisfies their lines of defence, lets 'em lie back and get on with what they want as much as I do. Nobody really means it.'

'Not when you were a lad, maybe. That was good enough for then, but you're a master now. You're taken more seriously, as well you know. You can be a little bastard sometimes, Gille!'

Gille flushed, but did not reply. They sat in gloomy silence, and the others, sensing that the mood had changed, left them to it. They had come to Saldenborg a decade past as journeymen, when their first master Kunrad forswore his craft in despair and won a great place of honour in the Southlands. He had been generous in his support of them, giving them ample money to study for their masterships, but finding a new place had proven hard. Kunrad, in his less prosperous days, had taken them on for qualities he found useful, such as Gille's versifying, ideal for the strong singing of virtues into metal; but as craftsmen they were, as they knew well, unremarkable. Without Kunrad they had the choice either to vegetate as sole smiths in some small village, or try for a place in the larger forges of great towns. This they had managed; but for masters to whom they were little more than day-labourers, and who gave them only occasional support and counsel. They had had to toil hard and against the odds for their mastery. Nonetheless, and perhaps because of that struggle, they achieved it younger than most men; and then they were launched upon a less than welcoming world. Since their skills and natures were so well matched, each supplying much that the other lacked, they had mingled the last of Kunrad's money to set up a forge together.

So far, though, despite desultory attempts to develop bright ideas, they were not prospering. There were too many other, richer smiths here, and their own forge lay in the less accessible and

fashionable end of the town. Merely keeping themselves fed took up all their time, and that with the
plainest and least rewarding of toil. Their friendship
had survived such stresses, for this time at least.
Gille knew that Olvar wanted him to seize his
opportunity; Olvar knew that Gille was unwilling
to leave him to struggle alone. But there were times
when the gulf between them grew greater.

Olvar considered his friend for a minute
or two. He was always sorry to break the man's
happy moods; it was like snuffing a bright light. He
himself felt like so much lead and iron to his
friend's quicksilver; but quicksilver has few uses,
and dangerous.

'Why don't you want to marry the wretched
girl, man?' he grumbled. 'Or some other one? You've
a choice, Powers know why, always. They throw
themselves in your path, and there's precious few
men can say that. Don't you really yearn after any
of them?'

'Any?' Gille laughed, his cheer restored by the
idea. 'All! But none of them enough, no single one. I
see them as if—'

'As if they're just facets of one big jewel, so you
said last time. It didn't make much sense to me then,
either.'

'I was *going* to say, fragments of a broken
mirror,' said Gille, in sudden dudgeon again. 'All
reflecting small parts of something greater.' To
Olvar's eyes he seemed more than usually serious.
'Maybe … some One greater. But I expect you'll
make little enough of that, too.'

Olvar's heavy mouth twitched. '*Maybe* you're
wrong. An ideal woman? Raven's claw, man, who
doesn't seek such an one? And who's likely to find
her? Who's so perfect in themselves that they could
match her if they did? It couldn't be that you tire of
a woman fast, could it? And find her flaws a

convenient reason to flit along to the next, like a butterfly that's drained all the nectar?'

'I haven't tired of Utte!' protested Gille, so indignantly that Olvar had to chuckle.

'True, young master. Perchance because she's not yet started to tighten the screw upon you. Let her but try, and I'll lay odds you'll be up and running.'

'I don't want to be stuck away out on a farm!' Gille muttered.

'Instead of our carefree, laughter-laden existence? Lad, from all I've seen, you wouldn't know your ideal woman if she had herself catapulted into your bed. You've always got your eyes fixed on the horizon, like in everything else. Like this trading trip south'ard you keep wanting to fix up! It's pretty girls with red hair you're after bidding for!'

Gille jangled the kantel impatiently. 'I could do it. You could do it with me. They'll pay high for Northern craft down there. We could bring back a hoard like Tanle's, and double, no, quadruple the profit. Then I might find myself able to settle – on my terms, not Utte's.'

Olvar shook his head. 'Might as well wish for your perfect woman, then, while you're about it!' He leaned across the table and rasped finger and thumb under Gille's nose. 'Gold's like livestock – you need to rub two bits together to get a third. And what do we see but coppers? It's hard enough for proper merchants to raise money for journeys south, let alone raggedy-arses like us. Who'd lend us the wherewithal?'

Gille's eyes flashed so suddenly Olvar sat back. 'Whom have we ever asked? Somebody might! Hear me, all of you!' And he sprang up on his bench, and struck a great flourish on the kantel, and sang, to an old slow air that rose and fell like the eternal ocean:

I would sail the seas to the wide world's end,
I would load my ships with the wealth of men
The North's precious things I would carry south,
And the Southland's pearls I'd bring back
   again!
Not for gold alone, nor to fill the mouth,
But the heart and the spirit of Nordeney men!
Who will fill me a ship? Who'll spread sail
   with me?
Who'll extend our reach to the farthest sea?

Olvar's eyebrows rose a fraction. 'My, my! This is the man who says he can't improvise?'

The listeners were startled into silence at first, but when they caught the drift of his song their response was not encouraging. Most smiled and shrugged and turned back to their drinks; some laughed out loud. Gille struck a ferocious chord.

'Do you not hear? So much that we make, smiths and the rest of us, goes south in the hands of sothran sea-traders! And a double profit is theirs, what they make from selling us their wares, and from selling the stuff of ours they buy. Those we send south are mostly pedlars by compare, bearing only what they can carry on their backs, or in a few wagons, selling what they bring back at the first market they come to, so that it never reaches us without passing through many profit-hungry hands. And that makes Tanle's prices cheap by comparison! No blame to him, he takes the opportunity we give him.'

'And do you know why?' demanded one of the older men there, a wealthy skin and hide merchant. 'Because he and his kind take something else – namely the risks. Even now that fellow Kunrad's showing the sothrans how to clear the corsairs from the land, he cannot altogether scour them from the sea – as you've seen for yourself. And there's winds and waves and worse, in the realm of Niarad Sea-Lord. You need good ships and good men to make the risk worth taking. We don't have that kind of money for ourselves, let alone to lend others!'

'Unless you bond together, Master Vangar!' snapped Gille, eyes glittering. 'Unless you take each a small part of the risk, no more than you can afford!'

'And unless we find a man we can trust,' said another, steepling his fingers censoriously. 'You can't garner riches for yourself, man! What makes you think you could gain them for us?'

'Because I'm ready to try!' barked Gille, eyes snapping. 'What have any of you done in the ten years I've lived here? What argosies have we sent out, as the sothrans have to us? As we used to?'

'Young Master Gille's caught the seafaring bug today!' smiled Altor the goldsmith, not unkindly. 'Wants to go chasing heaps of gold in foreign lands. More likely to leave your bones there, young sir! Or on the seabed, snug i' the arms of Saithana the Last-Comer. As soon go trawling for golden fish, laddie. Why should we venture so far, when there's surer profit enough nearer home?'

The mocking roar that picked up his words was a great deal less kind. Gille's temper blazed, and the strings flared under his fingers.

'Then stay and pick for coins in the gutters, if you will!' He worked the lever, and the song shifted disconcertingly into a harsher, more aggressive key. 'Drink your sothran wine at their prices, eat your meat with their precious spices!'

> *Over land, over sea, there our fortunes lie,*
> *Not in narrow ways that we know too well!*
> *I would venture once more, ere my spirit die,*
> *Sail to barter, to bargain, to buy and sell!*
> *Laugh your laugh as you will, you shall all*
>   *see me yet*

Sailing home to your shore with my
    cargoes bright
With the sights and the songs a man will
    not forget,
That shall warm his heart against bleak
    winter night!
You who scoff, you who mock, shall regret
    and pine
That you—

Olvar, acutely aware of the ugly atmosphere, tried to haul the furious Gille down. There were catcalls, and cries to turn him out. Somebody shied a crust of bread at him, another a greasy bone that bounced off his temple. Gille flinched, and his elbow caught the carven lever. Two of the strings snapped, unmelodiously, tangling his fingers. A roar of laughter filled the room. Lips pressed so tight they turned white, he stepped down from the bench, laid the kantel down on the table, and put his fingers to his temples.

'Here,' rasped Olvar, signalling for the reckoning, 'down your ale quickly! Enjoy it, it'll be a few weeks before we're welcome here again. Assuming we can afford it. Come, let's be on our way!'

Gille trailed after him, out into the chill evening air; a fog was rising. Jeers and whistles echoed after them, and a great roar of merriment. Evidently somebody had said something very witty. 'I can't imagine why they broke,' Gille said limply. 'They're not so very old, not like the body—'

'What in the world has got into you anyhow, my lad?' growled the big man. 'You're acting like a child, not a master. A spoilt child! What set you off at folks like that? And whence this sudden thirst for adventure?'

Gille shrugged. 'I … don't know. I felt, what should I call it? Stifled, maybe? Suffocated? I needed to open a window wide – or break it!'

'My talking about marriage,' grunted Olvar. 'That's what did it. Off like a rabbit at the very mention of the word.'

'Maybe, maybe. But there was more to it than that – I felt, I felt I should be able to *persuade* them, you know? That I could break through their bloody self-sufficiencies and show them, just this once, that I was right, damn *right!*' He sagged. 'And then I couldn't.'

He stopped beneath the warm light of an unshuttered window, fidgeting with the instrument, struggling to tie the plectrum back on to its wisp of wire. Then he stopped, peered at the soundboard and swore softly to himself. Olvar peered over his shoulder, but could make out nothing unusual.

'Come on!' Gille said suddenly, and went striding over the cobbles at his best father-dodging pace, so that Olvar had to stump along behind. 'Guts!' Gille muttered venomously.

'Er – pardon?' asked Olvar breathlessly.

'Gut strings!' snapped Gille. 'Should've known! Probably don't tan them properly down south. So they wouldn't stand up well to the sea air, not left tight like that. They stretch, they tighten – no wonder they snapped. The more so, as they're not meant to be there!'

Olvar was still annoyed and disturbed, but glad that Gille's grasshopper mind had sprung on to something new for now. It might be best to encourage him. 'It's got to have strings.'

'Yes, but not this kind! Look at these silver bridges, I should have noticed that at once – they're too hefty just for ordinary gut strings. And too hard – no wonder they snapped. Yes, see here, the others are wearing badly. They must have done that all the time. Might explain why nobody wanted to play this much.'

'Wouldn't affect its value too seriously if you wanted to sell it, though,' suggested Olvar hopefully. 'The name's the thing—' Gille wasn't listening.

'But what, then? Wire? Steel strings? I've heard of those – but they'd wear the silver off the bridge, wouldn't they?'

'It's steel beneath,' Olvar pointed out, getting interested in spite of himself. 'And it hasn't worn anywhere else in two centuries. Maybe there's some kind of virtue in the metal, the sort we sing into iron against rust.'

Gille nodded. 'You and I couldn't do that – but I imagine Vayde could. Maybe there's something to these unreadable swirlings... Steel strings, though! They'd harden the sound, surely. Still, let's have this home and take a good look under the lamp. Have we still got all that wire lying about? And the drawing gear, we'll need to thin it out.'

'Unless you've pawned it!' muttered Olvar. The wire-drawers had been bought for one of Gille's more disastrous money-making ideas; and he would have to see that this one didn't go the same way.

'Not yet!' said Gille breezily. 'Those bumpkins! Those bloody stick-in-the-mud stay-at-homes, I'll sing the ears off 'em yet!'

'Take care lest they have the ears off you less laboriously, laddie!' growled the large man. 'My ancestors used to risk that if they sang rude songs about the chieftain or the shamans. Some of our tight-fisted friends are from the same stock, and they've influence with the Guildmaster and the elders. They might revive the custom for your especial benefit!'

Gille laughed, his spirits restored. 'No, I don't fear that! That's what your folk fled from, after all, wasn't it? I mean, three generations of living with us has even managed to civilise you, after a fashion.'

'Think so, do you?' It was a bear's growl in the

still night. Huge hands caught him by his well-shaped ears, and began to pull apart.

'I'd – *ouch* – depend on it! Remember I might have some offcomer blood too, damn it!'

'Runs too thin,' opined Olvar, letting go. 'You pink people, you get excited too easily. Like tonight. What were you hoping for? 'Cause if it was to make us a laughing stock, your wish is granted. That's some more work we won't be getting, maybe!'

'Maybe so,' said Gille obstinately. 'But your ancestors and mine, they were great seamen, weren't they? All the way across the ocean they sailed here to Brasayhal, seeking freedom before the Ice. Yours from the West, mine the East, never once set eyes on land. Wouldn't they rise to a challenge?'

'Not like a fish to a fly.'

'I'll show you, all the same! The pack of you!' stormed Gille, and stalked on, close-mouthed and silent.

Olvar ambled after, with an inner sigh. He could not help remembering how their master Kunrad had run mad one day in much the same fashion, his old steady self dissolving in a tidal wave of feeling that had lost him his most prized possession, his home, his livelihood and in the end his land, even. Admittedly Kunrad had gained rather more, but painfully; and there was little chance Gille would be so lucky. Too many women, and too many songs; neither set a man's head straight as it should be. And Olvar would probably get roped along once more – or strung, with this infernal instrument that had erupted into their lives.

Back at the forge the big man began to stow the sacks of valuable ores he had brought home, sources of rare and precious metals that could be used to turn plain copper and steel into so many more useful alloys, imbued with the special virtues that only true smiths could impart. At first Gille helped him; but he kept wandering off to look at the instrument again, and Olvar left him to it. At last, when he had finished, he brushed off his hands and straightened up with a sigh, only to see Gille at the forge, tending pots and crucibles. 'Should've thought you'd be off to your bed, after the day you've had.'

Gille shook his head, engrossed despite the baking heat that streaked his face with sweat. 'Not yet. There's something here. Look at that paper pasted inside the soundbox.'

Olvar squinted. 'Common enough, isn't it? The maker's name or sign, a verse or motif – a dedication if they've made it for someone, or even just advice on playing the instrument, or caring for it. I can't read this.'

'I almost can. Some of the words, anyhow.'

'Mmm. 'S like what you call a cursed old script, ain't it?'

'Cursive, you human clinker! Hold it up to the hearthlight. Look for the shape of the characters.'

'Mmmh. Well, that word could be "copper" – and that silver-something, "silvered" maybe – and that "steel"—'

'Hey, don't get it too near the flame! I'll go fetch a lamp, that'll help.'

'No,' said Olvar slowly. 'I don't think so. This seems to come out a lot better in the firelight – see?'

Gille peered. 'Not wrong, are you? Must be something to do with colours. It's been varnished over with the rest. Here, I can read this! Though no wonder you couldn't.'

'Thanks *ever* so much!' growled Olvar.

'No, I mean it's really old-fashioned. More than that, positively antique. Must have been old-fashioned even when it was written. All tangled and poetic.'

'Oh, poetic, eh? Well, you'd know about that.'

'Yes,' breathed Gille, angling the soundbox this way and that. 'Yes! Weird. This is an old poetical form called *mhathlac* - really old, dating from ancient Kerys itself.'

'Like Vayde,' said Olvar, and his deep voice, suddenly hushed, set the strings humming in resonance.

'Yes, like Vayde,' agreed Gille, preoccupied. 'Pure Svarhath in style, wouldn't work in Penruthya - lots of assonance, agreements vague so you're never sure what refers to what. It's always a sort of invocation, two stanzas with a sort of participle ending, and a couplet to close. Supposed to be based on one of those temple chants they used, back in Kerys. Still do, down in the South, as I hear.'

Olvar shrugged; Nordeney built no temples. 'What's it mean? Anything interesting?'

Gille blinked. 'I don't know. The spelling's so antique it affects the metre, but ... well, something like this ...' He declaimed it haltingly, searching for the right words.

These are my voices, ringing, singing:
Hawk-high windwords in the sky-dome swirling,
Stark-deep stonespeech under earth shivering,
Wave-cold seasong on the shoreline rushing,
Sear-hot flamedance in the forgehearth leaping.

Copper my throat binding, steel my tongue
*   winding,*
From silver jaws my heart's song outpouring.
Whose heart to music beats, through my heart
*   spilling*
All he conceives, shall see it growing and
*   enriching.*

Only match your voice to mine, bind your
*   tongue with mine,*
And your heart's song shall not go unheard.

'Whew!' said Olvar. 'Sounds sort of conventional, hinting at things. Like one of those rhymes they put on seduction rings – only less obvious. What d'you make of it?'

'Don't know... There's the characters at the centre, though. *V* and *K* in the old style, and intertwined. So this is his work, as much as the rest of the kantel. And though they say he had a good few mistresses, I've never heard he was the type to go scratching out love-lyrics!'

'You never know. I had a go once,' said Olvar, a little wistfully.

Gille grinned. 'Well, I hope you didn't go on about copper throat and silver jaws. Silver? That sounds more like this – the two silver bridges... Copper and silver? That couldn't be what the strings ... no. Silver, maybe; but not copper...' He strummed the remaining strings, grimaced; and then suddenly held the kantel to his eyes. 'Look here! This little old tag-end of wire that holds the plectrum – see it?'

'Surely,' said Olvar. 'Looks worn – frayed, almost... That's strange.'

'Yes! It's ... a coil, isn't it? A complex coil, fine wire over a core, a fibrous core...'

Olvar rolled it in his huge forge-scarred fingers. 'Two kinds of wire,' he agreed. 'Reddish metal, and something white...'

'*Copper and silver!*' they chorused.

'Well, I'll be buggered!' said Olvar mildly. 'Around gut? Must sound a bit odd. And be damned hard in the making.'

'I don't know,' said Gille thoughtfully. 'No harder than any other coiled wire. Tense the core – this isn't gut, but gut should do. Draw the wire very fine, wind it close – with an adhesive... But how'd you temper the wire? What kind of alloying for the copper – what kind of virtues...'

'I need another drink,' said Olvar.

He thought, that night, that he had persuaded Gille to get to his bed and let matters rest till morn, at the least. But in the small hours he woke, and heard the creak of the wire-drawer, and along with it a series of those quick little notes that tense metal makes, as if ghostly fingers plucked it. The air smelt hot. Gille had fired up the hearth again. Through his ill-fitting door the red light traced a panel on the ceiling, hatched across with a web of fine lines that he guessed were wires stretched about the forge. They had plenty of copper in all gauges, so this suggested that Gille was busy applying hard distress to their meagre store of silver wire, drawing it still finer.

Olvar sighed. Gille should shape a few nails with such dedication, or something else to bring in a penny or two; but you could not force him to, he would simply forge bad nails. Not maliciously, but because his thoughts were elsewhere. Best to let him have his way, for now. As a child with toys he would tire of it, soon enough. Olvar turned over; but as he sank back to sleep he was woken again for a moment, by the muttering of curses and the slam of the outer door. He smiled and mumbled contentedly. Perhaps the tiring had already begun.

CHAPTER TWO
The Golden Shoal

THE wind whistled around Gille's ears, ruffling icy fingers through his dark curls, but he did not bother to draw up the heavy hood at his neck. The damp turf chilled his hams, but he did not move. He leaned his head against the flank of the kantel, and felt the remaining strings singing softly in the wind. The lacquered wood was cool, the metal colder, but they warmed up almost at once against his cheek. He looked along the bridge, seeing the strings vibrate like living things, and listened to their faint mutual music, reverberating with the force of the air. They could sound so much richer, the strings in his mind, the strings he had tried to make, and failed.

Below him, dark in the greyness before dawn, the sea crashed and beat on the beach, rolling relentless drums that echoed the black hopelessness in his heart. What was he? Where was he going? Nowhere, it seemed. And at an age when most men were settled already, even in that long-lived era, and plotting out the course their lives could reasonably take. Why was he not settled? Perhaps he was; and that was a thought too horrible to endure. To founder slowly in this slough of scanty comfort, year by year, with no prospect of better ...

The wind seemed suddenly that much colder, and the gull-cries mocking. There were the women, of course. Just over the point was the narrow sheltered beach where many came to bathe of a morning, the one steep path usually guarded by a frightful old masseuse with wrestler's arms. There were ways to evade her, for the nimble, while it was still half dark; but Gille did not even feel like trying. How long would he be welcome there, or anywhere else, as his youth faded and his poverty grew, his honour lessened?

He could feel himself decaying already, his eyes dimming, his teeth staining, his skin reddening and cracking and growing seamed and dirty with the constant rigours of the common forge, and the soot that penetrated every crevice and stained the very lines of the skin, even under clothes. The young girls on the beach would run screaming, then, and mean it; or else they would laugh at him. They already were, probably; the story must be all over the town by now. It would leave him doubly impotent. Gille was not much given to self-doubt; most of what fuelled his mood now, as Olvar had guessed, was wounded pride. But it forced him, for a moment, to look at himself and what he might be, and his heart withered.

He sighed, and the remaining strings sighed with him, but so feebly he struck them. The sound-box picked up the rough chord and flung it into the air, but still too weakly. He plucked a few notes. The overbearing crash of the surf did not drown them, but they sounded faint and strange. He heard the makings of a tune in them, that seemed to echo his own doubt and pain, and when he plucked them again, with a shivering tremolo that the missing strings should have picked up, his throat tightened. He was always improvising tunes, with dubious success. And yet this one was a real complaint, as lonely as a seabird's cry, as little understood.

You waves, you sentries of all the coast,
Part, and show me the hidden way,

The light is hidden by your spray,
And the tears it strikes from my sad eyes.

You waves, in infinite freedom born,
Hear, and share all my bitter mind,
How shall I ever hope to find
A sail that will bear me to my dreams?

You waves, your crests I may not subdue,
Nor stride across on a bridge of song!
The life and love for which I long,
Are shapes unformed in your endless play…

His voice faded. The sky was full of light, and
the first long ray lifted over the ocean's rim and
shone full in his face, as sudden and warm as a
caress. The wind seemed to lose some of its bite,
and become no more than fresh and reviving. Yet he
looked around, quickly; because something else had
changed, something subtle, the intangible loneliness
of the beach. It was like a touch laid upon him, icier
than the wind and more thrilling. Then he saw.

Perched on the steps of the bare black spray-
shining rocks at the cliff base, some hundred strides
away. Sitting with one pale-skinned leg extended,
one knee clasped in long arms, hair blowing in
the first light. Long hair, paler gold than the sunrise,
blew in fine streamers across the face, hiding it; but
the head was cocked his way, listening. At first he
thought she – yes, it had to be she, though the limbs
were long and shaded with muscles – at first he
thought she was naked. But as she rose, the wind
slapped the light shift back and forth about her
legs. Elsewhere it clung, soaked to transparency. She
stood, wavering a little on the slippery rock, and he
thought to run and help her, lest she lose her footing and tumble into the heavy surf. But she leaped
down to the beach and landed nimbly; then, a little

hesitantly, began to move towards him. He stood, uncertainly, letting the kantel slip down on its strap; but she gestured eagerly, her long fingers flung wide. He smiled. She wanted him to go on playing.

He struck the strings, and somehow caught the rhythm of her hesitant approach and wove a dancing theme around it, to the tune of a popular children's game.

> *Sweet girl goes a-gathering sea-flowers*
> *For her sweetest, sweetest sweetheart…*

It seemed strangely appropriate, and evidently she knew it; for suddenly she was dancing on the sand, a little clumsily at first, then gaining confidence, kicking out her long legs, spinning around. Her flimsy shift flew wide, and he saw it was greenish, with some kind of girdle; and though her hair still shadowed her face, he caught a flash of eyes as she whirled, light eyes. He speeded up the dance a little, and met a wide grin as she matched him, arms outflung for balance, at once endearingly coltish and suddenly, breathtakingly graceful, whirling faster and faster without the least false urge to conceal her body. He increased the beat to match her and beyond, and, forgetting himself, slid the lever up a key to make the music wilder and more exciting; until suddenly, with a vicious pinging sound, another string broke, stinging his wrist. Her feet flew from under her, her shift billowed wide, and she landed on her backside in the damp sand. It was a loud thump, and sent a guiltstruck Gille skidding and clattering down the layers of stone and leaping across the sand.

'Are you not hurt…?'

His voice petered out as he came face to face with her, even some yards away. Sea-bathing was fashionable for women of quality in the South, less so in the chillier North; yet the fashion was spreading. This one …

He should have been drinking in the sight of her, for little was concealed. It did not seem to worry her; there was no instinctive hunching down, no flutter of hands to cover breast and thigh. Yet he was astonished to find he could only look at the grey-green eyes, the shapely cheekbones and smooth cheeks flushed with excitement, pale lips drawn back in laughter, yet still sensuous and full.

'I fear I am little used to dancing!' she said, a slightly stiff, old-fashioned expression lightened by the breathless giggle behind it. Her voice was soft, quite deep, with a curious sibilant music that hinted at a delightful laugh.

'I thought you looked like one of the Powers, dancing at the creation of the world,' said Gille; and she smiled.

'That was a dance indeed; but they did not have you to play for them so wickedly!'

He laughed too, and sank down on his knees, still a little way from her. 'How do you know?' he teased her. 'How d'you know I'm not a Power in disguise, come to father his children upon the daughters of men, as all the old tales say?'

She smiled, lazily. 'Because you are Gille the Mastersmith, whom it is said has made of himself a hero and a fool in one and the same day, and now weeps over his fate to the unheeding ocean.'

Gille sagged. His mouth twisted. 'You heard.'

She laughed again, more softly. 'I could hardly help it. You were playing so well, and singing loudly, even above the surf. I heard you clearly from the beach, over there.'

'Yes, that one's more sheltered. Fine for your beauty bathing, but I just wanted to be alone.'

She sat up. 'Well, I am sorry, I should not have intruded. I can leave.'

'No!' he exclaimed. 'No, you can't – I mean, please don't! Seeing you there, listening like that … I don't think I've ever seen anything lovelier. It was like a song taking shape – the surf, all fury, and the rock, all grim, and you, perched calmly between them like…' He threw his hands wide, helplessly, and ran his fingers in a ripple down the remaining strings. 'Like life itself. Like the reason for being alive – ach, to Hella with it, I'm making a fool of myself again! You were beautiful, that's all. You are beautiful. More beautiful than any other woman I've ever seen, or hope to see.'

'You,' she said softly, 'are not the most beautiful man I have seen, though there are those who might think so. And not the tallest, nor the strongest, surely not the wisest. Many such men I have seen, and admired, worshipped even. And yet they have not stirred me as you do, my friend, with your fool's heroism and heroic foolery, your songs and your self-pity.'

She swept her legs under her and stood up, swiftly but awkwardly, and paced towards him. He had guessed she was tall, but not how tall; she seemed to tower over him, as he knelt dumb-founded in the sand. She gazed down at him, and her hair fell forward to shadow her face once again, leaving her eyes gleaming in the shadow. She reached a hand down to him, encrusted with the sparkling sand, and he saw rings gleam there, coursing with light deeper than that of their gems, virtues that betokened a hand of power in their making, and a high price.

The silken shift was greenish as it dried, a shimmering sunlit green that set smooth highlights on her skin, bound only by a low-slung girdle, its thin chain of silver set and hung about with pearls, stressing rather than concealing the fine shadow of her thighs. She was smiling down at him; and as she breathed, her breasts stirred the silk. He seized the hand and kissed it, finding the tang of salt on his lips, feeling his own breath catch. He felt as he had never before felt with a woman; but part of that feeling, incredible as it seemed, was fear.

Her other hand ruffled his hair, and the surf grew very loud in his ears. 'Poor Gille!' she said, almost dispassionately. 'The music is not right, not yet. Yet you play a powerful song, and you have earned it. Maybe you deserve to pursue your dream, and learn both the value and the peril of such things, and the penalties they carry. Maybe the choice is not yours, but destiny's.'

'This is my dream,' he said, drawing breath. 'If this is my peril, then for once I'll learn courage!' He leaned his head forward, against her belly, and kissed the girdle. The thin silken stuff of the shift left salt on his lips, and the warmth of the skin beneath. He sprang up, and found her less tall than she looked, but still smiling down upon him a little, taking his chin in long fingers and tweaking his beard playfully.

'Well, you dare in your dreams at least!' She tapped him lightly on the cheek, the merest token of a slap. Gille seized her fingers and kissed them.

'Does love offend you?' he demanded, with a quiet intensity which had worked wonders in the past. 'So much beauty in my eyes, so close – should a man not kiss what he worships? Lady, I have never seen the like of you before, ever! Your eyes are like the endless sea, your face—'

A long finger escaped his grasp and settled lightly on his lips, sealing them. A great wave crested and fell like violent thunder, and they were momentarily up to their knees in the flow as it fell back. Sand sucked at their feet.

'Save your words, Gille! It grows light, and I am expected back.'

Gille sighed. 'That's no surprise. You can't wander around the beach like that, swimming or no. Not a well-bred young lady like you.'

She nodded, still amused. 'Indeed. My father would be furious.'

That too was no surprise. Fathers always were. 'But surely I can see you again?' demanded Gille.

She gave a little smirk, the first of her expressions Gille did not like. 'That depends.'

'On what?'

'On a great many things. You would do better to play than talk, Mastersmith. Your sweet words have been used too often. Only in music does the truth of you shine forth. Play for me again!'

Another wave boomed, swirling cold sand and strips of weed around their legs. Gille hoisted the kantel hastily out of its way. 'How can I? I've hardly a string left now, and little hope either.'

She pursed her lips, and looked like girls he had failed to impress. 'Why so much self-pity, man? Have you not the remedy for all in your own hands? Make more strings! Are you not a smith?'

'Think I haven't been trying? That's what drove me out here. I know how they should be made. Like this fragment. I just can't shape them! The wire won't coil properly around the core, gut or whatever it is – yet it can't be steel, either.'

She rolled the tag of wire between her fingers. 'This is something smooth, with many strands. Gille, have you not heard old tales of the first of such instruments, crafted by the fiery hand of Ilmarinen himself – and strung by the Daughter of Air, with her own hair?'

In a sudden leaping joy Gille seized her hands, but the words faltered on his lips, as the air flicked her long pale tresses across them, leaving a tinge of salt. She openly laughed at him now, and nodded. 'Yes, yes, you may! Pluck as many as you will, I have no scarcity!'

He put his hand up to touch her head, hesitating. 'That'll hurt you,' he said lamely.

'Mmm. Then perhaps you should distract me,' she said demurely. Gille swallowed, unbelieving, and wound a pale strand around his fingers, drawing her closer. Her arms went around his neck, her eyelids sank, and he brushed his lips against hers. They were cool, surprisingly so, and slightly dry and papery; but as they pressed harder against his, her tongue darted from between them and teased his own. His teeth parted, his own tongue rolled against hers, and guiltily he tightened his grip and tugged. Her shoulders jerked slightly in his arms, bringing her tighter against him at breast and thigh. She rolled her head against his, and another strand was entangled somehow, and, appalled and excited, he tugged again, as cleanly as he could. The soft ghost of a cry sounded in her throat, but she only tightened her grip, pulling him off his feet. He fought his mouth free.

'Not here!' he gasped. 'The surf—' His fingers seemed to be full of the gleaming coils of hair. Callous he could be, but there was no cruelty in him, and he struggled against the excitement it awoke.

'The sea won't hurt you!' she said, her eyes gleaming beneath heavy lids.

'The kantel—' he muttered, struggling to object, but she was already sliding it off his shoulder, wrapping the hairs he had plucked loose about it, setting it back on a dry rock, all in one fluid, graceful movement that ended with her arms against his, sliding them down to her haunches as she leaned in against him. Her hair cascaded across them as she leaned her head back and thrust her thighs forward, and now he wrapped his fists in it and tugged in earnest. His elbows and knees dug into the cool damp sand, and the surging force of the ocean seemed to flow from him into her, and break again and again like scattering thunder.

At last, fighting for breath, they rolled apart on to the cool sand, caking on their sweat-run skin. A wave coursed about them both, and she spread her thighs lazily, as if to receive it, and looked at him with wry amusement. 'Now that was well played, Mastersmith! A merry tune you dance to, and lightly fingered!'

Gille shook a strand of weed from behind his ear. 'I ... You... You. You're wonderful. You're like no woman I've ever met, ever loved. You ...'

She stretched out a long finger to caress his cheek, and traced it lazily down from neck to chest. 'Loved? You love me, then?'

He laughed, a little crazy with the force of the passion that had passed through him. 'You're asking? Girl, woman, goddess! I want you, more than—'

The finger sealed his lips. 'Get your breath back, sooner than spin your old lies over again. They come too easily. You never said a word of love, before you had your way. And did I?'

Gille took the finger, and kissed it. 'We had little enough chance for speech. Well enough, perhaps they were the same old words, because I don't know any others for such a time. But - I do love you.' Her narrowed gaze had something stern in it, and he turned defiant.

'I do! At least, I ... feel for you, the way I've felt for no other woman. Oh yes, others enough, wonderful women, but always ... dragging me down somehow, reining me in. You don't feel like that. You look like beauty itself taken form, you're wise, you're strong, and yet you're honest, direct. With words ... with your body. At least I thought ... You don't feel anything for me? Not a thing?'

She lifted a long leg and ran it gently along his thigh. 'Now you're busy pitying yourself again. Just because I don't melt away and beg you to wed me and drag you home to take wine with my father, all on the instant. If I did you'd hardly spare me another glance. Don't you realise that's what galls you in those others? Sad man, yes, I feel something for you.' She ground her hips against him, then pulled back as he reached blindly for her again. 'But not everything, not yet. Not a long way yet. I'd sooner hear you sing a merrier song or two. And make more of yourself than you have.'

Gille sat up as another wave splashed him, and leaned his chin on his knees. 'Be damned to that! If my sorrows are only self-pity and there's no love or hope to lighten them, what's left to sing about?'

'I did not say your sorrows were self-pity alone. And there is always hope, Gille! Who knows how destiny will shape itself? Can you read the purposes of the sun, or the sea, or the Great Ice? Yet infinite as they are, they are far harder to change than a human heart. But the man will die of hunger who waits for golden fishes to swim into his net.'

'So what am I to do?' he demanded, bridling at the old saying. 'I can think of nothing! You are the one bright gleam among the stormclouds, and I don't even know your name.'

She laughed again. 'Better thus! But I shall leave you a token, Gille.' She plucked something from her girdle and dropped it on his thighs, a small leaping sungleam. He caught it deftly and felt it warm against his hand, warm from her body.

Then his face twisted. 'What's this? A fee for the poor player?'

She smiled. 'A reward for art. Are you too proud?'

Gille clutched the grubby gold coin, wondering if he could ever spend it. 'No. But only - mark this - only because I love you!'

'Well, then. I said it was but a token. Of

something I know that happened here long ago, that might help you. Of, say, what you might find if you trawled the harbour mouth, with a strong net of fine meshes. Just inside the bar to the east of the channel, where no ship moors because of the turbulence. Seek there, and be bold!'

Gille looked at her, uncomprehending, then more closely at the coin. The tarnish was heavy and sea-begotten, barnacle ring and worm train encrusting the heavy gold so that he could hardly make out the pattern beneath. 'Where did you get this? Do you know some secret—'

Again the finger stopped his lips. 'Many. This was brought up from there, and forgotten. No more words, lest you talk away your fortune. Play, Gille! You must find a truer song. But I will dance to your strings, meanwhile!'

As if in thrall, he drew out a long chord in its single notes, and she smiled and stretched as though it were her he caressed, lifting an arm in a graceful dancer's pose. He struck up a tune, a livelier one but not too lively, not testing her as before. She rose to her feet and stood over him a moment, rocking gently to the tune; and then she spun and whirled, much surer now, so graceful and lightfooted that it took him a moment to realise she was moving away.

His playing faltered, but she shook her neat fist at him impatiently, and he played again. She danced, one moment gliding like a statue of ancient grace above a sea of mist, the next leaping and bounding, all legs and delight. Another great wave roared in, but she splashed lightly through it, kicking water high like a delighted child. And then she was skipping across the rocks and away, more surefooted than before, and out of sight. Another wave pounded against his legs like an aggressive dog, and almost toppled him. Sadly he let the tune drop, and turned to gather up his tangled garments.

Then he looked at the coin he held, and over the hill to the town; and he swore a great oath to earth and sky and sea. And though he was only half dressed and dishevelled, his bare feet still wet and sandy, he began to run.

Olvar awoke again, startled. His dreams had that tangled feeling of sudden awakening, visions of green shores, wide seas, rolling clouds. Something had cut through them, something keen as a wire – something that sounded like one. He sat up, and realised it was already long past dawn, late by his usual standard. His mouth tasted foul, and by the sound of it Gille was already hard at work; he liked that almost less. He heaved himself out of the bed of ropes, and rolled through to the forge – and stopped dead as a wire sang tight across his throat. He choked and cursed. Gille looked up.

'Get some clothes on, for the Powers' sake, you'll put me off my breakfast.'

'You haven't had it yet?'

Gille shrugged. 'Too busy. Ten minutes more, maybe.'

'It's near mid-morn, man! Nearer your nuncheon. Why'd you leave me sleeping? I've work in hand, too.'

Gille looked around vaguely. 'That time? Sorry, Olvar. But–' He twisted something effortfully. 'Just – a minute – more – and ... Watch the wires, if you're coming through!'

'Watch the–' Speech failed Olvar. 'What, you want to live in a kantel, now? Go jump through a harp!'

'Clear it in a moment!' panted Gille. 'Just – now, then – *listen*!'

And there was that sound again, shivering the air, filling the forge. Every wire strung about the room resounded to it, blurring, humming. The very dust motes in the sunbeams striking through the skylights and shutters shook and danced, till the sunlight itself seemed to quiver. Even thought stopped for the first instant, as if to listen. It was not loud; it only seemed to be. Then it sounded again, more gently, plucked with another string; and the effect was different altogether. Less stark; gentler; and yet it still sang in Olvar's sleep-numbed mind, hinted at memories and visions tantalisingly beyond his reach. 'Urgh,' was about as much as he could manage.

Gille's grin flashed across the shadows. 'Now *that's* how it ought to sound - isn't it?'

Olvar stuck a finger in his ear and waggled it. 'You've got something, I'll give you that. Gille my lad, have you ever seriously thought of going in for making these musical knick-knacks you're so fond of? They fetch good prices, I know; and you seem to be finding a talent—'

'I found more than that,' said Gille, stretching. 'Powers, my back aches, and my reins! I found ...' His voice ran down. 'The right core for these strings.'

Olvar picked his way carefully through the web, though not without plinking and plunking noises. 'What's this?' He peered at the looped end of the wire Gille had been stretching across the kantel's soundbox. There were two strings there now, and more lay ready on the bench. 'Could almost be hair, couldn't it? It is hair - Gille, you little swine!'

Gille gestured impatiently. 'Olvar, listen - who in this town, a wealthy man, has a daughter blonde and tall and fond of sea-bathing?'

'Might have known it was a woman! A daughter - sure it wasn't a wife?'

Gille shook his head guiltily. He had been churning the same question over and over in his own mind. No blushing maiden, but one who knew a man's mind and her own, freely. More like a wife; but wives were always trouble. 'She said, a daughter. She seemed young, she wore rings, but no wedding ring.'

Olvar shrugged, as he turned back to his room. 'A dozen families I know of have such daughters. A hundred, if you take in the smaller towns around, and the richards with country estates. Though tall, that's not so common. Sounds almost sothran.'

'Her hair wasn't red, she didn't have freckles. She looked – I don't know, like one of the old blood, the first Northerners, the folk from Kerys you see in the old pictures. Olvar, her skin was so clear! Almost like the finest white calfskin parchment, as if the sun'd shine right through it.'

Olvar poked his head back around the door. 'And I'll wager you saw a lot of it? Don't appeal too much. Give me a nice silken copper-tits any day, but then I'm biased! Come on, I've got to eat. I've a pennyworth of fat kidneys on the cool slab, I'll fry us them up with bacon.'

'All right, all right,' grumbled Gille. 'I should have finished stringing this by then – it's not so easy, with that damned key lever. But then, no lounging about here. I've got to go out, and in all haste!'

Olvar, setting the griddle across a corner of the smouldering hearth, looked up in surprise. 'Why so? Which one's brother is chasing you? Or father, or husband?'

'Nobody,' wheezed Gille, as he wrestled with the tightening keys. 'Look at this.'

'Very nice,' said Olvar approvingly, as the gold coin rang on the bench. He made as if to bite it, then looked at the grime and put it down. 'But no reason to waste a pennyworth of kidneys. We can lash out on dinner later.'

'It's not for spending. I'm going to find more. And you'd better get dressed and come along, too.'

Olvar looked up from the sizzling griddle. 'Is the forge afire? Is the sky falling? Nothing less comes between me and a kidney. You'll be none the worse for it, either, by the look of you.' He patted Gille on the shoulder. 'Shows promise, all the same. Going after gold, instead of girlies and jinglies. How'd you come by all this?'

Gille opened his mouth, then shut it, firmly. 'We'll see.'

'Like that, is it? Secrets. Hmph.' Olvar prodded the bacon gloomily. 'Maybe I'd better make the best of this, while I can.'

Gille hated kidneys, but in his excited state he had eaten two before he remembered this, and had to drown the taste with ale. It did nothing to calm him. 'Sit down!' roared Olvar. 'You're hopping about like a drunken robin!'

'How can you squat there filling your face when there's gold to be gathered?'

'Easily,' replied Olvar, and demonstrated.

He took more time over his meal than he needed to, whether to calm Gille or annoy him he was unsure. When at last he finished licking his fingers, Gille more or less dragged him to his feet.

'What d'you need me for, anyhow?' demanded Olvar.

'You know about boats, don't you?' demanded Gille. 'We need one!'

The market square of Saldenborg was a great brimming churn of bright hues, loud voices and strong stinks, all of which spilled and spattered into the neighbouring streets and out along the quays that extended into the harbour it faced. This was the port through which all the seaborne traffic for the middle lands of Nordeney passed, the point at which inland traders bought for the great markets of their home regions. Here were merchants from near and

far, from the lands further north and the great
towns further south, stalking through the hubbub
rich of dress and haughty of bearing, save to their
better customers. Many such outcomers dealt, as did
Tanle, from the decks of their ships moored along
the quays, their rigging arrogant with banners and
flags, gaudy blazons of challenge to the dark sea
beyond.

In among these prosperous pavilions lesser
vendors sidled, selling food and drink from trays
Local men dealt from the landward side of the
square, the richest from their awning-hung shop-
fronts in the warehouses and other buildings that
surrounded it; but most from the rows of booths
and stalls at its centre. The best of these were canopied
constructions like miniature palaces, gilded and
ornate, others no more than trestle tables without
even a cover, but with their wares piled all the higher,
and the vendor lurking behind them to pounce on
the first curious face that paused. Embroidered tunics,
carpenter's tools, caps, candles and fine hide boots,
tooled and shiny, swayed like leaves in a breeze that
was a battleground of smells, from the pungent fish-
boxes, fresh and pine-smoked, to the great cheeses,
solid wheels marbled with blue or veined like a
drunkard's nose, that lolled in heaps and tubs, the
green earthy pungency of fresh-dug tubers and pep-
pers, the sharp dusting of sawdust over the sickly
blood-drip of freshly slaughtered carcasses, the singing peppery aroma of sausages bloated or skeletal,
the sudden sweetness of baskets of fruits and
berries. They all tangled fitfully with sudden sharp
wafts of spice, wine or ale as a bin was opened for
a special customer, or a barrel tapped to close a
deal.

In among these prosperous pavilions lesser
vendors sidled, selling food and drink from trays
and leather carriers, or even the bristling armoury
of tools and weapons hung about their bodies,
source and security both for their takings. Pedlars

poorer still displayed trinkets, cutlery and all kinds
of small stuff from their open knapsacks or even
their capacious pockets, cheap rings lining their
knuckles, strings of beads around their necks, and
all crying their wares in competition with their
richer fellows. On the cobbles underfoot that morning's fresh-strewn straw was rapidly becoming a
thick crust of trodden beast-dung, discarded vegeta-
bles and tops, dubious fishheads, bruised berries
and similar discards, sending up its own peculiar
fragrance to battle on the breeze. For all the filth,
there were many who simply sat or squatted and
spread out hides wherever there was a space, and
the larger booths often spilled out barrels and tubs,
so that moving among them was an awkward
business. Gille paid no attention at all, leaving tubs
rocking and trays tipping in his wake, while Olvar,
lumbering along behind, alternately swore at him
and apologised. He saw what Gille was heading for,
the great fountain at the heart of the square, and
clutched vainly at his friend's coat; and then at his
own head, in sheer despair.

Above the fountain, beneath the naked statue
the young apprentices loved to climb on, stood a
pulpit from which public proclamations were
made. Gille was already bounding up the short stair.
At the rail he struck a pose, and then a loud chord
on his kantel, a very loud chord. Even Olvar was
startled; the sound was launched like an arrow, to
shiver off the stone walls about the square. Every
voice stopped in sheer astonishment, every head
turned; and then Olvar winced, as a great shout of
laughter rippled across the square. The word, evidently, had spread.

One of the oldest and raggedest of the pedlars
piped up suddenly. 'Come t' beg the price of a ship,
lad?'

'Come to sing for his supper, more like!' laughed

one of the stallholders who had been at the Fountain.
'A better tune, Mastersmith, or it's back to beating
time on your anvil!'

'As you wish,' said Gille blithely, and flicked
the strings lightly once again. 'I'll keep it sweet and
simple for you.

> *The Masters of the Market,*
> *They lace their purses tight,*
> *They salt their gold in dunghills,*
> *To keep it from the light!*

> *Hail to the Masters,*
> *See their bellies sway!*
> *They'll buy and they'll sell at any price*
> *As long as it's we who pay!*

> *The Masters of the Market*
> *Are robed in wool and silk,*
> *Yet not a thought between them*
> *Save lesser folk to bilk.*

> *The Masters of the Market,*
> *They wine and dine and plan,*
> *Yet all to keep their prices*
> *Beyond the honest man!*

Olvar winced. The tune was well known, with
associations enough already. Already there were a
couple of voices joining in from the background,
prentices by the sound of them. This was the kind
of song folk would remember, and start adding
verses of their own. It had started with mild abuse,
common enough to be laughed at; but Gille was
cutting too near the nerve now, and that could spell
ruin. All the more so because it was, if not entirely
true, not entirely unfair either.

The Masters of the Market
They sell for golden pence
The things they bought for silver,
And ours is the expense!

The Masters of the Market
Buy heaps of treasures rare,
Yet where those treasures stem from,
They little know or care.

The Masters of the Market,
They will not venture south,
They send for golden fishes,
To fly into their mouth!

The Masters of the Market,
They fear a newer face,
They know a worthy rival
Can tip them from their place!

Hail to the Masters—

A tall man appeared in one of the warehouse entrances. Olvar recognised him; Stulte the clothman, one of the richest men of the town, and an elder and magistrate. He nodded to a few of his fellows in the square, Vangar among them, and they gathered around him. 'So this is the smith who'd teach us our trade! And with our own money, if you please!'

Gille bowed to him, most ceremoniously. 'No, sir. With the gold that awaits us all in the Southlands, if only we have the courage to go there for it.'

The merchants strode up to the fountain, and Stulte gestured with his stick. 'If only? That covers a world of risk and ruin! No, young man, my trade suits me very well. I have no need to range more widely.'

'Aye, that's so!' called another. 'Our trade's well enough for us. Do you stick to yours!'

Gille swung one leg over the pulpit rail. 'Why? Lest I disturb your profits, is that it? Lest I break all the convenient little cartels you and your friends operate, here and in other towns? Is it that you fear, worse than risk or ruin?'

The laughter was markedly less certain this time, among the stallholders at least. Olvar saw some of them exchange glances, when they were sure the elders were not looking.

'That is a cheap accusation!' snapped Stulte.

'Then it's all you've got that is!' said Gille cheerfully, tossing his coin in the air and catching it. 'You may up it by a third, like your cambric!' This time the laughter, though muted, sounded less hostile, and the elders cast quelling glances around the crowd. One of them, who occasionally brought his horses to Olvar for shoeing, cast him a bleak glance. Olvar bowed with overelaborate politeness.

'You should watch your tongue,' said another elder curtly. 'Even a master may be cast out of his Guild, for slandering another. Or bring upon himself some worse fate, who knows?'

There were men gathering at the warehouse entrance, as if they had been summoned, large men with the hooks and prybars of their trade. Olvar moved unobtrusively closer. Gille might be mad, but he wasn't about to leave his short friend in such a mess.

Stulte was seeking to swing the crowd's mood back to mockery. 'I bow to your judgement, Master Gille! You of course know all about the ins and outs of trade, about what is a fair price and what isn't. You, the shoddy tinker, the starveling, who seeks to win gold by begging it from us!'

Gille tossed the coin to him. Stulte plucked it out of the air with a rapacious snap, and the merchants stared at it. 'Just this? I'll wager you could get no more!'

'Any time I like,' laughed Gille. 'By waiting for golden fishes to swim into my net!'

Stulte snorted, and shied the coin back at him. 'You may wait a long time, for me. I'll wager you won't see more than this hoary old crown.'

Gille jangled a couple of strings. 'What will you wager, Stulte? Against my golden fishes?'

The marketplace seemed very quiet all of a sudden. Stulte snorted. 'You have nothing to wager with, that I'd give tuppence for. Even your forge is only half your own.'

Gille considered. 'I have my pride, as you have yours. I have my life. Do you not want to triumph over me, Master Stulte? To prove I'm only a dreamer, to show that all I sing about you isn't true?'

'What're you offering?' demanded Arkal the master grain-miller. 'Your miserable head?'

'That!' said Gille calmly, strolling down the pulpit stair. 'Against your penny-pinching riches, all of you. If you care to collect. Or that I quit this town in disgrace, to wander through the world. I care less and less for it, with such buffoons for its masters!'

'Write it down!' snapped Stulte. 'You heard him, set it down – he wagers his head!'

'Or banishment,' objected Vangar. 'We can hardly—'

'His head,' said Stulte evenly. 'Time enough to talk of mercy when we've sealed his lying tongue. Is it written?' He took the paper, and rummaged in his sleeve for his seal. Gille used the mastersmith's stamp from around his neck, an annoying reminder that in theory they were of equal rank. Even the elders could not touch Gille without permission of his Guild; though that, Olvar reflected, would probably not be a problem. He won through to Gille's side too late to stop him. Other masters were already adding their seals to Stulte's.

Olvar was not a man for extremes of temper. He simply blew out his cheeks, and growled, 'Well, you've been and gone and done it. Who's going to work the bellows for me now?'

Gille grinned irritatingly, poked Olvar's well-covered ribs and pushed past him to hail the crowd. 'You all heard the wager, eh? Well, who'll help me win it? Who'll give me the loan of a small boat for a few hours?'

Silence, as the market folk looked uneasily at one another. Many here had boats, but they were not things to risk in the hands of a madman, not to mention incurring the elders' wrath. Then a strong smell of fish heralded three brown-skinned young men pushing their way to the fore, heavy of build and feature, slow of speech.

'Reckon we'll stick with you, Master. Remember us, my brors an' me? From the *Sea Mare*? Us wi' the crossbows!'

Gille's smile turned a trace glassy. 'How could I possibly forget? But I thank you. We'll not need bows here, anyhow; but we'd better set out at once. This is my friend the mastersmith Olvar, born among fishermen like yourselves. He'll help...'

They measured up Olvar's bulk. 'Best not, by're leave, masters! 'Tis but a small smack, and if we've to carry aught...'

Olvar shrugged regretfully. Better, perhaps, not to be a part of it. It might help him shield Gille, afterwards.

The crowd cleared as the little crew passed, though perhaps their pungent scale-coated jerkins were reason enough. Olvar followed them down to the pier. The boat was as ordinary as any of the others it was moored alongside, beamy and heavy-planked, high-arched, one sweeping natural curve from stem to stern, with the traditional wide eyes painted at the bows, in the same green as the *Sea Mare*. Gille passed the kantel to Olvar and settled himself rather unsteadily amidships, looking to his friend as if for reassurance.

'Tight little smack,' he nodded. 'She'll serve you nicely.' *Whatever in the name of Lady Hella's curlies for,* he kept in his thoughts, and waved encouragingly as they pushed off from the quay.

From Gille's gestures Olvar thought they were heading for the open sea; but they made no move to hoist sail, and turned, still under oars, for the crooked end of the massive stone seawall, and across the bar, under the great salt-stained stones, weed-green and barnacle-white. The water there was deep enough to be dark, the waves still forceful. Even the brisk breeze whipped them white against the bar, and bounced the little craft unmercifully as it came about, working the oars hard, circling as if searching for something.

Olvar felt a sudden deep shiver, not only down his spine but through his whole body, a faint cool thrill like the tremor of an icicle on a branch. He touched the kantel, and jumped. The new strings were vibrating, as if in sympathy with some other sound; but he could hear nothing except the wind. Then he forgot it; something was happening out there. His eyes had always been keener than most men's, and he could see what was happening aboard the little boat clearly enough, the oars backwatering, the boat hove to, the oars shipped. Then one of the fishers, fighting to keep his feet, flung out his nets.

'What's he about?' demanded Olvar. 'A dredge trawl?'

'The Ice-demons a flatfish he'll scoop up there, gold or no!' snorted one of the town fishermen.

'A breaker amidships, more like!' muttered another, as the oars plied once again. 'Should we make ready to launch and rescue?'

A pot-mender sneered. 'The lads, maybe. Let the mad mastersmith walk home, if he will!'

Olvar rounded on him, but the other seamen were already shouting him down. 'Mad or not, we'll not leave a man to perish,' said an older skipper. ''Sides, he mayn't be so gyte as you think. D'you not mind, Torge? Maybe forty year back? That night of the great storms, when the ice-islands were driftin' in to shore?'

'Oh aye,' nodded Torge. 'Yon fine big ship. Sothran, they said.'

'It foundered there?' demanded Olvar. 'But surely that's too shallow – you'd have seen any wreck!'

'Nay, Mastersmith! 'Twas out beyond the bar it went down, and swift-like, beyond human help. But some said, later, they'd seen a boat driven in – maybe manned, maybe not, but in the very mouth it vanished. Dashed against yon stones, mayhap. Bodies fetched up in the harbour here, but all along the bay also. Great lords an' ladies some of them, by their jewels an' rings and garb of satins, sothrans wi' hair of flame or gold. But they sprawled and stank like the rest – ah, see there! They founder!'

For indeed the little craft was tossing wildly, and the figures in it waving their hands no less so. But Olvar clamped a heavy hand on the fisherman's shoulder. 'Stay! Look more calmly. They're in no great peril yet. They're excited at something, see – and who's that climbing over the side? Well, I'm ...'

It was Gille, recognisably Gille, and stripped to his breeches, so he had not simply fallen in. And he was not bothering to dress again, but kneeling, shaking his head; and after him the net was coming. A gasp ran along the quay. It was ripped open. Not so surprising, then, that the boat turned back to the shore.

That took a long twenty minutes or more for

Olvar. For even though the searchers had the inflowing tide with them now, they seemed to row unconscionably slowly, as if exhausted. Yet they turned, not back to their mooring, but to the low tidal jetty along the front of the square. It bounced and creaked under the weight of onlookers, but one of the boatmen roared at them to get back. 'We've burden enough as is!'

And he heaved a great muddy rock out on to the planks. 'Easy with that!' howled Gille.

'Well, Mastersmith?' shouted Stulte, from his dignified perch in the square above. 'Where's your catch? I don't see a single gilded scale. Have you just brought back weights to drown yourself?'

For answer Gille clambered awkwardly on to the jetty, picked up the lump. He had to be tired, thought Olvar, staggering like that. Then an inkling of the truth dawned, an instant before Gille raised the rock and let it drop, hard, on one of the quayside flagstones. It cracked with a hollow clink, and fell into large pieces. The crowd gasped as the sunlight flared up suddenly at their feet. It was not a rock at all, but a crusted conglomerate of debris; and its heart, shielded from the outer dirt, shone softly red in the morning rays.

Olvar blinked, dumbfounded. Stulte stared. But he was not a stupid man in himself, or a slow thinker, and he nodded. 'Very cunning, young Mastersmith! Happened on an old wreck, eh? You deserve your fortune; but I doubt that's enough to put you on a par with any of us, let alone fund your silly scheme. And you will have to enjoy it some-where else, or very possibly not for long; because, my poetic friend, it was gold fishes you wagered for, not gold coins. And I will accept no flowery figures of speech.'

'I would not ask you to, Master Stulte!' said Gille angelically; and hurled one of the smaller fragments up to the square. It burst with a pop, the crowd scattered instinctively as the bits flew; and then, with a soft gasp of wonder, fell scrabbling to their knees.

Gille held another coin aloft. 'Look for yourself, Master Stulte! Sothran struck, though by a Northern moneyer, I guess. New-minted when they went into the water, in chests and bags that kept them from being buried deep. On one face the proud towers of Ker Bryhaine, as ever – but on the other? In that encoiling style they're so fond of – can you make it out?'

'I see nothing!' protested Stulte. But from along the rail Tanle, drawn off his ship by the disturbance, shook his head.

'Master Merchant, I do! I know this minting well, struck a half-century back in my own home town, one of the best and purest ever, and now rare. I have a few in my own coffers back home. See the line there? And the curl there? That's the emblem of Bryhannec, Bryhaine the Lesser, our second port. The tail, twisting up thus to the head, there, with its armoured carapace. The great Fish, and golden as can be.'

Vangar was scrabbling around on his knees, looking at them. 'All the same! Fish everywhere, a hundred or more! Master Stulte, we're undone. But how?'

'I think the mastersmith owes us an answer!' grated Stulte.

Gille, swinging himself up the iron ladder, laughed aloud. 'All the debt's on your side, good master! Nothing was written of ways and means. And if you'd the wits to look closely at that first coin, you'd have made out the design! Now, honour your word!'

Stulte collapsed, rather than sat, on the rim of the fountain, and sank his face on his folded arms.

The other masters who had sealed the wager stood thunderstruck, leaning on their staves. One slumped down in the ripe market debris and began playing with straws, giggling nervously. Arkal shook his massive fist in Gille's face. 'Do you just try to collect, little tinker! Do your worst, and see if you don't end up between two millstones!'

Gille smiled, his eyes roaming seaward. 'Your fellows are less stupid, Master Arkal! They know the Guild courts will take a sterner view of a sealed agreement. And if it comes to force, why, my fishes will hire me men of my own. Not to mention my good friend the mastersmith Olvar, and my doughty crewmen here.'

The crewmen, heaving Gille's hoard up to the quay in a couple of fishy sacks, took their cue and turned to face the devastated merchants. Olvar did his best to loom impressively, but he was really suppressing startled sniggers. He could hardly recognise his friend in this confident bantam-cock facing down the master miller. Arkal's ruddy complexion was suddenly dusted down with his own flour. His voice sank to a hoarse whisper. 'If you mean to ruin us, you'll have this whole port down around your ears. It'll be the end of trade, of honest labour!'

Gille hesitated, then shrugged. 'The men who work your ventures now will do as much for me, at higher wages. But I said nothing of ruining you, though I could. Why do you assume the worst of me? Because you would do as much, in my place?'

Stulte shot to his feet. 'You won't enforce—'

'I most certainly will. But I am willing to come to terms, if you are sensible about them. I know you're the wealth of this town, or your businesses are, and I'll not scatter that to the four winds. I've no wish to pull you down. I want to be like you – only better, and wiser!'

Stulte gave a great sigh. 'I begin to think you

might, at that. Where has this come from, Mastersmith? Whence this sudden change in you?'

Those who knew Gille less well, thought Olvar, might not see his sudden discomfort. 'I am well advised,' he said curtly, looking away. 'So hear what I desire! Two good merchant ships, the best there are to be had – I'll pick them out for myself, with my friends. Fitted out and crewed for all the hazards of a long voyage, and filled with all the best goods this town can muster, yours and anybody's. We'll agree a bill of lading, and what you cannot supply, you shall buy. Smithcraft, most of all.' He stood, hands on hips, feet planted squarely in the muck of commerce. 'Thus much you can easily enough afford between you. Give me it fairly, and I shall call it quittance. Otherwise—'

'No man will cheat you!' said Vangar, with a black look at Stulte. 'Mastersmith, I set hard words on you i' the tavern, I thought you more apt to a plucked string or a maiden's skirt than your own craft, let alone mine. Now I have lent my seal to a braggart's wager, and you have triumphed. Maybe you are working out a purpose higher than yours or mine, who knows? But only a fool would cross you now. Come to a meeting of the elders this afternoon at the Great Guildhall, and we shall agree the bill as you demand. For now, you will wish to celebrate, no doubt?'

'I should like my nuncheon,' said Gille calmly. 'Celebration enough. Until the afternoon, then, masters.'

He bowed politely, and they all responded with elaborate courtesy, doffing their hats till they swept the earth, even the one still sitting among the dungy straws.

Gille, tucking in his shirt and straightening his tunic, retrieved the kantel lovingly. 'Thanks, Olvar. Think we can manage that little pile between us?'

'No need you do that, Mastersmith!' said one of the fishermen quickly, his dark hair flopping over his forehead. 'Ari and Ore and I'll bear it where you will.'

'Uz right!' said his brother. 'We're your men now, if you'll have us. Crew for this your voyage, if you need us.' The third one and youngest said nothing, but hoisted one of the sacks and stood waiting.

'A likely enough bunch,' said Olvar cheerfully. 'Will you take 'em, Gille? And for that matter, myself?'

Gille chuckled. 'I was about to ask if you'd come. I see gold makes other men ask the questions.' Then he swore, and added hurriedly, 'I didn't mean that! All of a sudden a friend has to guard his tongue, damn it to Hella! I need a captain, Olvar, and I'll not have any other. Partners as before! For the crew, Ari, Ore and Toste here, for a start!' He grinned at the fishermen. 'Won't ask you to bear that lot to the ends of the earth, lads - just to our forge and strongbox. And then a good feed! But little wine. We'll need a clear head to face that pack of sharks this afternoon.'

He strutted off cheerfully, as if he did in truth own the town. Olvar and the brothers exchanged wry looks, shouldered the gold, and lumbered after him. Olvar turned to Ari. 'You were with him out there,' he said quietly. 'Did you ... notice anything?'

'And what might you mean, Mastersm— I mean, skipper?' demanded Ari, slightly puzzled.

Olvar took a moment to adjust to his new title. 'See anything, well, strange. Or hear it, even.'

Toste suddenly broke his silence. 'Funny you askin' that.'

'Yes?' prompted Olvar, after a moment.

'Nothin' really,' said the taciturn brother. 'A feelin', sure. The breeze was brisk, but by moments there might been more. As if the whole air shivered. Like 'twas a music a man couldn't quite hear.'

Olvar glanced at Gille's back. Toste shrugged.

Sharks or no, the elders were still a very chastened pack by the afternoon, dealing with Gille as men who walk on eggshells and hot coals. The whole town was laughing at them, and Stulte was no longer their spokesman, but Vangar and Erkel the Guildmaster, who had had no part in the wager. 'I marvel at what got into them, as much as your good fortune, Mastersmith!' said the old man, his dry lips trembling. The merchants shrank into their shoulders. 'Arrogance and folly we suffer from, but seldom such a seizure. It could have brought ruin on us all. We owe your sense and restraint a debt beyond what is written, Mastersmith Gille.'

So it was that Gille left the hall with a scroll of fine vellum in his purse, heavy with stamps and seals. The largest was placed there by Erkel's fingers, age-spotted and fluttering, the heavy town seal; and tomorrow they would set out to buy ships. Their crewmen had gone back to the village to recruit others, and it was the first moment since morning Olvar had been alone with his transfigured friend.

'I also wonder,' he said idly, watching his own long shadow ripple over the cobbles of the main street. 'Is this Gille I speak to, or some sea-changeling? Whence came this advice of yours, Gille?'

The smaller man shrugged. 'The girl, this morning. I told you.'

'You did. But there's more, Gille, isn't there? What possessed you, human cat that you are, to cast yourself into cold choppy sea-water? And you came out of that boat not the same man that went in. Later, in the square, your eyes were forever turning aside. I could have sworn you were listening to something.'

'Into the water?' shrugged Gille, almost dreamily. 'There was little choice. We dragged up nothing on the first two casts, and then all at once the nets were snagging and snapping under the weight, all tangled on timbers and other things. I thought if I could only snatch up a coin or two, it might still salvage my wager; and the others were too busy handling the boat. So I tied a rope around me, and jumped ... you see ...'

His voice trailed off, puzzled. Olvar said nothing, which he was good at. His silence drew out an answer more readily than another question. 'I don't know. The first time I've ever felt really good about the sea. Even when that thing in the water brushed up against me, while they were hauling in the net.'

'A weedstrand? They can be slimy—'

'No! *In* the water, I told you. Like a current. And it didn't worry me. Not about breathing or drowning or anything. I felt safe. Anyhow, it was just for a moment, and then I saw what was coming up with the net!' He grinned, a slightly dazed and breathless grimace.

'Safe enough to jump, at the most difficult time,' remarked Olvar thoughtfully. 'And just about the time you hove to, you know something? This kantel of yours sang a little, by itself, very softly. A faint memory of a sound, no more.'

'A faint ...' Gille's voice faded. 'Yes, like that, almost ... the voice of the falling fountain ...'

Olvar looked sidelong, up and down the wide street. 'There's a name for folk who start hearing voices!'

Gille brushed the implications aside irritably. 'It wasn't like that! There weren't any words. There was just - something. Something I'd been told suddenly became clear.'

'Golden fishes!' jibed Olvar. 'Only reason I

might believe you. And Stulte stepping slap into that snare. Which he never would have done if you hadn't goaded him wild first. Handsomely done, lad, after a fashion; but not your fashion.' He jabbed a nervous thumb at the kantel, shining serenely in the sun at Gille's side. 'So … was somebody whispering the words in your ear then? Not … *him* …'

'I told you! Nobody's voice. Just - noise. The chatter of the fountain, the sounds of the square, the waves against the wall, even. But it helped me think clearly, somehow. Most likely nothing.'

Olvar bridled. 'Maybe! And maybe you'd best have a care. Who knows what you might be communing with, through that noisebox you bear? Maybe whoever took off those original strings knew what he was doing. Ever thought of that?'

Gille shook his head. 'No! No, that's not so. Look at it, man! Feel it!'

'Do I have to?'

'Damn it, you're a smith too. Look at it! Look!'

He practically thrust the kantel under Olvar's broad nose, so that the warm sun flashed on the ornate silver soundboard. Yet the eyes of a master-smith could not miss the deeper glare within the metal itself, the coursing veins of lightning. Olvar grabbed the kantel, tilted it this way and that. There was no mistaking it. The flows and courses ran now in different patterns, some this way, some that, some shifting and interweaving in an impossibly complex dance. From bridge to bridge they surged, like a ceaseless river of twisting serpents; and it was along the new strings, with their cladding coils of alternate copper and silver, that they flowed.

'The virtues are disordered no longer,' said Gille, more than a little proudly; for such triumphs of smithcraft were rare with either of them. 'I've made it whole, I've restored them. It has a purpose now.'

'Indeed,' said Olvar sourly. 'And have you any

better idea what that is? I still can't read them, any more than I could before.'

Gille took the kantel back gently. 'No. But what harm could there be? Whatever's there, I don't see evil. It's just meant to make music, Olvar. And that's all I've done – given it back its true voice. You heard it.'

'And if it's Vayde's, that voice? Would you really want to hear it?'

Gille considered, hefting the kantel lightly in the crook of his arm. 'I might do worse. He wasn't evil. And he was powerful, Olvar, very powerful.'

'He came to no good end, from all I've heard, though it was a lifetime at least too late. And he spared no man or woman, friend or foe, in his purposes. That one I could imagine leading you on, yes. To serve his ends, not yours.'

Their eyes met; but whatever Gille was about to say was halted by the patter of feet on the cobbled street behind them.

Gille froze. Olvar grinned, rather savagely. 'Hallo there, little Utte! What're you doing in town?' He took her hands, tiny in his immense paws, and kissed one of them. She greeted the two of them, practically bouncing up and down on her small neat sandals.

'Oh, Olvar, is it true what everyone's saying? I came in with my brothers to the market, and they were all talking about it! Gille's got himself hoards and hoards of money? And we don't have to wait any more?'

Olvar's mouth seemed to fall open before his mind was ready for it. 'Ah,' he said. 'Well...'

Gille slid between them like a greased snake, and took her in his arms. 'It's not that much money,' he said cautiously. 'Not yet. I can't take away all the merchants' wealth, can I? But now I've enough to make more. You'll see!'

'More?' she said dubiously. Her face fell. 'You mean, that dream of yours. The trading trip.' Anxiety quivered around her lips. 'Then ... you'll be going away? But that'll be for a long time!'

Olvar wondered if he could possibly just walk away, or whether he should simply run screaming wildly in all directions. He compromised by backing off across the street, slowly at first, then sidling swiftly away. Neither of them noticed.

'Yes,' said Gille bleakly. 'Yes, it could be. At least a few months; more, if I have to overwinter down south.' Her eyes fell, and he sought to cheer her. 'But I've got to come back sometime, haven't I?'

'Maybe,' she said flatly. 'Here, maybe. But what of me, Gille? Do you want to come back to me?'

'Utte,' he insisted, jogging her gently. 'This is my dream, Utte. My chance. Not everyone gets a chance at theirs. A sight fewer get two. What am I supposed to do?'

'I could say the same,' she said. To his immense relief she seemed dry-eyed enough, and not about to make a scene; and yet tears might somehow have been more reassuring. He was used to tears, and how soon they usually ended.

'It's more than just your dream, isn't it?' she insisted. 'It's a chance to get away – isn't it?'

'From some things, yes, all right.'

'From me.' Her smile was wry, and the twist of her mouth lingered. 'Do you think I can't see that? I half expected it. Then when your face fell the moment you saw me – then I was sure.'

He held her by the arms still, and she made no move to break away. At other such times he usually bubbled over with jolly reassurances, or, more rarely, found himself offended and picked a quarrel. Not on this day, though, that had slashed right through so many of his habits and assumptions. He had reeled through it like a drunken dream, like a child's bright ball bouncing from one wall to the next, his confidence at once wildly swollen and slashed apart by the encounter in the dawn. It was like no other; it had awoken feelings he could hardly put a name to, yet that tore at him with powerful claws. He had never felt so fulfilled as he had with the fair girl, nor craved so intensely what she gave him; yet he also felt lost and baffled, like a child shut out. Utte might look pale by comparison, and yet also infinitely closer and more comprehensible, open and familiar. The other was as fair as a statue, and as opaque; yet her blood burned hotter, and likewise kindled his. Too intensely, almost. The feelings she awoke engulfed him, rather than filled him with his usual self-satisfied delight at being loved.

'That isn't fair!' he protested. 'I was thinking of so many things, that's all. Exciting things – and then I realised I'd left you out of them. That was why I looked so crestfallen. That's all.'

She smiled again. 'Why, Gille – that sounds almost halfway true, for a change.'

Gille choked. 'For a— Utte, peach – you really think I've been lying to you?'

'Sometimes, aye. Gille, I may be just a little farm-girl, but do you really think I'm that blind? Or stupid? D'you think it wasn't fun for me, too?'

'What d'you—'

'Skating along the edge like that. The fun of being wedded to you, without each day's drudgery. Keeping it a half-dream, that we both half wanted and half believed. Keeping it alive with the intrigue. Gille, you're a fine and fancy lover, but that doesn't make you the best husband ever, that's daylight-clear! Have you not thought why you've not been snared before? Why all those others let you go so easily?'

Gille's tongue froze in his head. He had always

seen himself happily escaping a whole string of clutches; the idea that they might have been escaping him, or even tacitly speeding his departure, was appalling beyond words. 'There've been a hundred women who'd have been glad enough to wed me!' he protested.

'Only a hundred? Oh aye, I'm sure, glad enough at first. Glad enough if they could hold you. But when they knew they couldn't – they opened their hands. Let the butterfly flap away.'

'That's not true!' he insisted, and then, gathering his wits, 'Anyhow, who says it's true of you? Utte, you're different to me. You're special. And that's as true as ever anything was, ever!'

She twisted away now. 'I wish you'd not keep at saying that! It doesn't make it one whit easier. Can you not see I'm trying to – open my hand?'

'Well … I'm not.' He swallowed, and struggled to frame words where he had only ever needed easy lines. 'I … care for you. How much, I just don't know. It's been too easy to be just, well, conventional with you. But it isn't like that, not altogether. And I just don't know how far. I've never really felt like this. I don't know how I should feel. It isn't the romances. It isn't deathless passion, it's not being on fire. But it – you, you're not just another …'

'Am I not?' She was suddenly angry. 'Then who's the other?'

'The other?'

'The one who's got you feeling like this! Oh, it's not that trollop Laris, nor the fat flesher's wife neither – never want for a tranch of ham there, would you, Gille? I'd wager my blood and bed somebody's stuck a thorn into you for a change, my lad, and woken you up!'

'What do you want of me?' cried Gille, suddenly aware they were nose to nose like bristling dogs. 'D'you want me to bury my one chance in the dunghill and wallow down among the turnips with you?'

'Never that!' she snapped. 'You wouldn't last a week. You'd cut my throat, if I didn't get to yours first!'

'Well, what then? D'you want to come along and brave the seas with me?'

'You know I get sick in the millpond!'

'Well, then! What? Shall we end it here and now? Eh?'

'Well, you tell me. Shall we?'

They stood hands on hips, flushed, practically spitting in each other's eyes. Then they panted, subsided. They looked at one another, warily. 'Look,' said Gille, 'somehow... I might not want that. You?'

'I? I cannot say. But what *do* you want, then?'

'I told you. I don't know. You?'

'Sorry. Maybe I should, but I don't. I'd as soon see you come back safe, I'll say that much.'

'I will,' he said. 'Safe and rich. You don't have to wait, though. None of this fair-maid-at-the-spinning-wheel stuff. You could find somebody else while I'm gone. A better husband. I'd be happy for you. But if you do happen to be there when I get back – maybe I'd be happier, that's all.'

She considered. 'Maybe I would, too. You don't have to wait, either. As if you would! I'll think about it. I have time.'

He sighed. 'Maybe you'd be wasting your time.'

'I haven't thus far,' she said lightly. 'Scarce a mattress in the city that's had the pressing mine has. D'you know the seams are quite gone along one side?'

Gille was a little taken aback, as he always was by frankness in women. He preferred a decent reticence that it was his privilege to shock. He gave his most idiotic smile. 'Well...'

'Aye. I'd better be getting back to my brothers.'

'Your brothers. Yes.'

'Don't worry. I'll tell them I've refused to wed you until you come back with your fortune. Even though you begged me on bended knee. Which you've done, often enough. Or something after that fashion.'

Gille was embarrassed again. 'I almost wish—'

'Almost.' She wrapped her arms briefly around his neck and gave him a light peck on the lips, no more. She let go at once, and stepped back. They considered one another. 'It'll be growing cold and wet when you're back, autumn and all. Any time you see a light in the window, stop by for a stoup of wine. We can talk about it.'

He nodded, a little glumly. 'I'll do that.' He watched her turn away and trip down the street, not looking back, as if she hadn't a care in the world. The parchment crackled in his hand, crumpled tight. He wondered if he was not watching a still better fortune slip away.

And yet, for all that, the grey dawn light found him wandering abroad, as it had for many mornings since his farewell to Utte. Not down on the beach exactly, but wandering along the cliffs above; not seeking an encounter, but able to think of little else. Every morning he had not found her had been a disappointment to him, an aching emptiness; and this was the last before they sailed tomorrow. All the same, there had also been a tiny fragment of relief, that one more commitment, one more complication had not returned.

When the first warmth in the sky showed him the pale figure strolling through the grass, heading for the downward path to the bathing beach, he left himself no doubt at all, but began to run. The guardian was not yet at her place, yet even she might not have managed to stop Gille, so headlong was his rush, stumbling down the sandy path by its crude rock steps, tripping and sliding, clutching at the overhanging grass tussocks. He left himself too little breath to shout, and finished up leaping from sandhill to sandhill and racing out across the open sand to where the tall pale girl stood waiting for him, hair blowing about her.

Yet when he came within clear sight, and saw that it was indeed her, his feet faltered and he came to a foolish, breathless halt some strides away, uncertain what to say or do. She wore a tunic of blue silk today, less transparent than before but still clinging in the dampness. Her smile was muted but warm, and she wound a billowing blonde strand around a slender finger.

'Well, Mastersmith? Do I keep good tune?'

'The best!' said Gille, his boldness suddenly flooding back. 'What you gave me is clasped tight in fine metal, stretched out across ancient silver. Powerful virtues course through it, wonderful music awakes from it! Can you not feel them?'

And he swung the kantel up and drew a great rippling run across it, as sensuous a sound and key as he could imagine. She closed her eyes and breathed hard an instant, then raised her finger hastily to her lips. 'Hush, Mastersmith! Will you draw the locals down upon us, and my father with them?'

Hastily Gille damped the strings, though they quivered under his touch. 'Not I! Nothing to place you in peril. You've given me my life anew, and … and I don't even know your name, to thank you properly, or who you are.'

Again the finger to her lips. 'Don't ask! If you did know, how could I be so free with you? And give away such secrets? My father would never have recovered that gold, he has more than he needs, but still he would not take it kindly. Yet you may thank me.'

She stepped forward and placed her arms around Gille's neck, caressing it gently. 'Your eyes look shadowed. You haven't slept enough.'

He shook his head. 'I'm making ready a great venture. It's hard. I worry. About a lot of things. I don't even know why you're helping me. There's got to be a reason, hasn't there?'

'Greater than this?' she enquired, running a hand down her thighs. Gille caught his breath. Her laughter was gentle. 'We all have our reasons. Not all need concern you directly. Say that I might wish to spite one person and aid others; and there you were. I was sorry for you, I liked you. I wished to make you happier.'

'You have!' he said fervently. 'Every moment I'm with you! And when you're in my arms—'

'Put down your precious kantel,' she said gently. 'Carefully. I don't wish more handfuls plucked from my scalp.'

'I'm sorry,' he said, obeying her. 'I thought - that was a kind of pleasure to you.'

'Because I made it so,' she answered, lifting her hair high in her hands and letting it cascade damply about her shoulders. 'This morning, any morning, a different delight.' She put her hands to the base of her robe, and with a backward stretch drew it above her shoulders, so that her body arched to show every rib, and the taut muscles of her belly stretched flat. Gille shook a little with the sheer beauty of her, and her smile, as she shook the tunic free of her hair, showed that she knew its effect.

'You are the most wonderful woman alive,' he said fervently. 'And you will not say you love me.'

She smiled gently. 'Be wise, Gille. I give you much. Enjoy it, but be not too eager to cling to it. There may also come a time when you are required

to let it go as easily, some or all. See how wonderful
the world is! And yet beyond the horizons the Ice
has its hands about it, cruel and cold. Changes come.
In every fortune there is a tide, in every destiny. Be
sure you are as ready to release as readily as you
grasped, and cast your heart on the wings of
fortune once more.'

'Then may I not have the whole of it for now?
Can you not love me without restraint?'

'Perhaps I do, somewhat. We must make proof
of it.'

Gille looked around. 'Shall we not seek the
long grass? This place—'

'Is to my liking,' she said lazily, and unlaced his
jerkin with one sweep of her nimble fingers, and
slid them beneath.

'The sand—'

'I find it refreshes. And adds savour. And I
doubt any will intrude, so early.' She pressed her
long hands down hard upon his shoulders, forcing
him back upon the sand, and stooped down over
him, trailing her hair in his eyes, and down across
his chest as her lips sought it out and traced it,
breastbone to waist and so down. The sunlight
touched her flank, the angle of her breast, the faint
down beneath her arm as she ran it along his side,
and tugged the waistband of his hose away,
effortlessly.

'Now you have a long voyage ahead of you, I
hear, and little of love to ease it for many weeks to
come. So you must store up sweet memories, my
little master; and thank me as fervently as you wish.
Thank me!'

Later, limping half clad up a path that seemed
to have grown impossibly long and steep, he wondered if he had done the right thing, if he had not,
somehow, broken faith with Utte; and that was a
concern that had seldom bothered him before. For

any woman who sought to rein him in, he considered, was imposing an unnatural penalty upon him; and by that forfeited any right to expect it. Utte, by setting him free, had done practically the reverse, and somehow that constrained him to keep faith. Except that there was no faith to keep - was there?

And when he closed his eyes he could still see the fair girl arching over him and back, her long hair whipping, her thighs a lightning-burst about his own and the red sun playing rainbow flame across the tiny sweat droplets on her skin, and the sand that stuck to it like dragon-jewels. Or her head alongside his, her cheek to his, her long hair whipping him as her back coursed against his chest ...

He had said, again, that he loved her. And she had only laughed, and lured him to take her yet again, when he had thought himself spent.

He felt drained, in both body and soul. The tide of feeling had overpowered him once more, as it flooded the inlets below. He revelled in it, losing himself; and yet he feared it. He looked across to the port, figuring that he could almost make out the two tall mainmasts that were his, among the throng. His, to make truth of all the fond warm lies he had cuddled to his heart all these years; his, to bear him far from here. That would be for the best, maybe. No, surely. Yet, though neither woman had promised him anything, or extracted any promise of him, what he must face on his return made him almost more anxious than any peril of the voyage; for now.

He found himself not taking the way to town, but climbing the inland path, to the crest of the low hills. From there he looked out over the wide farmlands, to where in the middle distance Utte's manor lay, still sleeping in shadow, the sunbeams barely touching the tall stone chimneys, the shutters -

her shutters - closed. He could see through them as
if they were glass, to her bed in the darkness, her
fair skin. He sat awhile on the grassy slope,
breathless, with thoughts he could hardly give
shape to whirling around his brain. It was almost
without knowing it his fingers sought the strings,
and picked out a tune as dark and urgent as the
dawn wind hissing in the trees.

> *A stormbird is flying, silent and black,*
> *Unhindered by men or weathers,*
> *It wheels through the wide sky's driven wrack*
> *With the winds of fear in its feathers.*
>
> *No nest can that stormbird find to hide,*
> *No sheltering home or haven.*
> *Like a whispering shadow my yearnings glide*
> *Past the light in your window each even.*
>
> *You stirred as the moonlight touched your brows,*
> *Dark dreams brushed away with a finger.*
> *Now you sleep deep as your silent house,*
> *But my destiny, it cannot linger.*
>
> *Like clouds that are chased, like leaves that*
>   *are blown*
> *Across the dark waters in flight*
> *We unhappy children, we stormbirds unknown,*
> *We whispering wings in the night!*

At last he turned away; then stopped, listening.
Noises carried sharply in that waiting silence,
sounding larger and more immediate in their
isolation. Had he heard a bolt click, the faint creak
of hinges? He looked back; but the house seemed as
blind as before. If one of the shutters had opened a
crack, he might never know it. He turned again, and
trudged away up the hill.

CHAPTER THREE
Out of the Ice

GILLE paced back and forth on the narrow quarterdeck. In the quiet morning air the planking drummed beneath his boots. Olvar leaned against the rail, and shrugged. 'I don't care if she's the Queen of the Forests. We've got to go. Now, today, and that's it. Much later, and we'll find the solstice gales against us on our return, and what then? See our profit and maybe our lives blown away. And now means now! If we don't up anchor within the hour we miss the tide and Tanle's company. And we must sit twiddling our thumbs till the morrow with half the dock pointing the finger at us and laughing. A fine bloody start! A fine way to earn the crew's faith in us!'

Gille stopped pacing. The louring clouds rolled on overhead, and the cool breeze whipped at him, despite his heavy hide jacket. The water quietly lapping at the hull seemed to laugh gently at his unrest. He hugged himself and shivered. 'That's another thing. I should never have let you browbeat me into this captaining lark, Olvar. I'm scarcely up to it.'

'You have to be,' said Olvar brutally. 'No choice. Least of all now. But you took the *Rannvi* out well enough, didn't you? You learn quick, if you'll only believe in yourself.'

'On a fine day, a short jaunt in sight of the coast. But what if—'

Olvar held up his hand sharply. 'Not so loud! Don't let the lads hear you. Why d'you think you're so needful? You're the wonder-worker. You're the man who plucks gold from the sea and kicks our haughty merchants in the arse, the man whose bright idea all this is. We wouldn't have been able to sign half the crew we need without you, and we've still none to spare. You've got a fine sailing master in Nils, as good a shipman as I and a better navigator. Heed him, look to me and to Tanle, and you'll come to no harm.' He snorted. 'Provided, that is, you leave off your dreams of skirt once in a while. See, there she is on the quay, waiting to wave you off.'

'What? Where?' spluttered Gille, running to the side.

'Down there!' said Olvar sardonically. 'It's Utte I'm talking of. And so should you be, not some little biddy you've been rolling in the sand with. Go to her a moment, and then heed my signal.'

Without another word Olvar clattered away down to the deck. The narrow gangplank bounced alarmingly as he rolled on to the quay, waved to Utte and stalked up the gangplank opposite. Further down the quay a whistle sounded, and one set of rigging was suddenly aswarm with sailors. Tanle was already making sail. Gille cursed bitterly, and then, clenching his hands, he walked down the plank to where Utte waited, with a gaggle of other women, watching the ships silently. She looked at him, and said nothing.

Gille was not as hard of heart as he felt he could be. He opened his arms to her. She came to be kissed; a touch reservedly, but she came. 'I know you've been busy with your preparations, these past weeks. I felt you might fare better without me forever in your eye. Things being as they are.'

'Maybe,' said Gille wryly, wishing the interested spectators would walk off the dock and drown horribly. 'Thoughtful of you, anyhow. Wish me well for the voyage?'

'Of course I do!' Her smile was strained. 'Gille, whatever we decide – I do still wish you may come back safe.'

He clutched her hands, and smiled at her. 'I will. And richer. Maybe wiser.' A great rush of feeling overwhelmed him, and he kissed her again. 'You're too good for me, Utte. You should find yourself some fine steady fellow with a bit of his own land he never thinks of leaving.'

She giggled. 'What, like my brothers, you mean? A fine thing it'd be to drowse away my whole life with one more man the same. No, give me change and colour, Gille. Give me life and light and fun. But not on just any terms. There's got to be something we can share.'

He nodded. 'No, you're right. Not just any old how. There's got to be a centre, a purpose. Utte, don't you see? That's what I haven't found yet for myself.'

She giggled again. 'So meanwhile you and your wings go flapping about the place mucking up a few hats. Or beds, maybe? Ach, don't look as if I've trod on your little paw, then! Behave yourself if you can, but that's for your own good.'

He hugged her impulsively. 'I've never been too wise about that!' But even as he released her, the shrill pipe sounded from Olvar's quarterdeck, and she pulled away, suddenly more serious.

'So, then. Off with you. Find whatever of yourself there is to find. Then maybe we'll both know our minds a little better.'

'I must go!' he gasped, and scuttled up the gang-plank, almost overbalancing at the rail, uncertain whether he'd taken leave or been dismissed. The plank was hauled in behind him even as he leaped up the companion steps to where the burly sailing master waited. Nils and the man at the tiller saluted him.

Gille caught his breath and summoned up the

right words. 'You heard, Master. Make ready to set sail!'

Nils nodded, and put his pipe to his lips. Immediately the ship became a scurrying commotion, as men swung themselves up the ratlines and out along the mainyard, tugging at the lashings. Nils barked to the men on the quay, and the forward lines were loosed and cast aboard. 'Let fall!' Nils shouted, and the great mainsail dropped with a boom. Men on deck seized the mainsheets and hauled them taut, barely in time; the wind took it and bellied it, the men on the yard slid off it as it swung and creaked, scrambling and sliding back down stay and ratline to the deck. The *Rannvi* strained under the pressure, and her nose swung out, away from the quay. Gille gulped as the deck lurched under him. 'Cast off aft!' roared Nils, and the line came whipping back. 'Steer for the harbour mouth!'

The *Rannvi* bucked, the bows dipped and rose and its whole movement changed, like a horse breaking into a sharp trot. Gille staggered a little, caught the rail and felt his stomach lurch as the ship cleared the end of the quay and wallowed suddenly at the change of flow. He remembered abruptly, and leaned out to wave to Utte; but already he could not make her out on the quayside. Spray slashed at him, and the wind seemed suddenly far colder. Off to port the *Orrin*, which had had to pull away from the quay with sweeps, was shipping them hastily as its mainsail also caught the breeze. More sail blossomed out on its small mizzenmast. Olvar caught his eye and tipped him the wink.

'Sailing master!' called Gille.

'Make more sail, sir?' demanded Nils. 'Very good!'

Watching the extra sails hoisted, Gille smiled smugly. This wasn't going to be as hard as he'd thought. Ahead of him he saw the *Ker Dorfyn's* sail, already passing the end of the seawall and out into the open ocean, rising and falling with a great lazy swoop like a slow-beating wing. He glanced across at the *Orrin*, nerving himself. Olvar, back to the rail, waved cheerfully, as if to say, *After you!*

There was a noise like a rasp beside him, Nils running a thumb across his grizzle-bearded chin. 'Take 'er out, sir?'

Gille nodded. 'We must keep our station.' Which, if he remembered aright, was the word for keeping up with Tanle, who was to be their guide for the voyage south. It seemed to please Nils, anyhow, because he nodded back, and condescended to add, 'No worry, sir, he's but on a broad reach, we'll fetch 'im easy as yet.' All of which meant very little to Gille; but he memorised it carefully so he could go below and look it up in *The Skallas-book, or the Mirror for Mariners*, which was presently weighing down the shelf in his cabin.

In truth, that cabin was what had really got him into this latest mess. In this crowded merchant-man only the captain had one, and that doubled as the chartroom. Nils and the mate shared a cubby-hole in the fo'c'sle, and the crew slung hammocks where they could, or bedded down among the cargo. Gille, fastidious and fond of his privacy, would have been miserable joining them, yet as the instigator of the whole voyage he could hardly stay behind; and so he had given in to Olvar's insistence. He sighed, watching the bar draw closer and the shade of the sea change, colourless in the faint light; Olvar seemed to know what he was doing.

'Don't stick your nose into every detail!' had been the advice. 'The crew won't expect that, and it'll belittle you in their eyes. Leave it to Nils, they know he's after their own kind. The important thing's that they see you command him.'

It was only then the realisation struck him: Olvar was captaining for the first time too! Gille fought down everything that rose up, his breakfast included. Of course the big fellow had sailed as a crewman often enough, once even as a mate, when they were newly mastered and in need of funds. He would surely have learned enough, thus; wouldn't he?

Then the deck slid down under Gille's feet, and seemed to rise up in the same instant, and the hull boomed dully as the waves slapped against it. '*Ready about!*' rumbled Nils, and the pipe shrilled, and again the ship was an overturned anthill. Men tagged on to ropes and ran with them, the yards swung and creaked like ancient bones, the sheets stiffened, and when Gille got his balance again Tanle's sails were coming into dim view ahead, bleached whiter than his own by salt and sun, gleaming softly against the sweeping greyness above and below. 'Handsomely done, sailing master!' he said breathlessly, as the sheets were tied off and the ship settled into placidity once more. 'Er – how's she handling?'

'Like a baby, sir!' said Nils, almost cheerfully. 'Trim could be better, but 'tis always so with your overladen merchantman at setting sail, right?'

Gille ran desperately through all the meanings of trim he could remember, and decided it had nothing to do with the sails, and must refer to the angle of the ship, caused by the distribution of her cargo. He remembered something Olvar had said; and indeed the bows seemed to be rising rather high. 'Right. Down by the stern a bit, isn't she? She should even up as we use up our stores.'

Nils looked a little surprised, then ducked his head. ''Tis so, skipper. Not too much. No sweat.'

Skipper? Maybe he had said the right thing again. 'Take station, then,' he said, greatly heartened. 'And, er, steady as she goes.'

Hugely relieved, Gille strode to the rail and looked out at Tanle's ship. Olvar's was coming up to port. All well, so far. He felt fresh and free, and eager to see the sun rise; and he was even getting used to the changing motion of the ship. This energetic surging and plunging rhythm, with its accompaniment of light gasping creaks, reminded him of something. When he realised what, he grinned. For the moment at least he was free of all his entanglements in that line also. In fact, he was having fun.

He felt a little guilty at that. All the crew who were free to were looking wistfully astern at their home, already hardly more than a shadow in the mirk. He strolled back down the quarterdeck to do the same, and climbed up on the steps by the sternpost above the great tiller. Back there was Utte – was she weeping on her way home, or not? – and somewhere there the Other. He could hardly imagine her in tears, at least not at parting. She seemed above that, somehow; and when you thought of it, that was a very strange way for a woman, for anybody, to be. The things she said, too. *Can you read the purposes of the sun, or the sea, or the Great Ice?*

He gazed far astern now, beyond the grey mists to where the sky was still black and cold, beyond the reach of even this miserable pretence of light. All too easy to imagine the malevolence that dwelt there, stalled for the moment by the sharp young mountains that shielded the lands of men, and yet able to wait. To wait, it was said, until those self-same mountains wore down and crumbled, until their own snowpeaks blossomed and united to breed the glaciers which could reach out like fingers across the last fertile lowland, clawing, gouging, crushing the life it hated, and that of mankind most of all. And in the meantime the Powers of the Ice and their emissaries were working all manner of plots for the ruin of that mankind, its strife and disunity, to weaken the resistance of free minds and free knowledge that might hinder it.

That at least was no rumour. Once he had encountered such an emissary, definitely unhuman, and the experience still fuelled his nightmares. One terrible emissary; so the hosts of that darkness must be worse, and their masters...

It didn't bear thinking about.

And indeed, it was as if his incautious thought attracted some unhallowed attention; for it was even then that the dark void blossomed pallid white from horizon to horizon.

At first he mistook it for the moon breaking through the sullen cloud-roof. Then he realised the moon must be near setting. It was something stranger that suffused the sky, a translucent white glitter that shook and shifted like a windblown curtain, still in one place, shivering in another, as if the stars poured down the dust of forgotten years. Tinges of rainbow colour coursed through it, like a thread of gems. The height of it was appalling; the mountain peaks were less than gravel at its feet, and it soared up into infinite distances, dimming the stars. A chorus of dismayed shouts went up from the crew; and Gille felt much the same.

'The Northlights!' he whispered, through wind-dried lips. There was nothing new about them; he had seen them often, as they all had, every man of the Northlands, flickering across the skyline in the dark winter evenings, banner of the ravening barrenness the mountains held back. But he had never seen them from the sea. From here, even this short way out, the mountains were no longer a barrier. Out there, beyond their sight, the coast curved out northward, increasingly barren, to where the glaciers swept down to confront the sea, lining it with towering ice-cliffs, unstable, fragmenting in ice-falls, constantly advancing. Further north they overrode the sea itself, to form a single continent of Ice that stretched as far as the lands of the Far West, whence Olvar's copper-skinned folk had come, bridging both lands with the same dead grasp. It was high above that grim coastline that the North-lights shone forth now, marking the true extent of the dominion of the Ice; and incidentally making the ships, their voyage, their crews and indeed all human concerns seem suddenly very small and negligible indeed. Beyond all these, poised to over-whelm them, other forces were launching hostile purposes of their own.

Nils hawked and spat overside. 'Bastards!'

Gille caught the venom in the voice. 'You've seen them before, then? Like that?'

'That I have!' said Nils harshly. 'When I was a kid. A mine settlement, hardly a village, in the Nordenbergen, north of Harthaby even, hard land where the duergar themselves didn't dare go. Poor folk who thought to scratch their way to riches with raw courage. Then one night the Lights flared over the peaks, like green flame at the masthead. And a pack of snow-trolls came down on us over the passes. Just clearing the way, I'll be bound, for their masters; like sweeping the doorstep. My mother died, and my father couldn't help her; he fled with a few others to the coast, bearing me in one ragged blanket. They hunted us, and ate what they caught. That's when my childhood ended.'

Gille shivered. 'Yes, I know. There was a creature of the Ice— No, I don't want to say more. Maybe later.'

Nils's heavy eyebrows lifted a fraction. 'Aye. Wisest not to speak too loud of such matters. Most of all here before the crew.'

'But you don't think all that's meant for *us*, do you?'

Nils blew out his seamed cheeks. 'No wise. But there's something stirring, and always a chance it might snatch us up. You'd best say a word to cheer the lads.'

'Me? Oh well...'

It was little enough effort. Gille's fluent words carried the nervous young sailors along, as he pointed out that the Lights were far to the north, as far away as they had ever been, and that the mountain barriers stood as strong as they had for the last thousand years at least in this part of the world. The Lights only looked so bad because they were seeing them at sea, with nothing in the way; and it was at sea that the Ice had made least headway. That was because the waters carried warmth from the Southern seas to melt it back.

'The South, lads, Ker Bryhaine – and that's where we're headed, far away from rime and snow and spooks! A warm land, a wine-land, where the only light in the sky is the sun, and the girls have red curls all over. And even by night you can slip out for a leak without it freezing solid.'

That raised a laugh, even from Nils. Gille warmed to his theme. 'Believe me, I've been there. Only I had to ride all the way, and fast; and arrived with my arse better tanned than my saddle. You're travelling the soft road! And you'll be in a condition to take advantage—'

By the time he had finished expounding on sothran women, nobody was looking at the Lights; and, more to the point, he had almost forgotten them himself. He could not decide, thereafter, whom it was that Nils really wanted to reassure.

As dawn drew nearer, and the convoy made fine headway to the southward, the Lights faded. In the excitement of the sunrise, its first rays pouring a radiant track of molten gold along the ocean, he forgot them altogether. The long light-fingers that probed the ragged clouds tinged the sails with crimson, like a promise of the warmer days to come. The crew shouted cheerfully as they threw themselves into their labours, as if to tempt the Southlands closer. Before long the *Orrin* was overhauling the *Rannvi*, so that Olvar's boat could be launched back to them. He bellowed with good cheer as he swung himself up the side-rail, but his first quiet words to Gille, when they were alone on the quarterdeck, were, 'Any trouble?'

'Disquiet, yes. The Northlights. But Nils suggested I sweeten them. I seemed to manage.'

'Told him you could talk the hams off an elk. Would that I could. I came close to breaking a few heads, but they're quiet now. Maybe you should come over later and try there also.'

'All right. What about Tanle?'

'His men are sothrans. They expect that sort of thing up North, and they're on the way home with one more tale to tell. Never mind the crews, though – what'd *you* think of it?'

'Like Nils said. Nothing to do with us, unless a man get himself caught up.'

'That's usually the way.' Slowly, Olvar relaxed, slumping down on the helmsman's bench, leaning back against the rail, watching the taciturn Nils take a turn at the helm. 'Probably just shenanigans within the Ice itself – bickering, most like. Bloody Powers!'

'Bloody indeed!' growled Nils. 'Batteners on the blood and pain of men!'

'Some,' objected Olvar mildly. 'The Powers of the Ice, for sure. But most aren't too concerned with us unless we tread on their toes, like Tapiau. Or Lord Niarad!' He turned to the side and doffed his cap briefly. Gille smiled. Nils did not. 'And there's some who're friendly, in their fashion. Ilmarinen the Flame-Lord, our patron. Or Old Raven—'

Nils snorted. 'As bad as the rest! Interfering old sod! Mind you,' he added hastily, 'I say no word 'gainst the Sea-Lord or his kin. But the less I see of 'em, and they of me, the better it likes me. And them also, I'm sure. Meanin' no offence.'

Gille was thinking of the good wine sluiced over the bows of each ship when it was full-laden, the sothran as well as their own. What could that really mean to Niarad? A symbol, perhaps; an acknowledgement that they were entering his realm, and were aware of the need to keep the bounds and shut the gates. Smiths understood the power of symbols.

He gazed out over the vast expanse beyond the bow and imagined it tenanted not only by strange creatures and outright monsters, but by a mind as vast and alien as the compass of those lights, and by all accounts at least as powerful. Suddenly Olvar's gesture seemed a deal less amusing. 'Perhaps we should go talk to your men, right enough. Sailing master, will you overhaul the *Orrin*, please? And take command while I'm gone.'

The atmosphere aboard *Orrin* was palpably different from his own ship, sullen and uncooperative. From the moment he showed himself aboard it eased slightly; but it was not until he sat on the rail and struck up the kantel that they were ready to listen. He sang them songs he had learned in the South, sentimental songs of wine and women, and then, when he had them singing along, their familiar work songs. On those strings the lively tunes had them leaping to work with a will. The wind freshened, the clouds dispersed, the waves became a mass of white horses, and to Gille, already pleased with himself, it seemed the ship itself was dancing.

He was less pleased as the boat taking him back bounced like a cork, this way and that. He mistimed his leap for the sideladder, so that though he caught it the *Rannvi* heeled and dipped him waist-deep in the icy swell, with breathtaking effect. He was more concerned with saving the kantel, but when he arrived on deck dripping he dreaded a gale of laughter. Nobody gave him a second glance. 'It's common enough,' said Nils. 'Every man aboard'll have a few good soakings afore we reach these sothran ladies of yours. Want your breeks run up the mast? It's rare dryin' weather.'

Gille eyed him narrowly. 'You're not telling me *that's* an old sea custom? Flying 'em like a flag?'

'Well...' admitted the sailing master, without a tremor in his face.

Nils was well enough, decided Gille, as long as you watched him.

That day, on which he proved his hold over the crews, gave him a greater trust in himself. It was as Olvar had said: they did not expect displays of seamanship from him, for that they looked to Olvar and Nils. What they wanted from him in the days that followed was something subtler, a sense of direction and belief in their enterprise; and, curiously enough, he found himself able to provide it. The weather was mild enough, as they had expected, and though there were some heavy seas at times, there were none of the storms he had feared, and no mishaps that Nils could not cope with in his name. He knew it was best that he hold himself a little aloof from the men; but he found himself able to remember and point out landmarks from his previous voyage, tell them how far they had come, and tales of these places. That most of all raised him in their regard, for evidently he could be trusted to know whither they were headed. He did not tell them how that voyage had ended.

When they put in at Tensborg, last of the great Northern ports, for water and provisions, he took careful council with Tanle and Olvar, and sought out the latest news about corsairs in the area, and whether there had been any attacks. Everyone seemed to agree that there had not, and that it was high time trade was resumed. 'But so many ships were lost in those black years,' said one taverner, 'aye, and the boldest skippers and crews. So many that the habit of long seafaring sank with 'em, and the established markets. One or two convoys a year, when once there were twenty. And few ready to make the long haul, like Master Tanle here. You're welcome indeed, sirs, and no man'll raise his hand against you, for you may herald the return of our golden years!'

And that too was heartening. No man indeed but welcomed and encouraged the convoy, and they seldom had to pay for their ale; but still Gille was nervous. 'You were attacked, after all, Tanle. Other sea-reivers may have moved south as those ones moved north.'

'Well,' chuckled Tanle, beaming stickily over his flagon, 'your friend Kunrad'll give them a warm welcome! And we're three now, not alone as I was. But I won't put you off keeping watch, I'm sure!'

So Gille did, indeed, as they sailed out of Tensborg and along the margins of the Debatable Lands, that marked the end of Nordeney and the beginning of the bleak river delta, flat, tidal and swampy, that was known as the Great Marshes. Even that fell region had lost some of its terrors, since, a few years previously, Marchwarden Kunrad's army had made their way in great barges along the narrow waterways, to harry the last of the corsair army that lurked there, and throw down their tower. But the Marshes were still unhallowed country, plagued by the outflows of the Great Ice and its malign influences, the spirit-servitors of Taoune and Taounehtar, Lord and Lady of the Cold Realm, let loose upon the world of warmth and life.

That was a place no man would willingly find himself by day or night. Gille had passed through it, one corner at least, alive; but he said nothing of that. He paced the quarterdeck for long hours, watching the shore; and when they came to the first of the grey beaches that marked the outflows of the Marshes, he hardly left the rail.

'Why d'you scan the land so?' demanded Nils quietly. 'It goes beyond caution, it's making the lads jumpy!'

'Yes, I expect so, but … well. You see that stream there, the outflow with all the reedbeds about it?'

'Aye. What of it?'

'I was taken by corsairs from just such a place. Two longboats, bristling oars and crammed with men, out of the reeds like flung javelins. Then a near-massacre, the first I'd seen, and myself and Olvar and my master at cutlass-point.'

'Man! And you all lived?'

'They were part of the army. They wanted skilled men and smiths. They took and chained us, and made us swink in their damned forges.'

'How'd you get out of that with a whole skin?'

Gille shuddered. 'Don't ask. But you don't chain a mastersmith with iron.'

'I wager not!' Nils sounded almost impressed. 'Well, I'll not argue with you watching out, skipper. Only not so openly, maybe.'

'All right, but could we not steer a bit further from the land? That could make all the difference with those longboats, they're not seaworthy for a long run.'

Nils twisted his mouth and spat overside. 'This is Master Tanle's course, and he our pilot. We'd needs clear it with him. Want me to make a signal?'

'Ask him to send a boat. For Olvar as well. We should talk.'

To his relief, Tanle did not immediately laugh him down. 'Well, Master Gille, I'd have said the corsairs were gone from this stretch of the coast. But then I thought as much on the way north, and have you to thank for saving me from my mistake.' He tugged at his red pigtail and tapped his old chart. 'But see you now, this course strikes the best middle way between speed and safety. We're following a channel of sorts. There mayn't be any rocks along a delta coast like of this, but there's sudden shallows, there's sandbanks and shoals quite far out. Run aground on a good solid one and you'll dismast yourself, like as not; or stave in your planks. And there's great wide sands as have streams flowin' beneath them. They're like quicksand ashore, only greater - suck your whole ship down in an hour or two.'

Olvar nodded grimly. 'So I've heard. But I remember the corsairs, too. They came on us from the southern end of the Marshes, but it could be any one of these streams. I felt safe enough thinking about it at Thuneborg, but now we're here ...'

Tanle drummed his fingers on the *Ker Dorfyn*'s scarred but costly cabin table. 'Well, masters, the only way we'll clear the shoal waters is by headin' much further out from shore, as much as a league. And I'll confess I wouldn't mind that.' He nodded towards the shore, and Gille caught his breath as he saw the faint haze over the flat grey country of reeds. 'There's mists brewing up shoreward. Not riding seaward, like as not, but you never know. We might have to heave to and drop anchor, ride it out. Or even put in to shore, though ...'

'Steer out to sea!' said Gille and Olvar, in chorus.

By the next afternoon the low-lying shore was no more than a distant smudge, growing whiter and less distinct with every hour that passed. Gille, much more relaxed, sat against the sternpost watching it, strumming the kantel. The *Rannvi* was skipping along merrily enough, despite the greying sky; but Nils was silent and gloomy, and the kantel seemed to irritate him. 'See here, skipper,' he said at last. 'Would you could sway the weather with that thing, as you do men's hearts. 'Cause we could use a mite o'that right now.'

Gille sat upright. 'But we steered out here to clear the mist – among other things.'

'Aye, mebbe, but there's no law governs such matters. See there! If this wind holds…'

Gille glared at the long finger of whiteness oozing slowly off the point ahead, turning the grey waves paler. 'Signal the others!' he snapped. But even as he gave the command, long pennants were flying up *Ker Dorfyn*'s rigging, and sailors waving flags from the deck.

'Keep station…' read Nils. 'Or … out sweeps … down anchor … at need. That's as much as to say, do as we see fit. I'd say sweeps; slow, but we can handle her easier.'

Gille nodded. 'We won't anchor until we must. Not here; not in those mists.'

The pipe sent the crew racing up to take in sail; but Gille stood silently, looking past them as the white wall rolled inexorably towards him, bearing with it the memories of terrors long buried. It was on them with frightening speed, and the world grew momentarily grey, and vanished.

It was as if a sheet of pure white parchment had been thrust before his eyes. The immersion was complete. The masts, the deck, the rail, even the planking at his feet seemed to melt into the chilly whiteness. And with it sounds were curiously damped, the panicking cries of the crew, Nils swearing, his own fast breathing – all seemed to recede from him, leaving him adrift without a landmark. The terrified voices infuriated him because they mirrored his own fear so exactly. '*Down that piping!*' he yelled, as he had heard Nils do. 'Get those sweeps out, if you value your necks!'

'You heard the skipper!' roared Nils, startlingly close. 'Find them if you have to feel for 'em! And the first man loses one overside goes after it!'

Gille's eyes were adjusting fast. He began to make out slight shadings in the mist, faint flickerings of movement. 'Is that you, Nils?'

'Hope so, skipper. That was a timely word. Best we keep under way while we can.'

'All right. I wish we could signal the others – so we don't ram one another. Lodestones and direction bracelets won't stop that.' He ran a frustrated hand over the kantel, and was surprised at how loud it sounded. Then he jumped. One voice sounded really far off, too far.

'A hail!' growled the sailing master. 'They can hear that gut-box of yours, all right. No mistaking it, either. Give us a song, skipper!'

'Gut-box, indeed!' snapped Gille, but he struck a few strong chords. The clear tones seemed to cut through the mist. The voices that came back were faint by comparison, but they helped to define a sense of distance. Before long he caught the clanging of ship's bells and the clattering of improvised gongs and drums – galley-pots, guessed Nils, and empty barrels, anything to make a row. Carefully, slowly, the three ships inched together, eager to get within close hail, afraid of collisions. Before long the creak of their sweeps could be heard, and the shouts became words. Suddenly the mist flared red; Tanle had taken a risk and kindled a pitch-torch at his stern. Under the flame they drew together, until they could make one another out as fantastic looming spectres distorted by the mist, leaping shadows and skeletal outlines.

'*Keep your bloody distance!*' came Olvar's roar.

'Heave to, all!' shouted Tanle. 'Bottom at a hundred feet, pure sand. Drop anchor!'

The three chains rattled almost as one, and when they tautened, an audible sigh seemed to stir the mist. The dangerous torch hissed into the water, and a great silence fell. Gille could almost taste the uncertainty in the air. The mist was a chill hand on his face, but he found himself sweating. Almost instinctively he swung up the kantel again and launched into the first cheerful tune that came to mind, a favourite of Utte's. A few notes in, and a great roar of laughter from all the ships seemed to make the fog boil, drowning him out altogether. It was only then he remembered the first line:

I dance about in a mist of love…

So they sat, swinging lightly at anchor under the light swell, singing and laughing while the mist coiled and writhed around them. For a moment it would thin briefly so they could see the other hulls, then it closed in, blank as ever. Some fool tried to dance on the rail, inevitably fell in and had to be fished for. It all helped to pass the time. The pale light dimmed, and the hourglasses told them night had come. Gille grew weary of playing, and the singing faltered. Gradually silence began to fall again. Then it was abruptly broken, by a sudden sound from the mist, very loud, a creaking, groaning squeal.

'*What was that?*' yelled Gille, jumping up with the rest, his mind suddenly racing with images of mythical monsters, of Amicac the Sea Devourer and the Powers knew what more.

'That's my frigging timbers, that is!' roared Tanle. '*Orrin, Rannvi,* ahoy – something just brushed into us! Something large, we're swinging like – *fend off, damn your eyes, fend off! With the sweeps!*'

Gille heard the sothran's anchor chain clink taut in the water. 'Hope it holds, that sothran link!' he hissed to Nils. 'We've got good Northern virtues on ours, and the anchor too! But his—'

'*Gille! Nils! Watch out, it's…*' There was a bumping crash in the whiteness. 'Bugger! We're holed!'

Nils gave an anguished groan, and yelled, 'Out with those sweeps! Butt first, you stupid bastards, you're thicker than the fog! Fend it off, whatever it be! *Fend off!*' He staggered along down to the deck.

Just at that moment the mist was not so dense; they could see a stretch of black water below the port bow. But there seemed to be nothing else there, only the dense whiteness advancing once again, gleaming in patches as if it were frozen solid.

Gille gaped, with the horror of it trickling down his neck; then he managed to shout, 'There! Off the port bow! Get those sweeps forward and fend us off!'

'What from?' yelled someone. 'The mist?'

'That's not mist!' Gille yelled back. 'It's ice! An ice-island!'

A monster of the deep it was indeed, though not a living one. Barely in time, the butts of the long heavy oars rang against it, skidding and slipping. More men raced to throw their weight upon each one. Slowly, almost as ponderously, the *Rannvi* dipped and turned, the anchor-chain sprang taut with a deep sturdy clang, and the ship's angle changed. The appalling ice-cliff filled the air above them now, and even the fog seemed to be swept aside by its grim advance. The *Rannvi* bumped and bounced, her timbers groaned as had Tanle's, and Gille yelped at the sight of a long bluish outcrop advancing, gleaming just a little way below the water's surface. It was heading straight for the bows. 'If our luck holds, we'll lift and override it!' gasped

Nils from below. 'The keel's well built to endure it.'

'And if not?'

'Why then, skipper, may Saithana look to us all before the end!'

The bow lurched, creaked, lurched further. Men wielding sweeps lost their footing and fell slithering. Chill air wrapped around them like a giant's breath. The mast flexed, the rigging sang. Gille clung to the rail as a fearful scraping passed beneath; and then suddenly *Rannvi* was bouncing free again in the freshening swell, and the gleaming monster wallowing away astern, trailing ragged banners of mist.

'*Tanle!*' Gille screamed. 'Do you need help? *Orrin*, ahoy, *Olvar!* How d'you fare?'

'We thought you'd been crushed!' came the hail. '*Tanle*'s well, not too badly hulled, we're alongside and helping. And you – all well?'

'All's well!' breathed Gille, and then realised he had been able to see quite clearly for the last few minutes. 'And the mist's lifting! We're safe!'

'Are we indeed!' came Nils's grim voice from the deck. 'Then look you out at that, now!'

Gille looked ahead, and out to starboard, away from the land; and his heart froze an instant within him. Over sky and sea the mists were rolling back, like the cover of a tray of gems on black velvet. Over the clear black sky above the stars were scattered; but clustered almost as thick, it seemed, were the ice-islands glittering blue-white over the calm dark horizon. And the air was bitterly, unseasonably chill.

The one that had drifted among them was a mere outlier, and by no means the largest. It bobbed and swung clumsily in the wash behind them, as if reluctant to let them go. Gille had to swallow a few times before he could force out a word. 'Nils? This isn't ... normal – is it?'

Nils sounded as stunned. 'Up north, maybe, Harthaby way and beyond; I've seen nigh as many there, and more crowded. This far south ... ask Tanle. But I'd say never!'

'The Northlights!' exclaimed Gille; but Nils was already shaking his head.

'Think, man! The ice-islands would have needs drifted faster than we sail, to overtake us. Scarcely a stormwind could have driven them so far, so fast. No, these must have set out weeks before we saw the Lights.'

Gille listened to the hubbub below. 'Maybe we'd better explain that to the lads. Both of us...' Then his mind leaped. 'Tanle! They were holed!'

There was a general rush to the starboard rail, and the *Rannvi* listed sharply. There was *Ker Dorfyn*, with the *Orrin* already under sweeps and alongside.

'While we stand here gaping!' yelled Gille. 'Out sweeps! Up anchor! And hurry!' The crew ran to obey. Gille found himself boiling with anger, at himself and them, but still more at the forces that had launched these terrible agents of destruction. He had visions of great ice-cliffs cracking with explosions like thunder, and titanic blocks of blue-grey whiteness, as big as a Guildhall, falling in an eerie silence into the white-speckled waters, smashing the ordinary pack-ice beneath. And then rising in spray, rolling over, great jagged edges lifting like teeth; and beginning the long drift southward to the seas of men. Ill enough, if it were worked by nature alone; but with a living will behind them, in them even...

They were coming alongside *Ker Dorfyn* now. The sothran's deck lanterns were lit, and Gille could see Tanle leaning over the after rail, shouting orders to a boat below. 'Ahoy!' yelled Nils. 'Are you in need?'

Tanle looked up. 'We're holding, thank 'ee

kindly. No thanks to that bloody brute!'

'Were you not hulled?' cried Gille.

Tanle growled. 'That we were, and nicely! Caught us above the waterline, just, and hard by my bales of good Nordeney wool. That sprang the planking back out again, or we'd ha' shipped half the ocean in a moment. We're patching it now. A lick and a promise.'

It was miserable work, waist-deep in icy water, or in the heaving boat outside. The other crews swarmed to help, while the captains and masters conferred gloomily on the quarterdeck. 'I reckon she'll hold,' grunted Tanle.

'If the cargo doesn't spring her again,' said Olvar's sailing master, Kalve. 'You're mighty full-laden, Master!'

Tanle dismissed it with a wave. 'She'll not! Fother the spot, pump nice an' regular, and she'll hold till we make the Bryhaine ports, easy. A fother's a sort of mat,' he added to Gille in a thunderous whisper. 'Weave it out of rope and a sail, if you haven't got one. Tied over the breach like a bandage and held home by weight of water, see? Sail her nice and easy, and she'll do, I don't doubt. Which is why, b'yre leave, we'll set course shoreward once again.'

'I've no quarrel with that,' sighed Gille. 'Whatever the risk of corsairs, they don't compare with that pack—'

He was interrupted by a hoarse voice from the masthead. '*Sail! Sail ahoy!*'

Hands went instinctively to swords, and the heavy deck heaved more than usual.

'Whither away?' roared Olvar.

'*Seaward!*' came the reply. '*Out west by south-west a point! Among the ice-islands! Something small!*'

There was a general rumble of relief. 'What?' shouted Tanle. 'You're pissed, Firrig! What sail'd be dandering about among those? That's just an odd-shaped rib of Ice!'

'*Then it hangs ragged from a bloody mast!*' came the aggrieved reply. '*And it's black!*'

They looked at one another, uneasily. 'Who uses dark stuff for sails? None I know, save warmen and corsairs.'

'My folk did,' shrugged Olvar, straining his keen eyes into the dimness. 'I see something – I think. Masthead! Which way's he headed?'

'Been trying to guess! I'd say no way. He's adrift!'

Gille gaped. 'Adrift in that stramash?'

'Must be empty!' grimaced Kalve, shaking back his lank hair. 'Some derelict.'

'Or there might be folk need rescuing,' said Olvar crisply. 'We'll have to try, at least. Not your ship, of course, Master Tanle,' he added apologetically. 'But what say you, Gille? Are you game?'

Gille swallowed. But then he remembered the voice, that voice, speaking of destiny, and the hand of the Ice. The idea chilled him, but there might be something here; and there might be lives to be saved, as his own had been. The prospect terrified him; but he was more scared of not trying. He glanced at Nils. 'Are you ready to venture it, sailing master? And will the crew?'

Nils seemed completely undisturbed. 'Aye, if we're speedy. They'll feel first and think second. We'd best back to our ships, masters.'

'Truth,' said Olvar grimly. 'One ship goes in, the other stands off, in case. Master Tanle, do you stay here, make your repairs and stand ready to come pick up any who need it.'

Tanle looked grim. 'Anyone falls into that ice-cauldron'll be gone long before I could reach 'em. Best hold your boats ready.'

'We'll do that, believe me,' shivered Gille. 'Come

on, Nils, what're you hanging around for?'

Gille's ship lay to starboard of Tanle's, much closer to the derelict, and Nils had them under way even as the boat crew were hauling themselves over the rail. The sail barely filled in the light breeze, but it was enough. It was obvious who was going to be there first. 'Oh, wonderful,' muttered Gille. 'I didn't bargain for this!'

'Few do,' grunted Nils, and that was as much comfort as Gille got. He watched the ice-islands draw near, gleaming in the pale starlight like teeth in some vast submerged jaw, and tried to study the way they were moving, to predict their drift.

'That's odd,' he said, after a while. 'In – I don't know what you'd call it, a sort of wedge shape?'

Nils made a scornful noise, but after a while he nodded, slowly. 'Almost a formation.'

'As if they've all come sweeping down from the Ice in one great stream,' said Gille.

'Aye. Broke off in a storm, mayhap.'

Gille struggled to imagine the cataclysmic scene, but a colder thought overcame it. 'Or been sent.'

'What?'

'The Ice has purposes. Maybe this is one.'

Nils's scornful noise sounded less convincing.

As they drew nearer, Gille made out the derelict for himself, at first just a flash of ragged sail from behind an ice-crag. He caught his breath. He had not realised how alive a ready ship looks. This one did not. There was something skeletal about that half-bared yard, and the faint breeze pressed the lifeless shreds of sail back against the mast so they clung like rags. He thought uneasily of the tales he had heard about the Ice, and about ghost ships. This could almost be one, frozen in the Ice since an elder age, and set loose at last with its melting to wander the seas of night . . .

He shook off the idea, and turned to laugh it away with Nils. But the sailing master's face was frozen, its deep lines shadowed and pale eyes very wide and white in the gloom. 'What manner o' craft's that?' he whispered. 'Never seen the like of her, so long and low, with the bow upraised so.'

A hail drifted across the silent waters. '*Gille, ahoy! Do you mark her?*'

'We do, Olvar!' he called back. 'But we don't know what she is!'

'*I do! And I'll go in after her!*'

'We're nearer! It makes sense, man – we'll be with her quicker! Stand off and mark for us!' He looked at Nils. 'Was that the right way to say it?'

'It'll do,' said Nils curtly. 'Helm, suthard a point! And another! See how that ice drifts? So, steady. Now what fashion of vessel would a mastersmith know, and I not?'

Gille could not spare an inward grin. Nils evidently thought of Olvar as a landsman, too. They stared out hard at the shadow, looking thin and fragile in the shadow of a great half-melted arch of cold glass.

'We'll needs keep clear,' said Nils tightly. 'I hear they turn turtle a' times, sudden-like.'

'As they melt, I suppose,' said Gille, and realised suddenly that Nils was asking for orders. 'Oh. Well … take her in anyway. With sweeps, I suppose.'

'Aye, skipper. She'll handle more closely. But if we need to get out quick, we won't.'

Gille shrugged irritably, trying not to stare at the dim bulks that shimmered down into the depths. 'We probably wouldn't anyway. Can't we lower a boat?'

'If they got too far away, we'd have to rescue them too.'

'Carry on then. But steer as small as you may.'

The long sweeps dug their blades into the sea,

some clattering as they struck small fragments of detached ice. Above their wash the air was swirling with renewed chill. Ahead of them the shadow-ship seemed to slip into a narrow gap between two ice-hills, like a deceptive spectre drawing them deeper into a maze. They steered a crazy course, port a point, starboard four, then next moment hard to port and starboard again, dodging obstacles that were not there, but could be any moment. Beneath the surface the ice-islands thrust out their claws, long white reefs hard and sharp as starlight, jagged as the moon's rim, a hundred paces or more from their surface shoreline. Once they had to backwater fast, as melting changed a bulk's balance and it began to spin, ponderously, like a child's top. But it grazed another floating hill, in a crashing spray of cold chippings, and slowed, bobbing grotesquely. They pulled past, heads bowed, eyes averted, like those who fear to attract the wrath of higher forces.

The gap, when they reached it, was less narrow than it looked, and its shelter, killing the breeze, had slowed the shadow in its course. It rocked there on water like dark glass, awaiting them as they pulled nearer.

Olvar, steering the *Orrin* along the outer margin of the ice, saw them vanish into the gap, and swore. 'One breath of wind, one bloody little flaw... Sailing master! How long to reach them, now?'

Kalve, his master, was gloomy, but competent. 'Twenty minutes, at least, skipper. Too long. If they're caught between those two monsters...'

'I know. So we'll start now. Helm! Starboard a point, and be ready to port as fast as blinking. What was that?'

'That's Nils. They're hailing the ... the stranger, skipper.'

*

It sounded eerie in the still cold air, echoing between the high walls of the islands, raw and jagged as they had first split from the cliff. Nothing had melted here, and that nagged at Gille as they drew cautiously closer. The shadow-boat rocked gently ahead of them, low in the water. They could see it clearly now, long and narrow like an enlarged canoe, but with clean curving lines that swept upward to an overhanging bow and stern, sharply cut off. There was some sort of painted pattern along the side, bulbous and complex, but the moon had sunk too low, and the stars gave too little light even among the reflecting ice. It bespoke some level of craft and wisdom, but of no kind Gille could recall. Nils sent some men into the bows with boathooks, boarding pikes and ropes, and Gille went with them. He heard Nils give the command to lift oars, and the blades hung dripping into the water; and then to backwater, killing their way, letting the *Rannvi* slide silently alongside the derelict, nosing gently towards it.

The rowers, oars shipped, were twisting eagerly on their benches to catch a proper sight of the craft. From one of them came a sudden shout of recognition – and from others. But there was no time to ask. Dall the coxswain reached out with a hook, snared the derelict's backstay; others joined him, and drew the little craft bobbing in alongside with a satisfyingly solid bump. It was quite small, too, maybe ten to twelve paces; the mast looked overlarge. Another man threw down a rope, and made as if to climb down. But as he hung from the rail another man lowered a lantern. The climber screamed and clung, scrabbling to haul himself back up. The lantern fell loose and swung wildly at the line's end. Gille and the others sprang back also, with shouts of horror at what it showed them.

The black-hulled craft was a ship of the dead.

Four or five emaciated, bony corpses lay around its deckless hull, some laid out at the bow, a couple strewn anyhow around the stern, dark limbs akimbo, jaws sagging, eyes staring. But as the lantern swung and the shadows swept with it, back and forth, it lent them a grotesque look of movement, as if they swayed in time to music. That was horrible enough, and Gille wished he could close his eyes. Then one of the skeletal figures at the stern did move, lolling its lean head, lifting a faltering hand from the planking to claw feebly at the light.

'By the Raven himself, there's one left alive!' snapped Gille. 'Down with you, man! Fast!' And not waiting for that, he seized another line and himself went sliding down into the terrible boat.

It was the right thing; his men might still have hesitated. But he misjudged both the fall and the strength of the boat. It lurched heavily beneath his feet, and he almost fell among the corpses. Luckily the man behind caught him, and apologised as if the fault was his own. 'Get some water down here!' called Gille. A flask was already swinging down, and the quartermaster, who served as healer, came after it.

'Looks like thirst, right enough,' he said. 'Give him water, fast! But only in sips, and see he doesn't choke.' He cast about the bodies, swearing softly. 'The rest are a day or two done. Starting to stink. Easy, there! Don't give him too much. Pour a little over his face. The rest of you, make a cradle. We'll have to raise him. For the rest—' He shrugged. 'Over the side, with a word to the Powers for fair passage.'

'A wonder he didn't do that himself,' sighed Gille. 'Too weak, I suppose.'

The quartermaster shook his head. 'No, skipper.' He held up a small sharp dagger, of what looked like black glass, caked at the tip. 'He had a use for them still, poor bastard. He's been sucking their blood.'

They found also, when they turned over a corpse, that slices had been cut from the muscles of arm and thigh.

'A very determined fellow,' said the quartermaster grimly. 'The kind that lives, they say.'

'He didn't ... kill them, did he?'

'Not that I can see. No marks, and they're as shrivelled as he. None of 'em young, neither. They must all have died within a day or two. Thirst could do that, more surely if they took to drinking seawater at the end; and there's no water aboard. Not much of anything, save a few weapons, bows – no arrows! – short swords, spears.'

'Bring everything,' said Gille shortly. 'We can't linger here.'

Balancing awkwardly in the little boat, they watched the cradle hauled up. It seemed to be no effort, swaying like a feather in the breeze.

'What'll we do with the others?' demanded Nils at the rail. 'And the boat? No use to us. Sink it, with them?'

'I don't know what they'd want,' Gille said. 'What kind of folk were they, I wonder?'

'Didn't you hear?' asked Nils, surprised out of his taciturnity. 'Olvar guessed it. Some of the lads knew the cut of yon little craft the moment they saw't close. And the coppery skins, and those short heavy spears, they make certain. Offcomers from far over the ocean.'

'What?'

'From West over Sea, same as their ancestors came from, fleeing the Ice and its servants. Maybe a few of your forebears and mine also. Master Olvar's people were among the last, he told me. And now here's a handful more. Though how – all that way in such a wee craft ...'

'Fleeing the Ice...' mused Gille. 'Old men, in that shell. And to die within a day or two of deliverance! Well, they wouldn't want to sink here, right enough. Not in the dark and cold of the Ice, like this. We've some oil among the cargo, I'll gladly sacrifice a jar. We'll let them light a flame against it, as they might wish.'

The remains of the sail were torn loose from the mast, and the coarse heavy cloth laid over the bodies. The big jar of refined blubber oil, valuable for fine mechanisms, they emptied over this, pooling sluggishly in the folds, and Gille and the others clambered back up. Nils, relieved, gave an order, and the little craft was pushed away from the *Rannvi*, drifting slowly down the channel. Gille, at the stern-rail, lit a tarred torch, and held it high, and as the mast slid by he hurled it down. The oil caught at once. The remains of the sail blazed, and the light threw glancing gold and dancing red against the chill blue-white glass of the ice-walls.

A doubt touched Gille. 'Suppose they were these servants of the Ice? The same folk, by all accounts.'

Nils shook his head. 'The Ice clans? Doubt it. Their clan markings are different, I've heard; and their garb.'

They watched the flames rise higher. Fire in a boat was always to be feared, for so much of its fabric, tar and tow and seasoned timber, would catch in an instant. The light swelled, and drove back the shadow, shining over the still waters of the channel, and beneath. The watchers took it for a reflection at first, the strange whiteness that shone back at them from below; but then Gille caught Nils by the arm. It was rigid. The sailing master had seen the same thing, and for an instant it gripped them, the sudden loss of place and stability, as if the world had been turned upside down, sea above, stars below.

Then Nils whirled and shouted, '*Out sweeps, all! Jump to it! We'll needs be out of here, fast! For our lives!*

There was no mistaking that tone. Crewmen sprang this way and that, falling over one another to obey, and in a moment, no more, the sweeps were out and dipping at Nils's command. The black water swirled, the *Rannvi* surged, and Gille, still gripping the rail as if it would come alive under him, saw the column of flame slowly recede astern. A few strokes more, and they were gliding along, yet the rowers still bent and strained to Nils's frantic imprecations, the light flickering red on their sweating faces. The little longboat fell away astern, still flooding the channel with its defiant gleams; and Nils took one look back, and swore.

From this distance the sight was all the clearer. The jagged ice-cliffs plunged down beneath the surface of the channel; that was to be expected. But they sloped closer together, and the balefire's reflection revealed that beneath the surface, at no great depth, they passed, narrowed and met.

Now, at this distance, the black hull seemed to hang in clear emptiness, like a toy in a glass bowl. They were not in a deep channel between two tall ice-islands. They had sailed into a vast cleft or notch in one single, titanic island.

A shallow cleft at that, and probably irregular. At any moment they might run into snags or outcroppings half melted and so invisible within the water, or simply find too little depth to take *Rannvi*'s draught. 'Yet we'll not stay to pick our way!' muttered Nils. 'Such a weird shape as this must well be chancy. Might tip any moment with the slightest touch or shift of wind. *Row there, lads! Row!*

The *Rannvi* shuddered slightly as she grazed some hidden projection, and a soft, sourceless groan sounded through the ship. Gille's nose and ears were numb with the chill air, his eyes prickling, his head aching. But when he closed his eyes the horrible sight in the boat rose up before him. What kind of man had they rescued, eater of his fellows' flesh, drinker of their blood? And in such a case what would he himself have done? It didn't bear thinking of. Only a few strokes more to the end of the cleft, and clear sky. Only a few.

The air seemed less still now, the bite of it at once cleaner and clearer. The limp sail boomed suddenly taut, the bows dipped and rose, and the sweeps made one last great stroke that took the *Rannvi* gliding out into open air. Open only briefly; another pale crag loomed, the helmsman threw himself on the tiller, and Gille with him. The ship swung about sharply to port, so that the oars along that side dipped and rattled together, throwing the rowers from their benches. Then she was upright and surging smoothly out once more, though small floes half melted and barely visible boomed and bumped against the bows, clanking on the steel ram beneath.

'*Ahoy*, Rannvi*! There's a clear channel here! Clear for now, anyway!*'

The hail was startlingly close. 'Olvar! You were supposed to stay out!'

'*We lost sight of you! Then we saw the flame! What was that? And what's your catch?*'

'Later!' growled Nils. 'Let's be away from here, 'fore all else. Lead on, Master Olvar!'

Gille knew he could leave that to Nils. His legs seemed to be suddenly jointless beneath him, and he wanted to go below and throw himself on his bed; but he dared not before the crew, not till they were out of the ice-tangle. Instead he made his way forward to the fo'c'sle where the old man had been taken. He lay on the sailing master's bunk, and the skins that covered him outlined a strange, pitiful figure, a long skinny caricature of a man. He must once have been tall and handsome, for there was a nobility about the prominent cheekbones and high-arched nose, and the brow beneath the caught-back iron-grey hair; but it was the grandeur of a ruined fortress, subdued by time and hardship. Now his skin, lighter and browner than Olvar's, glistened with sweat in the light of the little lantern, and his eyes stared out into nothing. He breathed with painful effort, but his lips worked continually.

'Trying to say something,' grunted the quarter-master. 'Damned if I understand, even when he's not away with the fever. Some of the boys know a word or two of their grandfather's tongues he seems to understand; they've contrived to let him know he's safe and in friendly hands, but it doesn't stop him fretting. They can make out little of what he's on about; his friends, it seems. Poor old bugger!'

The air had a faint, ominous acrid taint. 'As soon as we're out of the Ice we'll get Olvar's healer across, and Tanle's, to help you,' said Gille. 'Will he last?'

'You'd need a better healer than I to say, skipper. I think not. We give him sips of water and fever draught, and we'll try a little broth, massage his limbs maybe, but he's far gone.'

Gille nodded. 'Poor bugger, as you say. Maybe somebody on Olvar's ship will know a few words more.'

As it chanced, they did. Getting out of the drifting pack was easier than getting in, thanks to Olvar's piloting and the flare of golden light that gave them a steady seamark astern; though it seemed to Gille that the islands were drifting closer all the time. But at last they were through, and saw *Ker Dorfyn* limping to meet them, with a clumsy swath across her side.

'Who has something of the old tongues?' boomed Olvar. 'I have myself, for one, and I know there are others.'

There were several, as it turned out, far more than on the *Rannvi*, dark-skinned men like Olvar himself. Gille reflected with amusement that he had probably picked them specially for the *Orrin*, to lend himself that little extra authority. They came swinging up the side, full of concern for this newcomer who had made the almost incalculably long and perilous journey their ancestors had ventured. The old man seemed to take heart, either through the healers' care or at the very sight of these men, and strove to speak; but though they had many dialects, none understood him properly until Olvar himself knelt by the bunk. He listened, and then beckoned another young man, a round-faced sailor named Palle with the same lighter skin. 'You're Elk clan? It has the sound of a speech between yours and the Morse which is mine. If we listen together...'

It was a laborious business, a continual struggle for words they understood, a piecing together of phrases, while Gille and the others fidgeted and muttered. The old man's tongue, still swollen, could hardly form more than a croak, and he needed long pauses to rest, while the breath rasped in his gullet like wind in a seacave. But Olvar and Palle conferred, and he turned to the others. 'He's Marten clan – old and honourable, never touched by the Ice that I ever heard. Farmers and hunters from inland territories, mostly, not fishers or seafarers from the coast. But they have come over the sea, many of them. That's what he's worried about.'

'Many?' demanded Tanle. 'Not in that little shell! You're not saying there's others out amid that mess?'

Olvar sat back on his haunches. 'I don't know. It sounded like a whole lot. His branch of the clan, or more than one clan, even. But where they are, and how he made it in that little cockleshell, well—'

He stopped short. The old man's hand suddenly clutched him tight by the arm, like a claw. The yellowed eyes were bright, but when they gave him a drink he spoke more clearly, words that sounded long and guttural. Olvar bowed his head to hear, while the young crewman listened, half shaking his head excitedly, passing on brief whispers as the old man searched for a word or a breath. 'He can speak some Morse clan dialect, I think – more than I. *Ashewayatate* – that's many great canoes, well, many ships. A fleet, I think he means – or is it two fleets? *Chatewa-ewa* … islands. And something about hunters… The *Akia*-something? *Aika'iya-wahsa*, that's it!' He scratched his head. 'No clan I ever heard tell of. And *telqua*? That's naught I can even guess.'

Suddenly the old man drew a deep, painful breath, that wheezed and bubbled deep in his chest. His voice seemed to burst through its thickness, and he spat out a stream of words. Olvar gave the toss of the head that was like a nod, and repeated a few, then jotted something down on his pocket tablet. He repeated it insistently, but the old man was rolling his head around to look at them all, thrusting out a hand and croaking something, over and over. The eyes held Gille's, and he read some great emotion in them, some demand or plea, both imperious and pathetic in its desperate intensity. Then he looked to Tanle, who appeared puzzled but moved. 'Wants something, does he?'

Olvar's voice fell iron-heavy. 'He wants you to save his folk. Thousands of them. I don't know what to tell him. I don't know if we can.'

'If they're at sea—' Gille began.

'They are and they aren't. But help they need, fast; and more after that. Desperate he is, for others.

Run is his hunt, he says.' Olvar had slipped back into the speech of his childhood, following the forms of the old tongue with the words of the new.

'What've you told him?' demanded Gille.

'What d'you think, man?'

Gille nodded. 'Then let him sleep with that.' He looked firmly into the overbright eyes and tried to shape his words reassuringly. 'Yes! We will help, as Olvar says. All that we can. Do you understand?' He held up a hand in reassurance, and the old man, after a hesitant moment, smiled suddenly, not the taut rictus of suffering, but a wide look of infinite relief. He breathed a few words that made Olvar tense, but he seemed not to notice. The taut body relaxed profoundly, the long limbs stretching as if only his will had held them so stick-like and rigid. His head lolled, and his eyelids fluttered. The quartermaster watched him intently, then shrugged, and began mixing another draught. Olvar heaved himself to his feet, and beckoned the other officers out on to the narrow foredeck.

'Well, Olvar?' demanded Gille. 'Come on, man! Let's be having the whole tale.'

Olvar leaned back against the rail and looked at him. 'Yes. I could wish you hadn't made your promise, Gille.'

'It was a kindness,' said Tanle defensively. 'I'd have done the same myself. It's no lie, after all. Who shall say what can and can't be done?'

'Wait until you hear,' said Olvar. 'He told me all too much, and I can piece in the rest. What drove my great-grandfather's folk from their lands, it happens once more. The clime grows colder, the glaciers advance, the living harder in a land already harsh. And with the glaciers come the tribes who serve them, the warriors, the slavemasters themselves enslaved, taught to sweep the Ice's path clear of all other folk. Since that last great incursion they have lain quiet, content with petty raiding, gathering their force in the lands they have stolen. Now they have invaded the last wide free lands, seeking to overrun and subdue the peaceable clans that dwell there. But these clans, taught by the past, at least had warning. And though little word of the last escape had come back to them, still they knew that there was another land far oversea, a deadly perilous distance but a place where they might well find their kin. So, though they're not used to building large ships, and have little enough timber fit for them, the most adventurous among them pulled down their very lodges and granaries to build a fleet, crude but strong.'

He fell silent. 'They must have suffered. Many died, and many no longer hale had to stay, or be left. But they were in time, barely. Even as the hunters poured in among them, they set sail, some three thousand or more by my reckoning, preferring the perils of the sea to a living death under the rule of these corrupted folk. They had little provision and less hope, but they felt they had escaped. Yet it was not so.'

He turned to look out to sea. 'The hunters too had had their spies, and time to prepare. They did not want their human cattle to escape in such numbers, lest it lessen their wealth of slaves and hearten the rest; and the Ice, it seems, had its reasons. They came by sea as well as land, in ships of their own, smaller but in greater numbers, lean and fast. They were too late to cut off the escapes; but they sent their fleet in pursuit. The refugees sailed northward, thinking to lose them, and encountered – that!'

His ham hand made as if to wipe the glittering horizon clear. The others stood silent, staring out at a sea that no longer seemed empty, but had become the board for a game of living and dying. 'They turned southward again, low on provisions and hope. They needed water, urgently, and when they sighted land, they made for it. They had no choice. But it was not the new continent they hoped for – only an archipelago of islands, out there to the south somewhere where the sea is warm, strange places. And the hunters had already espied the islands, and left a part of their fleet to guard them. Even as the fugitives sailed in, they fell upon them.'

Olvar slowly shrugged his shoulders as if to shift some vast burden. 'There was a great fight, and the hunters did not have it their own way. As the old man told it, ships on both sides were scattered throughout the archipelago, fighting and fleeing by turns, and in their fury falling foul of shoal and reef. But the upshot of it was that the fugitives were defeated, narrowly. They lost all their ships, but fewer lives; for the waters were shallow and sandy, and the majority made shore, men, women, children, babes. And almost all the hunters were destroyed; but four ships remained, and some warriors who had likewise escaped. They are out to hunt down the fugitives. And those islands – they are forested thick and lush, he tells me, warm beyond anything he imagined, and fruitful, for they are founded on smoking fire-mountains and the forests grow in the ash. But there are no rivers, no proper springs; only what the rains bring. There is little water beyond what they can catch. And, I guess, little enough food, fruitful or no.'

Silence fell again, as each man tasted the ashes on his tongue, and felt in himself the plight of those thousands marooned upon the islands – waterless, meatless, harried by cruel hunters. 'And they were bloody thirsty before they even got there!' muttered Tanle.

Olvar nodded. 'That decided the old fellow – his name is Telshakwa-tale, by the way. *Tale* means chieftain or headman, near enough. He and a few other old men felt they'd die soon, anyhow, and were slowing up their kin. So they salvaged a ship's boat from one of the sunken hunters, rigged a mast and sail out of the wreck and set off to seek help. They gave the hunter ships the slip by rowing with the mast down till they were out of reach, and that worked; but the strain told. Half starved, half mad with thirst, slopping down seawater.'

'Doesn't kill you, they say, if you get used to it,' muttered Tanle.

'If,' grunted Nils. 'Best cut your fresh water with it, a bit more each day. So I hear.'

'They didn't have any fresh water. A few fruits for food. They began to die. But they agreed the survivors could use their bodies, any way that would help. Getting through to the new land was all that mattered, getting help if it could be found. Then they fell among the ice-islands. I think it was the boat being so light saved it even that long. Even when he was the last, he swore by all the Powers that he'd get through to the new land, swore he'd offer himself up body and spirit to get through. His only living child's back out there, he said.'

'You always told a good story, Olvar,' said Gille quietly.

'I told it as he did!' growled the big man. 'And he never did get through, and he's precious little left of body or spirit to call his own.'

'He got through. And I wasn't denying the story.'

'But you were thinking over what it means. I know. I know. Out there, out there ...'

Tanle watched them narrowly. 'I was going to put into one of the ports for repairs, Iylan probably. We could send word from there.'

'Yes,' said Gille, drumming his fingers idly on the tiller-bar. 'To Dunmarhas, and from there to

Saldenborg and all the other coastal ports. They'd answer the call. They have ships enough and money to pay. All in all – a fortnight, would you say?'

Olvar snorted. 'Easily. Plus the time they'd spend in dickering about it. Weeks!'

'True,' said Tanle. 'I was thinking of your friend the Marchwarden Kunrad. And southward to Armen, where the March-fleet lies, against corsairs.'

'Sothrans?' demanded Olvar, surprised. 'Would your folk take ship so readily to help our kin?'

Tanle looked blackly a moment, then chuckled. 'Perhaps not,' he admitted. 'But Kunrad of Ker an Aruel, they'll do what *he* says. Within his bounds, anyhow. And from all you've told me of him—'

'Oh, he'll help,' said Gille darkly. 'Send to him, by all means, under our seals. But it could still take weeks. In that time the hunters may leave us nobody to rescue. Those folk need help now.'

Tanle's jaw dropped. 'You're not bloody serious? He is! Olvar, tell him!'

'I was thinking much the same,' said Olvar. 'Four ships. Without those—'

'Four ships of war!' spat Tanle, his face suddenly flaring red in the lamplight. 'Ours aren't fighting ships, they're merchantmen! And we're bloody merchants, not warriors! A sorry plight for those poor folk, agreed, but there's no need we should offer our own throats for the slitting!'

Gille held up a hand, a little wearily. 'No call for you, Master Tanle. These are not your people, and your ship is not fit, or you might not be arguing so hard against it. But we have no choice.'

Tanle was still breathing hard, but he spoke all too calmly. 'You're bringing ruin upon yourselves, you realise that?'

Gille shrugged. All this he had foreseen, the arguments, the protestations, all had come washing up into his mind as Olvar told the tale; and all the fears and horrors also, full-formed in an instant. They had battered against him, and fallen back, powerless. Not against his will; he no longer seemed to have any. It was the grip of destiny that held him against their onslaught. 'Yes. As merchants. But that ruin is less to us than it would be to you. There is always the anvil for us. We are not the best at our craft, but we will at least sleep easier after our toil. Easier than if our hands dripped with gold, at the cost of neglected lives.'

Olvar stared at him in surprise. 'Well, no need we should lose both cargoes. If we off-load one ship—'

Gille's voice came out colder and harder than he had ever heard it. 'One ship would not be a safe venture. We both go, Olvar.'

'Aye, maybe,' put in Nils. 'But whither away?'

'He gave me stars to follow,' said Olvar. 'You saw me write them down. Not a true reckoning, these folk lack our skills, but it will serve, I think.'

'The direction's only a part,' said Kalve severely. 'Master Nils is right. These are no isles any man of our lands ever even sighted. Do they lie a week's sail hence? A month's? The further away, the greater space to search. Who knows how long the old man drifted?'

Olvar's chuckle was grim. 'He knew. By the torment of every sunrise, and by the deaths. Remember, the corpses were still fresh enough to lend him their veins. They could not have been more than a week at sea, all told.'

'So near ...' muttered Kalve. Even his arid voice seemed moved. 'To come so near ... Then we should be able to bring you in sight of them, Master Nils and I.' Nils spat richly overside; which was assent enough, for him.

Tanle passed a hand over his brow. 'Well, I still say you're mad! But at least I'll be able to tell folk what became of you, and whence to send their ships. And since I'm heading for a nearby port I'll make shift to ship some of your goods, save you a little money. And leave you some more stores and water-barrels. And weapons.'

'We have steel,' said Olvar. 'Good Nordeney ramming skegs on both our bows. And weapons we brought against corsairs.'

'This pack of human bear-dogs sounds a sight more formidable,' said Tanle gloomily. 'But the powers of both our lands go with you. Wish I could.'

Olvar nodded. 'Our thanks. Well, let's go tell old Telshakwa-tale that we're on our way. It may buck him up a bit. Though just what we'll achieve – let's hope he doesn't ask, that's all.'

But the old man could neither ask nor be answered. He lay sprawled on his back, eyelids half closed, mouth wide and breathing shallowly but harshly. Now and again his fingers scrabbled feebly at the fur of a threadbare robe. The young sailor sat on the deck, watching him. 'In a swound, poor old bugger,' said the quartermaster, and shrugged again. 'I don't think he'll awaken. The lad and I'll keep the watch.'

'He said something,' said the young man Palle suddenly. 'Just before he went off altogether. Just a whisper, like; and I couldn't understand it all. *She said*... Just that, and he was smiling. *Kawat'eh*, that's said, isn't it? Then *She ... the* whatever the words meant ... *came to the side, and she said*... And maybe a few words more. But he smiled. Not like now. Really smiled. Happy as a lamb. Then he just ... let go. Like now.'

Gille sighed. 'This child of his, probably. Powers, it's sad. Well, let us know if he should awaken, after all. We've preparations to make.'

'*Kawat*,' mused Olvar, as they turned to go out into the now greying light. 'That means *said*, all

right; but in a special sense. *Kawat'eh* means
something more like "she promised", or "she swore
an oath". And the *she* is somebody important. Well,
we'll probably never know.'

It seemed so indeed. In that cold dawn light
they hastily unshipped the great booms that
doubled as cranes, and quickly shifted across as
much of their precious cargoes as Tanle's ship
would bear, while he made shift to pump his bilges
dry and cram in more stuff. That limit was easily
reached, however, for even emptied of all but one
water-butt, his damaged hull could stand little more
strain.

'This is going to be the best-travelled merchan-
dise ever,' said Gille ruefully. 'Think we can charge
more for that?'

'When we come back heroes?' grinned Olvar.
'Surely. They'll be queuing up along the quay.'

Gille did his best to smile, but he almost broke
down. He had taken refuge in thinking of cold
necessity and destiny, but the destruction of his
hopes and plans was being laid bare before him
now. It was almost a welcome distraction when, as
the booms were being slung back, the quartermaster and the boy came up to report that the old
man had died.

'So quiet-like we scarcely noticed – eh, lad? Just
slipped away, like. A breath like a sigh, and then we
waited for another, that didn't come.'

The young man looked moved, but also excited. 'Those words, though – I worked out what they
were! *Aoshu'we* – and *karakilwa'we*. Wouldn't that
mean – with the other words, I mean—'

Olvar snapped his fingers. 'Aye! Means
something like new place – and be buried. More like
find an earth-house, literally. So – she promised me I
would find a grave in the new lands. Well, she was
nearly right.'

'Maybe wholly right,' said Tanle, come aboard to say his farewells. 'Whip the old lad up in a bit o' sail and we'll ship him ashore.'

'Thought sothrans didn't like stiffs aboard,' grunted Nils.

'No more than hairy-arsed *nordinneic*,' retorted Tanle amiably. 'We'll plant him atop that promontory there, so his friends can come move his bones later, if they wish. Well, let's hope you can bring him some back. And yourselves also!'

'You'll get our letters off to Lord Kunrad?'

'If I have to bear them myself,' said Tanle. 'Well, it's been grand sailing with you two meatheads. May the powers that look after madmen go along with you, for you surely keep 'em busy!'

They watched as the overladen merchantman wallowed its way shoreward, the fothered patch over the hull showing every time it rolled. 'He'll make it!' said Nils. 'No fool, for a sothran, yon. See how he takes the swell there.'

'Hope so. Well, Gille, I'm off aboard the *Orrin*. Nils, have you the course ready?'

'I have that, and with Kalve's word, miserable bugger though he be. By the sinking of the Cross stars there, we follow. A good way to the soth'ard, but sure enough to within a league or two.'

'Then let's be about it,' said the big man shortly, and clapping Gille's shoulder briefly he swung down into the waiting boat. Within ten minutes he was back aboard and hoisting sail in the face of the dawn breeze. Nils's pipe shrilled across the *Rannvi's* deck, and the sailors chanted as they caught the cables and heaved. It was not a merry sound; its grim, heavy rhythm spoke of effort and endurance, rather than hope. The two ships swung about, and heeling heavily on their new tack, they rode the wind to an uncertain rescue.

CHAPTER FOUR
Sand and Ashes

'*FIRE-MOUNTAINS!*' exclaimed Gille, wiping his arm across his dripping brow. 'I could well believe it, in this clime. So there should be smoke or haze to guide us, a light by night, maybe. And what do we see? Nothing!'

'Maybe they're sleeping sound,' suggested Nils, sucking idly at his teeth.

'Lucky for them!' raged Gille. 'I cannot.'

Olvar, who had come over to *Rannvi* with Kalve to eat and confer, regarded his friend narrowly, but said nothing. Gille, stripped to the waist and with an ornate red bandanna binding up his hair, had great dark smudges under his eyes, and his mood was fractious. He paced back and forth within the shadow of the sail. 'I lie awake below, with hardly a breath of air, and what little water I've drunk trickling out of my skin almost faster than it went in. The cargo's just as hot, and every handspan of open space is littered with snoring crewmen. I've been climbing the masthead just to get cool.'

'Good a place as any to drop off,' observed Olvar mildly.

Gille glared at him with deep disgust. 'This is no sea for an honest Northern smith to sail! No wonder the sothrans' hair turns red!'

'Far 'way from the ice-islands, at least,' mumbled Kalve, chewing on a splinter he had been using to pick his teeth. 'Get down here, they melt.'

'Oh yes!' snapped Gille. 'And become invisible

lumps of glass just under the surface, like these great clumps of kelpweed! We've been lucky so far, but a big one could still stave us in as they did Tanle. At least they cool the air a bit, so I can think.'

He put his fingers to his temples and massaged them. Olvar regarded him stolidly. He rather liked this still warm weather, and his bronze-brown hide had less to fear from the sun. Gille, though, looked like a man with a touch of it. 'How's the water?' he asked.

'Oh … not too bad. But we're going to portion it to a couple of jacks a day. Leave more for the fugitives.'

'*If* we find them. That's too little, friend, in such conditions.'

'Yes, yes.' Gille sprang up again and prowled around the deck. 'I thought we'd know by now… Have I been doing the wrong things? Have I let her down?' His voice trailed away into a mutter, but suddenly became more businesslike. 'No, it's not too little. We've begun cutting it with seawater like Nils suggested, that does well with so much salt being sweated out of us. You could try that, too. But we have to make a move soon.'

'Due westward's the likeliest course, given that star sighting,' objected Kalve. 'If it's not here, could be anywhere. Bloody waste of time, then. Might as well go home and let the big ships do the searching, when they come. If!'

His words fell flatly into the silence.

Olvar leaned his head back, unobtrusively watching the crewmen nearby, seeing how they reacted. He saw some misgivings, some sullenness, little of the initial enthusiasm and concern which had carried them along these last nine days, to the region where the islands should be. At least there was no actual hostility. His own crew was much the same. Around the ship to every quarter the sea stretched away unbroken into what looked like infinite distances. Olvar knew it was barely a league to the horizon, but to the crew it might as well be a glittering eternity, a road to everywhere and nowhere. And to Gille, also, perhaps. He was unusually unkempt, his hair ruffled up in the bandanna as if by a fist and his beard burgeoning unchecked, like mould. His kantel hung from the rail untouched. The ring of it, audible even on the other ship, had not been heard in three days.

'We'll leave if we have to, sailing master!' Olvar said crisply and loudly. 'Not before. Remember, however sharp-set we are, there's women and children about those islands who're in worse case. At least we've water enough. What've they got for their thirst, save the promise of a spear in the throat?'

Kalve, whose gloomy nature had its better part, subsided. Olvar sensed that his words would have the same effect on the crew; for now. And, in a slightly different way, on Gille. He caught Olvar's eye, stopped pacing and made a huge effort to relax. As if to take out his impatience in another way, he squinted up at the mast. '*Masthead!* he roared. 'Have you fallen asleep, you blindworm? What d'you see up there?'

'Little enough, skipper!' came the plaintive reply. 'Too much sun-dazzle on the waves. Thought I saw another little boat a while back, but it's just some kelp and a treelimb.'

'*Treelimb?*' growled Nils, and was on his feet beside Olvar. 'Why, you shit-witted no-seaman, where there's logs there's land, didn't you know that? Whither away, man? Or shall we hoick you in to swim after it?'

The long dark shape bobbing in the water was no boat, indeed; but nor was it a branch, or kelp. It was a yardarm of unfamiliar type, with a tangle of rigging stretching out behind it in the water, like tentacles.

'*Wreckage!*' breathed Gille.

'Looks fresh,' said Nils. 'Look at that splintered end. Light and raw. Seaworms'd a' gotten to that if it were more'n a few days old. That's why we need coppering on the hull, and well sung over at that.'

'And the mast's black-painted; like the boat the old fellow stole. So it could have come from the fighting by the islands ... *Masthead! Eyes peeled for any more!*'

'*Any more? Masters, there's whole streams of the stuff, now I know to look! And all from the south and west!*'

Gille's ravaged eyes glittered. 'Sailing master!'

'Aye, skipper. You lads there! Ready about! Helm ahoy! And helmsman, the *Orrin*! South-west, and west a point! *Lee-ho!*'

They saw more of the debris as they ploughed on, some floating free, some entangled with the massive dun-coloured patches of stringy kelp. Evidently a current was carrying it out; perhaps even to the shores of their own land, eventually. Here, the sharp peak of another mast, of different pattern, poked out at a low angle; there, a crazy mass of splintered planking, or big withy baskets with things corrupted and shapeless in them – precious supplies, probably, past recovery. Once they saw what looked like a great sea-monster, wounded and wallowing; but it was an overturned hull far larger than their own, beamy and massive and quite unlike the sleek ship of the hunters. Its ribs gaped in many places, but some quirk of buoyancy still kept it afloat, just below the surface.

Only once, though, did they see a body drift by, still clinging to an irregular mass of wreckage. It was a man, a tall man with what had been copper skin, but strangely clad, in some kind of kilt and black body armour that might have been leather, painted vividly black and white, with bracelets and ornaments in his hair and along his arms. That much they could see, but not his face; for the seabirds were at him, rising like a cloud as the ships neared and wheeling, screeching, to settle again as they passed by.

'One of the hunters?' suggested Olvar, leaning over the *Orrin*'s rail. The ships were running a close course before the following wind, within easy hailing distance.

'Could be,' Gille called back. 'He reminded me of something – what, I don't know, but I don't like it. Powers, this must have been a bloody business!'

'All because of the Ice,' agreed Olvar. 'Grown a sight too used to it, we have, even back in old Athalby. All because the mountains have stopped it. Yet why should mere rock endure forever? It'd swallow the sea if it could—'

'*Deck!*' The cries came from both mastheads at once. 'On the horizon! Could be land! Off the port bow, two points! *Land ho!*'

There was a general rush forrard, but of course they could see nothing yet. But as those who had leisure stood and strained their eyes, something did indeed begin to take shape, a shadow lifting out of the shimmering ocean's rim like a gem in silver, a beryl or an emerald, polished and glowing green. And as they watched, it grew taller, and wider, and from its crest the sun struck a faint white haze.

'Fine seamen we are!' laughed Olvar suddenly. 'Small wonder we couldn't see any smoke! It blows away from us, like a banner!'

Gille's grim tone startled him. 'Fool! There may be other banners flying here, remember?'

'Truth!' Olvar called back, more than a little shaken. He had been so glad to see the islands he had all but forgotten why; but Gille's reminder was unduly harsh. Gille had always been the quicker thinker, of course; but now he seemed on edge, as if something more serious than the heat bedevilled him.

Olvar's suspicion was truer than he knew; for that thing else was eating into Gille as the corrosives he used to etch steel. He was a man used to woman's company and comfort, and the long voyage had left him deprived of it for the first time in years. That he could have endured, if it were not for the relentless haunting of his thoughts, by Utte, and by the Other. Against that quickening memory Utte seemed pale, mundane, stolid, her brown hair and eyes dull by comparison with the light gold and the green, the wild cool limbs among the surf and the kiss of shivering flame. And her words!

The few things the girl with the golden girdle had said to him, every word of them came back now, charged with strange oracular overtones he could only half guess at. Harmless in themselves, hardly noticeable, talking of destiny, and of choices that were not truly his. Yet it was surely true now that he had been singled out, though how and for what he could not imagine. Sometimes that excited and pleased him, remembering how she had melted against him. Surely there had to be love there, real love; surely that could only signify something good.

Then he would remember that as matters looked so far, his hopes lay in ruin; and he would decide it was all the world's baleful jest at his expense, that he was doomed and accursed, and sink into the blackest melancholy. And yet again he would see himself as neither blessed nor doomed, but simply an impotent pawn on a vaster gaming board, to be advanced or sacrificed as the game demanded; and that was worst of all.

But these three states of mind had one thing in common: they made Gille desperately impatient. He yearned to run around the ship screaming, which of course he did not dare do. Now, though, his worries might be resolved all too soon. Without realising it, his hand strayed to the half-forgotten kantel.

He winced. It was startlingly hot to the touch, wood and silver both. He had let the precious thing hang in this impossible sun, and he touched the tuning keys in anxious remorse. It was perfect; and he sent up a thought of awe and thankfulness to the Lord Vayde, wherever that ancient necromancer might now be; and then to the girl whose hair he stroked. He struck the strings, finding a rippling, strutting march rhythm, and grinned as heads turned among the crew, and among Olvar's men.

'What d'you say, brother Master?' he laughed. 'Shall we lower the sails and row the last half-league for stealth's sake? Or shall we charge straight into the enemy's hunting ground?'

Olvar shook his head at the sudden shift in Gille's mood; but found his own blood bubbling with the heady music. 'Well, rowing would be the prudent thing!' he shouted. 'But it will give us less speed, and tire us. So let's seize the day and swoop down upon them!'

'I'd hate to be anyone you swooped upon, my lad!' came Gille's reply. 'Have to scrape 'em up with a spoon.' The vision raised a laugh, as did Olvar's return gesture. Gille had an audience. His own music took hold of him, and he found words to string to it, cheerfully cocky and sinister.

> *Hunter of the seas,*
> *How's it fare, your chasing?*
> *Does the stink of death*
> *Set your black heart racing?*
> *Are you glutted yet*
> *On the women-slaughters?*
> *Have you slaked your thirst*

On the blood of daughters?
Time for you to dance
To a different fairing,
We will make you prance
Spit you like a herring!
Sink you in the tide,
Smash your bloody spear,
Reckonings we'll serve
That shall cost you dear!

Have you got the coursing mind?
Would you murder all you find?
Prey at bay may turn and rend,
Others flock to save a friend!
One brave cry shall summon up
All the pack to save the pup!

Hunter of the seas,
Turn and flee away,
Little though you know,
You are now the prey!

The crews beat the rowers' time-drums, that
normally they loathed, and stamped till the timbers
rang. Even Nils nodded in time as he leaned back
against the tiller, while the helmsman tapped his
foot. At Olvar's order the weapons were passed out
from their lockers, till the sides of the two ships
glinted in the midday sun like steel urchins, as Nils
put it.

'A bonny song! But these hunters are warriors
by trade, that's clear, and our lads aren't. Let's not be
forgetting that, eh?'

Gille nodded curtly, and struck the strings
more loudly yet.

Before them the nearest island grew, and the
next behind it, shining more than ever like emeralds
in gold; for wide beaches ringed them both, all but

joining them through a channel so shallow that the water was almost invisible. There was a strange grey underlie to the sand that puzzled Gille, until he looked to the white-wreathed summit of the further isle. The smoke was clear now, stretching out like a banner to the string of other islands which hove into sight now, stepping-stones to the horizon, some low and wide, some trailing plumes of their own, all dense tangles of green. Gille's heart rose. 'Better than we imagined!' he called to Olvar.

'Aye indeed!' came the reply. 'A few thousand could lose themselves a long while in that stramash. But where are our hunters? There's never a sail in sight. Don't tell me they've given up and gone home?'

'Or achieved their end,' said Nils quietly.

They agreed that they needed to see further, and that the nearest island would provide the best vantage. One ship would stand watch, while a party from the other landed; and that, argued Gille, had to be Olvar and his men.

'You're just trying to get out of a climb!' roared Olvar, scanning the formidable slopes ahead.

'But you and your lads can talk to any fugitives we meet!' shouted Gille. There was little arguing with that; and so, while the *Rannvi* stood off at the mouth of the sheltered bay between the two islands, the *Orrin* dug her anchor into that sparkling sandspit.

To Olvar, much as he dreaded the climb, the bay looked like an idyllic place. So clear was the calm water that the anchor chain could be seen right to the bottom, and the *Orrin*'s bulk seemed to float in midair. The boat taking them ashore moved silently over emptiness, like a strange insect on a window-glass, and only the swirl of the oars marked their passage. Then a crewman swore, and pointed. There

in the deepening water, already half covered in
sand as if a wound was healing, lay the debris-
strewn length of a ship's hull, as sleek and narrow as
the *Orrin* was hefty, and with the raised and
pointed prow and stern they recognised from the
boat in the ice-field. Only this was a full-fledged
ship, a black shark shape as long as *Orrin* or longer.

'That'd be main fast!' muttered one of the
rowers.

'Steer well, too,' said another.

Olvar disliked the tone of their voices. 'Yet a
cack-built craft full of raw no-seamen sent it to the
bottom!' he added loudly. 'Rammed it, most like! See
there!'

A great triangular wound opened in the black
flank, just at the head of the coiled creature painted
there. Every man jack could imagine the lurch, the
sudden onrush of buffeting water, the capsize amid
yells and screams. 'With no ram, even; just their bare
bow. We could do better than that, I'll wager! Maybe
we'll get the chance.'

The men cheered up, but they held their
weapons tighter; and when a strange bird screeched
in the wall of forest above, they almost lost their
oars. Olvar cursed them, then all but lost his seat as
the keel ground into the sand. He seized the painter
and sprang down into the lapping water, barely
knee-deep. The others followed, and drew the boat
up the beach, crunching the soft hot sand under its
bow. There was nothing to fasten the painter to, so
he let it drop; all the quicker to launch it – at need.
He waved to the *Orrin*, and saw Kalve at the rail
wave back.

Beyond the beach strange trees he didn't
recognise overhung the bushes, columns in a
tangled wall of greenery. 'A wall with no damn gate!'
he grumbled.

Adde, the bosun, pointed. 'That there might be

a path!' Certainly there was something, and so they trudged towards it, feeling the strange steadiness of the land after weeks at sea and the ashy sand baking under their toes, as if still hot from the heights above.

'Hope the whole place doesn't blow us sky-high!' grumbled a seaman.

'That's right!' scoffed Olvar. 'Hundreds of years the island's been growing all this tangle, and then it's going to blow just the day we come along! Look at the plume, man, it's just thin steady smoke, no tremors there. If you must worry, humans are a worse peril. Keep a weather-eye open!'

They came upon the truth of what he said almost at once, for the mark that had drawn them was a clearing in the foliage, with the scar of fire upon its sandy floor and debris strewn around.

'Rags and suchlike,' said the bosun, digging his toes into the dead embers. 'A cooking fire, this, but could be a week cold. Somebody had food, anyhow, to leave all these bones about—' He sprang back with a yelp of disgust. His casual kick had unearthed something from the calcined sand, blackened but still whole. A mass of small bones scattered, and out of them rolled a skull, a short way down the sand. A human skull, the upper part, grinning feebly from the sand.

'And a small one,' said Olvar sickly.

Palle, the young seaman of the Elk clan, suddenly gave a low moan. 'That word! That word the old fellow used for the hunters – I thought he was just rude, like. But it means what it says – man's-flesh hunters!'

'*Have you slaked your thirst…*' intoned the bosun. 'Stars and fucking Powers!'

Olvar broke the silence. 'Well,' he said wearily, 'we may bandy words with them sooner than we like. Climbing the hill's our best chance, and there's the semblance of a trail here. Let's be gone!'

It seemed hard, at first, to believe there was little water here, among such luxuriance of greenery, greater even than he had seen in the deepest Southlands. But as Olvar and his men slipped and stumbled and sweated up the steep flank of the hill, he changed his mind. The soil beneath him was soft and powdery, making every step a stumble and slither, sending dust and small stones down into the face of the man behind, on a level with one's ankles most of the time. He had drawn his sword to slash at the greenery, but more often he would dig it into the hillside and haul himself along, while small bright birds shrilled mockery from the bushes. Nobody spoke; their tongues stuck to the roofs of their mouths, until they took to sucking the gritty sweat from their arms.

Olvar watched for fruit of some kind, but there didn't seem to be much, only a few brilliant berries that looked highly poisonous, and a few shrivelled hard-shelled things. The ridge that would bring him to the mountain-flank was not far, rising out of the foliage above, but he began to feel he would never get there. At last, though, he pulled his bulk over the rim of the lower ridge, miserable and exhausted, and paused a moment beneath the shade of a heavy branch to put down his sword and help the others up. But even as he stooped there was a sudden flurry above his head, the branch descended, and something like the coil of a viper whipped around his neck with choking force. The hiss in his ear was wholly snakelike.

'*Eater of children, have we not taught you a proper caution?*'

A blade stung his side; but Olvar, though peaceable by nature, had been forced to fight often enough in his life, and he had the thews of a mastersmith. Instead of straightening, he was already bending further, hard, and sinking on one knee. The swordthrust slid by his ribs, and with a yelp of alarm his attacker was torn free of the branch and flung over his shoulder into the bushes. He sprang forward as the sword whistled back, and with one huge fist caught the arm that held it and stopped it dead. His other fist struck the wielder's stomach with a dull sound. The figure toppled back into the bushes, retching. He swung about, barely in time to face the first attacker, springing out at him with a long knife aimed at his navel; but by then the others had scrambled up, and the first of them Adde, a Nordeney inlander, brown-bearded, pale-skinned.

The knife-wielder faltered and stared. 'What manner of man are you?'

The speech, like the first, was Marten clan. The voice was a young woman's, though that was hardly obvious from her tunic and breeches of soiled grey skins. 'What manner?' she repeated, circling the knife from one to another as they scrambled up. Palle was as dark as Olvar, another pale like Adde, others of varying degrees between. Her hair hung tangled over her face, but Olvar saw the gleam of startled eyes. 'Skin, hair, what are you then? Minglings of man and ice-demon – *ah!*' A startled little cry. 'Are you men of the East, then? Of the Sweet Lands? Can you understand my words?'

'We are from the land we call Brasayhal, in the East,' said Olvar cautiously, as clearly as he could. The knife was still circling his stomach. 'From the realm of Nordeney. I think that may be what you call the Sweet Lands. I am myself Morse clan, and Palle here is of the Elk. You need not fear us. We have come to help you.'

'To help—' Her hand lifted, seemingly without thought, and, as if blind to the great knife in it, brushed back her hair. 'Then – you knew we were here? *Hayeh!*' The soft squeal, instantly bitten off, startled him. 'You heard of us, then? Who from? What is your name?'

'An old man. Telshakwa-tale, that was his name.'

Again the soft sudden breath. She ducked sharply past him, so close he almost overbalanced, and helped the groaning sword-wielder to his feet. 'It's all right, Ushkwawe – all right! These aren't the man-eaters!' She steadied him, a spindly, shabby old man with vague bewildered eyes and a dirt-smeared face, and looked to Olvar. 'How did you get here? How many ships have you?'

He retrieved his sword, grinning at her impatience. 'Just two. If we ever get up on the ridge there, I can show you.'

'Up there?' She seemed startled. 'Very dangerous, that would be. Did they not tell you there are enemies here, merciless killers? They watch the skyline. And two ships? Only two?'

'We were at sea when we found your messenger, drifting among ice-islands. We were on a merchant voyage. Help we sent for, but came at once, just because of those enemies.'

'Ah!' She gave that strange toss of the head Olvar remembered from his grandfather, a gesture of understanding like a nod. He realised she was hardly looking at him, always away, at the trees or the sky or the ground, and wondered if his own direct look was some kind of impoliteness. 'Ungrateful it must seem to you, my way of asking. You came at once to help a clan you do not know.'

He smiled. 'We are your kin. My great-grandfather was born on your shore of the ocean. My grandfather spoke a speech like yours, and taught it me.'

'You do not speak it so very well, you are hard

to understand. But I thank you for coming, though you are only pedlars, not fighters.'

The implications, and her tone, made him bridle. 'Maybe the word I used was wrong. A merchant is more than a pedlar, and at times he must defend his own. I have had to. And I am also a ship's captain, and a – what would you call it? A worker of metal, by ways of power, is that clear enough? A mastersmith.'

She looked round sharply for the first time, and he realised why he could not make out her face; it was darkened with smears of dirt and grease. 'A shaman? A shaman of metal? We have heard they are great in your land.'

'I had not heard that warriors were so great in yours. Save among those hunting you.'

She kicked at the dust, savagely. 'That is so. That is why we were so easily assailed, driven out, massacred, enslaved. Butchered – eaten. Too unused to fight, too unready, too weak. We younger folk have sought to change that. If we wish to withstand these brutes, we must become like them, be merciless and strong!'

Olvar shook his head impatiently. 'Then why bother fighting them? There's a better way, a … a middle way. Come to our land and see it.'

She was looking away from him again. 'That was what my father hoped. It does not sound possible to me, unless because you do not yet have the Ice near you, with its cold will setting men at each other's throats.'

Olvar laughed. 'Afraid we do. I've dwelt on its – how in Hella's name do you say *doorstep*? And suffered for it, aye, when our watch faltered. But we live in peace, for all that; and there are places where the Ice is no more than a distant name.' Something was making him uneasy, and he hesitated. 'Wait you now. Your father …'

She snapped towards him again, and seized him by the arm. 'Yes! *Yes!* Is Shakwa'telshakwa-oliwai-tale of the Marten-folk chieftain paramount. With him you spoke! He, say now, is he aboard your ship?'

Olvar realised the young woman had been bursting to ask, too uncertain of how much to reveal; in terrible torment, even. He struggled to shape the grim story in a way that might please her. 'No. All the others with him were dead, he himself almost, but fighting to live, never letting himself be defeated. We tended him, made him as comfortable as we could, and he revived a little. He delivered his message, to me myself, his hand on my arm as yours is now. Then he knew he need fight no longer, and gave himself to sleep.'

The bruising grip relaxed. 'Again I thank you.' He waited for some slackening, some sound of grief. None came. She seemed to sense his thought. 'He was near death when he set out, sailing into the sunrise. All of them were, the old chieftains. I thought they sought only a more honourable end. He was dead to me already. Now I know he found it, and am – in joy.'

'His last clear words were of his child, as he called you. And in his dying sleep he spoke of a promise or oath you had made, and that it was fulfilled. Strange that it should be his daughter I meet first, upon landing.'

She sneered. 'Strange it is not! I lingered here because it is the most eastward of the isles. No foot falls upon it that I do not know of, and the first blood is mine.'

'So you did hope he'd come back?'

She said nothing for a moment. 'This nonsense of a promise, what is it? I made none. What was there to promise?' She tossed her head again. 'No matter. This is idle talk, and can wait. What to do, that is our talk now, while our followers stand about idle.'

Olvar was startled to realise he had been completely intent on talking to this weird creature, forgetting all the others. 'Yes. My ship'll be watching – growing frantic, probably, when they don't see me at the ridge. We have to spy out the sea. And fast!'

'Now you talk like a fighter. Tell your men to wait. You, I will risk the ridge, if you keep low – if that great bulk of yours can ever do so!'

Olvar sputtered indignantly, but she was already disappearing into the bushes that led up the ridge. He gestured helplessly to the others to wait, and ploughed after her. An impatient hand seized his sleeve and hauled him along at a punishing pace, slipping and stumbling, losing all his dignity in puffing. He was all the more startled when the woman suddenly skidded as she climbed a narrow rain-worn channel, almost lost her footing and swayed into him. Instead of tugging on his arm, she clutched at it, swaying, stifling a cough. From behind the straggled net of hair her eyes shone in near panic.

'Haven't been eating too regularly, have you?' said Olvar, and then had to struggle to translate it. He remembered, and offered his water-flask. She seized it eagerly, began a greedy swig, but lowered it after a single swallow and thrust it back.

'There are others who thirst. There is no water here, save a poisoned pool in the hollow of the fire-mountain.'

'Better now?' He urged her gently onward, trying not to help her too obviously. Not that he cared much about her feelings; a fearful little vixen, though no doubt with cause enough. But there was no point in quarrelling with someone you'd come to save, and real danger. He hoped she'd have the sense to see that, too.

A short stretch more, and the foliage thinned as the ridge opened out. She ducked down without warning, so that he almost fell over her. She hissed impatiently and pulled him down by the front of his shirt. 'Keep those fat buttocks down! Morse indeed, all you lack is the tusks!'

'Well, thank you bloody well very much! And you're as vicious as a marten, I'd guess! Whatever your enchanting name is?'

'Teluqukulukwa-tal'eh!' she snapped, inching forward. 'For the Marten folk I speak, beneath their banner I fight! Yours?'

'Olvar of Saldenborg, Mastersmith and Master Mariner—' Olvar began, but she spat sharply in the dust, and hauled him forward again. The foliage was sparse, the view suddenly open across the bay and the sound, and out along the central channel of the archipelago.

At first he thought she was pointing at the *Orrin*, lying peacefully at anchor still, or at the *Rannvi*, beating easily across the baymouth with foam beneath her bows; and then at the ominous grey veil that was sweeping up from the distant horizon with visible speed. 'A rainsquall!' he said encouragingly. 'Big one, a storm maybe, be on us in an hour or so. If your folk can collect the water—'

She moaned impatiently, and stabbed out a finger again. Olvar's eyes were more acute than most, but it was only now he saw them, the black specks moving out from behind one of the middle islands, that swelled suddenly even as he watched. Dark sails were being unfurled, three at least; and they spread far wider than his own patch of discoloured white.

He felt the grip tremble, and saw in his astonishment that dirty tears were spattering the dust beneath her face. '*You!*' she spat. 'You came to help in all your weak good-will, and you have doomed us! You have drawn them back here!'

'What's so bad about that?' he demanded. 'About here? We'd have had to fight them sooner or later.'

'So bad? About here? You have brought us all into jeopardy!'

'How?' he snapped indignantly. 'Why? How can we know if you don't tell us?'

She spat again. 'Why? Because you have ruined our plan. They are few enough now so that if they spread to search every isle at once we could trap them, slay them, thin them down – this we have taught them! So it became a dance, splitting our folk up, shifting them from isle to isle ahead of the searchers, as they sought to herd us into a small space, like beasts for the slaughter. And this we made them think they had done.'

'How?' demanded Olvar.

'By letting them find some of us,' she said evenly. 'Those who are too starved, or sick, or thirsty. Or simply those who stay, or must be left. Men, women, children, so they would think us truly penned up. Most of the men are over there on the further islands, staying out of sight, leading them on, striking from cover when they can. The hunters think, the women, the children also. But they are not!'

'Here?'

'*Yes!* And now you have drawn their eyes hither once more. To the worst place possible.'

Olvar sprang to his feet, breaking her grip, and shouted. He tore off a long frond from some kind of giant fern and waved it urgently, pointing to the end of the bay, to the channel where the black sails were headed. Far below he saw the scuttling ants on the *Orrin* pause, and after a moment one of them on the quarterdeck waved back. The woman sprang up and tried to seize the frond from him. He let go, and she fell over.

'I've got to get back to my ship!' he snapped, and set off down the ridge, smashing the foliage out of his way as if it was hardly there, only vaguely aware she was running after him. The others, hearing the row, came running to meet him, but Olvar scooped them up and sent them scattering for the slope. 'Fall if you have to!' he snapped. 'But get down, fast, and to the boat! We've got guests coming!'

The blood roared in his ears as he blundered and bounced down the slope, leaping from tangle to tangle as if to tear them out of the ground. It beat the rhythm of Gille's march, and he grinned savagely to himself. 'Bulk, am I? Fat buttocks? Well, I'll show that vicious little bitch! This morse has tusks!' By the time they reached the beach he was leading all the rest, scattering the pathetic bones as he charged out on to the sand. It was only when he reached the boat that he realised the woman was still with him, though clutching her side and breathing painfully.

'Get back to your folk!' he said harshly. 'What we've done, we'll undo.'

'Take me with you,' she wheezed. 'I know how they fight at sea.'

He wasted no more breath, but half hurled her into the boat, as his rowers caught up. Palle and the bosun charged the boat down the sand, swinging themselves aboard as it bounced into the calm water, and they pulled back to the *Orrin* at speed. The grey clouds were boiling up now over the crest of the island opposite, on the freshening wind that would bring the black sails in its train. Olvar stood up, balancing easily on the planks, and hailed the ship.

'*Kalve ahoy!* Hoist a signal to Gille! Hunters to the south-west!'

Even as he scrambled up the side he saw

Rannvi come sharply about, and the *Orrin*'s anchor chain began to clank through the reinforced eye in the bow. As the boat was hoisted in they were already going about on their sweeps and tacking out as close to the new wind as they dared, racing to join Gille.

'*How many?*' Gille yelled across, as soon as they were within earshot.

'*Two, maybe three!*' Olvar bellowed back, counting them off on his fingers in case the wind drowned his words. 'Big, as big as the one below!'

'Greater,' said the young woman, reading his gestures. 'These are fine ships you have, but they are like whales to sharks.'

'Never seen an angry whale, have you?' grinned Olvar, and relayed her comment to Kalve. He was looking gloomier than ever, sucking his teeth and staring at the clouds.

'She'll likely mean those real big sharks, the deep-sea monsters,' he said. 'Rip a whale to ribbons, they will.'

'That's right, look on the bright side,' grumbled Olvar. But a roll of thunder drowned him, and sheet lightning flickered behind the peaks. A grey veil of rain trailed down the green slopes, as solid as cloudy glass, drumming down branch and frond before it.

From Gille's boat came another familiar tune, and everyone laughed.

> *Delicate as raindrops dancing,*
> *Nathe of the nimble foot—*

'Hi, Olvar!' Gille was waving. 'Who's your friend?'

'The old man's daughter!' shouted Olvar back. 'Tel—' He strangled over the name.

'I am often called Telqua,' she said unexpectedly.

For his gracious lordship's benefit, no doubt! thought Olvar sourly. It even works at this distance. He relayed the name, and as the two ships drew together Gille sprang up on the rail, and gave his most dashing bow.

Telqua surveyed him very calmly. 'Leaps like a salmon,' she pronounced, and it took Olvar a moment to understand that this might not be a compliment, exactly.

'He does, doesn't he?' he agreed cheerfully. But as he was about to relay this to Gille, he saw his friend was pointing down the channel, where the waves glittered now like steel. Against it the broad black sail stood out stark and menacing, and his keen sight even made out the high prow beneath. But there was only one sail there.

'Where are the other bastards?' yelled Gille.

Telqua clutched at Olvar's arm. 'I know what they plan! I saw them do this, more than once! They have seen you are only round ships, not ships of war, with no menace. They care more to cut off your escape to the east. So the one will engage you, hold you in play, while the others circle around the isle, thus.'

'Well, that'll take a while,' said Olvar, looking up. Again the thunder rolled, and the first of the rain curtain pattered over the deck.

Kalve agreed. 'Doesn't look as if they can sail as close to the wind as we. And this wind'll be a bugger and a half, good weight.'

'Then the thing to do is deal with that first brute as fast as we can, before they come upon us.'

Gille and Nils shouted their agreement, and the sailing masters passed a brief word or two of strategy while the rain lashed about them and the two ships ran for the heart of the channel, heeling and bounding in the growing waves. Olvar suddenly noticed that the Telqua woman, as he thought of her, was clutching the rail with both hands. He tapped her shoulder. 'Are you all right?'

She turned a rain-streaked face to him.

'Not into the wind, woman!' yelled Kalve, altogether too late.

'Well,' said Olvar, helping the staggering woman to slump against the stern-rail, 'the rain'll take care of it. Hella knows, she had little enough in her guts to lose.' She rolled on her side, drawing up her knees and dry-retching painfully. Kalve shook his head gloomily, but there was no more time to attend to her. Olvar was acutely aware that neither he nor Gille had fought in more than a skirmish at sea, and that this could well be very different. The thing that knifed its way up the channel looked larger by the moment, not far short of the great Southland warships he had seen in the roads of Ker Bryhaine, though much lower and leaner in the hull. And it looked not to have any of the sothran's great war-engines, at least. But Powers, it was swift!

White water seemed to peel away like a thin skin beneath that razor bow. Now he could see the rows of tall paddles working along the side, as regular and mechanical as a centipede's legs. It was chasing them, as it thought, fat prey wallowing away back out into the open sea. With no menace, the woman had said. So its unseen commander would be most concerned with coming alongside, grappling on and boarding ...

Olvar glanced at Kalve, whose face seemed to lengthen every moment, and for once he sympathised. This was going to be an appallingly perilous manoeuvre. If it went wrong—

No better time than now. Olvar thought longingly of his quiet smithy, and imagined he was shaping a difficult horseshoe. 'Now!' he said.

Kalve shouted to the men. Lines were shipped from cleats, sailors tagged on and hauled, their feet

skidding on the soaking deck. The mainsail strained
– and suddenly it was flying loose, flapping and
booming in the buffeting wind.

The *Orrin* wallowed horribly, and Olvar choked
down a cry. She swung to port as the balance of the
sails changed, the helmsman swore as he fought the
tiller, and then they all ducked as something long
and dark hissed through the rain overhead and into
the sea beyond. Others whipped by, and one smacked
into the sternpost and stood quivering, a huge arrow
with vividly painted black-and-white fletches. They
might not have catapults, but they had some kind of
rack-bow, firing salvoes of these things. He reached
for his own bow, laid ready by the stern, and found
it was not there. Telqua was on her feet and testing
it, with some effort. He sighed, and shouted to Kalve
for another. Telqua considered a moment, then
threw down his and snatched it.

'Yours pulls to the left!' she told him.

'And not too heavily?' he enquired sarcasti-
cally; but then he saw the black prow come sliding
out of the rain right at them, with water foaming
crazily beneath, and the rack-bow twisting on the
platform above the bow. A snap, a hiss, and the
vague shape of the man aiming it sprang up and fell
screaming backward into the sea. Telqua shrilled,
and Olvar found himself grinning.

'The bows are only distraction!' she shouted,
her breath sour in his face. 'Watch the paddlers!
They are the first to attack!'

'Eh?'

She stamped. 'The paddles! They swing them
up like warclubs, to clear the way for the boarders.'

'*Kalve!*' roared Olvar.

Other bowmen were springing up to the prow
platform, and he skipped aside as a shaft stuck in
the deck at his feet. His crewmen held their fire as
Kalve's order passed down the line, until the black

ship slid that little bit closer. He drew his own bow, trying to ignore the dark men trying to fix on him as the decks rose and fell; and as the prow came alongside for the first time he looked down into the lean hull, boiling like an ants' nest as the hunters came swarming forward. Hard faces upturned, smeared with lines of paint, grinning the grin of effort and fell excitement that turned them to skull-masks. Some brandished spears, strange things with long blades like a sword and short strong shafts; others swung grapnels. Big men, in the light breast-plates and kilts of the body he had seen, and some in robes, all jingling with metal.

He had never seen that before. Where had he heard of it, vividly? Recently?

With the same inhuman precision, and a snake's dry rattle, the paddlers swept up their blades, octagonal, black and lethal-looking, and scythed them along the *Orrin*'s rail. But Kalve's shout was swifter, and Olvar loosed with the rest. A cloud of arrows sang under the blades, into the faces of the wielders, and the paddles fell in clattering disarray. As the massing boarders momentarily ducked back, Kalve shouted again. Bows clattered to the deck, men sprang to the ropes. The rain curtain flared painfully white, and thunder blasted overhead.

The mainsail, that had seemed to fly free, was reined in hard on ropes that had never wholly been released. The wind played upon it, and the ship the hunters thought crippled leaped forward, almost joyfully, clear of the black spearhead that had sought her heart. Clear and fast, freeing the path for the *Rannvi*, which had gone about under cover of the seeming stricken *Orrin*, and now came charging in with all the force of the stormwind in her close-lashed sails. A great shout went up as *Rannvi*'s bows sliced the waves apart and the wicked blade of the ram threw up the spray, an instant before it lanced with terrible speed straight into the black ship's unprotected flank.

Telqua shrieked and sprang in the air, only to fall heavily as *Orrin* came sharply about in its turn, the waves bursting over the little foredeck in a leaping salvo of spray. A blinding levin-bolt welded sky and sea, the rain fell like chilling fire, and *Orrin* lurched around. She had less way than the *Rannvi*, but the waves were at her stern and throwing her forward. Telqua rolled to her feet and capered at the rail. Olvar barely had time to grab her by the greasy hair before the impact came. He felt it in every joint, a jerking, jarring crash and an alarming chewing sound, one beast gnawing at another. Then, in an astonishing moment, the whole black bulk of the enemy seemed to rise out of the sea before them, bowsprit high.

The hunters' ship, trading the space of beam and hold for greater speed and attack, survived heavy seas by its dagger-blade shape and flexibility; but now it was transfixed by two great shafts of steel, held rigid in raging waters. In the grip of the waves they tossed it in the air, two dogs fighting over a bone. Even that sleek hull had no such strength to support it. It cracked like a peapod, down the keel, and spilled its heart into the rain-lashed sea. Like glossy black ants the armoured warriors spilled out, this way and that, in a flailing horror of limbs. The mast fell across the *Orrin's* bow and slid off, bringing the black sail down on the struggling men in the water, like a shroud. The waves plucked the splintered remains of the hull from the rams and dropped it on top. Over the screaming, struggling mass, thrashed inexorably on their chosen courses by the wind, the two Nordeney merchantmen rolled. The rain-curtain flashed a blinding blue, and a moment later the thunder roared. The storm was passing.

Telqua had stopped capering. She stood and stared astern at the miserable wrack, jaw sagging open. 'Bring her about again, sailing master!' Olvar shouted. 'We've got to keep together with *Rannvi*!'

Gille's ship was already visible through the thinning rain, turning down the channel whence the hunter had come. Suddenly Telqua grabbed Olvar's arm yet again, and pointed astern, to the beach and sandspit where they had lately anchored. Black figures were coming ashore, wading, swimming, crawling in exhaustion. 'We daren't turn back—' began Olvar; and stopped. Out of the forest's edge other figures were emerging, very fast, swarming darkly about the struggling shapes. Some the swarm simply bore down and left lying; others, out of the water, were surrounded. Olvar could see little more, and was glad of it. Just as quickly the swarm dispersed, and the beach was empty of all save the dead in the shallows.

'The women and the children, you said?' enquired Olvar.

'And a few old men,' said Telqua calmly, still looking back. 'They bear a great hate. They would worship you for what you have done, you and your friend. But wondering I am what you will do next.'

Olvar shrugged. 'So am I. You couldn't hear what I was calling to the others, but I told them we had to draw the other ships away. That's why Gille's off down the channel.'

'*Ayeh!* So my people are safe!'

'Should be, for now. What we do when we get there, I don't know. Those bastards are *fast*. If we really had been hard in irons there as we pretended, they'd have had us. Ship to ship, without the rain, I guess they still might, by sheer numbers.'

'There may well be another ship more,' she said.

'Yes, your father said there were four in all.'

'No. This is one they were salvaging, though we made it very difficult for them. They had men enough to man it.'

Olvar clutched his brow. 'Another? You mean a fifth?'

'Not now. One of the first four has gone.'

'*Gone?* Gone where?'

'To summon their fleet, of course. Did my father not make that clear? It was a great number that pursued us, and swift, but able to carry little provision. So they must needs put back eventually. But here they left as many as they could spare, provisioned to watch for us. When we came, they drove us ashore, but not before we had reduced them also. So those hunters that were left sent back their swiftest remaining ship to summon the rest of the fleet, knowing they need only hold us pinned till it came. We know, because we saw it go; and one of them told us why. Eventually, when he had run out of other taunts to keep his spirit in his body, what of it was left.'

Olvar's flesh crawled, but his mind raced suddenly over times and distances, gauging, worrying. 'That would take weeks,' he said guardedly. 'And they left, when?'

'Twenty nights since,' she said. 'They could reach the fleet very soon.'

Olvar nodded despairingly. 'So in not much more than twenty more … *Kalve!* Any sign of the other bastards yet? No? Then signal Gille. We need to talk.'

The two ships moored in the shelter of a shallow bay, hidden behind a promontory low enough for the lookouts to see over. So far there had been no sign of the remaining ships; but strange smoke plumes had arisen from the lesser islands up ahead, and these Telqua was sure were the hunters' signals. Still nothing stirred. They held a hurried council of war slumped on the *Orrin*'s quarterdeck, while the crews quickly patched the sprung seams and other minor damage caused by the fight.

'Which could have been a deal worse!' said Gille emphatically. 'I was afraid we were too late, and you already had that rabble of wild dogs spilling over your decks. I'd not care to fight them hand-to-hand, not in such numbers.'

Nils grunted agreement. 'They'd have us. And now you say there's more?'

Olvar held up three fingers. 'In all. The two we've seen, that are probably still trying to work out what happened, and, so Telqua thinks, one more, the salvaged one. That would be who the signals were for.'

'Whither away for that one?'

'Probably left to guard the end of the archipelago, in place of the messenger they sent.'

'And which will bring the whole pack about our heels,' said Gille. 'While the folk here are held in check by the hunters. I see. And I think you do, too.'

Kalve scratched his gaunt chin with a noise like gnawing mice. 'We can't take more'n a handful of these folk, even if we offload the last scrap of cargo. They'll have to bide for whatever a fleet Tanle can scare up, and this Kunrad fellow. And if the hunters get here first, as well they might – well!' He sucked his breath sharply between his teeth. 'No telling. No telling.'

'I'll tell!' spat Nils. 'Our folk'll be sending merchantmen, big coasters maybe, p'raps even a grain carrier if they can get one seaworthy enough. Strip 'em out to carry as many as may be, leave off weapons even. A few ships of war for escort. That's all.'

Gille shivered, despite the warmth in the breeze. 'And they'll meet – *those*. A fleet of warcraft filled with howling maniacs. How many, did your princess here say?'

The princess knew she was being talked about, and glared out from under her dirty fringe. 'Hundreds of sails we saw,' she said sullenly, when the question was translated. 'All across the horizon, when the fleet first appeared in our pursuit, and we knew our doom followed us. Two hundreds, easily, I counted, to our hundred and twelve. Not all so large as these; but most. Thirty and five they left here only.'

'Two hundred!' exclaimed Gille. 'So there's still a good hundred and fifty coming! We've got to get back, to warn them.'

'And leave the folk here? Like this?'

Olvar clutched at his hair in anguish. 'What'd you have us do, then - take the children? The infants? Hammer of Ilmarinen, how do we choose? And in the time?'

Kalve shrugged. 'That'd be that, then. Best we run as we are, now. Do what good we can that way. Can't say I like it, but...'

'Man's right,' said Nils stolidly. 'If we stay to fight, we could both be destroyed, easy. Then the rescuers sail straight into the bear-dog's den!'

Olvar saw Gille sit up straight, with a light in his eye he knew of old; and simply knowing there was some idea seemed to trigger it off in his own mind. 'If we *stay*!' he rumbled.

Gille chuckled nastily. 'Or if we run - in the right way?'

A wolf's jaw seemed to clamp around Olvar's arm. It was Telqua's long fingers, nails filthy and chipped digging into his arm. 'You are deciding something. I can guess. Will you leave us whom you came to help, scarcely better off?'

'Less one enemy,' said Olvar, detaching the grip with difficulty. 'And perhaps more. But it may not go well for us, one or the other.'

She stared at him, unapologetically. 'Do you

risk so much? Then it is proper I share it. I will come with you.'

'As you like,' he muttered, for he knew how much her warnings had saved them. 'But I trust you've got your sea-legs by now.'

He and Gille clasped hands as the smaller man was about to go down into his boat. 'If this goes as we expect...'

'We'll have to make shift without one another a space,' shrugged Gille. 'It'll do me good. I've been relying on you too much for the rough stuff.'

'Be sure it's not too long a space,' said Olvar. 'I need your nonsense and your twangling to set my brains working, now and again. Like a purgative.'

Gille struck the kantel, and sang the opening line of a shanty.

Cast me loose and swing me pretty...

'Spare the innocent!' growled Nils from the boat below.

'We'll see these folk on our own shores yet,' said Gille, with something of his old impudent smirk. 'And our smoky old smithy, if naught better. At least we've lived a bit again. Fare you well, my lad – and to you also, princess.'

He kissed her hand, looked as if he regretted it, and went sliding down the rope ladder without bothering with the rungs. Olvar watched him rowed back to the *Rannvi*, full of sombre thoughts. He remembered their long trek southward together, dragged along behind their obsessed master, squabbling with him and each other; and the years they had shared since. They had been friends as boys because they were forced together, never especially close. If anything, they had grown apart in nature since then; and yet they had rarely been far apart. There was an understanding between them that was stronger than friendship, the knowledge that all folk share, men and women alike, who have faced a bitter test together. Now that might well be taken from him, perhaps forever. Silently he called on every Power he could remember to protect the fool, as he called him.

'And if they will not, then the seas and Saithana be kind to him at the end!' The old formula gave him little comfort, for Olvar was not sure how much he credited any sea Powers save one, Niarad Wave-Lord. He, it was said, had the sea's nature, too vast to be either cruel or merciful, or much concerned in mortal terms at all. In that Olvar could all too easily believe.

He was aware of someone watching him, and looked around into Telqua's glittering eyes. 'Well?' she demanded, with contemptuous challenge. 'Are you going to stand there forever? When do we do something?'

He bit back the obvious response. 'When we're ready,' he said quietly.

The hail from the masthead was almost a relief. '*Sail ahoy!*'

The same hail came from the *Rannvi*'s lookout, who added, '*Westward, down channel! Only one!*'

'At last!' muttered Olvar, and remembered to translate it for Telqua.

'You will fight it?' she challenged.

'No,' he told her cheerfully. 'We're going to run away.'

For some reason that left her staring; and, weary of being the only one she bothered, so did he.

The two ships raised anchor together, and swept out into the channel on a broad reach that set them bucking vigorously across the waves once again. Telqua, once she saw that no more seemed likely to happen, curled up in a shivering knot against the after-rail and said nothing; which suited Olvar very well. After a while he sent for the young seaman Palle, and told him off to talk to her when he had no more urgent duty, and try to teach her a little of their own speech, if she had the wit to learn. 'Give her some food if she can stomach it, that'll be a start. Show her where things are. And take care,' he added. 'She bites!'

Palle grimaced. 'A polecat! Aye, skipper, I'll try to keep her off your neck.'

'She has reason enough for being as she is, and a burden to bear. And we may need her, for her folk. Even if we succeed, there'll be hard counsels ahead.'

Palle knuckled his brow. Olvar got himself a drink of much-watered ale, and settled down to watch the chase. The oncoming ship was much like the other, but not as fast. That would be its repairs, probably. *Orrin* was pacing it easily enough, but they did well to remember the others were waiting somewhere up ahead. They would have seen the bodies and the wreckage of their companion by now – 'No menace, eh?' Olvar cackled to himself.

Probably they would set a snare of some kind, into which the newcomer was supposed to drive the two merchantmen. That would surely be soon, while they were still in the uncertain waters of the archipelago. Those the hunters must know by now, reef and rock and shoal, and the newcomers did not. He grimaced. He knew well why mariners preferred the deep waters, whatever landsmen might think. At least they *were* deep, with hazards well submerged. A man could drown as easily in one of these shallow lagoons, with a few razor-edged rocks poking up through the grey-streaked sand. Not him, though, if he had his way.

'Any change, Kalve?' he asked as the sailing

master came up to direct the helmsman.

Kalve wagged his head disconsolately. 'Nils just tipped me the nod, though. Thinks they'll be on us any moment, and so do I. Worse luck!'

'Have a word with Telqua; Palle will translate. She knows these waters and these bastard hunters. She may think of some chance we haven't.'

'If you say so, skipper. Can we not trawl her over the side and clean her up a bit?'

'Don't tempt me. But some of the grime was to help her stay unseen, and maybe kill a human scent; for they have keen noses, these hunters, it seems. We may be reduced to such measures ourselves, yet. Off now, Master.'

Olvar felt less like company than usual. He had never been more nervous, and he was afraid it would show. He stood there by himself as the hours passed, letting Kalve do the sailing, which was easy enough. Headland after headland slid by in building apprehension, and then sudden, almost sickening relief as the bays beyond proved empty, the waters free of reef or shoal. Where the surf beat upon the exposed coasts, washing back the sand, there the rocky bones of the islands stood out in jagged menace; but down the more sheltered channels there were mostly sandbars to worry about, nothing worse. And the only black sail in sight remained the one behind, gaining on them gradually. After a while the cycle of fear and relief became infuriating. 'Where the hell are they?' he snarled at Kalve, because he was the nearest.

The sailing master looked at him with his dead-fish eyes and shrugged. Olvar growled. 'They must be planning something. Look at all those smokes.'

'Plain earthfires, maybe,' suggested Kalve.

'Twisting and breaking like that? No! They're being changed somehow.'

'Maybe not,' objected Kalve. 'The tall one, where we landed – look at its plume.'

The banner of smoke, streaming to the heights when they first saw it, was sunken now, wreathed about the summit of the island like a sullen mantle, coiled and heavy, so that the forest seemed afire. It was a louring, sinister sight, and as Olvar contemplated it, something else caught his keen eyes, out beyond the island, in the open ocean eastward. A moment later, as he took in what it must mean, the masthead saved him the trouble.

'*Sail ho!* Two! East away beyond the island, out to sea! Black sails, both!'

Kalve nodded grimly. 'Wisdom, of a kind. They saw we'd smashed up their fellow, so they'll not play hunt-the-robin with us, but wait where we must go, due east. They've only to sit, then, while the other ship herds us out; while we must escape!'

'They can't sit for ever!' snapped Olvar. 'Warn Gille. Our plan still holds. And when we come out from behind the isle, make ready for strife.'

The two merchantmen moved out together, steering ever closer, and the black sails, angled like shark-fins indeed, stood in towards them. The sea-swell caught the merchantmen's beamy hulls and sent them wallowing and bouncing along, a sorry contrast to the skimming lances they faced. It was not long before Olvar, squinting, could see the motion along their gunwales, the warriors massing behind a gaudy line of raised shields. At Kalve's curt commands the crew were breaking out the sweeps again, seeking to take a leaf out of the hunters' book. The huge oars might not have sharp edges like those paddles, but they could surely fend off an attacker and perhaps do some damage among the boarders. But there had to be something else he could try, some other tactic; and perhaps the hunters had others, also.

They would go for the *Rannvi*, probably, as lead ship; then try to ensnare *Orrin* in the fight, cripple it as soon as possible. How could they manage that? He sighed, and leaned on the rail. He didn't enjoy thinking like a warrior. Suppose he had to do it himself? If he was as ruthless as they, he might pour men on board, take the losses and cut the rigging, probably. Then mop up at leisure. The young woman could tell him more, perhaps; but he'd had enough of her for now.

'They may shoot fire-arrows into the sail.'

He jumped, no mean thing in such a bulky man, for the voice was so close to his ear, as if it had caught the echo of his thought. 'How did you know?' he barked, furious at himself and her. Palle, trailing along helplessly, made himself scarce.

That sneer was in her voice again. 'It needs no mind-witch! You look, you think, a whale's-blow noise you make! Should I not know what you look for?'

'Of course,' he muttered. 'All these days you've been doing the same.'

'No. All these years. All my life. Watching was my mother to me. Now it must be my father too.'

Olvar was a kindly man, and the utter bleakness of her voice almost put tears in his eyes. She would despise that as weakness, of course. 'Fire-arrows,' he mused, and was surprised to see her relax, visibly, almost gratefully. She leaned beside him.

'The long ones, from the great deck-bows, tipped with tar-soaked wool or tow. The flame dies in flight, but the air feeds it. One, at least, will be hot enough to devour the blanket.'

'What? Oh, you mean the cloth. Maybe not. Our sails are of lighter stuff, and stiffened with twine – you don't know that word – not that tarry rope you use. Arrows would probably go right through too quickly to catch fire. Wouldn't hurt to have a pump ready, though. What else, now? It doesn't look as if they want to ram us.'

'Perhaps not. With our ships they did, sometimes; but they may think yours are too strong-built.' She gave a throaty hissing chuckle, more sneer than laugh, and jabbed him painfully around the navel. 'To carry you they must be.'

He glared, rubbing his stomach. 'Why d'you have to keep lacing into me all the time? Is it really that bloody hard to be grateful to somebody?'

She stared back, unreadably, and then she snapped out a hand and pinched the meaty muscle of his arm, even more painfully, and scuttled away down to the deck like a naughty child. 'If I get out of this—' grated Olvar between his teeth, then bit off the rest. No ifs and buts, not before the others. Nor could he run after her and tan her hide, not in front of the others, not now. As she well knew; and yet she was making his blood boil so much he could hardly keep his mind on the coming clash.

A sudden sound came to him, the ringing ripple of Gille's kantel, and the throaty rasp of voices from the *Rannvi*. They were chanting his march again; and some of Olvar's own men took it up.

> *Sink you in the tide,*
> *Smash your bloody spear,*
> *Reckonings we'll serve*
> *That shall cost you dear!*

That amazing kantel, if anything, grew louder, even over the rush and boom of the water between. It seemed to Olvar that the one mingled with the other, setting a sparkling fire in the sea, adding force to the voices, edging the very wind that sang in the rigging.

Hunter of the seas,
Turn and flee away,
Read it in our sails,
You are now the prey!

The merchantmen were huddling together now as if for comfort, and Olvar saw Gille for a moment, half dancing on the quarterdeck as he played, yet sparing a hand for one absurdly cheerful wave. Then the hunters were upon them.

As he had expected, they made no attempt to ram. Again the first attack was a salvo from the deck-bows; and some of the arrows were indeed trailing smoke. They missed the sails, though narrowly, but some stuck in the deck and blazed. Leather buckets dashed seawater on them; hands plucked them loose and flung them overside. Kalve had laid his orders well.

But the two sharks were drawing in now, and one closer to Gille. Clearly he could wait no longer. With the black bows almost alongside, the playing stopped suddenly, the sail billowed as the yard swung, and *Rannvi* heeled violently as Nils brought her about right in the path of the attacker. The black ship had either to risk a ramming, and perhaps shiver itself apart in the process, or backwater as fast as it could. And as it did so Olvar's ship passed alongside.

At his curt command the crewmen rushed out two heavy sweeps, sending them bouncing along the black gunwale, spilling shields, toppling boarders off their feet, smacking the rowers from their benches. But they swung up their own edged paddles, and Olvar winced. The young man Palle, yelling with excitement, leaned out too far with the forward sweep, and was cut head from shoulder, and the corpse dashed into the sea. Then Olvar himself dodged a hissing fountain of arrowshafts over the rail. Kalve yelled and doubled up over a black shaft, and Olvar, horrified, thought him shot through the body. But there was a boom of timbers as they collided with the black ship, spilling the wind from its sail, and, by the sound of it, doing some damage; and then they were clear.

As Olvar ran to him the sailing master brandished an arm transfixed. Olvar wondered crazily how the shaft had found enough meat on the old stick. He seized the arrow and snapped off the head, but Kalve held his hand. 'Leave the shaft for now, it'll stem the blood. We must make our move! *Ready about! Leap to it, for your bloody lives!'*

Other men lay hit, though mercifully few. Olvar himself plunged down to help with the sheets as the *Orrin* also came about, but on the bearing opposite to Gille's. All as they had planned, although the pass had been closer than they thought possible. Three ships in all, two out here and the third still a ways behind somewhere. If their ships ran in two opposite directions, how would the hunters hunt? All they had to do was stand sentinel, true; but only one ship need escape them.

And if the escapers divided their forces, they would stand a better chance. As the *Orrin* settled on her new heading he clambered back up to the deck and looked around for Gille. There was *Rannvi*, a surprising way off already, gybing wildly to the southward, with the hunter they had affronted in hot pursuit. And the other was coming about after the *Orrin*.

'So the honours are even,' he said grimly to himself. His lips felt ashy and swollen. 'But which way will the third rat run?'

Their pursuer had not been forced to slow, and he made his turn swiftly enough. Kalve, nursing his arm as the quartermaster plugged it with boiled rag and bound a cloth about it, watched the black sail sag and wallow around. 'Crude!' he said with dismal contempt, though he was gritting his teeth. 'Too large a sail, too shallow a draught for it, and a poor cheap rig. We'll manage a good point or two closer the breeze. That might lend us the speed we need. If we've only the luck. If only!'

'Can we not make ourselves some bloody luck?' demanded Olvar ruthlessly.

Kalve shook his head, as if to clear away the cobwebs that seemed to belong there. 'We might. With this wind from the north-east we could maybe risk a reach back behind the island yonder. It'll funnel the air, put it square on our bow.'

'A tacking duel,' mused Olvar. 'Side to side all the way up the channel, leaving him further behind at every tack. Then out into the ocean again. Fine idea – if we don't meet the third ship! But there's little choice. I'll handle her meanwhile, you get some food and rest. We need you whole!'

Kalve shrugged, but shuffled off. Olvar set course for the straits at the island's tip. The pursuer swung on to the same heading so swiftly that they must have been awaiting it. Olvar told himself that hardly mattered. The question was, could they do anything about it? Worries rose in his gorge, and the memory of the brief fight. Palle's was the only death, but there were five men wounded, one sorely; how would they fare in another such pass? These were warriors indeed they faced. He needed another weapon against them; he could not use the sweeps again. He shuddered at the thought.

'What are you thinking of?' It was the woman Telqua, still carrying her bow in hand, with an arrow on the string.

He answered her instinctively. 'The boy who was killed. A village fisherboy, as I was once myself.'

She ducked her head. 'Yes. Yes. Palle. He spoke to me, though he did not like me. To give life to others he risked his own. He was ready.'

'Was he? Are any of them? I never gave them any real chance to think about this. As Kalve said, feeling came before thought. I led them on.'

She snorted. 'The grey-face? A man who knows the sea, Palle told me; but not men. Palle said you did. You do not trust them enough. They know, yet they came to us, they help us more than I believed they could. They are good men. As are you.' She darted out her free hand, and he flinched impatiently; he did not need another bruising pinch. She held her fingers in the air a moment, as if puzzled; then she turned away.

Olvar stared after her, no less baffled; but then he had to pay heed to the helm, and bring the *Orrin* round another point less a half, to clear the white water at the advancing headland, and the rocks beneath.

He looked back unhappily at the black sail, and glimpsed far beyond it another, already small; and smaller still a white one. Then the masthead called out, and he saw, gliding out from behind one of the smaller islands to the south, the third sail.

Closer to Gille's ship – too close, though still well behind. So Gille had drawn the long straw, and had two enemies on his tail to their one. One damaged in the fight, perhaps, and the other patched up from wrecks, by Telqua's account; but still full of men and spears, and those deadly paddles. Gille might try the trick with the sweeps, and who would die then?

Olvar sighed. He had little enough hope for the *Rannvi* against such odds; so it was up to *Orrin* to break free, and bear the message home. He glanced up at the island ahead, its brilliance stifled under that encircling cloud. The sinking sun cast its shadow deeply across the strait, blotting out the sea's own green gleam and turning it to inky shadow. Not long before night now, of a terrible day; and before darkness lifted, perhaps, the fate of many would be settled, and himself one.

CHAPTER 5
The Dancers by the Tarn

The surf rolled and roared at the strait-mouth, and Olvar deliberately swung as close to land as he dared, hoping the hunters would either balk or strike. But they came through almost as closely, losing only a little way. Kalve, shambling back on deck with his arm tucked into his jacket, eyed the pursuer unhappily. 'Must be used to coast waters like this. Well, here comes the channel, and the wind. As I made sure.'

Being right seemed to cheer him not at all. Olvar cocked an eye at the madly fluttering pennants in the rigging. 'Yes, it's changing; and stiffening. Take the first tack when you think fit.'

Kalve nodded, tapped his foot briefly, then began shouting the orders. But as the *Orrin* swung about, head to wind and across it, he cast anxious glances up at the island-walls ahead, and the fire-mountain that crowned them. 'What's that bloody cloud hanging like that for?' he demanded. 'Wind like this, should be streaming out suth'ard, same as our pennants. Yet there it is, clinging like a quilt on a bed. Not natural!'

Olvar, surprised, scratched his head. 'See what you mean. Trick of the wind, maybe. Shouldn't worry us down here. Or maybe the fire-mountain's breathing out some kind of heavy airs, that lie close to the ground. Now that I think of it, I've heard of some such thing.'

Kalve grunted. 'Long as it don't blow its top off, all of a sudden. Steady now, helm!'

Olvar braced himself as the *Orrin* heeled against the waves, striking her now on the starboard flank. 'Here comes the bloody hunter about now, too. But you'll needs be smarter than that, my lad – hah! Look at that!'

From the deck below the crewmen whooped and jeered. The black ship, with half the merchant-man's freeboard, had to come about more cautiously to avoid shipping water or even capsizing. In his haste not to fall behind, its master had clearly mis-judged the angle, losing the wind from the sail completely.

Kalve sucked his teeth. 'In stays, in irons and wallowing like a grampus!' he observed with dour satisfaction. The black mast rocked wildly as the waves buffeted the low hull, and Olvar felt a sudden fierce hope that it might overset, while he was still close enough to aid Gille. But the paddles were beating the water, pulling the black hull into the wind to steady her.

'Still, it's a few minutes gained,' he consoled himself. 'A good start.'

'Ah,' said Kalve with dismal relish. 'But this is still just the first leg, isn't it? Plenty more to go. Back and bloody forth like skittles in an alley.'

This was true enough not to need pointing out, and Olvar's patience was already near snapping. He contented himself with sending half the hands to get some food while they could, and went down to join them. Halfway down the stair he remembered Telqua, crouched silently in a corner of the bridge, and called her along. She came, without speaking, except to bow her head over the salt meat and biscuit she was given, and squatted away from the others to eat. She must have been ravenous, Olvar realised, even more than he was; but she ate calmly, sipping water and chewing the tough mouthfuls carefully. He felt a pang of conscience; now young

Palle was gone, few of the others spoke much of her dialect. He was isolated, too, by command; he had nobody but a miserable bugger of a sailing master with whom to share his concerns. She would at least be a change.

'You should try to learn a few words of our tongue,' he said to her, as they made their way unsteadily back to the bridge. He sat down on the top step, and hesitantly she joined him. 'With any luck you'll be living in our land soon.'

'Palle taught me *yes* and *no*,' she said heavily. 'But I have little enough use for talk, it seems. I am not accepted.'

'Perhaps, not yet.' Olvar searched for words, which were never his strong point. 'My friend could put this better, but ... we have grown up in different ways. That does not mean that we can never understand one another, but it will take time. On both sides. And this, all this—' He waved a hand at the pursuing sail, now close-hauled and heeling as they were. 'It leaves little time. I want to understand you, you and your folk.'

'Do you? Truly?'

'Of course,' he said, and it seemed to please her. 'But this thinking in another tongue is hard, a tongue I have not used since I was an infant. I have to fit everything into the words I know, and they are not enough.'

'With me there are not even the words. Among my clan I am a leader, though young. I am known by all, and know most, or their kinfathers; and they hearken to me, though I have only been a chieftain for ten years. Here I am nothing.'

'You are one more hand on our side,' grinned Olvar. 'And a fell one, if I'm any judge. If you'd not stopped to whisper at me, we'd not have been sitting talking.'

'I spoke because I was in doubt. It was the old

fool who struck before I was ready. You were like none of the enemies I have ever seen, with no scars of rank or degree, and no paint or mask or armour. And so fat! In our land nobody grows so fat, not even the maneaters!'

'I,' observed Olvar painfully, 'am considered merely well grown, and a trace thick about the midriff. Don't judge me by the others; most of them are mere lads, and Kalve's a withered old ... fellow.'

'If you are well grown, he is a skeleton, only without the grin.'

'You don't know the half of it!' said Olvar feelingly. 'Here, that surf sounds loud. We must be getting near the coast—'

'That is not surf!' she said, rising to her feet. 'That is drums!'

Kalve and the man at the masthead, sliding down the stays to take his turn at food, confirmed it. 'From astern!' he said cheerfully. 'But not yon black-rigged bastard, or I'd'a hollooed! From the landward, I'd say, and naught of our concern.'

Olvar envied the young man his lack of imagination. 'I'm not so sure. Could those be signals?'

Kalve, as usual, shrugged. 'They can signal all they like, but it won't win 'em a hand's-breadth of way. We're gaining on them, and maybe we'll gain more with this next tack.'

Olvar looked to Telqua. She was standing rigid, with no sign of unhappiness now at the heaving deck. 'I think she knows better.'

She knew she was being spoken about, and glared at him. 'We must take care. They are about some shamanry, and on our island. My people are in peril. You must win us some war-luck.'

'Wish I could!' he said, a little surprised. 'What's all that likely to be about, anyhow? What can they do to us, out here, anyhow?'

She snapped a look at him, and he realised he

had never really seen her face, her expression even, under all that grime and paint. 'You are a shaman, and you do not know? How has the Ice not devoured you, long since? Their shamans are strong! War-craft they can dance up, in the image of their clan beasts. And a cruel fire of the mind that makes their man drive himself to the death-point and past, a bloodlust that overflows his heart to spill out all pity. The hearts of their enemies they can likewise blight, and set darknesses in their minds. And they can seek out destinies, some of them, and like-linesses – happen against not-happen. But there are mighty ones among them who can do more. Filled, men say, with such dark wisdom as the Ice itself doles out to them. I have seen such things at work, black dangerous things. I feel that some of those who wield them are here. We must guard ourselves somehow.'

Olvar felt a strange thrill in his spine. 'You *feel*? You mean more than just believe, don't you?' He reached up without thinking, and brushed the hair away from over her eyes, and looked down into them, wide, startled, yet meeting his own without flinching. No wonder they had seemed so bright! A slow glimmer came and went in their black depths, like a fire deep beneath the sea.

'So Ilmarinen favoured your folk also,' he mused.

'What is that?' she demanded sharply.

'I mean – that you also are a shaman. Of some kind; but most likely the same kind as I.'

'Much use that may be! I am a warrior and a chieftain, not a tin-tinker. But we have shamans, if that is what you mean. Not so strong or fell as our enemies, though; for they do not have the Ice to guide them, and must learn only one from another. They are our guides and our seers, they choose the paths we must tread; little more. I know you have

more power than that, among you; I have seen it.
Why do you not use it?'

Olvar was nonplussed. 'We have power over
metal, yes. And in it; the rams you saw strike that
ship apart, they had all the virtues a smith could set
in them. What else could you have seen?'

'Why, your friend the Salmon-Leaper, that song
he played, that thing he struck! War-craft dripped
from its wood, war-light danced on its strings, war-
luck filled his voice. You are a shaman and did not
feel it? How else could you have done what you
have done so far? He must be a master of great
power.'

Olvar bridled. 'The man who made that thing
was, yes. Our greatest of smiths and of other dark
crafts beside. And our sternest, some say; a cruel
man, to himself most of all. We knew it had power,
but not what you say. Luck alone made it Gille's,
and we here have nothing like it.'

He could have sworn there was something like
pity in her gaze. He was a pedlar again, he suspected. She glared up at the island, her straight lips
pursed. 'Then we may rue the day, is what those
drums say to me. Often they shape the beat like
their chant, to say their spell in a giant's voice. I will
listen awhile. Do not disturb me!'

'Wouldn't dream of it,' muttered Olvar. Now it
was Kalve who seemed like the relief.

'Ready to go about again, skipper.'

'On your mark, sailing master.'

Kalve nodded, picked a shred of meat from his
teeth and chewed it, and glanced up at the sail a
moment, then at their pursuer, choosing his moment. He scratched his backside vaguely; then he
spat out the orders, almost too fast to follow. The
Orrin heeled violently, Olvar's feet slid out from
under him, and the yards groaned and whined as
they swung about. Spray washed along the deck,

drenching Olvar as he rolled down against the rail.

'New tack, skipper,' said Kalve with grim satisfaction. 'And he's starting to come about, too soon. Next leg.'

'I'd never have noticed!' grunted Olvar, rubbing his bruises. Down below the crewmen were heating the air with oaths as they fought to stow all that had shifted. The sun had sunk low now, and to them it was already setting behind the island. The sky still held some deepening blue, but the white cloud wisps were tinged with pink, and the cloud atop the mountain looked very grey and solid. They surged on back across the channel, back towards the great island and the source of the drumming.

On and on it went, as regular as some huge machine rather than the hands of men; and it seemed to him that he heard faint voices, too, dull cries of insistent hate, deliberately crude even for such barbarians. He imagined the clan beasts, leaping silhouettes of savage, colourful masks with a cape or costume swirling beneath. His people had preserved some such masks, some captured in battle and some of their own. They were increasingly forgotten now, but as a child he had seen them brought to the spring festivals, vibrant, benign figures such as Raven and Whale and his own Morse, painted grinning past his long tusks and rolls of blubber. He had believed in them then, as they capered in the ancient dances or cast fruit and sweetmeats to enraptured children like himself, saw them as real spirits rather than men he knew in the masks. Somehow that depressed him now; or something did. The drums, surely; for the sound seemed to come leaping off the mountain at him, like a direct assault. What could they be saying to this Telqua woman?

She was clambering down the stairs into the waist. 'Where are you off to?' he demanded irritably.

'To piss,' she said casually, which took Olvar aback. Even his own fisherfolk were a little less down to earth. At least he didn't have to show her where. Palle probably had, poor lad. That made him feel guilty again, and he glared impatiently back to the mountain. Maybe the drums were doing more than just irritating him; and maybe not. The mood on board was bad, but the black sail was reason enough for that. The crewmen not immediately needed sprawled about the deck, muttering. He hardly blamed them; this was a long way from their dreams of a wealthy voyage and flame-haired southland girls, or even a swift and daring rescue. It was growing positively chill in this island twilight, and the greenery seemed no longer rich and exotic but hostile and bleak, the bird- and beast-calls from the shore sinister now, as the mists wreathed themselves more tightly about the mountain.

'They're up to something!' muttered Kalve unexpectedly. 'Look there! The bastard's changing course.'

Olvar stared. 'Is he standing in towards us? But that's daft. There's never a way he could overhaul us.'

'Not if we're flying along, no. Maybe he thinks we won't be. Maybe he has cause.'

There was a clatter on the steps, and Telqua reappeared, tugging down her hide shirt. 'Something indeed is in the sound now!' she said. 'Growing clearer every beat! What, I cannot tell. But it compels—'

The man at the masthead shouted. Men on deck cried out and pointed, for all Adde roared them down. On the bridge Olvar and the others simply stared.

Far to the south, the *Rannvi*'s lookout, weary of watching the black sails racing to leeward, also cried out. Gille had grown bored with the chase, which he could neither mar nor mend. He was sitting on the rail, idly strumming a love song and wishing for night and cool breezes; but his fingers faltered when he heard the cry. His heart went cold with apprehension. He sprang up on the rail, but could see nothing. Only when he clambered hand over hand high into the ratlines did he make out the cause. He lacked Olvar's keen sight, and at that remove could make out nothing of the chase; but he saw the island clearly enough. The sullen crown of vapours no longer clung about its crest. He watched in blank dismay. Down the green slopes, as if the stonefires beneath were suddenly boiling over, it rolled in an enormous, unearthly wave, and blotted them from sight.

Skimming the treetops, the wave vanished momentarily behind the crest of the ridge; then overleapt this with a force that made its silence all the more eerie. Down the beach it washed and out, without let or hesitation, across the waters. Olvar had a moment to cry out a warning, to hurl himself at the tiller. But even as the crew ran to the sheets they seemed to vanish. The bows were overwhelmed; the sail held back the flood a moment, but it streamed underneath and boiled madly in the breeze. Then the crest of vapour rolled up to the quarterdeck and over, and Olvar flinched, expecting furnace heat and suffocation. But though hot enough to sting his eyelids a little, it was not the choking smoke it seemed to be. It clung.

'Steam!' he exclaimed, as he felt the dankness settle about him, dewing his cheeks and forming droplets on his hair, making his clothes stick unpleasantly to his skin. Then he did cough violently, for it was more than steam. It had a bitter, acrid tang to it, sulphurous and vile, worse than the worst smoke a smithy ever unleashed. His eyes watered, and down on the deck men were retching and swearing, in utter confusion. The wind was dropping, or so it seemed, for though the stuff swirled in the air, it clung about the ship, and sight came and went by the instant. One moment the ship was a dim grey outline; the next he could not see the hand that wiped the stuff out of his eyes. Even the hubbub below sounded stifled, and he raised his voice to carry over it.

'*Move, you stupid bastards!* While there's still a breath of breeze! Get the sweeps out! *Fast* – faugh!'

The breath made him cough and heave again, but no worse. The voices became marginally more purposeful, and he heard the clatter as the sweeps were pulled from their racks. He blundered his way back to the helm, colliding heavily with what turned out to be Kalve, in mid-plaint. 'Ah, there, skipper! Might've known they had some deviltry planned!'

'Good of you to tell us! Listen, can you get us moving?'

'Aye, maybe, but whither away? I can't bring us about—'

'I don't want you to! I want you to use whatever way we've got, keep her heading straight ahead, as far as we can. And as swiftly.'

Kalve shook his head. 'Ahead? But we don't even know we're still on the same heading!'

For answer Olvar pulled the direction bracelet from his wrist, and set it swinging. They peered at it in silence through the steam. Olvar hissed with relief.

'If you've a better idea ... ? No. Then jump to it, sailing master! Remember, the hunters were standing in, and fast.'

Kalve spat out a dry oath, and went sliding down the stair, shouting for Adde. At Olvar's side something seemed to sidle out of the mist, a ragged ghost that collided with nothing: Telqua. 'Now I know what,' she said, spitting liberally on the deck. 'The pool, in the fire-mountain. The waters bubble yellow, too hot to touch, and have the same taste. The shamans hold the steam down upon us. Strong indeed!'

'Then I'll wager they can't keep it up forever,' he said grimly. 'Thank you, princess.'

'What is happening?' she interrupted fiercely, swaying as she stood. 'The water changes its song against the hull—'

'What I hoped, maybe,' he said, and seized the tiller. 'Better hang on to something!'

The *Orrin* swung slowly upright, and any trace of wind about them died. In the dull stinking air there was only the muffled beat of oars – and, beyond it, nearing fast, a fast fierce splashing. 'Cease rowing!' wheezed Olvar. 'Ship oars! Any man makes a sound, I'll cut his bloody throat!'

He must have sounded sincere. Perhaps he was. There was suddenly no noise around him save the soft lap of wavelets, the trickle of water from the hovering oars; and, drawing nearer with the same relentless intensity as the drumbeats, the rhythmical splash of paddles. Closer it came and louder, as constant as a machine, as quick and deadly. So close they could hear the soft thudding of the time-drum, the fast controlled gasps of the paddlers, all in time with the pulsing command from the heights. Olvar was strong even for a smith, but he thought of the sinews and the staying power involved, and resolved to himself that if he came up against these fellows, he was going to be very, very careful indeed.

Closer still it came. He felt his own sweat join itself to the fog and run stinging into his eyes; and the arm he dashed it away with was also sweat-soaked.

The pulse seemed to fill all the mist about him, coming from every side, with those barbaric grunting breaths; and then, very suddenly as it seemed, it was past and away, vanishing into the mist. Only then did he realise Telqua had a deathgrip on his tunic, and she was quivering like a pine frond. For long minutes they stood without moving, in the silent ship; and then she let go, sighing. 'At least they will not ram us now—'

There was a soft low thud, a booming, scraping sound and the whole heavy ship shuddered. A hard hand seemed to crush the life out of it, the living lilt of the water, with a force that twanged the rigging like Gille's strings, and threw them both off their feet. Olvar, clutching the tiller, swung by his arms; Telqua was flung against him, bounced off and struck the deck with a thud.

'Aground!' said Kalve, aghast.

'Yes,' said Olvar, picking himself up. 'In the shallows. Better than paddling in circles out there, at the mercy of those bastards. They'd be over us like rats the moment they got wind of us.'

'S'pose that's true,' conceded Kalve grudgingly. 'We can refloat her when it begins to clear. Or the tide'll do it in a few hours.'

Telqua, rubbing bits of herself, was looking over the side. 'Your best move, as things were,' she informed him, spitting copiously. 'But there are other pieces on the board. We lie near shore, and now there are warriors here. By land they may come at you.'

'Yes. We'd better post sentinels, then. Maybe get a fighting party ashore, to delay them.'

She shook her head slowly. 'Your young men are bold, but not used to land. The hunters are cunning, even in this terrible forest. We must get word my folk, who have learned some of their tricks. I will go ashore.'

'Alone? With those vermin loose out there? I'd better come too.'

She sighed. 'I cannot stop you. But do not expect me to carry you. Not such a bulk!'

'Charmed, I'm sure!' muttered Olvar, and gave Kalve his orders. 'No more than common sense. Two men on shore, one at the masthead in case this stuff sinks. When it thins enough to sail, piss off out of here whether I'm back or not.'

'I'll give you a few minutes, at least,' protested the sailing master.

'In Hella's nightbound bum you will! That shark is still cruising around out there, and you'll have enough of a time dodging him as it is. I'll be all right here till you get back, I can live on my f— my reserves.'

The dour sailing master seemed ready to rebel. Instead he shook his head angrily. 'We'll ne'er see either of you again. But it's never heed me, go you must. Have a care, skipper!'

Olvar, unsure how he understood that, clapped him on the shoulder. 'Give my best to Gille, if I can't.'

There was some murmuring among the crew, but Olvar knew he was not being foolish; they could do without him sooner than he without them. He looped his bow and swordbelt over his shoulder, though he would have been happier with a good cudgel. Telqua took more arrows for the bow he had found her. As silently as possible they swung down the ladder into the water. It came up to Olvar's neck, and Telqua nearly vanished, though she held her bowstring obstinately above water. Her feet floated out from under her, and he towed her along, to avoid splashes, while the grey sand sluggishly invaded his sandals. Suddenly heavy and dripping, they stumbled up on to the beach, casting around in the eye-watering mist.

'This must be the other end of the island,' whispered Olvar. 'Will any of your folk be here?'

'There are watchers everywhere!' she hissed. 'Unless they have been taken. Little I hear and less I see!'

That was true; even the chattering birds had fallen silent under the dismal pall. 'We must get among the trees!' she whispered. 'But carefully, whale!'

Olvar had to fight down an urge to kick her skinny buttocks as she scuttled forward, hunched down. Instead he did his best to imitate her, to be greeted by a stifled but unmistakable outburst of giggling as he plunged in among the leaves. She said nothing, but led him on at a great pace. With leaves slashing at his face or dripping dew down his neck, he stumbled on after her, struggling to breathe in the foul airs. She had to halt before he did, though, bent over and wheezing in real pain. Sorry for her as she fought for breath, he rubbed a comforting hand along her back. It felt like a rack of bare bones. She straightened up suddenly and shied away, glaring. Then she grabbed both his arms and pulled him down, hard.

He had enough sense to obey, for then he heard it, too; the soft metallic jingle, the rustle and clink from out of the mist, faint, slow, but advancing fast. She jabbed a finger to her lips, then grinned mirthlessly and tapped her teeth. They were remarkably sharp-looking, and it took little enough in these surroundings to see her as a maneater herself. Before long the sound stopped awhile, then cautiously started, and a little later stopped again; and in this dreadful mirk it could almost be upon them already. They could not tell from where; they could only lie low and hope.

Sweat and condensing mist slithered in equal amounts down Olvar's neck, pooling in ticklish little droplets around every fold of his fleshy body. He took a tight hold of his sword, and wondered how he would fare against those broad-bladed spears. Even as he wondered, he heard the rasp and clink again, and suddenly, out of the mist to his left, he caught his first close sight of one of the hunters.

The man advanced in the same half-ridiculous crouch they had adopted, leading with the spear-blade, squinting narrow-eyed into the churning obscurity. In look and garb he could have been the corpse on the wreckage: black kilt, black body-armour of stiffened leather slashed and splashed with crude white patterns. They left his limbs bare, long and sturdy, though desperately lean, with cord-like muscles playing beneath skin like fired copper; darker than Telqua's or her father's, disturbingly like Olvar's own. What might he have been, now, if Great-great-grandfather Akhote-something-or-other had not joined the clan migration? Might this not have been Olvar leading the hunt, his bloodline absorbed into the merciless fraternity that served the Ice? Was that very man there his clansman, his cousin?

A cousin ready to pull out his kin's guts; or his own, if the cold Powers should require it.

On they came, round shields on one lean arm, spearblades poised, short, crude-looking bows and black arrows at their backs, the metal that was their nomads' wealth chiming softly at wrist, neck and in their short-braided hair. For all that, if he had not been forewarned and silent he would not have heard them beyond twenty paces away, so smoothly they slipped through the tangles that had tripped him. Their stance, the way they moved, their expressions even, under the cruel lines of cicatrice and paint, gave them an eerie likeness. There were twenty of them, but they stayed close to one another, glancing around, too alert to be called nervous. The last men in the line were especially vigilant, swinging on the least cause; but the watchers in the undergrowth remained hidden. The column filed past and Olvar found Telqua's quick gesture immensely reassuring; the patrol was evidently headed around the island, away from the beach. He let himself relax a little.

What came next startled him all the more. The watchers looked back once more, and it was as if there was a brief flurry of movement, and their outlines blurred a moment. Then, slouching now, they padded on after their fellows. But helmets, armour and all made little difference to Olvar; these were not the same two men he had seen a moment earlier. He looked round for Telqua. She was not there. Suddenly chilled, he pushed forward, as quietly as he could, and almost fell over something that moved. Two bodies lay stripped and sprawling in the leaf mould, the hand of one still scrabbling faintly at the blood that spurted dully from the deep slash in his throat. Even as he saw, the hand fell, and the pulse faded. Then he himself was seized.

He made no resistance, save to turn from the hand that sought his mouth. He found himself surrounded by crouching figures, grotesque in trailing black kilts and tilting helmets too large for the skinny limbs beneath. But there was a fearful earnestness about them, and he made no move that could alarm them. A shadow slid up alongside him. 'If you are not stupid, you are safe!' said Telqua's hoarse whisper. 'We could not let you make noise, not now!'

He nodded, and the hands around him relaxed a little. He heard her breathe out. 'You saw.' It was not a question. 'Two less. In heartbeats fewer still ...'

Olvar smiled grimly. Telqua whispered something, and the hands released him, unwillingly, he felt. There was little trust here. Another voice spoke, fast and light; but he understood. 'We must not wait here. They may need us.'

'The East-over-Sea men need us,' said Telqua to the fog. 'Only they can help us now. We must lift this mirk.'

There was a burst of whispers. 'It is the shamans' will!'

'I know,' she said impatiently. 'Where are they? Where do they dance?'

'In the mountain-cauldron. High above. I have seen them.'

Olvar listened to the rattle of whispers with some disbelief. Some were women's voices like Telqua's, some the dry quavering of old men, but others the piping lisp of children, small children at that, yet without light or laughter. All were in the same cold earnest.

'You hear?' demanded Telqua. 'We will go now, to stop them, for a time at least. You get back to your ship and be ready.'

Olvar struggled up. 'No. I'm coming along.'

'You?' She was sneering again. 'Do you think we can haul you up by a rope? Besides, how to rejoin your ship? They sail the moment the mirk thins. That was your own command. Why mix yourself in this—'

There was a sudden brief furore in the mist, a choppy mingling of sounds never completed – a clash of arms silenced, a shout cut short, a burst of dull drubbing impacts, low moans and stifled cries, as if even mortal agony muffled itself lest it betray others. It was over as suddenly, leaving their thudding heartbeats abruptly louder than the drums above. Hands moved instinctively to weapons. The scarecrow figures about him stood poised to fight or flee.

'Because of that,' Olvar whispered harshly.

A rasping birdcall cut the mist. Another answered, beside him, and was answered again, twice. Telqua breathed out, harshly enough to stir the stinking clouds, and made no move to draw her bow at the shapes that formed in the fog ahead. The hunters' garb and weapons they bore, but they moved in silent parody, stalking, scuttling, sidling, some half dancing with the exhilaration of the bloody spears they brandished.

A curt word from Telqua silenced them; and he saw the captured helms turn and lift, doubtfully, towards the island heights. 'Come then!' she said. 'But if you hinder us, you are left behind. Just as one of our own people.'

'I am one of your own people,' he said, and was astonished when she stooped suddenly and scooped up some ashen earth. Her fingers drew quick grey slashes across his cheeks, but their touch was surprisingly gentle.

'Now you are.' Without seeming to move she vanished into the mist. The ragamuffin army, armour creaking, helms lolling, spears trailing along the ground, sidled away almost as easily. Olvar loped heavily to catch up.

Gille stood silently, watching the black sails move once again, struggling to outflank the *Rannvi*. Nils too was studying them. 'One's slower than the other – the rebuilt one, I'll wager. But I'd allow that one the better captain.'

Gille's smile returned. 'Better than you?'

'Not in yon ship,' answered Nils, without the slightest smile. 'I can outrace them for you – just, for now. But miracles I cannot work. They guess our mind and mission. They've made sure to come between us and our best course home, and we dare not risk closing with 'em.'

'Then what's your counsel, sailing master?'

'Steer south still. We don't know how well provisioned they are, or how long they can endure such a chase. They are heavily manned, they were not expecting us; they may have to fall back. Then we can risk a break eastward.'

'South!' groaned Gille, mopping at his neck. 'This is as bad as the Southlands already. They say it gets worse very soon, south of their borders.'

Nils nodded. 'So I've heard, too.'

Gille turned his eyes back to the bearing of the islands, already hull down and hidden against the glowing clouds of sunset. They made him think of fires, below the earth and in the sky. 'How much can we endure?' he muttered.

'How long do you want to live?'

Olvar toiled on up the hill, through what seemed to be an infinite course of dripping, stinking leaves. Strange blooms spattered him with damp pollen, fungi smeared him with slime or squashed under his skidding boots. Despite Telqua's harsh words, he was never left. The strange bobbing helmets surrounded him, and at difficult points hands would seize his arms to haul him up, or unceremoniously boost him from behind over an obtrusive rock. He was acutely aware how small most of these hands were; it was like being guided by the Little Ancestors in whom all his folk believed, and which he thought were some memory in their own land of that enigmatic folk the duergar.

They were surprisingly strong and wholly silent, these small creatures. He began to understand Telqua rather better now, and guess at her own grim childhood. To his surprise a rare hot pride flushed him at the thought of these folk, his own. His forefathers had been welcomed by the pale-skinned Easterners, themselves outcasts, and seldom if ever made to feel lowly or lesser. Yet they could not help some sense of inferiority, in the face of these wise folk with their strange arts of metal and miraculous devices and laws and living; and still more so of the fire-haired sothrans, with their arrogant strength and wealth, that could carve beauty out of living stone, tame wide lands, spread fertile fields and build vast cities, yet drive their own kin like oxen to achieve it. He saw now that his folk had their own achievements, although these were shaped by a hostile land and savage foes, and the Ice beyond all. Malformed and misshapen they were by the impress of that crushing heel, but not destroyed. Given the chance, they too would live and grow straight again.

He blundered on with still fiercer determination; and it was a shock when a hand pressed against his shoulder, and bore him swiftly down. Light flickered in the mist above. 'We are here!' whispered Telqua. He was startled to find he had no wind to reply. 'And you must crawl. Slowly, silently! Sentinels watch.'

He inched forward on his belly. No doubt Telqua was comparing him to some immense slug; he felt little better. After a while it dawned on him that the throbbing was not only in his ears, and that the soil beneath him felt strangely hot and dry. It was mostly ash, he realised, and thinning at that; there was stone not far beneath. He glanced up. He was in some kind of shallow cleft, nothing visible above its rim. The bushes here were scanty and gnarled, less tangled than below. He could see between them, almost, a confused pattern of glows and movement his sight was slow to resolve. Just as a light hand held him back, he saw.

Below him the cleft dropped away in a slope of loose ash and crumbled stone, into the hollow heart of the fire-mountain. He had never seen such a place before, and expected the earthfires to blaze and boil openly; but they did not. The walls sloped inward in a shallow curve, and at their outer edge below there were still clumps of bushes clinging to the sides, rooted in the crumbled surface. But the centre was barren and desolate, and from beneath the rocks and between the soil constant smokes arose, filling the air with foul taints. Yet at its heart lay not a fire but a tarn, startlingly wide and seemingly deep; but like none he had imagined. He would never have known it for water; he would have taken it for the tainted humour of the earth, oozing from this chasm as from an open sore. It was thick and yellow, and all around its margin ran a solid band of yellow crust, smoothing out the outlines of the rock beneath; and it boiled and bubbled violently, while from its heart the steam arose in a thick column and bowed over them like a spectral tree.

Fires did burn in that dreadful place; but they were not the work of nature. Along one edge of the pool three high pyres blazed in a line, forming a circle of light in the murk; and around its margins, as far as they could get from the fumes, tall warriors sat or slumped about. Before them, at the brink, six stakes of half-trimmed saplings had been driven into the soil. Smokes wavered and spurted about their bases, wreathing the shapes that were fastened to them by rough lashings in the lee of the fires. Olvar winced, but he could not tear his eyes away.

One or two of those shapes sagged deadly still, their half-naked bodies streaked with darkness, and he was almost glad. Some hung or slumped apathetically, but others writhed and twisted frantically against their bindings, their skins shining with sweat in the firelight, struggling to twist away from the fearsome figures that bounded and capered about the fires.

To the tune of drums and tambours and other instruments like dry wooden clappers those figures moved. Some were played by men who sat so far back they were barely visible save by their glittering, intent eyes, some by the shapes themselves; for they who danced were human, beneath the massive masks they bore. Yet Olvar had doubted that for a moment, so fearful were their aspects, so deep they struck into his inner self. It was as if his body remembered them as keenly as his mind, and looked deeper than his eyes, seeing not themselves, their garb, but what it was they summoned. Of the same kind they were as the masks he remembered, and yet not so; for these were more elaborate, more forceful in their crafting, as if secrets were graven into them greater than most makers knew. Their contours were rough, their colours harsh and crude, but so chosen, by art or chance, that the firelight lent them its flickering, searing life.

The Hawk-Owl danced with wooden wings outflung in its silent glide, and the dancer's body beneath seemed lost in the suggestion of pale sharp talons outthrust, to strangle and stab in the same sharp action. The Viper swayed and swung with tongue that darted and fangs that folded down as the red mouth struck; and Olvar saw no legs beneath the swinging robe, only glistening belly scales, though yellow dust kicked up around the dancer's feet. And a shaggy, sullen thing that lounged and shambled, a red tongue lolling between its fangs, was a Bear in far more than the fur robe and the carven snout.

Before the fires and around the stakes they danced, striking with claw and fang and talon at the figures slung there. And with them, also dancing, moved a tall figure with ashen skin and blank white mask. At a wave of his pale hand the drumming redoubled its pace; and he too struck at the stakes, but with a darting black blade. Back, forth, it slashed, a small arc; the figure hung there stiffened, and a thin scream sounded over the drum-pulse. Then it fell back, twisting feebly again; and the white man tossed a collop to the Hawk-Owl, which caught it deftly in its beak with a wooden clatter, and twisted its mask in glee. The lounging warriors bayed and clattered their spears.

Olvar felt his mouth dry and twist, his throat flood with a sudden rush. He turned away and managed to stifle his retching, and found Telqua's face close to his own. 'We can put a stop to that!' he grated.

Telqua's hand clenched in his sleeve. 'Then we turn their eyes to this island, away from their fruitless hunt in the south-western isles. They will realise there are many here.'

'You destroyed their patrol. And those are your folk hanging there. Your children.'

'One patrol is nothing! And those are our sacrifices also, to save the rest. This will expose our strength. But I did not say we would not do it. It is worth the risk.'

'They may be too busy chasing our ships, anyhow. They may even blame us!'

'That's likely, yes. So!' She let herself slide back from the crest, and faint insect chirrups sounded in the mist.

'Some of the sentinels, on this side,' she whispered, sliding back. 'The same trick we may work upon them. That will give us time. Watch now!'

For a long time there seemed to be little more to watch, save when the drumming grew faster again; and then he could not. Yet from this height he was somehow aware of a change in the deeper shadows of the slope. He turned his eyes from the firelight, accustomed them to the dimness again; and it came to him that darkness slid over the stones, like spreading patches of thick oil. The sentinels sat lazy but alert, their eyes scanned the dark; but they were drawn back always to the cruel spectacle at the tarnside, and the light. They saw nothing. And then he noticed one, the outermost, seem to stretch out idly, shift his position. Another's head bowed where he sat, as if he were sleepy or bored; and then the small group of three beside them looked around, and vanished as if a cloak were thrown over them. A flicker, and then three figures lounged among the firelit stones once more, to any casual eye the same.

Telqua's whisper tickled his ear. 'Come back now! We have found an easier way clear, though you must still crawl.'

Olvar's breeches were torn, his knees bleeding; but he had seen too much already. He shuffled along with grim care, and surprised himself at how well he managed, how little he feared. His sickness at least helped him to ignore his growing hunger. Lower down the slope a wider cleft opened, and most of the bushes had been cut away within. It was down this he wriggled, with elbows in his ribs and feet in his face, and more than one clambering over him as if he wasn't there, amid a smell that overpowered even the stink of the mist; but at the mouth of the cleft there was no scramble. Hands pulled him carefully through, eased him across the stones, guided him on his way.

With the sentries in place here he could never have come so close. He could not tell which of the firelit sihouettes were hunters and which hunted, but of the ten or twelve nearby not one head turned as they crawled closer. The ease of it chilled him; the hunters must have been complacent, believing there were only a few stray fugitives here. They would be less careless now. Telqua's hand stopped him, and they lay still and waited; and it came to him suddenly that he had not strung his bow. With agonising care he rolled over and caught the end between his feet, heaving on the arc and sliding the loop into the notch in the horn tip, biting his tongue with the effort. He glimpsed Telqua's eyes, wide with alarm in the shadow beside him. Then it was done, and he relaxed, slowly, with little specks of coloured light dancing in front of his eyes. Carefully he drew an arrow from his belt; and his elbow struck a small rock, that pattered away against another. One of the watchers turned sharply, then jerked forward as a crowd of hands reached up and snatched him down, like Hella's demons claiming a prize. As perhaps they were; for the sentinel sat up again limply, head down, and dying tremors racked the body on the spear that propped it up.

'Any moment they see!' whispered Telqua in his ear, and tugged him on. Below them the white figure halted his cavorting, visibly shaking with lack of breath, and gestured. Two warriors cut one of the still shapes loose, and flung it on a pyre with a great splutter and sizzle; two more dragged out a new victim, kicking and screaming, and the watchers leaned forward and laughed.

That was Telqua's moment. Olvar heard no signal, but it was as if the darkness about him lifted and rushed forward. He staggered under the jostle of bodies, saw three last sentries on this side vanish under the tide, and heads turn all around the firelight, men spring to their feet. A shrilling howl of demons split the dark, drowning the drums, and he yelled with them as all the silent tensions of recent hours boiled out. Arrows came hissing across the light, but the hunters' bows were less in range or power, and in the mirk few struck home. Olvar stumped down the hill, drawing the bow as he ran, seeking the mark he wanted; and seeing it, stopped, aimed, loosed, and ran on.

His shot vanished high into the mist and plunged down between the stakes, to spatter into the tarn's rim at the white-masked shaman's feet. Startled, the tall figure cast about, sought to duck behind a stake; but Olvar was far closer now, and his next shot, almost level, took the ghastly figure full in the breast. The impact toppled him backwards, arms flailing, into the bubbling cauldron of the tarn. The mask coughed up a spray of scarlet, and sank. Running from the fires, the Hawk-Owl shaman threw back his winged arms and screeched, as if about to take flight; then fell forward into the ground with a cluster of shafts in his back. The men at the drums, less encumbered, sprang up as arrows and stones flew past them, and tried to duck back into the dark; but it was suddenly alive with black shrilling figures. Some fell, others ran back; and the attackers reached the fires.

The moments of disorder were over. The hunters had been surprised and split apart; but swiftly they rallied. A group gathered quickly about some of the shamans, raising shields to form a wall. The Bear, braver perhaps than his fellows or with freer arms, tore off his cumbersome mask and seized a spear; but even as he ran forward to join the others he was seen and pelted with stones. One struck blood from his face, he staggered blindly, and like a bear indeed he was encircled. Spears rose and fell, he staggered free with one thrust right through him and sank to his painted face on the stones, crawling. Then his fellows were around him, and the attackers scattered screaming into the steamy confusion. Other hunters fought their way through to join the group; other knots formed and forced their way through also. In seconds what had been a scattered rabble was a solid phalanx, with archers at their back, pacing forward over the scattering stones, forcing the milling attackers back. From behind the shields their short spears stabbed out, or slashed like swords, and the small shapes they cut down were trampled and borne down into the mist that swirled around their feet.

Olvar, alarmed, looked around for Telqua. She was on the slope above him, launching arrows into the line, but arrows from behind were striking sparks from the stones about her. 'We've got to get back!' he shouted. 'You can't fight this. We've done what we can.'

She pointed suddenly. The Viper still danced down by the stakes with a spear in his costumed hand, stabbing frenziedly at the figures slung there. To Olvar, struggling to aim, it seemed like wanton viciousness; but then he realised it might be a rush to conclude some arcane offering. The Viper stood still a moment, the scale-painted arm swung high, and he loosed. In the instant the blow fell, Telqua's shot took him in the back; but Olvar's pinned him writhing to the same post as his victim.

Olvar seized Telqua's arm. 'Come on!'

She pulled the other way. 'I thought you wanted to fall back.'

'We've got to free those victims.'

'What for? They are already our sacrifices. We cannot support them.'

Olvar shook his head, as if to dash something out of it. 'Look, saving them might foul up the ritual.'

She shook her head also, but let herself be drawn along the slope, across the flank of the advancing phalanx. Somebody had taken command, for suddenly it seemed to split in the middle and range back to either side; the blank wall became an arrowhead. Telqua stopped, stuck her fingers in her mouth and blew an earsplitting whistle, twice; and the attackers gave back swiftly into the dark. The arrowhead paced forward. Olvar and Telqua went skidding and scrambling down the slope towards the fires. He choked as wafts of smoke bore a still worse reek about him, of the burning bone and fat from the ghastly pyres. From the furthest stakes he turned, for there was nothing left alive to rescue; even that last blow had fallen. But on the last the child there, scrawny and pitiful, still lived and bled from her grievous wound; and Telqua's knife slashed the coarse rope away to free her. Olvar plucked her loose, and ducked hastily as an arrow splintered the top of the stake. Telqua shot her last shaft, and the two of them bounded up the slope, out of the light by the fastest way. 'There's another track out around this side!' she shouted.

Olvar, carrying the stunned child, struggled to staunch her bleeding with a scrap of rag as they ran, but had to free his hand to haul himself up the uncertain slope. Telqua heaved him up on to a ledge, and then the going was easier; but the jingle of metal from below kept them running as fast as they could, up into a steep and narrow crevice where vines both helped and hindered them, and out at last, drenched in sweat and brimstone stink, into the sudden shock of a cool fresh breeze.

He was so stunned and exhausted he did not at once see what that meant. But then he looked wildly around him. He stood just below the cauldron's rim, among the low trees; and through them, though they trailed white wisps like shrouds, he could see a darkly luminous horizon, mirrored in a restless sea. He was facing east, he realized; towards the dawn, and towards his distant home. He sought, for an instant, a glimpse of a sail, Gille's or his own. But Gille would be too far by now, he hoped; and there was no hull visible in the wide bay below, though he could almost make out the sandbar glimmering with the waves that rolled against it. The attack had succeeded, the mist was clearing. Obedient to his orders, the *Orrin* would already have pulled herself off the sand, and set sail.

A feeling of great loneliness swept over him,

and he resisted unthinkingly as Telqua sought to pull the child from his arms. 'Let her go, shaman!' she said flatly. 'She is dead.'

Dully he released the body, its limbs loose against his, and still warm. So was the blood that soaked his coat. 'At least she will not serve their purposes,' said Telqua, more softly, laying the child down beneath a bush, and kicking the loose ash down to cover her. 'Nor fill their foul bellies. She died free.'

A sudden rush of feet and clash of arms behind them jarred them from their exhausted trance. 'So may we!' she gasped. 'Fools that we be! Run, man, run!'

An arrow winged at the sound of her voice, but she was no longer there, leaping downhill in great bounds. Olvar, less agile, kept pace with her as much by swinging through branches by his hands like an ape. Even the stones he stood on would turn in the soft soil and bounce down ahead of him. One of his pursuers went slipping and sliding straight past him on a fall of the stuff, yelling, to collide with something hard in the half-light. Time passed, how long he had no sense or notion. It was getting lighter, but Olvar hardly noticed; sweat flooded his eyes, his heart pounded, and he hardly knew whether Telqua was still in front of him. Then there were no more branches to grab at, and a scarlet light dazzled his eyes.

Telqua's hand smacked across his jowls, back and forth, and he realized she had been shaking him. 'All right!' he gasped, as she hauled him along. 'All right!' It was his own tongue, not hers, but he was past noticing such things. They were out in the open, the sky was red, the sea blazed before him. They stumbled on, and then she was fighting just as hard to hold him back. Stones rattled beneath his scrabbling feet and bounced out into emptiness, and with a sudden chill of understanding he saw that he stood on the edge of a cliff. He looked at her, gasping, and coughed out a crazy laugh. 'Well,' he said, still in his own tongue, 'nice try. Maybe we won.'

She was staring past him, not to the forest but the sea beyond. He followed her gaze, and saw white sails bobbing on the breeze below. The *Orrin*, with all sails set, rounding the point they stood on. 'That bastard Kalve!' he coughed. 'The mist's been gone for bloody hours! He waited! I'll—'

He stopped suddenly. 'Telqua—'

'That's too far!' she said, breasts heaving.

He jerked his head at the sounds among the forest behind them. He could not remember the words to ask her if she would prefer what snarled at their heels, but she took his meaning. She skipped back a pace or two, pulling him along, and then with a truly horrendous ululating cry she ran and sprang. He almost balked; but he was hot, and tired, and covered in blood, and he longed for the cool clean sea. His cry was no more than a croak; but at least like a frog, he thought, he jumped.

The slap was a shock to him; he had expected rushing air, and death. Instead, almost at once there was a flat hard blow, and he was very much awake, and in fearful agony and frantic confusion. Winded, his chest on fire, he fought to breathe, and drew in only water. Hot iron banded his brow, his eyes bulged and his ears roared. He flailed uselessly at the green dimness that pressed in around him, and at the thing that seemed to be rising from the depths below. Long, pale, it swirled about him, spinning him with the rush of its passage; and something touched him, brushed him like fine weed, yet with a startling warmth. The water was suddenly a mass of bubbles; and the fire in his chest sank and died. His heart laboured less, the crushing pain in his head sank away, and he was able to move his limbs, though the pain in his back was still blinding. He kicked out, and bobbed up suddenly, coughing and spewing, into the light.

His eyes cleared, and he felt a hand seize him. He was looking into a face, surprising and surprised, a strong lean face with broad flat cheekbones not unlike his own, but a nose keener and less blunt, high-bridged and proud, framed by straight straggles of black hair. Above it bright open eyes, alive with delight, and a wide laughing mouth below. A young face, a lively laughing face that seemed at that moment like the embodiment of a life regained. A face he had never seen before.

'*Telqua?*' he spluttered, doing his best to tread water and ignore the twinges of agony it caused him.

She laughed still, too breathless to form her words, and pointed. The sails, so huge they all but blotted out the rising sun, were standing in towards them now, Kalve disobeying his orders yet again to see whom he could rescue. He waved an arm and hailed, sank, rose spluttering and hailed again, and heard a hail in answer.

'*They see us!*' he said, and Telqua laughed.

'No ... wonder, with the splash you made! And you brought down half the cliff edge upon my head.'

'Sorry!' he spluttered. 'More careful – next time. Thanks for pulling me up.'

She laughed, a little surprised. 'I? I couldn't find you.'

It made no sense, so he laughed; it hurt him, and he turned on his back to float. That was easier. There was the cliff, not so high as it had looked, evidently; though he could see the hunters clearly, baffled at the brink, and they showed no urge to jump. One of them hurled a spear, and it splashed into the green water quite close by, but Telqua broke into peals of laughter again, and, when he caught her eye, so did he; it seemed like the funniest thing in the world. A thought struck him. 'You said you'd been a chieftain for ten years!'

'So I have! Since my coming to womanhood, as is the custom.'

'At – what? Thirteen years old?'

'Eleven. You see me long past the age of marrying.'

Olvar shook his head gravely, though his neck was a mass of fiery needles. Above them, from the crest of the island, the plume of steam trailed out in the fresh southerly breeze, free and untrammelled. The *Orrin* would have to come dangerously close inshore, in that; but of course they would lower a boat. A few minutes lost; but then, let any black ship dare to catch them now!

CHAPTER SIX

The Shifting Stars

Gille hammered on the tiller in his frustration.

'That'll not be changing anything, skipper,' observed Nils calmly. 'Except maybe our heading. Leave the poor wood be.'

Gille glowered at him. He had wanted the sailing master to accept him, which he had; and become a lot less respectful in the process. 'How long till dawn?'

'A few minutes, no more. Then we'll see. 'Tis best you contain yourself till then. Let the crew see you calm.'

'They know well enough I'm not, by now.'

'Not the point, skipper. Play the man, and they'll feel they must themselves.'

'Will they? When they see...' Gille shut his mouth, closed his eyes, did his best to calm his breathing. 'You're right. As usual. Play the man, you say? I'll sooner play the kantel awhile.'

'You could do worse. If there's a power indeed on our side, it lies in that thing. Times are I think there's more untapped.'

Gille tuned a string against its neighbour. 'So do I. But how to get at it? I don't think it's got the right player.'

'Or the right audience, just as likely,' Nils suggested. 'At the least you're a mastersmith in Vayde's line, and a singer. But for what ears did he make that thing? Not serenading a bunch of roughneck sea-rats, surely.'

The tuning, as usual, revealed that other strings needed a slight refinement, and Gille twisted the keys gently. He hadn't been aware of telling Nils so much about the instrument; but in the sleepless night-watches of the past ten days he must have revealed more of himself, of his thinking, than he knew. The sailing master had said little in return, till now; but evidently in his quiet way he also had been at thought.

'I think he made it to, well, to catch attention,' said Gille. 'To do more, maybe. To intrigue; to compel. Maybe no one person, but a mass of them, a crowd. It seems to work best on people in a group. Maybe there just aren't enough of us.'

'Or maybe it was meant to speak over spaces and distances. Or to things greater than people,' suggested Nils, with an unusual sense of mystery. 'Things that are the equal of many people.'

'It's said he spoke with strange forces,' admitted Gille, wondering where Nils had suddenly picked up an imagination. 'And with the dead.'

'No distance greater than that,' said Nils. 'And, man, would it not be wonderful to speak with the souls that once inhabited Kerys the Great? The mariners who sailed the round seas roundabout, 'tis said. Or Svethan of Morvannec, or ...'

'I'd talk to the women!' grinned Gille. 'Deyadarye of Pentynon, ever hear of her? Two kings died cursing her. Or the Lady Kerhalt, who kept a guard of forty lads and forty lasses, all of the handsomest? Or Berie the Gold Lady of Tor Daveth, who seized one of the kings of Kerys in battle and imprisoned him in the tower for a year and a day? I saw their pictures in a book once.'

'I can imagine,' Nils smirked. 'Education's a wonderful thing. What did the king do when this Berie released him?'

'Asked her to marry him. She refused, unless

he brought along a regiment of his best knights to assist.'

Nils gave a dry chuckle. 'And did he?'

'No. But they signed a friendship pact. With a parley twice a year. Probably he found that about often enough.' Gille plucked out a little phrase, and found the kantel was back in tune. And so also was he; as, he realised, Nils had intended.

Whistles down below told him the watch was changing, sailors scrambling out of their stuffy hammocks, leaving their stink for the next man. Clothes and bodies and bedding were foul after so many days, but there was no slowing the ship to sluice down, make and mend; not unless the sunrise showed them anything different from all the other mornings past. And Gille, with a return of his bitterness, knew it would not. The sailors were groaning and griping, but it was with weariness of the mind more than the body; they had all too little to occupy them, save worry. By day the sailing was easy enough, save that one did not dare make a single slip. The night was an unhappy time for them, too, when they started at shadows and dreams, fearing what lay around them, and ahead.

He swung himself up to his favourite place on the rail, resting against the sternpost, leaning on the anchorage of the backstay, and began to play, watching the sky and sea to the eastward. In mornings previous, small clouds along the horizon would already have been tinged with pink, and the whitecaps would have taken on a tinge to match. But now there were no clouds.

The colour of the sky changed quickly, kindling swiftly from horizon to horizon a sullen red glow. The sun's rim blazed over the world's edge, sparking the wavecrests to scarlet fire. And Gille's hands struck bitter chords from the kantel's strings,

as against that growing disc of fire, as at every
sunrise since they fled the isles, the two black sails
barred their way into the east, herding them like
beaters to the kill.

> *Two black ships there were, that sailed out
>   from the West*
> *The sea is wide and the wind blows free*
> *Now half their crews were Ice-ghouls, and
>   maneaters the rest,*
> *Running hard before the breeze to Old
>   Nordeney.*
> *They raced us, they chased us, they worried at
>   our tail,*
> *The sea is wide and the wind blows free,*
> *But catching us is sorer work than goosing up
>   a whale,*
> *Running hard before the breeze to Old
>   Nordeney.*
> *They couldn't catch us on the land, they will
>   not on the waves,*
> *The sea is wide and the wind blows free.*
> *They'll never down and geld us, boys, and work
>   us as their slaves,*
> *Running hard before the breeze to Old
>   Nordeney.*
>
> *For we sunk the others in the swell-a,*
> *We'll send these ratbags off to Hella,*
> *We're leading them to her front door,*
> *We'll smash their ships and flay them sore,*
> *And when we've beat them to the skin,*
> *She'll open wide and ask 'em in,*
> *And we'll sail on our homeward way*
> *To home and beauty on the quay*
> *Mooring safe and happy home in Old
>   Nordeney!*

It was Gille improvising as he went along, new words to an old work song and little enough of poetry in them; but they caught the raw bite of resentment in his own heart, and turned it into cheerful defiance. And that awoke an echo in the listless men as they emerged and set about the usual minor morning tasks. They hummed along, they caught the refrain and took it up; and for a while the ship seemed to lighten a little, and the burden of the chase. Only Nils stood wholly still, for he was carefully taking a sighting, the device he used flashing fire as its brass pendant weight caught the sun.

'Well?' demanded Gille. 'How far south have we come now?'

Nils closed the quadrant with a snap. "Tis too far. My moon-bearings were near enough right. Skipper, we're south of any bearing the sothran charts recognise. South of Bryhannec, south of their southernmost borders.'

Gille's heart sank. 'But beyond them there's nothing but the *daveth*! The *Daveth Loscaouhen*, the Burning Wastes.'

'S'that what *losca*-whatever means? Well, skipper, long years back I saw an old chart with this quarter of the sea set down as the *mor losca*— that word. So that must mean...'

'Yes. *Mor* is one word for *sea*. It fits all I've heard of it. And *loscaou* doesn't quite mean *burning*. It's a word they use for the action of ovens, furnaces, that kind of thing. Roasting; baking; reducing...'

'Spare me, skipper. See what you mean. But remember...' He jerked a calloused thumb at their pursuers. 'Whatever tells upon us, tells on yon bastards every bit as much. More so, maybe, for they cannot have come provisioned for so long a chase.'

'We're not doing so well ourselves. Though

that trick of cutting the fresh water with seawater's a good one.'

'Maybe. But I'd say they're wrought of sterner stuff than we, skipper.'

Gille glared out at the black sails, seeking to put himself in the place of those iron-faced men with all their grim intent; and an understanding grew in him, that made the growing heat seem for a moment leaden cold.

'Sterner? Or just harder driven? Nils, don't you see? If they're running short of provender now, there's only one place they're going to get it. No wonder they're sticking to the chase so close. They've *got* to catch us!'

Nils whistled, long and low. 'Damn! Right you are, skipper, though I wish you weren't. Our vittles – or if you'll credit that Telqua critter, we ourselves!'

'Oh, I believe her. Remember what Olvar found on that beach. Those bastards are driven in another way, too. The will of the Ice is in them, in their whole way of life. They're born to hate.'

'Well,' said Nils calmly, 'not I. But I'm aye a fast learner. We'll needs sit tight, and bear the burning, and pray the wind holds. For 'tis not the Ice that's our main foe now.'

So they sat, and endured, as the light climbed the sky. It was a new experience for these men of the North, to whom the sun had once been a welcome friend after the grey hours of winter. Now the light they had loved fell on them like a lash, dazzling on the bleached planking. Its pitch bubbled and seams popped under that heat, burning their bare feet, so they had to weave rough sandals of rope. Everything was dry as tinder, and the cook dared not light the fire even in its oven of clay brick; they gnawed their dry provisions cold, and the salted meat and fish burned their throats. The water ration was meagre already at two jacks, equal to three tall mugs a day, for every need, and that cut with seawater. No man washed save in the little water that could be gained by slinging a bucket overside. That was hard work, with the ship making such a way. The bedding was brought out to bake in the air; but it was not enough. Skins were already peeling, flayed by the light, and garments stiffened by salt and dirt began to rub painfully at neck and wrist and groin. Gille still sang, and the crew still listened; but as the day drew on his voice dried up in his throat, and he yearned for night.

Legend said no man could live for long in these latitudes, whether on the dunes of the Wastes or the shifting waves they rode. Gille felt the truth of it, as the sun poured down from its zenith, with enough weight, it seemed, to collapse the makeshift canopy. Another sail sheltered those of the crew not required to labour, and every so often someone would make the effort to haul up a bucket or two and sluice down the canvas, to cool it as the sun sucked up the water. Gille took his turn, but did little else; the songs he started faltered in the stifling wind. Around that time the masthead lookout fainted and had to be lowered down and revived with seawater; he was not replaced. There was little to look out for in this empty expanse, save those sails; and Nils and the helmsmen could see them all too clearly.

A few gulls had followed them from the isles, making the sailors laugh as they strutted possessively along the gunwales, or pecked and squabbled over scraps thrown to them; but those had fled, the day before perhaps – or was it earlier? All days were becoming the same, in this fearful chase. There had been porpoise-kind, too, the Sea-brothers sporting about their bows; those too had left them. They saw none of the great whales, either. The whole expanse of horizon around the *Rannvi* stood clear.

There was nothing save them, those black sails, and the sun; and the open ocean, mirroring the glare above, seemed nothing but a vast empty arena in which their flight had little meaning.

For the first time night brought no relief at all. The sun was gone, the stars glittered down; but they were not the stars of home. The wind felt like the sun's withering breath blown from the skies beneath the world. The timbers cooled only slowly, with much cracking and creaking; metal grew merely lukewarm. Men abandoned their hammocks below and lay sprawled about, unable to sleep or moaning in haunted dreams. Often they would start up with cries of fear; and sometimes those who sat awake would cry out, and challenge some flickering shadow or sudden uncanny creak. And sometimes, in the sea around them, men seemed to see things stir. Most often it was no more than a quirk of the cool radiance that shone around their wake, and the wakes of their pursuers; but now and again there seemed to be deeper glows, faint stirrings coursing this way and that far beneath the surface, and dark suggestions of great inchoate bulks that rose momentarily almost to the surface before sinking silently and swiftly back into the deep.

When Gille, having doused himself with seawater, won a few moments of uneasy slumber, he dreamed that a great beast of shaggy white fur squatted on his chest and blew its foul breath into his mouth, and he awoke sweating no less than before. After slow wretched hours the sun struck its brass gong over their heads, the first rays lit the sail a mocking blood-red, and they hauled themselves wearily up to see the predatory sails as before; only, this time, that little bit larger, that trace closer.

Nils, rubbing inflamed eyes, grunted at Gille's greeting, and nodded to the rigging pennants. They were flickering still, but after a while he saw, or thought he saw, the fitful, fishtail fluttering that had not been there yesterday.

'Blowing yet, but no life in 'em, see?' said Nils.

Gille wished he need not ask. 'Then the wind's dropping?'

''Tis so,' said Nils, no more willing to answer. 'No wonder, in this heat. Even the sea's going glassy. I'd give it another few hours, no more.'

Gille swore as he found himself peeling a thin tissue of skin from his bare shoulder. Sweat stung him where it had been. 'Then that's how long's left us to think of something.'

Voices rising round the water barrel caught their ears, as the men drew their morning ration. Gille ran down the ladder, feeling how weak his legs were, and pushed his way into the growing ring of men.

'And there's but one lousy sod it could be!' roared Dall the coxswain, his huge fist bunched to strike, the other clutched in the steersman's jerkin. 'Lurkin' loose about the ship all night, sookin' away other folk's lifeblood!'

The steersman was practically spitting with fury, his own muscular arms flexing, his long bony hands bunching. He was nearly as hefty as Dall, and ten years younger. Others milled around them, trying to separate them, taking sides or both. Gille, dreading a general brawl any minute, plunged between them.

'What's this?' he demanded. 'Want to behave like those carrion beasts in the black ships, do you? Why don't you bloody well swim over and join them?'

'There's water gone missing!' roared Dall. 'Broached this new barrel for last night's ration, I did myself, and set it astern for to be watched like you ordered.' Nils had given that order. 'And all night long there's comings and goings all over the ship, stealthy-like and scary, light steps on deck and wet marks o' feet, and here's the level near half down – and who else but...'

He stopped. It could, of course, have been Nils or Gille; and they could not have the crew thinking along those lines. Gille shook his head to clear it. 'You left it open? With just the top balanced like that?'

'Well, yes, skipper. Lads like it, 'cause it cools it—'

'It cools it because it turns to vapour, you idiot! The heat sucks it up, even at night.'

Dall looked horrified, then relieved. 'Well, you bein' a mastersmith'd know about things like that – er, skipper. Sorry, chum,' he said to the steersman, who grunted. Gille sighed. There would be blows over that yet, unless something happened to distract them. The water was stretched a little further with seawater, and though it tasted like a brackish pond, it went down well enough. The salt even seemed to kill off the greenish scum that always grew in the barrels once opened, for all the virtues set in hoop and fastening. But when he went back to the quarterdeck, Nils was looking as gloomy as Kalve.

'That's how it starts. Wet bloody footmarks! Looking for somebody to blame. So far it's not you or me. But it will be.'

The day wore on as before, and led them into another night. Only in that night there was a new thing, because at dawn the pursuing sails were far closer, sailing almost in file themselves.

'With this weak breeze they can dare to run closer,' grumbled Nils. 'And with that huge spread of a sail, and the low hull, they take better advantage of it.' He laughed, without mirth. 'While it lasts.'

And though the hour before dawn brought them a brief breath, by the time the sun was wholly over the horizon the last force of the wind was all but spent. The sails hung exhausted from the masts, bellying a moment with a dull crackle of canvas and then sagging back in wrinkles. *Rannvi* glided with barely perceptible motion over a sea sunk to a mosaic of mild wavelets, and here and there patches like a glassy pond that barely shivered with the dying riffles that played across them, and were gone. The heat punished them like a torture press, squeezing the breath from their chests, bending their bones as it seemed. The crew barely moved, and looked listlessly at their pursuers, as if any end was becoming welcome. They muttered, too, about strange things seen in the heat shimmer now, as well as by night. These were realms, they said, where men should not be, home to things of another order; and Gille could not find it in his heart to rebuke them.

As the sun sank, though, he took one last look eastward; then he cursed with a force that brought Nils running. 'Hella's ruin! Look back there! Are they readying their damned paddles?'

Nils gaped in disbelief. 'I'd wager you're right! They'll labour? In this?'

'Maybe. I hardly believe those bastards can be human!'

Nils squinted in the fading light. 'They are. They must think it's too dark for us to see them. They'll wait, I think. Get as much rest as they can. That's what I'd do. Then make one great effort. Try to surprise us, at dawn maybe.'

'Suppose they do start after dark ... How long till they'd overhaul us, would you say?'

Nils, trying to take a bearing, spoiled his calculations three times and gave up. 'Ach, a guess is as good!' He massaged his neck. 'Yon bloody oven's boiling all our brains, curse it! I could almost wish for the Ice now, in the face of this.'

'No!' Gille told him, savouring the grim irony of it. 'You don't understand. This too is the Ice, its creation, its counterpart. It creates these burning realms, just by being there, by tipping the balance of the world. This is the shadow it casts.'

'I could well credit that!' The sailing master supped the miserable portion of water Gille had brought him, and relished the mouthful before he spoke. 'Skipper, they could be on us before dawn.'

'Could we not lower the boats, and draw her along?'

'We could – if we had no pursuers. Suppose they contrived to come down on us quickly, with half our crew in the boats? No, skipper. Whether they wait or move now, we've only one answer. We'll needs get the sweeps out. Row like Hella's hams the moment there's too little light to see us.'

Gille was momentarily afraid his order would not be obeyed, though he took care to explain it. Dall nodded grimly, and prodded the others about their task; but he added in a low voice, 'That's done, skipper; but, by're leave, we can't row for long!'

'I know that. I'm hoping they can't, either.'

'Aye, skipper; but is there not summat else you can do? With that there music-box of yourn?'

'I can play you a rowing chant,' said Gille sardonically. 'But I was going to take my turn on an oar.'

'I was minded more of singing up a wind, skipper. You being a smith, an' all.'

'I've no power over any elements beyond my forge, Coxs'n.'

'You harness wind in bellows, skipper, don't you? D'you not have a bellows song like what I've heard the village master sing?'

Gille considered. 'I could try that. We have the sun for a hearth and the sea for an anvil, why should we not have bellows too? Only tell the lads, or they'll think I'm clean mad.'

So it was that, with a larger sip of his portion of

water, he went to the bows in the gathering dusk, and began to strum an old chant that he and Olvar often set over their work in its first few minutes on the hearth, with the bellows blasting to build up the heat. As he sang, darkness settled about their heads, and the sea-glow washed around the blades, dripping as they lifted in thin curtains of chilly fire.

Swarthy the smiths, soot- and smoke-blackened,
Heavy their hands, for hammering hearthside
Hard shall it go, if they burst not the beastskin
Bladders of bellows to boil up the fire!
Leaning on levers, side to side swinging,
Strong in their smithcraft for smelting and
*   shaping,*
Winding the wind in to waft their fires
*   skyward!*
Breathing and blowing, strong in the
*   smokestack,*
Sighing in furnace, sucking and filling,
Wheezing out skyward, set the coals spitting,
Come as they call you, sough as they summon,
Breath of the world, blow now steady and
*   strong!*

He chose it because its rhythm made it a fine rowing chant as well, and their way perceptibly increased as the night grew cooler. His voice began to fail all too soon, but the tune was simple and repetitive, easy to strum against the rhythmic creak and rattle of the rowlocks and the sluggish splash of the sea. After a while he seemed to sink into it, and lose his conscious thought in the pace of the music, breathing in and out like immense lungs. It was Nils's ripe oath that jolted him out of his trance.

'By the Sea-Daughters' short an' curlies! Look at the sail!'

For a moment Gille thought it was some effect

of the air as they pulled. But the canvas was filling and billowing on its own, beginning to strain at the sheets and give them some way.

'No, don't stop playing, skipper,' grated the sailing master. 'Whatever you do! Sing some more, even.'

'I'm too dry,' croaked Gille.

'Whistle, then!' snarled Nils, and took up the tune a moment in his own toneless whistle. 'Wind for wind, that's old sea-lore.'

'It makes sense,' admitted Gille, and licked his lips to try and catch the tune. He felt foolish, but as others joined in, the tone of the kantel seemed to pick it up and grow stronger, and he could feel the breeze on his cheeks, hot as a girl's breath. As Utte's, anyhow; the Other's had been cooler, perhaps. What was Utte doing now? What was she thinking about?

A vision came to him with startling clarity – Utte, on the high leads of the old farmhouse, gazing far out to the distant sea. The sight of her, with her brown hair whipping about her eyes in the sea breeze, wrung his heart and pricked his conscience, and he struggled to blot it out. The other girl – what of her?

Nothing came save darkness. Infinite darkness, though it was tinged with a coolness and peace he found achingly welcome. But it was overwhelmingly strange, and there was a sense of motion in it also, of great masses churning in the blackness, mighty and slow; and he fought clear of that also. If these were truly visions shown him by the strange music under his hands, what could that one mean?

Far better let the old tune carry him back to where he had first heard it. His first bewildered day as prentice in the smithy of his new master, Kunrad the Armourer, learning to pull the bellows, to make the hearthflame leap beneath the crucibles dangling from their chains, ready to tip out their molten brews. Learning that song, then, from the thickset fellow-apprentice with the red-brown skin who was the enormous span of eleven months senior to himself, and who would become, after a fashion, his best friend. Could the music tell where he was now?

Gille found himself afraid to wonder. But it would be good to know Olvar still lived. He looked towards the horizon, past the skeletal shadows of the mizzenmast and loading boom to the still stiffening mainsail, tinged with starlight. And suddenly he was seeing poorly, his eyes blurring. The sharp-cut silhouette of sheet and halyard smudged like lines of smeared ink. He feared he was losing his sight, that thirst and heat and salt were somehow taking a sudden toll. But as he struggled to focus his eyes on the stars above the masthead, it came to him suddenly. He saw them double, because of each shimmering point of light there truly were two; similar, but not the same.

Olvar, pacing *Orrin*'s quarterdeck on the night watch, stopped suddenly and rubbed frantically at his eyes. 'What's that?' demanded Telqua, curled up cat-like beneath the tiller, as she always seemed to be. She was on her feet with no visible effort, and pulling his hands away. 'Rubbing makes them worse, if there is sickness there.'

Olvar shook his head, impatient yet touched by her concern. He blinked rapidly, glanced about, glared suspiciously back at the patch of night that ran tirelessly in their wake, as if this could be some dark sending. His sight seemed as clear as before, and he sensed nothing ill or evil. 'Just weary, I'd guess. Yet ... it was as if I saw the stars ... differently. There was something, something in my ears, too. An old song. And another thing. A memory, yet that I seemed to see with new eyes.'

'Then shake off your dreams, Olva'.' She pronounced his name flatly, without the rolling ending.
'For they are surely gaining.'

Olvar squinted into the night once more. 'Are
you sure? Kalve wasn't.'

'He has old men's eyes. The hunters ride
swifter than this fat-bellied pedlar's basket.' She
spoke without any strong emotion. 'This trick you
have of shaving the wind's edge, they are risking
much to match it. See their sail belly as if with child!
Sooner or later we will have to fight.'

'Maybe. Yet it seemed there was something for
me in that dream, something that might help, in the
last moment.'

She drew a deep breath and held it, like a bow,
before a sudden sigh. 'That is not so far away.'

'Two skies!' said Gille harshly, though he went on
strumming the chords of the chant. The breeze was
well in the sails now, and though he could not be
sure, it seemed that the black ships were already
lagging a little. At Nils's advice he had commanded
the sweeps kept going, every man an hour at a
stretch. Every stride's length between them might
count. 'And no, no, it was not my tired eyes! It was
as if … as if the stars took a step to the side!'

Nils considered. 'As if you saw 'em from somewhere else, you mean? Maybe further north?'

Gille shook his head dazedly. 'You don't think I
really did reach out to Olvar, somehow?'

'Why not?' The navigator shrugged. 'Do I know
why the wind blows, or how an albatross rides it, or
how a smith pours power into his handiwork? Were
they not witnessed, I might say none of these things
could be. So perhaps others equally strange may be,
also. Not least with such strong songs at your
fingers' end. This other thought, what was it?'

'I … I don't quite know. It was more like a

memory; something we shared. You may be right about the song. This kantel was made by a great mastersmith, after all; the greatest. Maybe the hearth-song tapped some more of its power, somehow.'

'Maybe it just liked it.'

Gille's fingers fumbled for their stops. That was perilously close to how he was feeling about this strange instrument, as if it had a will of its own, and that will not his. 'Anyway, I don't know. It was something in the memory, like ... noticing something, something we'd both seen and overlooked. If it came from one of us, I don't know who. It was something there, by Kunrad's hearth ... If I could only *think*!'

Nils gave up, and glanced astern. 'Wouldn't linger, were I you. When those laddies wake up and realise we're within a few breaths of monkeying them – why then, they'll grow truly desperate. And then, who knows?'

Gille struck a miserable discord. Even now the air was hot enough to crack his lips. Panic rose up in him; he did not want to face another merciless dawn, live through another searing day. His brains would boil in his skull. He played on, but he made more mistakes, faltered, and finally let the strings fall silent. The music faded from him; and slowly, as the night wore on, the breeze also died.

When the first red light came, it shone upon a sea like molten glass. Hardly a ripple stirred the dark surface, save where the great sweeps worked, two men to each, bending and straining to catch every hand's-breadth of a lead. The water dribbled listlessly from the blades. Gille had taken his turn, in the dark hours, and his hands were raw with the effort. 'Can you not play some more?' demanded Nils, as he soaked them in strong brine from the food barrels. 'Not a few measures, even?'

'It is not in me, not now.'

'Yet that thing – if you could summon a wind—'

Gille winced. 'It was made for stronger hands. Stronger songs. More craft, true craft that would speak clearer to the virtue within. If I were a great smith I could sing up a whirlwind to disperse our foes, maybe. But I am not.' His head bowed. 'Even this little has drained me of strengths I never knew I had. If I could only rest! Or remember! My mind worries at memory like a hungry dog, and I cannot put it to anything else.'

'Don't crack on us, skipper,' said Nils softly, and there was a note in his voice Gille had never heard before. 'Without you we're lost for sure.'

'Without me?' Gille's laugh sounded a little cracked already. 'How 'bout you?'

'Think I could have held these lads together? Think I can? Never believe it, skipper. Not without your hand behind me. It's you they trust.'

Gille laughed bitterly now. 'With little enough cause! But yes, I'll try—'

'*Skipper!*' The helmsman's cry brought all hands to their feet.

Gille and Nils did not need to hear which way to look. There was only one thing to expect; and there it was. The exhausted crews of the black ships had awoken, and seen how the *Rannvi* had stolen a march on them in the darkness. It was enough; it was the sign that they must make their play, or perish unrelieved. The helmsman had seen the lines of paddles on the nearer ship run out. The rest of the crew, running to the rail, shook their fists as the broad blades poised, their metal edges glinting, and struck down into the black water as one. And again, with a fierce stabbing force, and again, gaining speed so quickly that the tempo changed, the line changed its sequence, so that the black hulls seemed to come rippling after them like sinister centipedes.

'They'll never keep that up for long,' grated Nils.

'They don't need to,' said Gille, so calmly that Nils looked around quickly. It was almost a relief, after all this, to have the end forced on him. 'That leading ship'll be on us soon enough, won't it? Half an hour, maybe; the other, maybe ten minutes after. Half an hour in the sun – yes, some may die. Maybe they're dying now. But they're different. That's a ship of war. We came prepared to trade, they … to fight …'

'Skipper?' demanded Nils, for Gille's voice faltered. But when he turned to face the sailing master, it was with a devouring grin.

'I'm all right! Get the men off those sweeps, Nils. Deal out an extra portion of water, and food. And pick me a working party – Dall, and the strongest hands. We came prepared! Of course we did! I saw it, only I didn't understand. And with any luck they won't either.'

'A working detail,' said Olvar quietly. 'Into the hold with them.'

Kalve's long jaw sagged. 'Now? What's to do there?'

'Get those maneating swine off our stern, maybe. Be ready for them, at least. Move, man!'

Dall and his men threw themselves on to the line and ran it back. The rigging creaked and complained as it tautened, and the blocks took the strain.

'That's enough!' called Gille from down below, with a new satisfaction in his voice. 'Take it a few turns around the capstan, and stand ready!'

'They're getting damned close now!' Nils shouted down into the hold. 'Will you not come up?'

'By Raven's blisters!' exclaimed Gille, oblivious.

'I think there's more down here we can use!'

'Play the trick twice?' protested Nils, bending over the edge of the hold. 'They'll never weather it!'

'Not quite the same way,' grinned Gille. 'Theme and variations.'

There was shouting on deck. Nils shook his head. 'Best tune up your strings tight, skipper. They come!'

'As a jape I might risk this!' complained Kalve, though he could hardly have looked less amused. 'But we cannot be more than a half a day's sail from sight of the land now, so—'

Olvar, covered in the dust of the hold, cut him off impatiently. 'The land, maybe! But where, man? By your own best reckoning we could be days away from any ports; and the moment we alter course more than a hair's-breadth, that brute'll be upon us. Think he'll be scared off by the mere peak of a mountain?'

'We could try and lose him along the coast.'

'You said it yourself, he can sail such waters as well as we, that one.'

'Well, then,' said Kalve, 'at least I suppose I might find you sea-room to make your move. But it's unchancy.'

Olvar sneezed. 'Bugger! I know. Better break out the arms. If it doesn't work – well, we'd face it soon enough, anyhow.'

Kalve touched knuckle to brow in brief salute, though his face was grey with the strain of the chase. Telqua was there as Olvar clambered out of the hold, stringing her bow and testing it.

'We fight soon?'

'Only when we have to. We'll have to change course soon; that might give them the edge they need. Let's hope the sea is with us.'

'The sea is with nobody. Some it helps, some it

betrays, but its hand is always cruel. We feared to
fare on it, even we who set sail.'

'Do you regret it, then?'

She turned a sudden flashing smile on him.
After so much of Kalve's company he found it
brighter than the sunrise, and marvelled at how it lit
up her blunt features. 'Never! Never! If I die now, I
die free! Better than scraping a slave's living from
barren rocks, or fawning on the hand that holds the
whip!'

Olvar's own grin awoke in answer, and he
suddenly felt less weary. 'I wish you may see real
freedom soon.'

Her hand on his arm surprised him. 'I have
seen it already. In you. And the Powers know, there
is enough room for it.'

Gille scrambled out of the hold barely in time.
Crouching like an ape below the rail, he scuttled up
to the quarterdeck, fretting because he could not
see properly. He winced as he looked up, expecting
arrows at any moment; but there was nothing.
Nothing except the sound, and that was enough: the
drumbeat, louder by the moment, the swift splashing stroke of the great paddles and the soft guttural
grunts of the men who wielded them. Soft, but
inexpressibly menacing, speaking of a fierce discipline and determination beyond his own, a consuming need and hatred. They blended like the breath
of some huge sea-beast, and drew the picture in his
mind of the longship inching ever closer.

His own throat was impossibly dry, and the
sweat trickling across his sun-flayed skin made him
mad with irritation. The sky was a dome of hot
copper. It hurt his eyes, but he kept watching the
patch to port of the sternpost. He drew his sword. It
felt not at all romantic, dull and slippery in his
sweaty fingers. Surely he was watching the right

place, the way they would come? The side they were approaching. They had nothing to fear from ramming now. So he would see them in good time, he could choose his moment—

He nearly choked. It was too sudden. The sun was blotted out. The immense billowing blackness rising behind the sternpost sent its shadow along the deck, like a vanguard. In that same moment came the loud dull snap of the enemy's deck-bows, and the grapnels they fired snaked over the rail, slithered and struck. The lines tautened, and he could not force the choking air through his dry throat. Desperate, he sprang to his feet and screamed. He might as well have howled like a wolf for all the words he could form; but there was only one command the hands awaited. That drew the arrows, long iron shafts from the deck-bows, thinner ones from the archers, hissing around him to strike juddering into plank and rail. He did not move; he hardly saw them. Part of him, somewhere distant and detached, gave thanks there was no fire; they dared not kindle it either, or feared to destroy the provisions they fought for.

From below the rail harsh shouts came, like the cries of fell beasts on barren lands; and from the hold another cry, the fierce chorus of men who make one violent effort. The rigging groaned, the great boom moaned as it took the weight, the tackle whined through the blocks, and the huge bale came soaring out of the hold, as if the costly dyed hides it held, Vangar's best, had sprung suddenly back to life.

The black sail billowed hard against the sternpost, the arrows whined, and Gille stared as if transfixed at the lean brown hands that clamped on the rail. But over them, across his gaze, the crane-boom swung like a child on a treelimb, faster than he could blink. Lifted, as he had lifted the crucibles from the hearthfire, with their precious burden of metal. Swung, as he had swung them with swift and desperate precision, over the open mouth of the awaiting mould. The whole ship lurched suddenly, grinding against its attacker, timbers scraping hideously. Out, out and over the rail—

'*Cast her off!*' screamed Gille.

From where he stood he vaguely noticed Dall's hands fly up; but it was as if the great bale itself broke free, the scream of the rope in the smoking blocks a burning, exultant yell of liberation. Out it flew, a precious costly thing. Down it plummeted, a fearsome dead weight from the height of the boom, down past the *Rannvi*'s deck and out of sight, into the lean and vicious hull alongside. One shrill scream vanished in the rending crash as it struck.

The *Rannvi*, freed of the weight, lurched upright. The unladen boom swung wildly, caught the black mainyard and smashed it back against the stays, tearing the sail half away. But the worst damage was already done. The black mast heeled, and the ragged fabric billowed wildly in the swift spurting fountain from below.

The warrior who had seized the rail hung a moment, staring, then swung himself astride it and stabbed his spear straight at Gille. Gille parried, awkwardly, but though the force threw him back, it also tore loose the hunter's handhold. He wavered; Gille struck back. His lunge skidded off the leather armour, but the man toppled with a cry. Gille fetched up hard against the rail, staring down into the chaos beneath.

The longship's hull was filling fast, a turmoil of brown-skinned rowers clambering over the benches and one another, grabbing for what would float. But the warriors who had stood ready to board were all the fiercer, leaping to seize the rail or the merest handholds on port and plank, swinging on the looped anchor chain, scrabbling up like rats. Some slid back, with harsh cawing cries; but not all. Nils and the hands sprang to meet them, and the rail was shouting, flailing confusion. Another hunter leapt up on to the quarterdeck, but Dall took him in the chest with a boathook and sent him flailing down on the heads of his fellows.

Another clambered over the sternpost, landed on the deck, rolled over and to his feet in one fluid lunge, spear poised, gold jingling in his greasy greying wolf-locks. Gille hewed at him, uncertainly; the hunter caught the uncertainty and trapped the blow against his small bronze buckler. Then he thrust it back at Gille, and lunged with the spear. Gille ducked, the blade went over his shoulder, and they collided.

For a moment, staggering, they looked one another in the eye. The man's face was as dark as Olvar's, but the cheeks were sunken and bloodless, so that the cruel patterns of cicatrised scars stood out. The mouth was thin and twisted with habitual wrath, the jet-black eyes sunken, intent and cold, mocking Gille as he struggled to bring his sword to bear. The spear-haft struck it down. Gille was hurled against the sternrail, guard wide, open to the thrust. Then the man jerked and cried out, and his stroke cut splinters off the rail. Instinctively Gille struck home. The point sliced down the jerkin and sank in; the man doubled up. Nils, behind him, took careful aim, as he might in chopping wood, and brought his axe down hard once more. Gille looked away.

Nils clicked his tongue. 'Got to watch those buggers – whups! *There she goes!*'

The black mast, listing cruelly, vanished abruptly as if a hidden hand snatched it from sight, and stifled the screaming confusion. Gille and Nils looked down. The black hull rolled in the water beneath, keel upward, and slid smoothly beneath the water amid a shower of bubbles. Bits of wreckage and flailing bodies came boiling up. One warrior, almost at the *Rannvi's* rail, slipped back with a despairing howl and splashed into the wreckage-strewn sea. Men clutched at spars, or at one another, at anything, cried out, slipped back and vanished. On the *Rannvi* all movement ceased suddenly, save for the crane-boom flailing to and fro. The hands stood stupefied, staring. Gille, tearing his eyes from the turmoil below, was astonished to see how many black-armoured figures strewed the rail-walks and quarterdeck, as if they had dropped from the sky. Blood pooled beneath them, and none stirred. Then another shadow crossed the sun.

'*Hands!*' roared Nils, and Gille jumped like the rest. He could hear that deadly breath once again, panting, pulsing, amid the rush of the still water. The second ship was upon them.

'Get that crane in!' Gille shouted, and the men in the hold, stumbling over the tops of bales and boxes, threw themselves on the flailing lines.

'That was a handy trick!' said Nils, quietly. 'Let's hope the next one's as good.'

'Agreed!' said Gille breathlessly, watching them shackle the cargo net. 'By the by, thanks for saving my guts.'

'You'd have done as much. Nobody was bothering me just then. But it was hot enough, for a few moments. Hard bastards, these. We barely dealt with the stragglers. We'll never hold off a proper boarding.'

At Gille's word the crane tackle creaked again, and a new bale swung out of the hold, looser than the last, shifting within the net.

'They'll have seen!' Nils protested. 'They'll never come within reach of the crane now!' And indeed, the black sail was drawing level with the

Rannví's stern, but at a respectful thirty paces away.

'They'll have to, if they want to board,' said Gille, whistling between his teeth. 'And hard men or not, they can't keep up that pace much longer. So they'll try something else. Let's hope it's the obvious.'

'*They're coming in!*' shouted the steersman, and then ducked as arrows sang past him. The pulse of the drum rose to a frenzied rattle, and the windless black sail lolled heavily about. The black prow's blunt edge swung around towards them. 'Coming in astern!' grated Nils. 'They can risk ramming, at that speed. Take us in the rudder, maybe. And present a slim target for whatever you've got up there!'

'But still a target,' said Gille, and gestured. The steersman left the useless helm, and ducked down the ladder. Dall and the others hauled, dodging the occasional shaft that spat down among the cargo. The shapeless net creaked about sternward, to the extent of its travel.

'Almost - a little more—' hissed Nils, dashing the sweat from his face. 'Too short - ach, just too short—'

It was obvious. As the net swung, their missile might just reach the enemy's advancing prow; more likely it would not. Dall and the others jerked the tackle as best they could, to increase the arc. Back and forth it swung, ropes trailing, as the cruel black beak crept closer, near enough now so that even those fell faces flinched a little as its shadow touched them. Until aboard the black ship, at last, somebody gave an order.

The black bows swung around, and lifted. The spiked grapnel heads winked in the harsh light. Then they loosed together, the grapnels hissing out high over the water with their lines looping out behind them, not at the deck but at that ponderous swinging threat, the hunter's claws swiping out to catch and tear it away.

The first ones flew under, snaking down to splash into the sea and be hauled back. But then one caught, another and another, crashing into the menacing bale with loud shattering noises, right at the outermost arc of the swing. The hunters sprang to seize the lines; but they were already too late. The impacts had been enough. The overstrained net gave way, and the bulky load spilled through.

It fell; but not in a mass. Through the rent net jar and barrel cascaded, some shattered to pieces by the claws, spilling as they fell. A few plummeted down upon the black ship's deck, and the warriors at the leading paddles dashed aside or were struck senseless where they knelt. But the boarding party flung their shields above their heads, and were little scathed; the bulk of the load spilled harmlessly into the sea around them. And as the shower of debris passed, the warriors waved their shields and hammered their spear-butts hard against them, hooting and jeering, a cruel, chilling sound.

It was then Gille flung the torch.

Plucking it from the steersman's hand, he sprang up to the rail, and whirling it around in a great arc he sent it sailing outward. The pitch-tipped shaft fell some way short of its mark; it struck the black prow and bounced off into the sea. But that was enough. There was a sound, a great soft exhalation. Flame spattered where the drizzle of rich oil had fallen. Flame blossomed from the surface of the sea surrounding, where staved barrel and broken-necked jars bobbed viscously about in a small but spreading pool, directly under the black ship's bow.

From above and below fire wreathed the sun-heated wood. It could hardly help but catch; yet still its devouring suddenness startled Gille. The jeers turned to angry shouts, and the hunters poured forward with shields, buckets, lengths of sail, anything they could find to beat at it. They sprang upon the high prow to stamp it out with their feet, sandalled or bare; but it had caught hold beneath, at the curve of the bow where they could not reach, and the flames came crackling up on either side of the prow, like spray. They sought to fling water at it with the forward paddles, dipped skins and balers overside and hurled it bodily; but the oil-drenched water fed the flame. As also, perhaps, did the heavy black paint that sheathed the timbers, and the pitch and fibre that caulked them. The patches of fire hissed, sputtered, smoked and blazed out anew, gushing out a stinking black smoke that hung heavy in the windless air.

Aboard *Rannvi* Gille's men sprang out of shelter to cluster along the rail, whooping and jeering in their turn, loosing the odd arrow to spur the firefighters on. One hunter, hit in the thigh, tripped and tumbled screaming into the crackling oil below. The splash sent a bobbing barrel of lard, sputtering stinking sparks, against the enemy's flank, and where it touched, new fire took hungry hold. The flames lapped around a trailing halyard above; another few minutes and they might climb to the sail. But the warrior discipline still ruled. From the black ship's stern, archers returned the shots; and along its flanks, even where the fire was taking hold, they saw the paddlers ducking back to their benches, and the great paddles biting the water. The drum rolled out through the thickening smoke.

'What's he doing?' demanded Nils; and then cold fear edged his voice as he roared to the crew. '*Hands!* All hands to the sweeps! We've got to get away!'

There was no way they could have moved in time. All this time, even though the paddles had stopped, the black ship had drifted closer. Now hate and desperation drove it forward like a flaming lance, towards the *Rannvi*'s unprotected flank.

'*Run them out!*' screamed Nils, his voice cracking. 'Get poles, anything! Fend the bastards off!'

Dall and the hands were running out the massive sweeps, not into the locks but over the rail, blunt butt-ends outward. On the quarterdeck Gille and Nils struggled to do the same, but the high rail made it harder. Gille hopped up and heaved, the long oar slid past him, and he grabbed it to steady it. Then Nils cried out, and there was nothing he could do save fling up a futile arm.

He was wrapped in flame and smoke, stinging, blinding. He had a momentary sight of a dark deck warping in the heat, the planks writhing like tormented beasts, the caulking boiling up bubbling demon mouths at him. Then the flaming black prow crashed against the *Rannvi*'s flank immediately below his feet.

A burning hand slapped him up and away, as a wanton child its toy, and the smouldering sparks in clothes and hair burst into full flame. He screamed. A cool hard hand slammed the breath from his lungs and dashed his mouth full of salt water. His eyes blurred, his blood roared deep in his brain, flooding out thought. He flailed around frantically and caught at something drifting up before him, clutching it close to the tearing agony that was his chest.

It gave him the impetus to kick, and suddenly his eyes were full of light, the water was heaving out of him, and he managed to suck in a breath. It hurt, but it was so good he kicked again, coughing violently, and kept his head above water, and breathed again. For a time that was all there was, kicking and breathing, until the pain went and exhaustion took its place. Stunned, only half understanding where he was, he sagged back in the calm warm water, unable to panic as his legs floated up.

That, perhaps, was what saved him; for he turned back to the habit of childhood, and gave himself up to the ocean, floating spreadeagled, using only the faintest effort to raise his head. Something bumped at him, nudged him like a friendly dog. It touched off the panic again. He began to struggle, half sank, kicked out again and grabbed the thing, gradually aware that it was solid, unthreatening. It sank when he leant on it, wallowing just below the surface, but it drained away the need to struggle. He clung, and let his head slump forward on his arms.

Time passed; not long, perhaps. But somewhere among it a faint breath of wind came up, stirring the glassy sea a little. Wavelets lapped about him, and eventually one slapped his face. The sensation shattered his dazed trance. He blinked around, as if half asleep, and saw what he clung to. It was a spar, and black. It rushed in upon him all of a sudden who he was, where he was, what had happened, why. Anger and fear shook him, and a consuming worry for his men, the sailors and fisherlads he had talked into this ill-fated voyage, into trusting him. He hung, gasping, and managed to raise his head to look around. He saw nothing; nothing at all between him and the cruel glare that was the horizon. He twisted his head frantically this way and that, dreading what he might see, still more what he might not see. And indeed there was nothing but the steel shield of the ocean; until the plume of smoke caught his eye.

The smoke only; for its source was no more than a shadow, impossible to distinguish, already on the very margin of the horizon.

CHAPTER SEVEN
The Summons

He had never, in all his adventures, felt more desolate. Emptiness poured in upon him, and its invisible burden bowed his head. It may be his ship-schooling had not yet taught him how much closer the horizon is at sea than it seems, the nearer are one's eyes to the surface. His could not have been nearer. The unbroken distance seemed vast, the smoke plume inexpressibly remote, and himself forgotten and abandoned by his comrades, if they still lived. He clung to the spar, because there was nothing else. He wept, perhaps, a little, and shouted, railing against fate, for there was none to see. But he looked up sharply, soon enough, when it came to him that he heard an answering voice. Again he stared about, and saw something wave, no great way off. An arm; another survivor.

He shouted back encouragement, took a tighter grip on the spar and kicked out fervently, splashing foam. The labour was welcome, his legs surprisingly stiff, for all the warmth of the sea. He moved slowly, but the wind was with him, and the other man, again, closer than he had thought. He found himself passing among a carpet of debris, everything from splinters of painted wood to those half-drowned provision tubs, and realised this was the remains of the ship he had sunk. One piece, the shattered frame of a heavy bilge-grating, floated well and was large enough to make a healthy raft; so instead of going on, he clung and hailed the other man, who was clutching what looked like one of the great paddles. He understood, and splashed his way closer; then let go and dove like a seal. There was an instant of emptiness; then Gille jumped where he clung as the other shot out of the water less than an arm's length away, and clutched the side of the grid with lean brown fingers.

It was one of the hunters.

He could have been the brother of the man Gille had fought, save that his features were more lined and more scarred, the cicatrised outline heavier and harshly outlined by black tattoos. His high-bridged, blunt nose had been savagely slashed and poorly set. His hair ornaments jangled softly as the water caught them; they looked like tarnished silver. The deepest likeness lay in the cast of the features, the set of the expression, as if it were a common stamp upon them all. It was something Gille had never encountered before, and in its way more frightening than any corsair savagery.

The man seemed no happier to see Gille. The thin lips drew back, and the deep narrow eyes, uncannily like Olvar's, glittered with fury. His hand splashed to his side, then he hesitated visibly. Gille, for all his fright, laughed aloud.

'Dropped our pigsticker, have we? No, wait,' he added, as the dark man seemed about to lunge at him anyway, and held up a hand. He pointed to the distant smoke. 'Your folk, or mine – understand? Maybe you win, maybe we do.' He spread his hands, trying to force his meaning across a barrier wider than language. 'There's room for two here. If we fight, maybe we both lose.'

The dark man looked at him with evident contempt, but did not move. Then, abruptly, he placed his palms flat down on the edge of the timbers, and shot himself right out of the water on to the makeshift raft. Gille tried to do the same, but it turned into an undignified scramble, punctuated by a musical thump. Horrified, Gille realised he still had the kantel at his side. That was what he had clutched to his chest, floating from its strap; maybe it had lent him some buoyancy, trapping air.

Hastily, his feet still dabbling in the sea, he tipped the water out of the soundbox, thoroughly, and looked at the inside. The strange label seemed no worse, and nor did the finish; water beaded on the age-polished lacquer, and found no entry. Even the strings were sound. He strummed a chord or two; then remembered his adversary and looked up at once. He did not trust this barbarian one finger's-breadth; probably he would think a musician a weakling – and not be that far wrong, Gille added to himself. But the gaze he met held not a sneer but a wide-eyed glare; the man was as far across the raft as he could manage. It was not a face to show fear, that; but tauter than any string of Gille's, fear bridged the air between them.

Then both men jumped. Another figure bobbed up next to them, and swung himself on to the raft with the same sinewy swiftness. His weight pulled it down to the water-level. Gille's heart sank; for this was another of the hunters, a younger man, his cheeks less sunken, his scars fewer. Some looked new. The markings on his light leather armour were the same as the older man's, but not his aspect. He was paler-skinned than Olvar, his face less round, his cheekbones more prominent, his nose sharper; more like the woman Telqua. Gille, carefully keeping his composure, shuddered inwardly. He guessed that he was seeing different bloodlines drawn and absorbed into this terrible folk, lost as metals in a hardening alloy.

The newcomer glanced curiously from one to the other; who had caught who? Slowly, smirking, he drew a dagger from his belt, a blade of what looked like chipped black glass. The elder snapped a word or two, and he stopped short, dagger half drawn, squinting sullenly at Gille and the kantel; but he did not put the dagger back. Gille, trying not to breathe too heavily, plucked a couple of ominous chords, and relished the young man's nervous twitch. They thought he was some kind of shaman, probably; gifted with the evil eye and who knew what other dark forces? But the young man's face was a frozen mask, and his throat bobbed as he swallowed; and Gille understood suddenly that these folk would be taught to attack anything they feared so greatly, sooner than betray it. He was nerving himself to spring.

A hail broke the silence so abruptly they all swung around, and so close. '*Skipper! Ahoy!*'

Gille gaped. '*Dall?* What're you—'

The coxswain's round bald head came bobbing towards them. 'Why, same's you, I'd guess, skipper. Over the rail, eh? Thought I was headed straight down into Saithana's little jolly-box, I did! Ach, Hella's hurdies, what's these here, now? Nice wee playmates!'

'No, Dall!' yelped Gille hastily as the coxswain tried to hand his bulk up on to the raft. It sank deep, spilling them all off into the sea. The young man let loose a spluttering stream of abuse, till the elder cut him off. Carefully they tried to clamber back on, but though the raft stayed level, it sank so deep under Dall's weight that they had little joy of it. 'Well, I don't suppose it matters much,' Gille sighed. 'At least the water's warm as a bath.'

Dall glared at the hunters and shook his head. 'Now it is, skipper. Come tonight it'll be a sight cooler. Not so much as I'd mind that; but there's more. Big fish that'll whip your toes or more off in a sweep; and worse, so I've heard. 'Member them deep lights we seen? Maybe them. They come up by nights, men say.'

'Take turn!' said a deep guttural voice, unexpectedly. 'You – then me! Him – then him! Two hour.'

Dall and Gille whipped around.

'So you talk!'

'How in Hella's pink—'

There was another hail.

This time it was Ore the fisherman, and another crewman Gille knew less well, Kol by name, thrown off at the collision as he had been, and clinging to a splintered tub. It was taking in water fast, and foundering. Gille bade everyone look for more wreckage that they could add to the raft, but there was little of any size. They recovered another spar, and joined that to the frame, so that men could lean on it as Gille had. Towards twilight they came upon another of the warriors, floating with a slab of loose planking, which broke up when they tried to seize it. He was injured in the head and leg, and could not climb aboard the raft.

'His blood'll draw 'em down on us!' muttered Dall, bunching his fists.

'He hasn't drawn anything yet!' snapped Gille, glancing at the elder. To his surprise the hunters made no move to help their fellow. The elder's stare was as hard as Dall's. 'Maybe this ocean's too hot for your big fish. But just in case, better bind him up a bit.'

The warriors bunched defensively when Gille moved towards him; but when the elder understood, he gave a curt nod. 'So! Too much blood if we kill, also.'

'You'd slaughter one of your own?' demanded Gille.

The elder's eyes were as opaque as the black dagger, and as cold. He gave a slight shrug, and said nothing further.

The two warriors left Gille and the others to help their fellow up and wrap what rags he could tear from the man's tunic around his wounds. His eyes were no warmer than theirs, and when Gille had finished he turned away at once.

'Nice polite shower!' muttered Ore. 'Reckon we beat 'em?'

'I was too stunned to see,' sighed Gille, now taking his turn in the water.

'I wasn't,' said Dall. 'Flung well out, but no harm done. Swam back, when my head cleared. Would've made it, too, only the old girl was swingin' so with the crash, and the savage ship locked to her, them just wheelin' slow around like that. And then that bit breeze got up, and away they went. Just faster'n I could swim, and I got weary. Still fightin'.' He grinned suddenly. 'But I don't reckon on these scarfaces gettin' the best o' it! Not with their ship sizzlin' under 'em, an' no clear way to board. Must've had to drop into the sea and clamber up. My guess is, that's what these bastards were tryin', when they came unstuck.'

'Could be,' said Kol, dangling next to Gille. 'If only yon fire didn't catch the old *Rannvi*-girl, too.'

'I'm sure it didn't!' said Gille decisively, though his own heart was chilled. 'They'll be back for us, you'll see. Our job's to be here when they come.'

'Aye, but without any scoff or slop—'

'I know. But it shouldn't take them long. Hours more than days. Nils took a bearing not long before the attack, he'll find his way back to us. Before noon tomorrow, if our luck holds.'

'And the wind,' muttered Ore.

Silence fell, as they listened. The breeze was slackening, but that was normal enough at this hour of the day. The air hung about them, suffocating, as the light drained from the sky. Gille was glad enough to be in the water, but he was uneasily aware it was cooling. Would the warriors go on taking their turns? For now, he thought so. Later, weariness might shatter the fragile accord. They would have to watch for treachery.

When his turn ended, the wounded warrior slid off the raft with an ill grace, and Gille felt a guilty relief as he scrambled up and retrieved the kantel from the splintered post where he had tied it. He exclaimed as the sea-glow dripped fire along his skin and across the raft, and the warriors mumbled superstitiously. He ignored them, and strummed a quiet chord or two to cheer himself, while the air warmed his chilled limbs. He was bone-weary, but there was no room to lie down, even if he felt like huddling against the others. The moon was rising, but it was old, and giving them little enough light. His fingers felt clumsy and heavy, and slowly he bent forward over the warm smooth wood, and fell into a drifting shadow of sleep.

Sound jerked him awake, voices raised, splashing in the water. 'What is it?' he demanded, into the darkness. 'Dall? What's going on?'

'Dunno, skip! This bastard don't want to stay out his time. Taken frit at somethin', or so he says!'

He heard the elder's growling voice. 'There is some thing, he says. In sea, below. You look!'

Cautiously Gille peered over the edge of the raft, alert for any attempt to dislodge him. The sea-glow around the raft was dim, but he could make out the faint outlines of the men who hung there, especially the warrior, kicking furiously as he tried to scramble up. The glow seemed strongest where the water was churned up. 'I don't see anything. But tell him to stop kicking. If anything'd attract attention—'

A screech split the night. The glow was blotted out by a long dark cloudy shape, then frothed green-golden in its wake. Under the raft it lanced, twisting sharply to show a flash of lighter underbelly, and the struggling man screamed and threw up his hands. He was jerked violently into the blackness, faster than any man could move, his screams and splashes suddenly cut off. A faint shimmering trail along the surface faded to nothing.

The younger warrior yelled in anger, but Gille felt the raft rock as somebody hauled him down. 'Stop it!' barked Gille, though he himself was trembling. 'Stop, you lackwits! Do you want to draw something else down on you? If we haven't, already.' He turned to where the elder clung in the blackness. 'We still have to take turns. But everybody stays *quiet*, see?'

There was a moment's silence. 'Hear you. Soon your turn ends.'

'But not yet,' said Gille quietly. He closed his eyes, but sleep was impossible now. The air was cooling, but it was still a stifling curtain about their heads. Another commotion jarred him, but it was only the younger warrior scrambling back aboard with noisy satisfaction, and the elder, it seemed, telling him to keep quiet. Again the sea-glow glimmered in the disturbed water, and Gille cursed.

Dall came aboard, more quietly, which relieved Gille; his strongest man would be there to keep an eye on the two warriors remaining. This time, as he prepared to slip into the water, he wrapped the strap of the kantel round his wrist, and laid it carefully where he would cling on. Then he stretched his legs out, and let himself float easily off the edge, resisting the urge to wriggle at the clammy chill of the water. The elder warrior slithered aboard with a quiet swift urgency which unnerved Gille; as soon share a dark wood with a daggertooth cat as these folk. But there were fiercer hunters than man or daggertooth abroad already.

He could feel just how visible the raft must be

from below, the one dark spot floating in this vast expanse, the one source of sound and disturbance, smell or taste or whatever; visible to senses men did not have, probably. He felt very small and very vulnerable. He looked down, and saw nothing stirring, and tried not to think how fathomless that darkness was, the Sea-Lord's shadowy realm.

Curiously, he came closer to true sleep then than at any time that night, though the cooling seawater was becoming less than pleasant. He hung limp, pillowed his head against the timbers; at least the gentle rocking was soothing. He hovered on the edge of dream, and it seemed to him that people were out in a fog, looking for him with lanterns. Then his head slipped from the timbers and splashed into the water, and he was abruptly awake – but seeing the lanterns still, soft glows that came and went in the misty sea below.

Glows within a glow, as if something truly large was disturbing the depths, passing unhurriedly back and forth below them. Hovering a moment, then sliding easily along again; but never going far, never away.

Gille raised his dripping face. 'Nobody move,' he whispered. 'No sound, more than you need to. Hang limp! Pretend you're weed or something!'

The others may have been asleep too. The men in the water beside him stirred slightly, and one let out a sleepy oath. Gille wanted to strangle him, though he shut up at once. Did one of the dim glows veer a little? Probably not. Passing, repassing, hovering, they circled below like great slow bees or glow-worms, while Gille and the others hung on and clenched their teeth. Along the raft he heard somebody whimper, and then knew why, as the rush of water stirred around his legs. Whatever was beneath them, it was solid. Quite large, too.

The glow was bright enough now to silhouette

parts of the raft, and cast dim shadows. It lit the young warrior's face as he sprawled out, half over the raft's edge, and Gille saw with a thrill that it was a twisted, anguished mark; he was staring down at where his legs must be, afraid to move. Then Gille stiffened involuntarily, in just the same way, as a little spurt of cold water traced across his torn trouser-leg, and was gone. He sagged in relief – and then the rictus seized him again, as the cold touch returned, and lingered.

It was no current. It was colder than the seawater even, and soft. Soft, but solid, a distinct touch. It might have been a frond of weed, if weed could move with purpose. It slid over his leg with slimy ease, delicately, teasingly, as if it were tasting something – pondering the contrast between the torn canvas breeches and the warm skin, maybe. It seemed to broaden as it moved, and something on it scratched at him faintly. Gille bit his lip, tasting the bitter salt, forcing back the overwhelming urge to kick it away. He lowered his face to the cold wood, the stink of the oily black paint filling his nostrils; some kind of pitch—

The thing felt far heavier than weed now. Muscle played beneath the spongy slime. If it went any higher, he thought, there was no way he could possibly stop a scream.

Instead it tightened suddenly – lightly, without effort, but enough to ring Gille's thigh and swell it like a bladder, deadening his lower leg. He gasped and choked with sudden pain. An immense dead weight hung on him, gently, unhurriedly, hardly even pulling, yet growing irresistibly. He would not be snatched, as the warrior had been, but he would be pulled away in seconds, no more. It was like being towed by a ship. His hip strained, the muscles cracked; what felt like a dozen mouths sucked at his skin, and bit hard. He let out a cry.

He was almost flung off the raft. The thing whipped off his leg so fast it raked his skin raw in patches, and the salt stung it. A scream rang out, and the sea splashed in cold fire around another man, threshing; Kol, or Ore.

'*Dall! Skip—*'

Kol. The glow subsided and was still. The lights below were gone. Blackness enveloped them once more. Around him Gille could hear the hard breathing of terrified men, his own loudest of all.

'Poor bastard, who could help 'im?' groaned Dall softly. 'You all right, skipper?'

'More or less. It had me there, Dall! Then it let go, and took him. Why not me? Why him?'

A heavy hand took his arm. 'Up you come aboard, skipper. C'mon, jingly, you hop it back in sea – see? S'long past your two hours.'

There was a brief explosion of shouting in the blackness, broken by a smacking thud and a soft clatter of ornaments. The makeshift raft rocked violently. 'Yeah, and you're another!' said Dall to the spluttered curses in the dark. 'You can 'ave another like that any time you like it, laddie – and that goes for you too, you old vulture!'

The elder warrior's voice was calm. 'For now I do nothing. Keep pact. When ship returns – we see.'

He was speaking more clearly now, as if the memory of words long unused was coming back to him. There was even a hint of a Northern accent. Gille, dripping on the raft's edge, shook his head dazedly. 'How can you speak our tongue? You're from half a world away, an ocean apart...'

Then he remembered the man in the corsair ship. The man he had shot by the mast, tumbling back across the hull. The scarred copper features and the ornaments jingling...

'You've been among us!' he said flatly, though the implications were making his heart race and his flesh crawl. 'Slinking about our bloody country! How? When? A spy, was it? Who for? Readying an invasion?'

The sudden crow-like laugh in the blackness was chilling in its contempt. 'Maybe! Maybe! One day, maybe! Long after you and I dead! More like, you do worse to yourself. Fools fight in a burning house.'

Gille nodded. 'Oh yes? So you and your little friend aren't that kind of fool right now? This may not be a burning house, but it's sure as Hella a sinking one! Remember this – if it's our ship comes back, you'd better have us to tell them to keep you alive – right? Right?'

Silence was the best answer he could expect. He brooded. 'Anyhow, how come you're so sure we'll war with each other? How d'you know?' The answer came tumbling in on him, and like the boulder that starts the avalanche it brought a whole shower of others after it.

'The corsairs!' he hissed. 'Merthian's Revolt, fifteen years back! Those bastards took in fighting men from anywhere, any kind. That other man; he was about your age. A fine chance, that must have been, to smuggle in some spies!'

The soft contemptuous breath was confirmation enough.

'Well,' said Gille decisively, though he was shivering still with the shock, 'we broke your precious corsairs, our two lands between them. I know; I was there. I watched them run through briar and bramble, so fast the hounds couldn't even catch up. Maybe I caught sight of your scut in the crowd, who knows? And there were men of both lands in the Marchwarden's force, that threw down that rathole fortress of yours in the Great Marshes. So—'

Another scream shattered his words. He

whirled about. A hand hovered in front of his eyes, close enough to be seen, quivering, beseeching. The cry again, with no words he understood; but there was no mistaking the sense.

'*Help me!*'

Hard and sinewy the grip was; the younger warrior's hand, and Gille almost let go, fearing a trick to drag him down. Then he felt that awful, inexorable burden, and saw the dull shimmer deep in the water below. He threw himself flat on the grid to try and hold on, the kantel bouncing and twanging beside him. The burden was already too great. The fingers, for all their convulsive clutching, tore through his own, and a hoarse scream was suddenly silenced. The sea shone and bubbled convulsively, but it sank to nothing.

Gille, gasping, rounded on the elder warrior. 'You could have helped! You could have held him!'

The dry sniff said as much as a shrug. 'Warrior dies before chieftain, always. Why other?'

'*Skipper!*' That was young Ore in the water. 'Can't you—'

'We'll try!' said Gille. 'Maybe if I lie flat at the edge like this - and you, chieftain or not, you lie along that side. Dall, can you haul him in now?'

The makeshift raft sank alarmingly. Wavelets washed around Gille's spine, and the kantel floated up and bumped against him.

'Doing my best, skipper! Up you come, Ore - bloody little room! Can't we just turf ...'

'No!' said Gille sharply. 'He's kept the pact. And a fight might spill us all off.'

There seemed to be chilly arms and legs everywhere, Ore's greasy hair in Gille's eyes and an elbow in his side. 'If this were a barn full of hay-wenches, I might just stand for it!' grunted Dall painfully. The chieftain let out another croaking laugh.

'Join us! Strong man, skin like us, you do good.
All wenches you like!'

'Piss off, bandy-knees! I don't like my women
toasted!'

'Nor I. Not always.'

Ore started to laugh, and then tailed off. There
was that in the elder warrior's voice which drained
even the shred of desperate merriment they clutched
at.

'Not much of a shield, is it, with the raft this
low?' said Ore, after a while. 'Them snakey worm
things come wrap 'emselves about you ... Maybe I'd
be just as well back in the water ...'

'No you don't, lad,' said Dall. 'My turn, eh?'

'*No!*' said Gille; but Dall was already moving,
sliding down the side of the raft. For all his hostility,
the coxswain had not realised how that could
change the balance of power upon the raft. It left
the chieftain more room to move than any, and free
of Dall's strength. The raft listed further – and then
gave a violent jolt. The disturbed water flared into
stark phosphorescence.

Ore was pitched over Gille's back, entangling
them both. Gille heard a heavy crunching thud, and
Dall bellow in pain. Ore toppled into the water,
crying out in fright, thinking it was another attack.
Gille, on his back staring up at the faint sky-glow,
saw the elder warrior loom up against it, his bone-
lean silhouette straddling the raft, raising high over
his head some irregular length of .wood he seemed
to have worked free.

Gille swung the kantel on its strap. It whipped
hard about, and rang out clear as its silvered edge
caught the warrior with a sharp popping crack, fair
and square across his left knee. The man howled
and staggered, fell on his side, half in the water,
clutching his shattered kneecap and screaming.
Gille turned to Ore, pulling him in, shouting to Dall.

The coxswain was swimming weakly in towards the raft. They saw him clearly, by the huge soft glow that swelled suddenly in the depths, no longer circling but rising steadily.

'The spar!' yelled Gille. 'Catch the spar!'

Then the splash behind them, soft but weighty, had them whip about, to see just below the surface a glowing, inchoate bulk, and at its heart, rolling upward, pale and lidless, an eye so tall it could have been a high window; the look that fixed them was as inhuman as some implacable divinity. For a long instant even their hearts seemed to stop; the glow shifted and shimmered, shadows rolled within it, but the eye never moved. With easy slowness part of the bulk before it broke surface in a scummy splash, a tangle of heavy serpentine writhings welling about a thick dark base. They looked like serpents mating, and yet they had common roots, that was clear; like fingers, or arms.

The faint breeze was flooded with a choking, cloying fishy stench. The sea bubbled and frothed with pallid crackling scum. 'Don't move!' hissed Gille, as more arms welled up, sprouting an obscene forest. 'Don't splash, don't even breathe!'

Then, as swift as they had been slow, the writhing things struck serpentlike at the raft. Around the chieftain, as he writhed and splashed in agony, monstrous whips lashed. The longest plucked him effortlessly straight off the wood and into the air, flailing this way and that, while the rest wavered idly.

Moonlight and sea-glow glistened on their undersides; and for all his caution, Gille yelled with the rest. Innumerable, awful circular mouth-shapes like a lamprey's jaw lined them, standing proud on stubby stalks, flexing, sucking, working, ringed with innumerable blunt teeth little smaller than a man's. There was no escaping those without leaving gobbets of flesh behind, and no time. Ore sat rigid, but he giggled hysterically as the warrior, still struggling frenziedly, was weighed, as a fisherman among men weighs up a fine catch, and drawn down towards the massive calm of that enormous eye.

Down, and beyond, into the water, into the threshing thicket of limbs that might be one beast, or, as Gille guessed, several, but no less vast for that. He could glimpse surfaces of colour in that glow, shifting, pulsing, blossoming flowerlike in a second and fading again, here and there rippling into patterns long as a fair-sized boat. Then a spurt of darkness marred them, like a stormcloud in the water, killing the deep glow and the phosphorescence together. The stench became suffocating, and Dall, lying on the surface, choked out an oath. The raft rode upon inky blackness, flecked with pale trails of slime. Slowly, as the seamen clung silently, the stench faded. A faint knot of light still circled in the deeps beneath, like a lantern swinging above the abyss, at last flickering, dwindling and going out.

They hauled Dall's bulk on board, still cursing crazily, stinking unbelievably with the dark sticky slime that engulfed his body. 'Like a nest of worms! Feeling round my legs they were, flamin' great worms and worms and worms! An' I had to jus' dangle there an' pretend I was a bit o' weed, while they pulled that bastard down! An' there's those eyes an' worms and beaks like a bird's all snappin'! An' then there's this shit, all over me so I can't even fuckin' *breathe—*'

They got him calmed eventually, though they themselves retched at the stench. The stinking stuff still clung around the raft, so one could hardly wash even if one dared. 'At least we don't feel so hungry,' said Gille, seeking to lighten the mood; but it was met as all such encouragements deserve.

'Well,' said Dall thickly, 'we're alive, give you that. So far. But come morning, if our sail ain't in sight ... I'll wonder why I bothered, that's all.'

'Uh. I too,' was all Ore could say. They lolled exhausted on the uncomfortable wood, and though Gille's fingers told him that the precious kantel was still all right, he had not the heart to play it. He suspected a thing which the others did not, and he had to keep it to himself for now.

But his care was wasted; for, as the first light grew in the sky, Dall sat up and cursed more violently than before. 'It's sinking! This bloody bolt of firewood's sinking! It's gettin' waterlogged!'

Ore clutched the wood and looked wildly around. 'No bloody sail in sight! Skipper! What're we going to do?'

'We'll have to take turns again,' sighed Gille, knowing the answer even as he said it.

'That's death,' grunted Dall. 'The big fish'll come back, even if yon bastard worm-beasts don't.'

They looked at one another. 'Could be it's death anyway,' said Ore thinly. 'Another day o' that heat, us with no water.'

'They say you can drink piss,' offered Dall. The others winced.

'We won't have time to find out,' sighed Gille. 'Not with three of us aboard. I know what they do in all the old sea-tales I've heard. We'll draw lots for who goes in the water.' He snapped off thin fragments of the wood, and found his fingers wet. The draw might not make too much difference. He offered them in his hand. 'Two long, one short. I know which, you draw.'

They looked at one another. 'Come on!' he snapped, hating them for making the only sensible way so hard. 'No stupid bloody heroes here, by're leave! We've all got lives to go back to.'

The crewmen hesitated again, but then Ore

drew, and Dall, shrugging, followed suit. Gille sighed. The splinter he still held barely reached his palm. 'Well,' he said, 'it's a decision, at the least.'

'No!' exclaimed Ore. 'That's not right, Master-smith!'

'It's as right as anything can be,' said Gille.

'Best out of three?' suggested Dall. 'Or the old sea-way – let the ocean choose whom it wants itself. Cast your lots overside, and see which sinks first!' Without waiting for approval, he dropped his splinter in the water. Ore tossed his in also, and Gille had no choice but to follow. The two splinters bobbed obstinately side by side, waterlogged as they were; but Gille's, though lighter, sank a little, and was suddenly snatched from their sight. The other two stared, their faces bloodless beneath the flaring sunburn. Gille said nothing; he could not trust his voice.

In truth, after the first sick moment he had begun to feel rather imbecilically pleased with himself. There was the makings of a good song here, and with any luck he was going to be the centre of it. These two would get picked up, surely, and the tale would reach the singers back home. Lightheadedly he imagined the merchants having it sung before them in the inn, and feeling bad about the way they'd misjudged him. Olvar and old Kunrad wagging their heads at it, raising a glass, telling tales of his escapades. He thought of it spreading all across the Northlands, and a whole train of girls in tears; some in the Southlands, too, if it ever got there. Especially the ones who'd turned him down.

Utte in tears too, of course; or maybe not. He couldn't decide which he liked less. Still, she would have no trouble finding a good man, not so exciting as himself, naturally; and she would never forget him. And the Other? He wasn't so sure. She didn't strike him as the tearful kind. If she had sorrows, nobody would know. But he could imagine her approving, and relishing a memory or two. She would think better of him, and that suited him just as well as tears.

He swung his legs over the side, careful not to splash, and slid in. The others moved tentatively to stop him, but faltered.

'Do as I did, skipper!' said Dall harshly. 'Grab ahold o' the spar, lie dead still whatever happens.'

'Not much difficulty in that,' sighed Gille. 'I'm worn out. This is almost restful,' he added, floating idly on his back, watching what he thought would surely be his last sunrise. It worried him surprisingly little. He toyed idly with rhymes for *Gille*, and decided the songs would have to be in blank verse. That would be more heroic, anyhow. His eyes were sore with the salt, his sight blurred, and the long low rays pained them; his crusted eyelids fluttered and drooped. He clutched unconsciously at the kantel, and slid into sleep.

He floated on darkness, and beneath him something was rising, some grim shadow, with a glimmer of light about it. His eyes flew open suddenly, and he flailed about for a handhold. The kantel's strings jangled. There was nothing else around him, nothing at all, and he twisted about and sank. He kicked desperately back to the surface, and caught a brief glimpse of the raft, a speck on a shimmering mirror, with two still forms sprawled upon it, as if pinned down by the towering mass of the sun.

Then something cool caught at his ankle, and drew him inexorably down.

Olvar looked around, so sharply that Telqua, tightening her bowstring against the wet, sprang up. 'What is it? Have you seen something?'

'In this? Scarcely.' He dashed the rain out of his eyes. 'Yet ... it was as if something came to me again. Just as before... I think Gille's got himself into trouble again.'

'Then he still lives, at least,' said Telqua, with a gentleness that was surprising, considering she was testing an arrow's point.

'Maybe. I thought ... there's no telling. Well, I can't be much more certain about us. Hella's curse upon this rain! If they're ever going to stand in on us, it'll be soon!'

He had said that a hundred times in the last hour alone, struggling to see through the shifting veils of grey. Kalve, having more sense than to answer him, had drawn his oilcloth hood over his face and retired to the relative shelter of the great tiller, lashed tight, where he was passing a long-treasured flask to and fro with the helmsman. All the rest of the crew who could be spared were down in the hold, but the tarred canvas covering flapped loose. They were growling in discontent, but there was no help for it. The crane had to be kept ready, the more so now. They had lost a lot of way in these squalls, and it could be their pursuers were level with them now.

Olvar wiped away the rain again, wincing at the stink of the oiled wool sleeve, filthy with wearing. A sword dragged down his belt, but he missed a solid cudgel to slap into his palm. He longed to be ashore again, and at peace; but the shore too was a danger, for after the wild shifts of wind in this last day, they could be driven upon it. Till they had clear air to take a sighting, they would hardly know whither they were headed, where they were at all, even. Only Telqua seemed curiously unperturbed, and Olvar suspected it was because a fight was imminent.

'How are we ever going to live with the likes

of you?' he sighed, hunching down beside her in the
shelter of the rail. 'We rarely fight – not even
between ourselves, as the sothrans seem to every
fifty years or so. We don't have armies, just city
guards. Against bandits, corsairs, wild men of one
kind or another. How will you ever amuse yourself?'

She smiled at him. 'More changeable, I, than
you believe, perhaps. I too shall learn peace, and the
growing of little things from the dirt, and these arts
you tell me of. I shall. Honestly!'

'And like them better than a fight?'

'Perhaps not. But I shall, all the same; because
they belong to a world where children can grow
and not fear, as I did. Not see my mother raped and
slain, as I did. What I am is what my growing made
me. But if that must languish, so that our children
may sleep in the peace I was denied – so be it! And
these arts…' Her fingers plucked open the grease-
shining neck of her tunic, and the water beaded
upon it. 'You see this?'

'I see…'

She growled at him. 'Not me, oaf! The thong.
Take it!'

He touched her skin, and it was a surprise to
find it so soft. The thong lay warm across his palm,
and he stared at the dark lump at its end. It was
blackened with dirt, worn to shapelessness almost;
but the thing at its heart, stained and yellowed, had
once been a pearl. And as he looked, he saw a
flicker within the metal, the last faint ghost of a
craft not unlike his own. That held the shape of it,
like a ghost indeed, long after all the corners and
textures had been polished away. A shape with
wings, a face defined in the body, a long beak
grasping the pearl…

'Raven stealing the sun!' he said. 'The same
emblem we so often use. Showing it in a different

way, but it's still so much the same...'

'I did not show you before. I thought, this *mastersmith*, he would find it crude. Savage.'

'No! Not at all, Telqua. It's very old, isn't it? And worn. But I can still see it was fairly made.'

'We had these arts too, once. Homes in great gatherings behind walls, and rich lands. Before the Ice rolled over them, and the men who serve it drove us to huddle in cave and tent, and claw our living from a stony land. Clans keep a few things, treasures to prove the tales are true, when the dark around the campfire closes in.'

'You'll have them again, you and your folk.'

Her face twisted, halfway between smile and wrath. 'Yes! Some you shall teach us. But some we will make anew for ourselves.' She stared at the tarnished lump of metal. 'What is their worth, those arts, I do not know. I might scorn them, as the one I was. But that your folk put store in them – that such a man as you... I see there is much I do not know.'

'They say that's the first sign of wisdom,' said Olvar. 'But thank you. For what you said.'

She stood up sharply, tilting her cheeks to the rain. 'It was little enough. I am not good at speaking. I have not been taught. More I would say; but I do not know how.'

Olvar was about to say she would learn that, too; but her tone warned him. He tumbled the words over in his mind for their meaning, as he would tumble gemstones for polishing. He heaved himself to his feet, and put a hand on her shoulder; but it was stiff and hard, muscles tense.

'Something stirs, out there,' she said.

'I don't see anything.'

'I did. For an instant. Shining like a whale's back, black. A few lengths of this ship away, no more.'

Kalve leaned over beside them, breathing out

wine fumes into the wet. 'It's gusting,' he said. 'Wind's rising, should take the rain off soon. Could be they'd make a move then.'

To Olvar's surprise Telqua understood a word or two. 'Tell him, sooner!' she said. 'If they sighted us, they might lower the sail, and paddle. For short ways, that is fast.'

Olvar waved the helmsman to his station, while Kalve padded across the rain-slicked deck to alert the crew. Feet trampled below, men cursed and skidded and dropped their newly issued weapons with a clatter, but the ship came alive again more quickly and quietly than he had thought possible. In a moment or two the crane-ropes creaked taut, flicking out a shower of droplets, and the weighty bundle lifted to the hold-mouth, twisting gently. The rain curtain blew and billowed a moment, and there, no distance at all away, he saw the glossy black flank slide into view; and above it, as if floating among the cloud, the black yardarm with its sail gathered in. The rain billowed in his face. Telqua hissed softly, 'So they do in reiving, run beneath a rain-cloud!'

She nocked an arrow to the string, testing its tension. Kalve was leaning down from the quarterdeck, hissing instructions, and the tackle moaned as the crane ran up its load. *Orrin* listed sharply as it swung about, twirling at the end of the rope. Olvar, squinting through his streaming eyes, held up his hand. It was hard to be sure...

The black bows, painted with a pouncing beast, knifed the mist apart. Men crouched there, behind the huge deck-bows. Olvar's hand slashed the air. The crane swung violently around, the *Orrin* rolled sickeningly, and the burden, whirling, smashed straight into the oncoming bows. The thud and crack was clearly heard, and the black mast was momentarily visible, heeling violently. A man was hurled from its top; Olvar's keen eyes saw him clearly, his painted armour, his bow, the arrows spilling from his quiver. But the mast rose again, rocking; and the bows became visible, a great crack crossing the skull of the beast and half the platform's planking hanging loose, the remains of a deck-bow shattered into them on top of the half-pulped corpses of its wielders.

The men on *Orrin*'s deck cheered, as the mighty weight swung; and had the black sail been lowered it would have been carried away, and the mast with it, no doubt. But the load spun past, harmless, while Olvar's crew sought to haul it in again. Too late; an iron shaft, some two strides long, by fate or fine marksmanship, crashed in among them. Three fell, slashed and stricken, and one of the ropes whipped free. Others sprang to it, but it leaped through their hands like a live thing, steaming through the blocks. Into the sea it splashed before they caught it, dragging the *Orrin* over with it. And then the *Orrin*'s hull boomed dully as the black ship slammed home against it, right amidships.

The impact was not great, but it rocked the *Orrin*; men staggered and fell. And with the impact came the grapnels, drawing the hulls together, and more arrows. A warrior sprang over the maindeck rail, howling, and slumped back over it with Telqua's first shaft in his throat; another scrambled up to the quarterdeck, and by her next shot was hurled screaming into the sea. But his fellows were behind him, firing also, and an arrow struck down the helmsman. The crew's crossbows snapped, and some men were already wielding the long-handled boarding axes, Kalve with a fury which belied his usual gloom. But the paddles with their sharp edges were scything the crew back from the rails, and warriors were leaping wildly into the gap, shrieking what might be war-cries or the howls of hunting beasts.

Olvar slashed this way and that with little swordsmanship, but striking down spears and dinting shields with his great strength. Telqua knelt and shot, and no warrior ran up against her but was struck down. But it may be that these were men more hardened than those whom Gille had faced, not weakened by heat and labour, and better provisioned; and there was no fire here to stop them boarding. Over the rails they poured in a flood of black, pushing the defenders swiftly back. Olvar's sword was growing slippery in the wet, and he knew that any moment it would be stricken from his hand. He swung back, and suddenly slashed at the heavy tiller lashings. They sang loose, the warriors and crew alike ducked to avoid them. He dropped his sword, took the mighty beam upon his shoulder and heaved.

Even for Olvar's strength it was a test. The tiller was meant to be massive and stable, slow to shift. But it came free, and he hefted it with a triumphant cry that came out as a scream, for he had no breath to spare. This was a weapon after his fashion. The deep-carven patterns gave him a good handhold, and he swung the hard wood around, this way, that way, driving the invaders back upon the spears of their fellows. Shafts splintered where it passed, shields were not merely dinted but smashed, and the arms that bore them. The press gave back before him, back to the rail or leaping down on the heads of their fellows below. For a minute it seemed there might be hope, as Olvar came up against the rail with his ram thrust painfully hard against the breasts of the leading intruders, pinioning their weapons. They struggled and hissed at him in fell voices, their black eyes glaring with strain and blood-rage; their rank smell filled the misty air, amid the steam of breath and blood.

Telqua had a sword, his sword, and she was beating at them with it, wounding them, felling them as they fought to scramble back over the rail. But he saw then that there were as many or more still trying to board, clambering even over the shoulders of their fellows; and there was no help to come. His men were fighting for their own lives below against those already aboard, and the archers who were raking the deck with their black shafts. Olvar, arms cracking, saw one spring up to the bow and take a steady sight upon him. He ducked down; and that was what his tormented enemies needed. They heaved against the tiller bar, and he staggered, unable to react. There was a flat snapping sound, Telqua screamed; and to Olvar's eyes the dank air seemed to blur with the flight of a single huge arrow.

The crash of its impact rocked him where he stood. He staggered, and the tiller, slick with dew and blood, slipped from his straining arms and boomed against the planking. For a giddy moment, he faced his foes empty-handed, arms wide; but it was Telqua who sprang before him, with a cry as wild as any of the warriors, flailing the sword at their faces. Yet their eyes, he saw, were not on her, but on him; their heads were turning away, their jaws dropping. From somewhere came a sudden tang of smoke. Again the snap, too loud even for one of their deck-bows, and friend and foe ducked as one before the fearful singing in the air.

Another crash; and this time the *Orrin* hardly rocked. But from below came shouts of anger and alarm, and suddenly the rattle of the time-drum, coupled with the high shrilling note of some kind of pipe; and at that, the wall of black armour broke before him. The lean men were clambering over the rail, vaulting it even in their haste; while below the warriors driving back the crew also broke off the fight, swung themselves up to the walkways, out of the hold, the fo'c'sle, everywhere they had carried the battle, hardly heeding the blows that were aimed at them as they turned.

Olvar and Telqua stood transfixed, unable to comprehend what change was afoot, realising only slowly that the rain had thinned to a fine drizzle, that the clouds had broken. It was a pale light that came upon them, and drew a sullen gleam from the surface of a cold iron-hued sea. But it was a blessed light for all that, for they were alive, though they could not yet know why.

There was cheering from somewhere, from the bows, from the waist; but why, at what, they could not see. It was the sail, rain-ridden and sagging, that hid it from them, as the *Orrin* rode sluggishly into the wind. The air sang again, twice; and two more huge bolts came arching high over the sail, trailing smoke and sparks from their broad glinting heads, and down upon the hunters' ship.

The shouting there was redoubled as they crashed home, the black mast rocked and the yard swung; yet the warriors had it under control already, and men were shinning up the ratlines to let fall the sail. The black fabric, crossed with its hatching of tarry cords, boomed full in an instant, the high bow turned, exposing its splintered side, and the huge bolts that stuck in its outer flank, smoking peril to the timbers. But it was already too late.

A great shadow darkened the *Orrin*'s sail, and high above it a masthead whose bright pennons flicked like a serpent's tongue, and behind that another; and the sails that billowed from them hid the sun. Out into their sight rode a high bow, blunt and massive, and set upon it the figure of a great bird, carven and painted, long claws outthrust, dark

wings flung back in the onrush, pinions spread and
golden beak screaming wrath as it swooped upon
its prey; and upon its white head a crown.

Between and beneath those claws thrust out
a heavy pointed prow, a massive shaft that tapered
to a faceted spearhead of black iron. And though
drums rattled defiantly, and arrows soared up
against it, they could no more deter it than a carrion
crow defy the crowned eagle. Down upon the black
ship it rode, driving the water cleansing white
before it. So low lay the black hull that the huge ram
rode right over it, shattering the gunwales, and the
full force of the massive bow-stem struck it on the
fore-quarter.

The great bow lifted a little. The black mast
snapped and flew wide, like a windblown twig. The
black hull heaved as the white wave struck it, and
with a fearful splintering crash it rolled and tipped,
its gunwale driven under, its warriors, archers,
rowers flung down into the foam. Heads bobbed
among the wreckage, arms flailed, voices screamed,
but nothing could be done for them; nothing could
stem the high ship's onrush. Over that general ruin
the huge ship dipped and plunged, its bow-wave
boiling, and the heads and arms vanished in turmoil,
the voices were blotted out. In its wake, like a
wounded sea-beast, a black thing rolled once and
sank slowly away, into the empty sea.

Telqua stared, aghast; and Olvar could hardly
blame her. 'I told you of the strength of the
Southlands,' he said, a little less than steadily, 'and
their wealth. You see one of their great warcraft,
such as I have seen only once or twice myself, and
never at sea.'

'Is such a monster made by men?' she demanded
tremulously.

Her answer made her jump, for it came as a
flourish of trumpets sounding from the high stern.

A group of tall men appeared at the ornate taffrail, all clad alike in white surcoats with a device at the breast, of high towers that seemed afloat upon water, as if to embody such a seagoing fortress as this. The tallest of them, a man middling young with dark red curls spilling around his golden collar, raised a hand in solemn salute. 'Ahoy there, *Orrin* out of Nordeney! The Marchwarden of Ker Bryhaine his ship of war *Sea Eagle* bears you fair greeting and salutation, in the person of Ervalien Ardrhennan her commander! Do I have the honour of addressing Captain Olvar of Saldenborg?'

Olvar's laughter bubbled up at the sothran politenesses. 'The honour's all Captain Olvar's, Commander Ervalien! And so's the gratitude! How came you upon us, may I ask? And how know of us?'

'Small mystery there! We were sent ahead in great hope to scout out you and your consort vessel – though we little looked to find you entertaining such savage guests.'

'You sped them nicely on their way. But sent ahead of what?'

For answer Ervalien simply stretched out an arm to the horizon. The rainsqualls had cleared, the dismal clouds parted to reveal a more solid bank of grey along the ocean's true margin, and rising out of it, blue and blurred by distance, the misty slopes of distant hills. Here and there above them, as if riding on the cloud, arose the jagged peak of a still more distant mountain, sharp and thrusting. But in between, more distinct, stretched a broad phalanx of white wings, like stormbirds riding the swell. Telqua thrust her hands on Olvar's shoulders and sprang in the air with a yell of delight and wonder; for these were the sails of ships, a mighty fleet of them. And most of them, it was clear, were as great as the *Sea Eagle*, or still greater.

'Enough to bear a small town!' marvelled Olvar.

'And the wherewithal to feed it,' nodded Kalve, chewing on his toothpick splinter. 'See you now! Ships of war. Big merchantmen. Even those wallowing great sothran grain-carriers that ply the coastal estates – your Marchwarden must have raised every one he could find. Not only in his own domain, either – skipper, this is Northland and Southland together here. And we've not seen the like of that at sea in my lifetime.'

'They do, then?' pleaded Telqua, unable to accept what her sight told her. 'They come? They... *save*?' The men turned to her in surprise, for she was speaking their tongue.

Gille spluttered and kicked, but though the grip did not feel hard he could not break it. Water rushed into his nose, he fought not to let his mouth open, but as his lungs strained and hot iron bands tightened around his chest, his control slipped away. Was he breathing or screaming? He hardly knew, but as his head burned and his vision blurred, his mouth flew open. His last breath fluttered out of him in bubbles that flew upward like the glittering moment of life, and were gone.

Water rushed in to fill their place. His lungs heaved against it. He convulsed in agony, eyes blurring in the green dimness, ears roaring, too maddened by panic even to long for death.

Then a voice spoke in his ear. He heard it all too clearly, above the thunder of his heart; and he knew it was impossible even as it rang in his tortured head. The single word had the force of a command that could not be ignored; and the word was '*Cease!*'

A message of hope? A command to die? Either or neither, it tangled the tiny thread of understanding left him. A voice meant a helping hand, that much he understood, and threshed wildly about to grab it. Then something floated up in front of his unfocused eyes, something pale that filled his sight, long strands of uncertain whiteness streaming wide in the water, something very close; and he hung motionless with the shock, forgetting to struggle.

'That is right,' said the voice, and suddenly an immense burst of tiny bubbles erupted around him. It came to him suddenly that the grip on his ankle had gone. 'You need not fight so hard. See, you are not dying. It is given you to breathe.'

Forgetting himself, he opened his mouth, felt the rush of water in his throat and retched violently; his throat ached, straining to form words against the weight of the water.

'No!' said the voice quickly. 'You cannot speak, not yet; nor sing. But the water will sustain you as well as the air, otherwise. Breathe slowly, and be at peace. Come, Gille, give me your hand!'

Stunned at the sound of his own name, where no sound should be, he reached out instinctively. And then his vision cleared, and almost he choked once more at the sight.

It was a human face that floated before him, level with his own, in an aureole of trailing swaths that might have been weed or fine silk, shimmering translucent. Within that aureole another, finer yet, a spreading crown of hair that glistened against the dim green glow as gold against mottled jade. And within that, in turn, the features, slender yet strong, utterly unforgettable, changed in only one respect; and that was the scatter of gems that hung about the high brow and around the slender neck, jewels that shone blue and green and the purple of dark wine or waves beneath a passing cloud-shadow, impossibly beautiful gems in settings of entangled gold that trailed down between the high white breasts, floating free.

Brightly the gems glistened; yet the eyes beneath that diadem were brighter yet, emerald fires that held Gille transfixed as easily as ever. The lips that parted were pale and firm, the hands that reached up to frame his cheeks shapely but irresistible. Their touch was as cold as the kiss she placed upon his lips and let linger there, while his heart leaped and his eyes went wide with the miracle of it. Gold rings rounded her wrists and arms, heavy things of ancient patterns like none he knew, yet spoke to him of craft and wisdom even as he hung there, lost in wonder.

He was dead. He was sure of that, and yet it seemed impossible to care. Already the raft and all about it lay in another world, the terror of drowning a shadow slipped away like an evil dream before the sun. It was enough to be where he was now, and wish no change; to feel, as he put out his hands, the waist beneath the draperies with the fine ceinture still about it, hanging low beneath the fine soft curve of her body. Yet there too, now, he felt the facets of gems, and saw, as she lifted her head once more, the pearls that were woven into that streaming hair, yet paled against its lustre.

His heart, overburdened, bade him speak; and again his chest burned and heaved. 'Y–'

Suddenly the gems were very much a diadem, a glittering beacon of command about her brow as she lifted it.

'Peace, I said! Yes, I. Little singer, clever lover, I have been seeking you out, in all your wild careerings about the ocean. You have done well; and yet your greatest task remains. Your greatest, and our greatest hope, that all this effort shall come to a good end. We have someone to see, little master of metals, small cunning fingers! Someone of much moment, whose merest glance is an honour to few accorded. Someone whose goodwill I wish you to win, for so much now rests upon it, so very much.'

Gille was fighting desperately to make a sound. 'Y... Whhh... S...'

The lips twitched delicately. 'Peace! You will hurt that golden throat of yours. The water about you is soaked with the spirit of the air, and no more salty than the sea you bear within you, always. It will sustain you, but cannot shape sounds as you are used to. As I can, because it heeds my will in all things, within my compass – and because I shape it that I am shaped for. And you ask who I am, do you? Have you not guessed?'

Her lips had ceased to move; yet the water around him was suddenly alive with her laughter, rippling across his skin, stirring his hair. Her breasts brushed his chest, and the silken aura about her trailed clinging chills across his skin, so that his heart skipped beat upon beat. For a moment he was absurdly delighted he was receiving such personal attention; then he reflected that he would very much rather be alive.

'Perhaps you have. The Child of Waves am I who has trodden the shore for you, who has lain with you upon the margins of my world, who has searched the oceans for you, the Lady Saithana Sea's-Daughter. But have no fear, little singer. You are not drowned. Not yet!'

He could no more have closed his arms than embrace the sun. But the wicked smile that crossed her face was the same as ever, and her frightening quickness as she slipped free of him and dived, doubled over, so that her thighs flashed past his helpless face and the draperies slapped at him, gently. Her lean hand closed hard about his ankle again, her bare feet kicked, and he was pulled down once more in a rush and swirl of water, into an abyss of green that grew steadily darker.

There was a strange sound in his ears, metallic,

faint. He looked up, and saw only the kantel, floating in the rush and bubble, trailing as helpless in his hand as he from hers, against a sparkling sheet of green glass. Beyond it lay light and life; but he was being drawn away, down into his living dream.

CHAPTER EIGHT
Fortress of Glass

Olvar stumped impatiently up into the *Orrin*'s bows, revelling in the openness of his view, sea and sky spread out before him and the steep green slopes of the islands rising between. Even the white plumes that trailed from many summits no longer heralded dark memories. The awful scene in the crater that had haunted him this past two weeks had lost much of its power. That barbarity was something he could help to end now, not merely strike at and run. The power to stop it was at his back, to sweep the scene clear as firmly as a sleeve across a crudely chalked slate. The wind was fresh, and to either side the great warships of the South rode like islands themselves, under taut sails as sparkling white as their bow-foam, a vision of strength and reassurance.

The airy expanse looked oddly new to him, without the familiar spread of mainsail in the way. He was slightly shocked to realise how seldom he had seen it. In all their long voyage he had hardly been forrard at all. That was what it was to be skipper, hardly moving from the quarterdeck. He had never been up to the masthead, even.

'Though chances are I'll be driven up there yet!' he muttered.

Telqua, sitting on the bowsprit, smiled. 'Now what was that?'

She spoke a strange mix of the Northland tongue and her own, quite unselfconsciously dropping in words where she did not know them. It made Olvar, never the fastest thinker, feel he was climbing a ladder with missing rungs.

'Oh … I was just wondering where they all are.' He waved an impatient hand at the yellow-grey fringes beneath the greenery ahead. 'You'd think they'd be flocking down to the beach at the first sight of us. They must have seen we're not those bastard hunters by now.'

She smiled again, more ruefully. 'Remember, trust comes not so easily to our folk, even within our own clan. And these great ships are wholly strange to us. Had I seen them approach, I would not have come rushing out of cover, merely because the sails were white instead of black.'

'Fair enough!' grunted Olvar grudgingly. 'But us they must recognise, the *Orrin*. We sank one foe in their sight, drew off the rest, and you went off with us. Isn't that enough?'

Telqua shrugged. 'If I were there, perhaps yes. But without me they may be more cautious. That is why I am sitting here, to be seen. But with the black ships gone, the elders may have moved the people to one of the other islands. There may be only watchers left here. They would send back for orders. Be patient, great blundering morse! All shall be well yet.'

She leaned back on her elbows, smiling lazily, and swung her thighs lightly open and closed against the bowsprit, straight in his line of sight. The effect was startling. The sun suddenly seemed much fiercer, and a thin trickle traced an infuriating course down from Olvar's shoulderblades to between his buttocks. Once again he cursed the lack of privacy on these ships. There was his cabin, of course; but they could hardly be seen disappearing into it all the time. Gille might not be around with his ribald songs, but the sailors could do pretty well on their own account.

He looked swiftly around before letting his hand rest on her thigh and slide upward, squeezing gently. She clasped it hard and squirmed lazily. She felt disturbingly lean compared to the other women he had touched – and when was the last of those? Ancient history. Her leg was rubbing up and down the inside of his, and that was still more disturbing, and he did not want it to stop.

What there was between them, he was not even sure. From those moments in the water together, when he had first seen her true face, when they had sustained one another until the boat reached them, an attraction had grown. But it was a strange, stunted growth, forced to take its course in what little intimacy they could find, in stolen moments of the night watch, in brief unsatisfying grapples in his bunk, narrow enough for himself as it was. Neither was romantic, neither in thrall to the other, surely. And she was fierce, uncertain, wholly unpredictable. It was hard to call that love, or anything approaching it; more like petting a caged daggertooth. Would you get your hand back licked, or savaged – or at all? Yet he was drawn to her, wanted her, and he persisted. And in that there was something of thrall; for so did she.

'You wait,' he murmured, 'until I get you home.'

Telqua smirked. 'Do I have to? Will all that forest not be enough?'

Olvar exhaled hard, and detached himself. 'No. Not if you go on like that.'

'I thought, you are so old and fat, you will need encouragement.'

'About as much as one of those fire-mountains. I'm just afraid all your bony bits will leave bruises. You being just a bit young and skinny...' He squeezed her thigh, less lightly, and was rewarded by one of those stinging tweaks on his arm. Some sort of love-play from the beginning, he now realised; her idea of a gentle tease, maybe. These people! What was he letting himself in for?

She swung herself up again, feet dangling high above the white water. 'Where are they, fools? See, now you are making me impatient! At least they have left no warnings that I can read, no danger signals. They would have done that, even with the skies falling. This would have been the place, this beach. But no, nothing!'

Behind them Kalve began calling orders. The crew clattered into life, freeing the sheets for a change of tack, leading the fleet in towards the islands. Olvar struggled to call his mind back to mundane matters. 'Well,' he decided, 'we'll head into the main channel and drop anchor there. Give 'em a chance to see we're friendly, and the crews to go ashore. Ours especially. They've had a swink and a half, good weight!'

He had been worried about the men, even when their desperate chase ended; had given them the choice of going on to the Southlands, or back to Saldenborg, rather than make the long voyage to the isles and back once more. He and Telqua could easily have transferred to the *Sea Eagle*. But when they heard that, Adde and the rest of the men became mulish. They could replenish their stores from the fleet, and what was a few more days afloat to a hardened sailor? Like him, they wanted to see the whole rescue through. And like him, also, they were hoping that they might find the *Rannvi* back there, too. Or, if they did not, then whatever was left of its pursuers.

That awoke an unwelcome thought. Olvar scanned what he could see of the bays. 'I wonder. Could one of the ships that chased Gille have come back already? Could that be why they're hiding?'

'One ship?' she scoffed. 'They would not hide from it, they would try to seize it. Or even two.

They would succeed, too, now that they have more arms. Wait now, and watch, and we shall see.'

The channel opened wide as before, but now it was almost free of flotsam, save for a black ring marring the tideline of the white beaches. Olvar brooded at how little sign remained of human strife. Telqua had told him tales of that first battle, when the crude, lumbering refugee ships with their precious cargo thrashed and struggled for life against the biting black predators, of heroisms and sacrifices that left him feeling the risks he had taken were nothing by comparison. And yet now, barely weeks later, sea and land and sky were reasserting their dominion, and erasing the scars. Most of the larger wreckage had sunk by now, and even the foundered hulls they passed over were already half covered by the drifting sand or the burgeoning life of the water. Bright seaflowers waved their fronds over rough-hewn timbers and sleek black planking, seastars crawled and long eels rippled where grim captains had stood, wielding their ships like swords, and the lives aboard them like scattered darts to hurl in the face of the hated enemy. The bones on the beach, the bodies in the crater, the shattered hulks below were already fading from sight, and heroism and villainy alike blended into the natural elements as if they had never been.

'Not so,' said Telqua, answering his thought. 'We are here. And so long as we live, so too will they. To live is to bear witness, and give thanks.'

Kalve had to lay his course into the islands with especial care, to mark the deepest water for the huge vessels following. That meant sending a sailor into the bows with the lead, spoiling Olvar and Telqua's brief idyll. They picked their way back along the narrow decking alongside the hold, but they had not yet reached the quarterdeck when they heard the sounds from either side.

'What's this?' demanded Olvar, over the racket of trumpets and cries, as he bounded up. 'Some stupid sothran aground—'

Then *Orrin* rounded the point, and he saw for himself what the higher mastheads of the sothran warships had espied first; and even his oath stuck in his throat. They were looking along the length of the channel now, the island slopes framing the narrow straits and the bay between the isles, and beyond its mouth the open ocean. In itself that view was surpassing fair, an infinite blue-green mead glittering under the sky that dove to meet it at the world's edge, strewn with streaks of fresh bright cloud. Yet it was as if these cast their shadows on the sea beneath, and in the distance gathered into an array of frowning storm.

All across the horizon black sails were growing, dark tares strewing the ocean with the threat of bitter harvest. That was ill enough; but before them, far nearer, sprang up a scorched stubble of barren black stems, masts without sails. Even Olvar could not make out more; but he could guess at the relentless digging of those paddles in driven hands, thrusting the black bows onward. A dark vanguard was racing with all speed to the bay between the isles, and the straits it commanded.

'So!' said Telqua. 'Now we know why they hide, my folk!'

The fleet of the hunters had returned.

Gille trailed helplessly down into the gathering dark. Only above him was there light, the distant glow of the surface, growing ever less distinct. How deep he was, he could not guess; how much deeper he might go, he did not dare to wonder. The water around him fizzed and bubbled with the breath of life. It was beginning to feel chill, he noticed; then as suddenly as that, it was not. The water was barely cooler than his blood; yet when he reached out, much colder currents played around his fingertips. All he could see of Saithana was the trailing ends of her drapery, her writhing hair, and now and again a flash of her flexing thighs; that now appealed to him a great deal less than it had. The grip on his ankle never slackened. The bar upon his speech chafed him more. He longed to speak to her, to beg a hundred answers and explanations; but she was silent.

Not so the strange world about them. He expected a vast dead silence; yet as his ears grew used to the rushing descent, he became aware of sounds in the watery void about him, sounds such as he had never before heard. Faint crackles, throbs, grunts; animal sounds clearly, though what made them he could not imagine. Now and again he caught glimpses in the haze – a vast silver sphere, as it seemed, its highlights shifting and shimmering, then suddenly exploding outward. A shoal of fish, he guessed; scattering suddenly before some predator. Then he saw the cause, two of them, long grey monsters, sailing unconcernedly past the throng with powerful tail strokes. He knew those dorsal fins; here were some of the big fish he had feared so much. With cause, he thought, as he saw their half-open mouths, spiny thickets of teeth. They turned towards him with an air of lazy curiosity, and he made a flailing attempt to attract Saithana's attention; but they circled about him once, well beyond the stream of bubbles, their jet-bead eyes staring inanely, and suddenly vanished into the gloom with powerful tail-beats, leaving him shivering. It was fear, for the most part; but anger flared in him briefly.

Time passed, though there was no measuring it. Sound shivered the darkness again, quivered through his clothes, playing like a blown flame

across his flesh, a huge sound he could associate
with nothing he knew, not even the tentacled things
that had assailed them on the raft. He thought of his
men there, Dall and young Ore; would they be
picked up? If he could ask Saithana ...

The sound boomed around him again, one
moment a throbbing sensation below the level of
hearing, the next a sobbing moan in his ears,
daunting, inhuman, like the sorrows of a world. He
saw nothing, whatever way he looked; and it came
to him that he was hearing noises from afar, an
ocean away perhaps. They seemed like the voice of
the vastness itself, and he felt wretched and small,
utterly out of place. The kantel tugged at his wrist,
and with some difficulty he drew it to him and
clutched at it, wondering if the miraculous instrument would yet be ruined by this terrible soaking.
That felt almost worse; he had few hopes left for
himself. And yet neither of them had played their
last chord yet. With the firm wood to hold on to he
felt better, stronger. Sooner or later this had to end.

Very suddenly, it did. Shadow rose on either
side; then the grip on his ankle vanished, and he
floated free. The girl was before him, eyes dancing,
hands on his shoulders to press him gently down.
Something jarred against his bare feet. In the same
moment there was a tremendous rush in his ears,
something wrenched at him, but the hands on his
shoulders held him firm. With the suddenness of
nightmare he was dragged down by a massive
weight, and his chest was one inflating agony. He
fell on his knees, his chest heaved, he coughed,
spewed, felt the water flung out of his mouth, saw it
pour away across bare grey rock, spreading brown
on yellow sand, soaking away. A cool hand touched
his arched back, and the knots in his muscles
relaxed. 'Have no fear. Breathe calmly. The spasm
will fade. You stand as safe here as in your own

land. More so; for you are under my protection.'

Suddenly he could draw one long, heaving breath. It felt impossibly good, but it set him coughing violently again, clutching the kantel to ease the spasms of his chest. The ugly sounds echoed among the silent rocks. The fit passed, and he looked up at the tall girl standing quite unconcernedly beside him, acutely aware what she had seen him doing, and that he was half naked, barefoot, on all fours. 'So,' she said. 'You bear it better than many. As I thought you would.' She stretched out a hand to him, but he was already struggling to his feet. He was afraid the rock would be slimy and slippery, but it was dry and firm, the sand in its crevices as crisp as a sunbaked beach. Fronds of bladdered weed hung blackened around it, crunching and popping underfoot. He wavered a little on his legs, but had to admit he felt better than he expected. He looked around him suspiciously, wondering where the light came from in such an echoing cavern. Instinctively he looked up; and his knees almost gave beneath him.

He was surrounded by rocks. He stood on a smooth rocky shelf at one end of a shallow bowl, almost like one of the great amphitheatres of the Southlands; but though at the further end higher shelves climbed to a tall rock wall, he was not in any cavern. High above his head there hung suspended, without any support he could see, a curving vault of green glass through which the pale clear light filtered down. From the rocks around it rose to the height of a tower above his head, airy, unsupported, suffused with the glow from above. But within that very wall the weedfronds waved, green, brown, full; and small fish stirred in wonder, darting this way and that about the green. There was no glass, no surface at all; and what power upheld it he could only guess at. The mighty weight of the ocean itself overhung his head.

He could not speak again, though he opened and shut his mouth; but the girl smiled, and stroked his cheek. 'What is this place?' he burst out. 'Where – why – the bottom of the bloody sea?'

'This? Our realm, as is all between the shores of the world, from the height to the abyss. But that is a place of darkness and crushing weight of waters, remote from all that you know. Where you now stand is no great depth, barely beyond the threshold of the land, one of the places we sometimes set aside to speak with those who dwell in other elements. There are many Powers who cannot endure the ocean, or will not.'

'Amazing!' said Gille faintly, hoping his knees would not betray him, or some other region.

The girl nodded, very earnestly. 'Indeed! Can you conceive such a thing? Yet they have naught to fear from it, beings of light and motion that they are. Whereas you, you stand firm! Ah, my choice was right in you, my little sweet singer, my hero...'

As quickly as that her arms were around him, sliding the kantel out of the way, her lips pressing home on his, her breasts cool against his bare chest, the jewels stinging cold on his burned skin. The kantel rang gently as she ground her flank against him, and Gille, to his great surprise, found himself responding. The weariness, the burning, the dull ache of short commons and hard labour seemed to have sloughed off him in his long descent, like a skin he had shed. His head felt light, and all about him had the semblance of a dream. The more so, as it came to him that she was somehow taller than she had been, and stronger, so that he had to strain to reach her lips, and his ribs creaked.

She released him no less abruptly. 'Time enough later, perhaps! We have little enough now, to prepare you. Ere *He* comes!'

Gille could not form a word. 'H... Your *choice?* Who is *He?* What does he want with me? What do *you* want?'

'*Peace!*' Her finger touched his lips. 'Little singer, I have brought you here to speak, to play, to sing, to dance and caper if need be. To please, to divert, to plead a case. To move the Ocean by your music, if you can; and that I most truly believe. To touch the heart of my father.'

'Your ...' Gille ran his fingers through his hair.

Even down here, he thought, in a sagging kind of way; they *always* had bloody fathers.

'I didn't know you... creatures, I mean people... like you... had fathers? I believed you just *were*...'

She laughed. 'We do as all life may do! Two join to shape a third from their common substance, for that is how growth is best infused with change. Unlike your fleshly coupling, of course; at once simpler for us, and vastly more complex. Though in that, as in all else, when form is upon us we happily share - as you may recall?'

She smoothed out his tousled hair with an affectionate gesture. He smiled weakly. She sighed happily. 'Some despise it, the cold spirits of the Ice above all; yet even they cannot wholly escape its lure. I am sprung of the Daughter of Air, who stretched herself out upon the Sea in the first forming of the world, and there grew great with the waves, and so brought Beauty into the world. A part of that am I, Air's offspring still. Though in my father's august realm I dwell, yet may I roam about its boundaries, and pass at times into my mother's light domain, to dance in the free air. The human shape serves me well for that, and comes easier to me than most of my kind, mirroring what I am. And so also, human thoughts, and the hopes and fears of human hearts, the desires of human blood, the pain and fragility of their lives.' She smiled again, serene as a summer shore. 'I am not of you, little singer, but do not fear me, or hate me; for I know what it is to have a heart beat in my breast. And all I have done is by that dictate.'

Gille looked at her for a moment, and bowed his head quickly, like one who has gazed too long into the sun. 'Lady, I do not hate you. But what *have* you done, in all this? And why?'

'Why?' She laid a hand upon his bare arm. 'Because I do not understand humans, though I have known so many. Known, and loved. Because I see how one will happily tear the flesh of his fellow, one people another; and I have never truly known why. Long ago I saw a folk come to our shores, far in the west. I heard there their songs of pain and lamentation, I saw their sufferings upon the banks of stone. Yet I could help them little, for my father will not have the conflicts of the upper realms intrude upon the Deep. But I knew the Ice was behind this, and its cold masters; and I longed to spite them. Then I saw ships building, crude, desperate things, and a harried people embark on one last bold venture, hunted and alone; and my heart became a fire all Ocean could not quench. Myself forbidden to deliver them, I was yet free to seek others who might. So I sought along your rugged shores, where there were bold adventurers of old, and found none; only wary merchants I could not trust to value lives above gain. Until the sound of the kantel came to me, a voice of power out of the abyss of time, won in an act of valour; and bearing with it your sad song.'

Gille closed his eyes a moment. 'So that was why you gave me what I lacked.'

'No. Not for that alone. For I had to look within your heart, truly, to know if you were the man I needed; and I pitied you, Gille, as I pity all humankind whose desires must forever outstrip their dreams. So indeed I gave you what you lacked, and what I wished also. I do not speak of the gold.'

'Neither did I,' said Gille quietly.

She reached out and caressed his cheek. 'So. I had found my adventurer, and won his heart, and sent him to sea. But I knew too little of the malice of the Ice, or the implacable hatred of its human hounds, that came up against my poor people, and wrecked and stranded them. Then I would have warned you outright, defying my father's express command; but I came upon the old man instead. I could not save him, but I spoke to him, made solemn promise and left him in hope. I turned the Ice's own weapons against it, to bring you two together. And, my little singer, you did not fail me, you and your friend!'

'But did you fail him?' demanded Gille bitterly. 'As you failed me?'

Sudden shock and hurt crumpled her face. He felt as if he had slapped a child for no cause. 'Failed? I? But I have not, no! Neither of you. Why do you think I summoned you?'

'Summoned... Could you not have done it otherwise? And not through so much terror and death?'

Tears might have streaked those perfect cheeks, had she been human. She had none. 'You wrong me, Gille! The encircling Ocean is my father's realm, yet even he cannot be all places within it, still less I. I had to help your friend also - you wished that, did you not? He might have drowned, fallen from a height, but for me. Then I sought you out, I watched over you. I walked your deck, and kissed you as you slept, Gille! But in the fight I lost you. I watched over your ship, and only knew you were gone when I heard your men lament you.'

'They're safe, then? It's safe?' Gille clutched her arm, hard enough to bruise. She only nodded.

'They, and the two on the raft; the *Rannvi* will come upon her lost children soon. The very creatures of the sea sought you out, Gille!'

He shuddered. 'Aye. They found us. Like the one of my men your great fishes seized!'

'The fishes have not wit enough to tell one from another, or to be held back from their natural course. But it was through them you were discovered, and others sent who could tell and judge, to shield you till I came – the many-armed ones, the Children of Deep Night. Did you not wonder, that only your foes were taken, and that as they threatened you? My little poet, even if I needed you no further, I would not have left you thus!'

He gave a jerky nod. 'You walked our deck ... yes. We found wet footprints, and feared somebody had been at the water rations. I wish ... I wish you'd woken me, that's all.'

'I did not dare! My father ... Gille, our venture is still in peril, and so are your friends. Olvar, your friend, even now he returns to the isles, with his wild princess and a mass of ships sent by this kindly lord. That is why I summoned you. A terrible peril comes upon them. The great fleet of their foes has also been summoned; and it too descends upon the islands.'

'And Olvar doesn't know?' Gille all but tore at his hair. 'Lady, can we not warn them? They won't have warships. A few, at best. Those devils will slaughter them!'

'Did you not hear? I hardly dared risk warning you outright, lest my father turn upon us in his wrath! Nor can I blame him. He hates the Ice, that has already stolen away so much of his realm, locked it in sterile solidity. But he will not lightly attract the wrath of the Powers its overlords once more. Still less at the behest of intruding men, whom he despises as wastrels of the world, without worth or achievement. And yet, and yet...'

She broke off, as if listening, her breasts heaving. Again that shuddering pulse ran through water and air alike, up through the very rocks beneath, trembling through their legs. The watery vault blurred as if a breath had passed over it. She spoke again, in haste. 'Gille, you must speak for us, sing for us! I can do no more, not in the face of his power. He would undo all, simply to punish my defying him. You must stand before him, win him to our aid.'

Gille giggled a little hysterically. 'Won't he just reach out and crush me? Will he even hear one little human voice? One limping song?'

She smiled, excitedly. 'I did, Gille! I heard! One voice, but a strong one! And your songs need not limp, Gille. Not when you could set the world dancing, with what you hold.'

Again that deep thunder sent its reverberations through the deep, and she caught at him, held him as if she were the one seeking comfort. The touch of her cool skin set his aflame, and it was as if light shone through his veins, the light of a summer morning. 'I healed your hurts and your weariness, Gille! Nothing now holds you back, but yourself. Look, and find the strength within, little poet! *He comes!*'

The echo took her voice, the very air seemed to blur around him, and the shudder of sound rose in pitch to become a moaning cry, ever too vast for human throat. From rock to rock ran her words, like scurrying messengers, while the green ceiling darkened. Around its margins massive forms seemed to well up and diminish. '*He comes! He comes!*'

'What the hell are they doing, Kalve?' demanded Olvar.

The sailing master surveyed the scene with

cold disdain. 'Is it not clear enough? They seek to deny us the open water.'

Ervalien snorted. 'Those? Their rig is crude, they cannot outsail us. And they lie so low that *Sea Eagle* and *Javelin* could simply ride over them, let alone the lesser warships. The grain-carriers, even!'

The sothrans chuckled. Olvar kept his temper. *Orrin*, riding between the two chief warships, made a handy place for a council of captains, but he was well aware he was the least of them, a former fisherlad with his first command. His mastership meant nothing to the sothrans, and he suspected only his association with Kunrad made them ready to consult him at all; but he would not improve anything by rudeness.

'My sea-lords, I take leave to doubt that. Especially the grain-carriers! With half a crew, and hundreds of those stony fanatics swarming up her flanks? From two of those sharks, or maybe three? They manoeuvre with paddles, not sail, and swiftly. And they are hard as iron, they can paddle for hours.'

'That's right, Master. They'd have any of the carriers in minutes, and then sink them, maybe in the channel.' Kalve's gloomy satisfaction seemed to be complete. 'Bottle us in, depend on it, that's their mind; just as the first ships sought to. While the rest of the bastards circle around the isles and close in on us from the side – see you there, how they're setting their sails even now? Look at their numbers. We'd be overrun then, for sure.'

Olvar looked at Telqua. She understood, no doubt about that; beneath her tan the blood had fled from about her mouth. The sothran lords glanced uncertainly to Ervalien, though he was obviously the youngest; none of them had ventured to say much, save him. Olvar wondered why Kunrad had appointed this Ervalien captain of the fleet; and then the answer came with the force of a cold thrill. From his time in Ker Bryhaine he knew that the sothrans often appointed lords to command simply because they were lords, or to placate their factions in the Syndicacy. These might be no better seamen than himself. But Ervalien was Kunrad's man, and Kunrad would choose with care; a younger man, a hungry man maybe, who would not think it beneath him to learn true seamanship. Or had it already, through some chance of birth and training, and the proven power of command. There was a steely cast of thought about him now, as he stared out beneath a shading hand at the advancing menace, that reminded Olvar of his old master in his most fell mood.

'Our orders are to rescue these poor folk,' he said at last, with a courteous nod to Telqua. 'This lady and Master Olvar have shown us what will become of them if we do not. And so has the Ice, by taking such great pains to prevent us. We cannot with honour abandon the attempt, and I think it unwise we should. What image of us would we leave in the minds of these Ice-slaves, if we turned and fled? In the minds of the Ice itself?'

Olvar could see the stiffening effect that had on the sea-lords. Honour would drive them where their care for a few dark-skinned outsiders might not, and the unwillingness to flee before the face of their ancient foe.

'The Ice had no such hordes as these when Morvan fell,' said one of the older lords doubtfully.

'Which is why it endured so long,' drawled Adryel Kerkarron, captain of *Vayde's Javelin*, the other great warship. 'And why, no doubt, the Ice Powers have been gathering them, and other renegades, as with those dreadful corsairs these last few years.' He bowed elegantly to Olvar, acknowledging his part in their suppression. 'The Ice learns to pit man against man, where its own arm cannot yet reach. I' faith, what would please them better?'

Lord Kerkarron was the kind of caricatured sothran fop Olvar detested at sight, the sort he was afraid Gille might imitate; but he was beginning to see a mind beneath the exquisite manners.

'If that's so,' said another of the wavering lords, picking up the thought Kerkarron had trailed before him, 'then we cannot back off from this encounter, can we? Neither for honour – nor for the safety of our land.'

'If we do turn tail, who knows?' spat one of the captains of the smaller warships. 'We'd be shouting weakness. We could have 'em on our necks in a year. Not just in the North or the Marchlands, but in Ker Bryhaine itself.'

Even the less eager lords bridled at that. 'They'd never dare!' barked the oldest, blowing out his whiskered cheeks. 'But still, we have little choice, have we?'

'Indeed,' said Kerkarron languidly, his pinched cheeks flaming suddenly red. 'We must teach them to fear us.'

Ervalien raked back the red curls that blew around his hard-boned face. 'Then we are agreed. Let the lesser ships land, with some that may speak with the fugitives, and start taking them aboard. They at least may run and escape while they still can. All the warships and the largest carriers will sail out meanwhile, and engage that vanguard. *Sea Eagle* will lead, in line formation across the bay-mouth. Stay close, and heed my signals; we may be able to defend one another's flanks. Need we say more? Then back to your ships, my lords and captains. Master Olvar! I thank you for your hospitality, and I regret we must part so soon.'

Olvar considered. 'I thank you also – but must we? You'll need every ship that can fight out there.'

Ervalien's green eyes narrowed. 'I know you have fought them already, bravely; but yours is still only a merchantman.'

'Lighter and swifter than your great sea-beasts, my lord; and it has a ram of Nordeney steel. My heart tells me that we'll have to fight wherever we are. And if we must, it had better be well clear of the rescue.'

'Yes. If even one of these shark-ships you describe breaks through, it could wreak terrible havoc.' Ervalien wound a curl around one finger, evidently weighing the odds once more. 'Very well then! But it is your charge to stay clear of the larger vessels. And if the tide of battle goes against us, it is my command, as far as I can command you, that you break away and take charge of the rescue. See that at least some rescue ships escape in time, together or scattered as the situation demands. Somebody must, and I would feel happier if it were you. I will command the other captains accordingly.'

Olvar, rather to his own surprise, bowed deeply. 'Good of you to entrust sothran ships to a Nordeney man, lord. It won't be forgotten.'

Ervalien smiled thinly. 'It may, with all else of us. But I hope for better, as one always must.' He stared out to sea. 'Though in this clear weather, with naught but a light breeze in our favour, and their sheer numbers, I confess to you I have no great hopes. Heavier weather might tell against their ships, but they seem to be brave seamen in their fashion.'

'Brave, aye, as mad dogs are brave!' muttered Kalve, nursing his arm. 'Glad they stuck me and not bit me!'

'Indeed. And if we are to gain the bay's mouth in time, we must move. Since you insist on coming, you will lead us, Master Olvar, and mark the channel. And sailing master, have an eye to our greater draught, if you please!'

As Ervalien went down into his boat, Olvar ordered their own made ready. 'For you!' he said gruffly to Telqua.

She stared at him haughtily. 'Am I a coward or weakling, to be packed off in shame?'

'No,' he said, fighting his crowded mind for the right words. 'You know I don't believe that. Everyone aboard has seen you fight, better than any. But you should be with your folk.'

'I am with my folk!' said Telqua emphatically. 'We are one, yours and mine. What you have done for us proves it. I fight for them here with you. My ancestors – ours – would reject me if I left you now!'

Olvar nodded. His people no longer made a cult of their ancestors, but the echoes of it, in word and implication, ran through the very tongue they shared. In his mind also the long shadows of his race reached back through time. The truth they shared was so strong that for once he had no difficulty; it flowed into his words.

'*We* are ancestors,' he said, clenching her long fingers firmly in his own. 'It's given to us to look after those to come. If your folk – ours – are to have any chance at all, we have to get as many of them on board and away as swiftly as possible, while the fight still goes on. You said yourself that they'll follow you. They won't hesitate, or squabble over who goes first or last. Who else shall we send? An ordinary sailor-lad who can string a phrase or two together, less even than I? Even assuming they believe him, how can he command the boarding? You shall have a couple such with you, to help you speak to the sothrans; but to your own folk, only you can speak.'

She looked down at the deck, and her small

breast rose and fell more deeply; but when she looked up, her face was calm and composed, her manner stern. 'Very well,' she answered, as if conferring a favour. 'I will go. I know the men who speak my tongue best, I shall choose them. And I shall take the bow you gave me.' He saw not a flicker of feeling in that smooth countenance, and wondered if she had bade farewell to her father thus. 'Tell the crew for me that I thank them for all they have ventured for us. *Orrin* shall return safely, or live on in our songs. And yourself with her.'

'Don't forget Gille,' he smiled. 'He'd like that.'

'I will not forget anyone,' she said. She bowed her head over his hands. He was startled at the touch of hot tears. They stopped as suddenly, dammed by a stubborn pride.

'So, then!' she said. 'But you have named us ancestors. Together.'

'I meant it.' Olvar grinned. 'We may yet come through all this. And then I mean to have children, chieftain's daughter, and by none other than you.'

She gave a harsh little laugh. 'We shall see, man. But I will make him who would father children upon me sweat and slave for them.'

'I will feed them. As many as there are.'

She looked up at him beneath heavy eyelids. 'In the making of them. But feed them he shall. They shall eat before he does, the fat off the bowl, and he shall grow lean and lithe!'

The little boat bobbed away, bouncing over the *Javelin's* wash as it took station behind *Sea Eagle*, and one of the lesser warships hid it swiftly from view.

The sothran trumpets were signalling from ship to ship, and Kalve was growing hoarse trying to match them with a speaking-tube. But there was little enough need for orders now, as the line moved into the narrow strait; they had only to follow, to keep clear of reef and bar. Olvar scowled up at the fire-mountain, and at the plume that drifted banner-like into the blue. The chase seemed so remote now, and so much might have gone differently had they only managed to ground their pursuer on that first tack, and stay clear of that ill-omened cloud. A day earlier coming on the rescuers, and they might have been aboard and away before the black fleet hove in sight; half a day, even. But that was all past now, and the sea opened before them, a fire-stripped forest.

Even now, while the enemy were still easily a thousand strides'-length beyond the bay, he could hear the pulse of their time-drums. Feel it, almost, through the clear air, setting his own heart fluttering. Olvar told himself firmly it was excitement, not fear. But surely not even the hardest paddlers could keep such a pace; and looking more keenly, he saw the figures that cavorted on the bow platforms of many boats, masked and costumed with savage richness. War-luck, weapon-luck in their leaping and posturing, mimicking the beasts and birds they represented, flooding the hearts and souls of those grim warriors with the totem-spirits of their clan.

Yet in some wise they warred against themselves, though they knew it not; for in Olvar, and in all those who had heard tell of the crater, they brought that grim vision to sudden life. Anger woke in them, hatred and contempt, and a bitter determination not to bow down or be taken living by the evil that pranced and capered before them. When a moment later, at Ervalien's behest, the trumpets of the fleet split the air, the cheer that answered was scarcely less savage, the fell cry of cornered beasts who yet had claws.

Out of the mouth of the channel swept the fleet, and, coming about on the freer wind within the bay, they peeled away smoothly past the *Orrin* on either flank to form a wide shallow crescent, denying all passage to the straits. In the centre loomed the two massive warships; at either arm the next largest, and between them the lighter craft, the least of which was far greater than *Orrin*. 'But we've one small advantage,' grunted Kalve. 'Those buggers don't know we're squattin' here behind.'

Olvar put a hand to the sailing master's brow. 'No fever. I was worried. That sounded a whit encouraging!'

Kalve's answer was cut off by a sharp dull thud. Something arced high above the *Sea Eagle*'s deck, trailing a cloud of yellow smoke, and plummeted downward. There was a distant crash, and a howl of triumph from the warship's deck.

'Yon big sothran war engines,' said Kalve. 'A catapult or some such, with fire-stuff and stones. When they draw closer, they'll use bolts, that you can aim better.'

'Not doing too bad now!' put in the helmsman happily, as another crash sounded along the line, and more cheers.

'It means the sea's so full of the bastards you can hardly miss,' said Kalve; and then a different kind of shout went up. A lean low hull ran alongside the *Eagle*, bouncing wildly in her wash, and closed in to board.

'Shouldn't we— began Olvar, but Kalve held him back.

'Wait! Yon maneating laddies will have a longer climb than they did with us.'

Indeed, many grapnels were not reaching the *Eagle*'s rail, falling back on the heads of their throwers. Some stuck, and warriors were already swarming up; but then Kalve released Olvar's arm and hissed, 'Watch!'

With a ponderous grace, languid as its commander, the *Javelin* was standing in towards the

Eagle, the wide tumble-homes of their flanks much of a height above the water. The warriors on the lines saw first, and some let go at once, to drop into the boiling sea; but others climbed more frantically, or clung helplessly to face the most immediate doom. The great ships boomed together, flank to flank, and the raider simply vanished beneath them in one splintering, grinding crash. The impact flung warriors from their ropes; but some were caught. Olvar winced; and then pointed. Another shark was sliding through the gap the *Javelin* had opened; but a flaming bolt shot from the *Sunfish*, next in line, smashed down through its hull. The paddlers lost their rhythm, it rolled in the wash and spilled them out. Another streaked towards the gap, and another; but the *Javelin* was already closing it.

'They don't seem to care!' Olvar muttered.

'I'd say these are but sacrifices, skipper. As soon as the big ships are hard enough beset, others will start slipping through.'

So it was; for no crushing or sinking seemed to deter the onslaught of the black vanguard, not even when *Sea Eagle* caught one raider with a bolt and line, like a harpoon, hoisted it dangling from the water, and dropped it, with men still clinging, flat on top of the next assailant. Another went scudding through the confusion, came hard about under *Eagle*'s stern with a speed she could not counter, and fired a hail of arrows and grapnels over her richly carved transom. So intent were the raiders on this greatest prize, though, that they failed to see *Orrin*, racing up before the freshening wind. Kalve had to take care not to strike *Eagle*'s rudder; but he still ran the ram right into the raider's high black stern, and cut it clean away, so closely that some of the climbing men plummeted down on to the *Orrin*'s deck.

'Daylights up!' roared the helmsman. 'It's rainin'

crazies! All rotten ripe windfalls – should've plucked 'em sooner!'

Alive or dead, they were tossed overboard, and *Orrin* came about to seek another foe. 'Not so ill for a mere merchantman!' said Olvar.

But from then on there was little enough of triumph; for though they sank two more raiders, rescuing one lesser warship that was all but in irons, the sight that faced them all along the line was terrible. No ship but had at least one raider grappled tight against it. No deck but there was fighting on it; in the rigging, even, as the boarders strove to climb and cripple, hacking at halyards, severing the very sheets and sail-lashings, or carrying fire to hurl down into open hatches. Smoke billowed from two ships already, and those who ran to quench it risked arrows in their backs, or had to drop their buckets and fight. The line still held, and from *Sea Eagle* and *Javelin* bolus and bolt rained down into the churning confusion; but clearly it could not last.

'You heard Ervalien's command,' prompted Kalve. 'More than one may make the next breach. Then we'll be beset ourselves, or lose the strait.'

Olvar squinted through the smoke. 'You're right. That one, the *Jay*, if they've wrecked her rudder, she'll be done in no time. Just a moment more – damn this smoke, it's ruining the light!'

'Not the smoke!' exclaimed Kalve, staring. 'What in Hella's name—'

He had no need to finish. All could see. Above the islands the fire-mountain's plumes were whipping and curling crazily. For a moment Olvar's heart sickened at the thought of more dark shamanry at work. But clearly this was something far more fell; for the brown-grey wall that arose over the sharp green summits reduced mere earthly smokes and steams to wisps of seed-silk. The gust it rode sang crazy songs in the halyards, and blew a sharper scent in their faces.

'Where'd that come from?' roared the sailing master, as *Orrin* rocked in a sudden trough. Swell struck her flanks, spray spattered in Olvar's face.

'A squall!' he shouted. 'Ready about there! Ready, leap to it!'

The wind veered sharply, sucked in every vessel's sail till the rigging protested, then blew it out with a seam-splitting boom. Kalve swore horribly as he and the helmsman struggled to turn the helm aside, as the *Orrin* was driven down against the sterns of the line, all rolling and corkscrewing wildly in the suddenly inconstant waves.

'A squall? A *squall*? Skipper, the skies were clear not twenty minutes since! What's brought this upon us, save the breath of Hella? More evil off the Ice?'

'They're not sparing their servants, if so!' panted Olvar, all his weight on the tiller beside them. A black ship was being lifted and dashed repeatedly against *Sunfish*'s rocking flank, smashing the timbers and spilling out the remaining crew. 'We're handier for heavy weather, remember? This may be our luck, not theirs!'

'*Luck?*' screamed the sailing master. He had to, over the wailing wind. 'Master, a blow that rises so damned sudden has little of luck behind it! Wherever it's sprung from, something fearful spawned it! This could make flotsam of us all!'

Shadows passed over the rocky bowl, like clouds across the sun. Gille looked up in fear and wonder at the shapes that circled in slow descent, while the throb and moan grew louder, shaking the little vault of air, rising and falling by laws and scales of its own. Not one voice, but many, a pulsing harmony that swelled and separated to become a much greater music, tones that held his ear with the elusive promise of vast words, of meaning momentous and unhurried as the sea itself. Rising and falling with great beats of their winglike flukes, the creatures spiralled down towards the fragile bubble of air, and the two who stood there. Over one end of the dome they passed, and it was as if the water turned to hammered glass, a shivering pattern of ripples in motion so constant and so regular it seemed almost solid.

Then the ripples changed again, split, formed more complex patterns and split once more. With an eerie suddenness the smooth surface bulged fiercely outward, as if some shape were flung against it from behind. Yet nothing made that outline; the water stood as transparent as before. Dents deepened within, like thumbmarks in clay, defining features fluid, half formed like a primitive image, smooth eyelids closed, lipless mouth gaping blankly in the cry of a newborn. That hypnotic moan did not seem to come from them; it grew louder, but from every side.

Slowly, like the ghost of one drowned, the face sank back, bubbled, dissolved in ripples that coursed across that vertical wall as if it were the face of a pond. Then, as fiercely as before, another outline burst through them – a shape, human, this time complete. Its glossy surface shimmered like a soap-bubble, then shivered and grew dull, grey as a windblown river. Waterfalls poured off it in ragged sheets, pooled about it this way and that. Its feet already touched the rock; its head, still streaming foaming rivulets of water about the shoulders, touched the upper margin of the dome. The air grew strong with the smell of salt and weed, the sea-cry boomed and moaned, and the great shadows beyond the barrier swirled back and forth in the green light, swelling to vastness and diminishing in an instant.

The falls about the head, as if they froze, grew greyer still and ever more solid, till steel-dark curls and beard spilled in an immense mane about the bare shoulders. Below, the streams swirled closer about the colossal frame, bearing fronds of glistening green weed, as the grey surface took on the shadows of muscle and skin, until it stood a vast stone image, blind and staring, wrapped in a flowing robe shaped of darkly iridescent glass. For a long moment it rested there, an awesome solidity, while the droplets scattered about it like gems outflung, and the rock ran dark beneath. Then with titanic ease the limbs stirred, the head bowed, and the figure stooped and settled down upon the rock shelves, leaning back against the tall wall beyond. Only then did Gille's sight take in what those shelves were, a crude, almost accidental shape in themselves, yet in their totality a token of sweeping, careless power: a gigantic throne of sea-worn rock. As the trickling falls streamed about it, the stony surfaces lost their dullness and sparkled with flecks of colour, gold, green, ruddy, blue, flashes of rainbow light in the shimmering green shade.

The head lifted, and quite suddenly the grey skin flushed as white as ivory, shadowed with touches of green. Just as suddenly, although the features did not change, life shot through the face like sunlight streaming through water. The rushing beard fell away below the great jaw only, baring a face uncommonly firm and fair in its fashioning, lofty in the brow, straight in nose and jaw, tinged with no blemish of youth or age, but only commanding lines of maturity and strength across the brow and about the deep mouth. Gille called it a regal countenance; but he came of a land that put no trust in kings.

Then the blank eyelids lifted, and he looked into the abyss. Storm-dark and swirling, they seemed to open on infinity; but for a moment only. Then they were eyes much like a man's, save that the pupils were long slots in what might have been green glass; and that against them a taller man than Gille might have stood. The look in them was terrible, and upon him it played an instant. He sank to his knees, shaking, and felt no shame in doing so.

The figure stretched out an arm, its dark robe shimmering with the pearls that trimmed it, plunging half the amphitheatre into shadow. From the arc of the roof a narrow shaft of water spurted down to strike the stone with a force that flung droplets into Gille's face. It stopped at once; and the hand held a staff of glass, headed with dark weed fronds. It struck, and the stone rang. Gille struggled not to whimper. Around the margins of the air the shapes were clustering closer, like sinister outlines circling a campfire's light. The cries tailed away to silence, yet the rock still trembled beneath his knees. Then, to either side of the rock-chair, the water-wall bulged and ran with inward-thrusting outlines.

All were huge, all greater than men, yet none even half so great as the enthroned figure. Some were the shapings of evil dreams, minglings of limb and fin, skin and scale, that ran and re-formed even as they grew solid, as if their forms were only matters of the moment, of convenience, or even wholly random. Yet side by side with gaping apparitions, men and women took shape, great and graceful, some in forms of races he knew, others he had never seen. Even among them, though, some had skin that glistened with green scale or brown slime, or glinted dull grey and white about the belly, or eyes that bulged too large for their faces, with slotted pupils that fastened coldly upon him. A few wore the heads of seabirds, or the wings. The air bore him faint fishmarket stinks that might have made him smile, elsewhere; but laughter here was beyond thought.

A mirror of madness it might have seemed to many. To his own surprise, though, Gille was not wholly daunted, for wonder drove out fear before it, and hope surprised him. This was a world not of sense but of song, and he felt more at home in it than most, and knew it. He had been made a speaker for his kind; well, the role fitted him better than many he had been thrust into, the shadow of a shipmaster, a weak warrior, a mediocre smith. But words, now; he could give those his best.

He felt that gaze settle upon him once more, as one might a stinging gust of icy spray; but he raised his eyes to meet it. It overlooked him utterly, fastened upon Saithana. Her long fingers settled lightly on his shoulder. There was silence; even the cry had died, yet that tiny islet of air seemed alive with meaning.

Saithana spoke, softly. 'He asks how you differ from your kind, that I have dared to bring you here. He asks if you know who He is. At least He asks! Speak to Him!'

Gille's throat felt crusted with salt; but the breath he drew tasted suddenly very sweet to him. 'I know. The Powers are mighty, their lords great among them. I know of none greater than the Ocean-Lord, Master of the Encircling Deep, whom men call Niarad Sea-King. And even that name I would not have spoken, did you not command me.'

The girl's fingers stiffened on his shoulder. 'Lord and father, I see you wear the shape of his kind; you speak in his fashion. You mean, I see, to ask him yourself; so why not now?'

The tremors in the stone grew swifter and lighter, as if it were a string tuned sharply tighter, and suddenly it was a sound rumbling in his ears. The lips did not move, but words beat heavily upon his hearing.

'*Man.* Denizen of Light and Air. Bastard child of base earth. Do you know where you are?'

'Lord,' said Gille, 'I am brought before what men would call your court, I think.'

The Sea-King tilted his massive head, as if considering. 'The word will serve,' said the voice, vast and bleak. 'Consider this my court, indeed; and these, obedient to my will, my courtiers. No nearer could you come, in human terms. Why are you here, where you are scarcely welcome?'

'Lord, on behalf of the Lady your daughter, who has shown herself our friend in great need. We thank and revere her for that, as we revere you.'

This time the pale lips parted, the words came higher and clearer, like wind over a bay. 'So. She who is sprung of me is ever of the surface, the body of her mother the Air-daughter that presses forever against mine, yet may not hold me back. It is in her to favour men; but not in me.' The glassy staff made a sweeping gesture, and the court in their half-formed shapes shook and bowed. Some, the least ready, half melted back into the wall.

The voice grew more fluent as it spoke, yet still with the timbre of the winds, breathy and soft as a whisper, wholly expressionless, limitlessly vast. 'This was our world before men intruded themselves upon it, to shape and steer as our several natures bade us, and make a home for Life to burgeon in. I am not as the Ice-lords, despising all that grows and is glad, seeking the lifeless perfection of the Unliving. In my oceans life was cradled. In my realm, as I nurtured and sheltered it, the first shred of substance that could make itself anew grew strong, and grew to its first great fullness, and blossomed into infinite richness.'

The creatures who flanked the stone chair waved and bobbed like weed in the current, and a sound arose from them above his own, as the hiss of foam on pebbles follows the tumbling surf-roar. 'And it is into this treasurehouse primeval that the worm called man intrudes, hungry to reshape these wonders to his own callow will, as he lays waste the land and all realms else he touches. Tearing down the ancient balances, gnawing and fouling as rats do in your holds of grain, staining the waves he sails with his own blood. Born of life, he rapes his parent, takes all, gives nothing, shapes nothing save shoddy toys to serve himself. Very well, then; let him try, and take what consequence he finds. I will neither help nor shelter him; and in my depths he perishes.'

Again the hiss of the surf, with a hungry edge to it. The soft thunder grew muted. 'I bear you no special ill will, creature of your realm; but that must be your destiny now, when my countenance is withdrawn.'

'Yet,' said Gille quickly, fighting the sheer immensity of the sound, 'your greatness and your court have not come so far, and in such guise, simply to drown me like a trapped rat. Will you not hear me first?'

He could not read the vast features. No living human face ever showed so little expression, no voice so little change of tone. 'I came to see what my daughter wished of me. This time she promised me some new thing. I do not see it. Nor can any hearing serve you yourself, for favours, boons or stays of natural consequence I may not grant. The way of the world must take its course, the balance swing without mercy or cruelty.'

Gille's mind caught flame. 'Lord, if that were so I would have less complaint! The Powers of Ice tamper with that balance, they cast cold Ice into the scale against us. They claim to loathe life, to despise our kind; yet they make use of us, enslave us, breed us to destroy one another. Lord of the Oceans, all I ask of you now is to undo one small part of that merciless cruelty. To restore the free balance!'

Gille stared up into that vast face, trying to suppress the urge to shake his fist and scream at its unyielding calm. Its lack of expression was beginning to seem not merely statuesque and blank but actively horrible, filling him not only with awe but with fear and revulsion of the actively inhuman. The voice blew around him like the clifftop breezes, cutting, indifferent.

'Man, even if all you said were true, why should we confront those ancient Powers, older by far than we ourselves and strong still? Why should we venture so, in a matter that does not concern our realm? We owe you nothing, we can ask nothing of you. Nothing you make, and nothing you are worth.'

'Lord,' said Gille slowly. He flashed a sudden look at Saithana, and caught her pale and tense of face, lips pursed; and yet was that truly an expression, or merely one copied? She was a hundred times more human, this creature, than the towering monster she called her father; yet she was tinged with the same remoteness of feeling. She would rather the refugees lived. She would rather Gille lived. If not, she would mourn, sincerely; but there were years to pass, ages, aeons. There would be others. 'Lord,' he repeated, struggling to choose his words, not to let them bubble over his tongue in the heat within. 'Lord, you - have perhaps been misinformed. We do create, within our lesser compass - many things, and with some lasting value. I myself am a mastersmith—'

'I know of that art. It is not yours. It was the gift of a great Power, to enhance your survival in the face of the Ice. Yet that too you misuse, to no lasting end.'

'Do we, Lord?' Gille unslung the kantel, shaking the water from it; but it was already dry, and lacquer and silver alike shone new even yet. He held it up in both hands. 'Then what of this? Made not by me, but by the greatest of our smiths many lifetimes since, a time even the seas must notice. Yet it endures, is fair, and makes a powerful music still.'

And, greatly daring, he struck a soft flowing chord, string after string, a chord of a tone that he always felt sang of mystery and power. It chimed lightly among the rocks, and the creatures of the court rustled and squeaked among themselves.

'Music...' said the voice, and for a moment there was a strangeness in it, something that belonged more to Gille's world than its own. 'I have heard ... sailors on your ships. The sounds they made with their voices, and with such devices as this, perhaps; they moved oddly, stamped their feet. Disturbing the deep, through the thin hulls with which you think to bar me. I have never cared to know more of it. Save once, perhaps...'

The head bowed over him. Gille, plunged into shadow, hoped his gulp and start had not been too obvious, knew they had.

'Once...' mused the voice. 'How old did you call this device of wires and wood, mastersmith among men?'

'Two hundred years at least. Maybe three. He who made it lived longer than any man I know of.'

'You made a sound with it. Make another.'

Saithana's breath hissed softly in Gille's ear, wordless, encouraging. He struck a chord, and another in the sequence, with a flourish of the fingers. The acoustic in this strange place was good, at least. The kantel had never sounded better, resonant and larger than life, almost.

'Three hundred years...' breathed the voice. 'Yes, it could be... A man, one man in a little ship, little more than a shell, its sails ragged with the claws of tempests. Naught I would pay heed to; save that it set a faint burning upon me, almost as when one Power comes up against another. One man, standing, with a black sword girt about him on a belt of gold, who leaned upon the tiller and struck a thing of wires, and sang. Sang to me ... and I listened, and forgot my waves and weather, and let him pass. Some Power was in him or about him, or I would have looked at him closer, seen what lay beneath his guise. Save for that singing...'

'Vayde,' said Gille, stunned. 'That was Vayde as the *Vaydagest* has him, on his great voyage from Kerys to Morvannec, alone.

> *The barque that bore him onwards,*
> *He steered with idle hand,*
> *He set his course with music*
> *From ancient land to land.*
> *A long black sword beside him,*
> *He leaned upon the helm,*
> *Stood, singing to the ocean*
> *The songs that overwhelm.*
> *The chants of steady breezes,*
> *The words that calm and quell...*

'Lord, this very instrument indeed you heard. In greater hands than mine; but its music is still mine to awaken.'

One or two of the court creatures, with the bodies and faces of women almost as fair as Saithana, spread the wings that served them for arms, sprang aloft and wheeled about the dome of air, filling it with their cries.

'There!' soughed the voice. 'Is that not music? Is

there skill in that? Can man match it? Can even that clever little device?'

'There is music in that, Lord Niarad, as there is in so much of nature,' said Gille, very carefully. 'The sounds in the cries of birds, the drumbeats of thunder, the patter of rain; rhythms in the wash of waves, the ebb and flow of tides, the pulse of hearts. Of all these things men surely compounded music. Yet the art of music is deeper, for they sound only of themselves, without shape or direction. To the bird, its cry speaks only of itself; but to work its cry into a tune, with the wash of water on the shore, and the shiver of reedbeds, is to speak of vast spaces, grey heavens, solitude.'

'Why should a man work such a ... tune? Of such things men can take no delight in?'

'They may give us less pleasure in themselves, Lord. Yet in a song they can. That is part of its power.' And he strummed a few lines, and let his voice pick up the quietly lilting melody.

So lonely are your shores,
Yet still for them I yearn;
So sadly in the night winds
Hangs the cry of the tern.

In the night alone and lost
It calls against the cold,
Searching through the reed-beds
Nestless, weary, old.

I've watched your stone-grey waters
Through eyes that filled with tears.
I shed them first on your shores,
And mourn the passing years.

In me the sight is carven,
I long to go back there.

Through the long nights I listen
For the tern in the lonely air.

The last echo of the strings faded away eerily in the dome, into absolute silence. Gille licked his lips with a certain complacency. He had sung a lot worse than that, in his time; in fact, he had never sung better. Something about the renewed tone of the kantel, maybe; he seemed to feel his own voice resonate through the strings, as if they acknowledged their maker. And he had made his impression, that was obvious. The quiet was as good as thunderous applause.

What broke it, after a moment, was the creatures of the court in rustling converse, peering with their strange eyes down at Gille. Some of them came forward, striding, shuffling, slithering. One who would have seemed the image of a man, were it not for the sleek dark fur that covered his frame, gave a barking laugh and casually cuffed a clawed finger at Gille. Instantly Saithana was before him, hand raised. Her jewels flashed, and the seal-man stepped hastily back. The courtiers laughed, a weird sound of barks and squeals and guttural bubbling. The great voice cut through it with the crash of a cresting wave.

'*Enough!* Man, this sound you make, this *song.*' The word boomed out on a rising pitch. 'It is not without some worth. It captures the run of waves on a shore, indeed. Yet it is a very mortal thing, then, this music, full of your sadness of loss and decay. Small wonder it does not interest the Powers, who see instead growth and renewal and return, and rejoice in it.'

Gille bowed. 'I am glad the music did not displease you, Lord. Clearly you understood its mood well. Yet that is only one of the many feelings it can create. Music is just as good for rough merrymaking, as you have heard; or finer rejoicing, or praise. We praise our great men and our heroes in music both while they are alive and in songs that endure long after they are gone.'

'Indeed?' The great figure of Niarad tilted its head once more, almost the only human gesture it showed. 'And do you praise the Powers?'

That was the question Gille wanted; but it still made him perspire. He weighed every word twice before he spoke it. 'There are songs about many of them, Lord. I know of most, perhaps, concerning the one we call Raven Man's-Friend, ballads, epics, praise of the Sun that he stole and restored to us. And in my Guild we have songs of homage to our revered patron Ilmarinen the Fire-Lord, Master of Mastersmiths. And of course there are many among seafarers in praise of the Lady Saithana, her beauty, grace and kindness.' He did not want to add what terms some of them were couched in; not, he suspected, that that would bother the lady herself.

The great head tilted sharply. 'And of the Sea-Lord?'

Gille glanced at Saithana, and ducked his head. This was his chance. 'As you say yourself, my lord, you have little to do with men. Chiefly it is awe of your might, and fearful reverence, that passes human tongue concerning you.'

The laughter was unexpected, and horribly cold.

'That, thrall of the Air, is barely true! Do you think I have not heard what men say of me, when the slightest commotion of the surface sends their ships sprawling and their stomachs rising? When their own folly leads them into storm or reef, and sends their feeble masts crashing about their ears, their hulls polluting the deep? Man, do not lie!'

The booming laughter shivered the water of the dome. The great shadows that rose and fell continually beyond it swept high against the light, so that Gille saw at last something of what they were. And for all his peril wonder held him.

Legion they were, great and small in vast numbers, fish of all shapes and kinds, far more than he knew or even recognised. Hanging almost suspended in the water, barely flicking their fins, ignoring one another, predator and prey alike; shark, skate, salmon, a million forms he could not name, around the dome they circled in one wide halo. Beyond them, circling more slowly, moved shapes less solid, shoals of tiny creatures in constant motion, great idling clouds of translucency clearly visible only when the sunlight angled off their milky forms and trailing tendrils. But closest of all, swooping in to brush the very base of the dome itself, were creatures he had seen and knew, yet still could hardly believe.

Great whales. He had seen their kind at sea, blunt-headed and bulky yet strangely serpentine in their swimming. In constant motion they flowed about the dome, in their hundreds perhaps, soaring to the distant surface and back, drifting and twisting about the margins of the glassy wall. Long jaws snapping, they twisted and frolicked to the booming thunder of the voice, as if they were the dolphins their cousins, responding far more to the life in that titanic laughter than the statuesque figure of Niarad.

Gille could see the great chest heave, but somehow it seemed to answer that chilly merriment, rather than originate it. It gave form to an eerie feeling that had grown upon him, that this awesome creature that spoke and laughed before him in the Sea-Lord's name was not Niarad himself, but only some part of him, too small, monstrous as it was, to contain the whole. Some segment; some facet, given human shape, yet moved and manipulated like a puppet, to create some point of contact with the

tiny human before him. That in itself Gille could
understand, even be thankful for; but it led him to
another thought he did not want.

He looked to Saithana again. It must be true of
her also. This was not her, not the whole person,
this shape she set before him for his benefit. She
was simply a more practised puppeteer.

Small wonder she had seemed like his ideal
woman. There must be so many elements of her
being to pick and choose from, to shape this
particular creature. He had heard of great fish, that
to lure the lesser dangled a smaller shape before
them, as it might be a tempting worm. So this must
be, that had captured his heart – as slight a reflection
of whatever lay behind her as that worm, or as the
tentacle-tips that had touched him on the raft were
of the fearful beast beneath. Less malevolent, surely,
but scarcely more human; too great for him still, too
far beyond his reach. As well love a shadow, he
thought, traced large upon a wall, as long for her.
Desire did not die in him, not altogether; but a great
sadness grew.

Then the laughter died, and he must not wait
to speak. 'Lord, all you say is true, no doubt. We are
mortal; what can we do but curse what pains us
without pity? Yet there is more you have not seen,
or heard. There are songs that speak of the beauty
and power of the Sea, songs to which men dance
and revel. In your name!'

'Then put your supple tongue to better use.
Prove what you say, ere the Ocean fall in upon you!
Play me one, now, this instant! Play, and sing!'

Gille struck a great rippling chord, which gave
him time to draw breath. He knew what he had to
sing, but the thought of it unnerved him; if it was
taken badly ... Only the clear tone of the kantel lent
him the strength he needed. '*Vayde!*' he muttered. 'If
your power in this thing's more than a memory,

lend it to a fellow mastersmith now!'

Saithana heard; but the look that flashed across her keen features he could not make out. Was it dismay, or terror, or simply eagerness? He dared not wait. He launched into the melody with a will.

> *Lordly and mighty face of the Ocean,*
> *Depths of the waters, wine-dark and deep,*
> *Who shall dare measure all that you treasure?*
> *Who was your builder, fortress of glass?*
> *Who holds your rampart, encircling the earth?*
> *King of the wide seas, terrible Master!*
> *Hail to the Sea-Lord, glorious one!*
> *All hail to him and to his daughter Saithana,*
> *Hope of the helpless, saviour of men!*

It was an ancient, rolling tune, with lines that rose, crested and fell again, very like the waves. As Gille gained his wind and his confidence his fingers fairly flew across the strings, and the old kantel's tone seemed to burgeon and swell into the heavy air.

> *Sun in the heavens is mirrored in waters.*
> *Moon in the heavens reflects in the sea*
> *The stars and the planets, the dawn and the*
>   *dark clouds,*
> *Celestial light and the lowering storm.*
> *In the depths shines all that passes aloft!*
> *King of the wide Seas, terrible Master!*
> *Hail to the Sea-Lord, glorious one!*
> *Glory to him and his daughter Saithana,*
> *Hope of the helpless, saviour of men!*

The song was taking hold of him now, sweeping the rough stone out from under him, sending him twisting and turning up through the waters, frolicking, free. And not only hold of him;

the monstrous shapes of the court were swaying in time, shuffling a little from side to side even. Saithana was skipping from foot to foot, tossing her head lightly so that her jewels clinked and rippled merrily. He would have been dancing himself, if he could. His heart thrilled within him as he saw the massive fingers begin to sway faintly, in time.

He struck and stroked the strings with ever greater freedom, sporting in the sound as the porpoises had before his bows, leaping and racing. The kantel quivered under his fingers, with never the least hint of strain or weakness, and he laughed aloud. Even in this oppressive green light he could see the flash and flow of its virtues, glittering around the shimmering strings. He had striven to shield the thing from harm; but if after such rough handling it could still unleash such reserve of tone, maybe he should not have worried. Perhaps he had only woken it more fully from its centuries-old sleep. He struck a final flourish and bowed deeply with hand to heart, panting.

'There was a song!' cried Saithana, clapping her hands high, in human fashion. Astonishingly the court imitated her, wings and fins and flippers as well as hands – the most illustrious applause Gille had ever received, and the only ovation he hoped he would be able to forget. 'Lord and Father, see you now what his voice and his music are? And why I love them? Why they make me wish to dance? As a white gull he soars, as a golden fish he skips through the waves!'

The voice rumbled around them. 'Indeed, he praised the Oceans well, better than I deemed that human could. A new thing indeed. I will have more. Play on, young singer among men! Play, and let my daughter dance before me – and sing my praises further!'

Gille swallowed. He wondered if he had not

unleashed something altogether too new. There was a wilful edge to that command which reminded him of an insistent child, discovering some new delight and demanding it again and yet again. He strummed the strings, ignoring the ache in his fingers, and struggled to summon up his words. Saithana, lithe limbs outflung, spun about on the spot, so that her long hair flicked damply against his shoulder, then wheeled around him.

'Dance!' thundered Niarad, drowning out all else. 'Dance as my daughter does, my people! Dance in honour of your lord!'

The sun in the sea is the power of its master,
The moon is the ebb and the flow of his bounty,
The stars and the planets, the eyes of his
*   princess,*
The storm is his rage as his kindness, the dawn!
Beauties and wonders that dwell in his realm!

'*Beauties and wonders that dwell in his realm!*' she echoed him, her voice pure and strong, cutting through the shuffling stamp of the court. To his wonder and horror they were indeed dancing, some gracefully, some clumsily; yet not even the winged women had the grace of Saithana as she swept about the rock, and joined her voice to his.

King of the Waters, ancient Sea-Father,
Hail to the Master of Storm and of Calm!
Turn the sun to us, set the moon o'er us,
Light of the Ocean, red Dawn of the Sea!

Gille's fingers faltered, he made as if to end his verse; but the gigantic figure jerked to its feet, robes swirling like shot silk. '*No!* Do you think so little of me, child of Men? This music of yours is wine, it inflames the spirits of the very Powers itself! Play and do not falter! Play on, praise me!'

Gille gaped in horror. He had had hopes of that song, an old one whose tune was lively and bright enough to catch the fancy of someone new to music, whose words could be made fulsome enough to flatter the hearer. Like Saithana, he had hoped it would catch the Sea-Lord's fancy. But this much…

He was drenched with sweat. His hands were hurting, yet somehow he could not mistake his fingering, and if anything the power of the kantel's tone was growing. It should not have been possible, but he heard it, felt the shimmer of the sound in the enclosed air. He had run out of words, he was singing the verses over and over again, mingling lines at random. His throat was beginning to dry up – though that was as much through terror. If what he feared was true –

He had heard of the mania that went with dancing, of cults who sought to whirl themselves into ecstasy with it, so that they could commune with the Powers; of some, even, who would dance themselves to death thereby, as sacrifices. And those were human minds accustomed to music – and without this infernal instrument in their ears.

The robe swirled, brushing the rock with the rush and whisper of surf. The great feet tapped the time. He felt the same power; he could hardly keep his own still.

If that monstrosity was going to *dance*–

He had to stop. He would shift the melody to something simpler, improvise something less exciting with a jolly shouting refrain, then gradually let it wind down…

> *Glory to the Great Sea-Father!*
> *Hoi! Hoi! Hoi! Hoi!*

Lord of near and distant sea,
Every lake and stream bears tribute,
Every river feeds the Sea!
Hoi! Hoi! Hoi! Hoi!

'*Hoi! Hoi! Faster!*' thundered Niarad. 'Faster, maker of music! Faster play, and louder sing our praise! *Hoi! Hoi!*'

Gille cringed in horror as the dome above his head seemed to shatter. Water burst through it, jagged columns that struck down upon him like spears – and stayed, frozen, like the columns that descend from the stone ceilings of caves, a looming, overpowering threat.

'I cannot!' screamed Gille, as the great hand blotted out the light. Yet it was only the index finger, longer than he was tall, and its nail, clouded green as seaworn glass, that touched him, and that lightly. It felt like a bolt of lightning, coursing down every limb, every nerve with keen cold fire; and suddenly he was playing faster than ever, and the sound of the kantel was a jangling ring of plucked steel, and above it all roared the thunderous laughter of the Sea-King.

Around the ring of stone and sea the figure of the Power whirled and plunged, while his court scattered before him, back into the water or across the rock. Saithana was caught up in the rush, and vanished. And Niarad himself smashed into the water wall, vanished into it and out again, sending sheets of spray crashing through the amphitheatre, drenching Gille. He could not help himself. He played, and played, feeling his fingernails splinter, his fingertips skinned raw, and still he played, faster than ever, with the white fire driving his limbs, fastened to the spot, wholly unable to stop.

Faster still wheeled Niarad, while the sea wall quivered and shook with the impact of his passing, and his court hopped and capered in his wake. Suddenly he changed direction, whirled across the rock; and Gille screamed again. The vast foot fell directly over him, where he stood transfixed; and for a moment he thought he was crushed indeed. But though the impact was terrible, it was more as if a huge wave crashed down upon him. It passed, and left him on his knees, still screaming and coughing with the water, still playing, still transfixed.

The court swept by him; but what led them was no longer even remotely human. From glassy vault to rocky floor there stretched a whirling column of water, hissing with the force of its spin, a mighty waterspout that plucked up stones and weed as it passed, swaying with sinuous force to the demonic rhythm of the kantel, howling with insane laughter. Other vortices sprang up, as the court followed the lead of their lord. The vault roof turned from green to grey above them, and the dome sank into the sullen light of storm.

CHAPTER NINE
The Hand of the Maker

Rampart upon rampart above the islands, the stormfront surged up the sky to the zenith. The men of the *Orrin* flinched as it plunged their decks into smoky shadow. A deep shudder seemed to run through their bones, as if from the very roots of the earth. A mighty rolling crash split the air, and a flash; yet it was not lightning, not yet. High above their heads, the crater spewed a jet of yellow steam skyward, and among it, sparkling like stars, gledes of scarlet fire.

And out of nowhere, from the heart of the sea, a vast iron anvil-head of cloud came boiling and swirling, swift beyond all nature, and its followers wrapped hungry jaws about the sun. Blue flashes leaped in its belly, and behind the summits sheets of glaring lightning paled the dwindling shafts of light.

'Below there!' yelled Kalve. 'All hands, the hatches! Leap to it, lads! Batten down all, stow every bit of gear you can, tie down every tarpaulin!' He looked to Olvar, and his stubbled mouth was working.

The sun was consumed, the battle blanketed in a sudden grim twilight. The air, full of flying spray, flooded with steel-grey shadow. The fighting all but stilled, as men lost their footing on decks and holds on ropes, and fought to control their ships that flung and bucked in the swell. Raiders fell from their grapnel lines, sailors from their high mast-heads as they struggled to reef sail, to deny the snarling air its bite.

'Never seen its like!' yelled Kalve. 'Steady breeze one moment, the next the whole sea boils like my lady's washpot! And see you now!'

Into the twilight, here and there, a few red cinders, flared by the wind, came smoking and twisting. Great fat droplets splashed and spattered on the deck, startlingly cold against the skin, a few first then faster, drumming hard. The cinders fell among them, hissing like serpents, but some were not extinguished. Again the sharp concussion, and the island summits exploded smoke at the sky; but this time it was heavy, rolling, contorted columns of ash and dust, and through the heart of them the lightning came branching and blazing down.

The sea was a meadow no longer, but dark and metallic, a churning, treacherous mass of clashing crests and leaping surf, the black ships struggling as fiercely as they. They heaved and tipped, while the sothran warships rolled like bloated whales with sharks nipping at their bellies. The straits were a mass of booming surf, the channel a stream of foaming white, while in the distance the rescue ships swung this way and that at their anchors, among surf that smashed against beach and bank and rebounded into the veering wind.

'And let's hope they're anchored clear of one another!' shouted Olvar.

Kalve shrugged gloomily. A wave crashed over the bows in a thunderous spray, and the *Orrin* pitched and rolled like a child's bark boat in a stream. 'This is no common slew of sea and air!' he growled. 'Something higher takes a hand!'

The fury of the air drove across both fleets, and left no time for command or order. Both line and vanguard broke, yet neither had an eye to spare for the other. The waves battered them in the wind, and waterspouts sprang up to smash against their bows and smother them in spray. And in the bay's mouth, as the wind lashed from one slope to another, stripping the trees, and rebounded upon itself, the steely surf sank and churned into wide clashing currents, which tore at one another as they met, opening up brief but vicious whirlpools.

The *Jay*, her rudder jammed by the remains of a black ship's prow, drifted out of the line and across one such, and was whirled violently about, tipped all but over, and shot no less violently back. Halyards snapped with the shock, and her three tall masts wavered like aspens. Foremast and mainmast, under weight of sail, gave and folded, sending rig and tackle down across the deck, the sail trailing in the sea, where the whirling waters took it and worried at the hapless ship again, like a dog with a rat. She drifted, helpless prey for weather or warrior.

There was nothing *Orrin* could do to help her, or any other of the ships. The waterspouts were rising now to the skies, and upon the horizon a giant black column of water spun and swayed, dizzily. The waves were black now, heaving against a dome of grey cloud, their white crests spraying out in long plumes like the mountains above. Over every deck they burst with a meteoric clap, and the spray struck faces like a barrage of sharp pebbles, stinging, numbing, blinding. The captains could do no more now than reef what sail they could, toss out a floating sea-anchor, lash the helm, cling on and hope.

The islands offered no protection, for the forests bent and groaned, and the beaches lifted in blinding clouds that sprayed as far as the tormented ships, spattered the decks. Still the wind wailed and whirled, its force redoubled, stirring up fearful eddies and sidewinds till it caught the larger ships by their sheer size alone and hurled them together in grinding chaos, tangling rig and snapping spar. The helms flew free of their lashings, or were torn free by desperate masters. Olvar, wrestling the sea's insanity with all his stolid strength, had one fearful vision of the *Javelin* spinning like a great slow top through a clutch of black ships, smashing them from its path, but heeling horribly, its gunwales pounded by the surf. Then the black skies closed over him, and the light was lost in a slashing wall of rain, so dense he could tell the waves' way only by their whipping blows against the *Orrin's* hull.

The world was reduced to a frenzied struggle with the helm, in which he could hardly see the men who lent their strength to his. There was no way it could be lashed again, for the waves were slewing this way and that with every flaw of the biting wind, crashing over the gunwales and across the deck from one quarter and then another as the ship heeled, and swift reaction was the only defence. So great were the thunders of earth and sky that they could not hear or speak, but must go by instinct and common will alone. Storm and sea were the antagonists, and they merely caught between their blows, their fate foredoomed. In no more than a breath or so the waters would surely close over them all, and ruin be complete.

And then, no less suddenly, the world was changed.

A strong hand shook Gille's shoulder. Saithana knelt beside him, eyes wide, face aghast, panting with all too human horror. '*Gille! Stop!* The sea is all in ferment, near and far! He dances here, he dances everywhere! Storms are raging, ships are foundering, friend and foe alike and folk you have never heard of, falling into the deep! The very shores are besieged, sea walls overwhelmed, cliffs crumbling! *Stop!*'

'I ... *cannot!*' yelled Gille, over the roaring of the waterspout. 'Break the command he laid upon me!'

'*I* cannot!' she cried. 'If it were only his ... but it has awoken a greater power! Gille, *it is the kantel!* Smash it, if you cannot stop!'

'Even if I would, I could not,' Gille snarled. 'You are stronger than I.'

'Stronger?' she wailed. 'Gille, upon that thing I dare not lay a finger! There is virtue in it greater than all the Seas! It would drink me in and redouble its power! *I dare not!*'

Even through fear and pain, the marvel of her words took root. Gille laughed incredulously, even as his fingers flew against his will. 'A single small work of man greater than the infinite Seas?' He felt the frenzy within himself, and drew it together, as a dying man might his last torn lungful of air. 'Well then! If he can, let man amend it!'

> *You who shaped the source of singing,*
> *You who forged the fount of music,*
> *Master of my art and mystery*
> *What of you is left within this*
> *Wood and metal I have woken,*
> *Livened with my cunning stringing,*
> *Quickened with my play and singing,*
> *Hear me, Vayde! Hear the smith's word,*
> *Virtues set within the metal!*
> *Though I am not born so mighty,*
> *Though my hand has no such cunning,*
> *Though my art is scorned and slighted,*
> *Though my craft burns low and feeble,*
> *Still I too have song within me,*
> *And the power of making music!*
> *Mine the hand that forged your stringing,*
> *Mine that gave you back your ringing,*
> *Mine it is to call upon you,*
> *All that lingers yet within you—*
> *Loose your ancient song-enthraldom,*
> *Free the foot and free the finger,*

Break the spell of mighty music!
Vayde!
    I too am a Master!

It seemed impossible that anything so small as
the kantel could have issued that awesome sound, a
chord struck not by his fingers but his voice, and
become part of it. The wood leaped like a live thing
on his arm, the metal rang, the strings were a blur
that did not fade and die, but hummed and sang
with eerie harmonics.

The last words thundered out into silence, absolute, immediate, shocking in their completeness.

Vayde – I too am a Master!

They echoed off the stone, and Gille hardly knew
his own voice, so great and commanding it sounded,
so proud and calm; and through his lacerated
fingers, he felt the wooden soundbox shivering
with it still. 'I too am a Master!' he repeated, half
laughing, half weeping. 'D'you hear me, Lord Vayde
the Great, Master of Masters! *I too, damn you! I*
too!'

Nothing moved. The dance, the maelstrom, the
whirling shapes, everything was as motionless as
windless cloud. The dome of ocean above his head
hung arrested in its half-frozen collapse. Even the
vast figure of Niarad, human once again, stood
stock still against the cloudy wall, eyes closed, lips
parted, head tilted back, as if listening. Gille was
vaguely aware of Saithana at his side, on her knees.

Then the light changed; and the cavern filled
with what seemed the thing least possible, the
devouring roar of flame.

The air in the bowl tore like a taut sail before a
gale's blast. Gille ducked his head as wind bellowed
about him, and it was the breath of an oven, a blast

of steam. The light around him flared from pallid green shadow to roaring, rippling glare. The water falling inward above him screamed like a living thing and sprang hissing back as if spilt on some red-hot griddle, sizzling into a shower of steam that stung Gille's cringing shoulders.

Had he not been a smith, he would have been hopelessly dazzled; but his eyes had learned to bear the light of furnaces. The glare of the flame curtain that blossomed about the far end of the bowl, enshrouding the Sea-Lord's empty throne, was appalling; but, shading his eyes, he could make out, just barely, the awesome presence within it.

The form was as vastly human, perhaps, as Niarad's; but though it had no single solid shape, it seemed less carelessly sketched. Only the random flicker of flames defined it, yet it was as constantly renewed, a constancy of continual change, a fearful solidity of fluttering fire. It had a face, features, eyes; wide eyes, brilliant fire-gems that sprayed out light as those of humans drank it in, so that wherever their gaze fell the bowl and all within it flashed and coruscated.

Yet at the heart of the flame a glare still brighter struck Gille's squinting, shrivelling gaze – a light within the light, purer, whiter, more sustained. Throughout all that terrible figure it radiated like the leafless ribs of a winter tree, like the mass of veins that branch through human limbs. Its pulses played with the outer fires, beating the pace they danced to. It was a light Gille knew well. Within him also it pulsed, though dim and feeble by comparison, and through the works of his hands, as through those of every smith of true craft. And not even amid the whirl of the sea had he felt smaller and less significant.

The apparition raised one incandescent arm, and the fires leaped up about it like fawning dogs.

With the explosive thunder of a fire-mountain, echoing about that great amphitheatre, it spoke.

This man is mine!

The flames fell to a devouring hiss. Gille's ears rang in the silence, as it seemed. He stole an anxious glance at Saithana. She was beside him, still solid and human, hunched into a terrified crouch that hid her face against the rock, her head wrapped tight in her arms. Then the voice of fire roared out again, as if to a reply unheard; and at the sound her whole body shook.

Mine the art, mine the instrument he wields!
   You have no claim on him, Sea-Lord, to heal
   or harm. Nor upon his praises – not when
   you so sorely neglect your own great charge.
   Your duty you betray, and your very nature,
   to be so intent upon a mortal value and a
   human whim!

Your realm it is!
   But not to do with as you will. Against all
   others it must be balanced, against every
   least thing that makes this world a whole!
   You have tilted the balance, and laid open a
   way through which the Ice might strike. You
   have lost the innocent lives of men, and set
   many more in peril.

No, do not scorn them!
   Not when you have drunk in their flatteries
   and danced to their tune!
   Not when one day you and yours must
   become as they are, or slowly fade to nothing

Still Gille heard no response but the faint trickle

and flow of water, and the soft hissing of the fires that nothing fed.

> *You need neither the praise nor the hatred of*
> *men, Sea-King. Nor such sport as they*
> *provide.*
> *I end it!*

Olvar gaped. The *Orrin*'s helm was still beneath his hand, but it fought him no longer, save with the easy life of a ship hove to. He looked out over a sea of light and calm, without even the brisk breeze that had preceded the storm, and over the amazed faces of his crew. Kalve's dour jowls sagged with a child's wonder, while the helmsman blinked about like a baby, unable to take in so drastic a shift in his senses. A young seaman raised his hands to the skies in awe, and shaped strange words silently.

The rumbling of the earth was stilled as if it had never been, and from the mountaintops the calm white banners trailed in the breeze, as before. Only the glow and smoke of fires among the dense trees bore witness to what had passed. The clouds, blown ragged, were melting away even as they looked. Between them the sun shone down in the great beams men called messengers, playing and shifting across the surface of a falling sea, turning it from lead to silver. They picked out the rolling hulls of the sothran fleet around him, sorely changed from their pride and pomp of the morning. Like lost sheep the line huddled together across the bay, stricken, stunned and stupid.

In the water around them a few dazed heads bobbed still, men of both fleets wallowing in a sea they could hardly believe had not devoured them. They struggled reflexively, or trod water helplessly, too amazed even to seek rescue or strike out for the shore or the surrounding ships. These were in little better case. Spars were torn away, masts snapped, sails hung in rags. Here and there men, losing their thrall of shock, ran to extinguish the few fires that still smouldered, or to man pumps and bail frantically as sprung planks and stove-in timbers took effect, and cut loose encumbering debris. The *Javelin* was listing to port, pulled down by the wreckage of her mainmast; a few men hacked awkwardly at the ruin with axe and sword. The *Jay* lay aslant and aground upon a long sandbar, dismasted but whole, among black lines of wreckage bobbing about her. The *Sea Eagle* still rode proud and secure, but without her foremast, and tremendous scars upon her timbers. But so swift had been the passing of the maelstrom that, save *Jay*, all the ships were still afloat.

And all around them, in terrible masses of splintering ruin, floated the mangled hulls of their enemy. Seaworthy they were in their way, those black spearshafts, when only the sea was their foe; they moved closer to the life of wind and tide and current, and in heavy seas their hulls flexed with the waves sooner than against them. But, as Kalve had predicted, they were more vulnerable to sudden weathers than the heavier hulls of Nordeney and Bryhaine. In this narrow place, in so violent a tempest, to those same hulls they had fallen, caught and been ground among them as gemstones are polished in a mill, roughly. Not a single one of the vanguard had survived.

Olvar looked quickly back down the channel, to where the remainder of the ships must be, and Telqua. He could see masts and hulls, but how many he could not tell, nor in what state. He could only hope the extra shelter had spared them the worst of storm and fire.

The bay lay all but clear now, a mass of dark wine purple patched with clear green as the cloudshadows passed. To Olvar it might have been a vision of hope; and yet he saw beyond it only a menace more imminent, and a surer doom.

Out across the open ocean the clouds were still sinking apart, as the turmoils slackened that had sucked them in; and they showed him a truth disheartening and grim. The black vanguard had perished, the swordtip shattered; but the edged blade yet remained.

Over the black fleet of the west the storm had also passed; as a plough through an ants' nest, thought Olvar. In the confined bay it had created whirling turmoil, but in the open ocean it had blown straight across them; and here the lean and vicious lines of the black ships showed their strengths. Lower in profile, with simpler, more bendable masts and rigs, they had given the winds a lesser target, and their flexing hulls had held them closer to the waves. Colliding only with one another, their lighter frames had suffered less harm, and even gunwale-deep with water they stayed buoyant, so long as they were whole. Many had succumbed, none-theless, their hulls flooded or smashed to floating flinders by the waves, their crews and warriors scattered in the deep; yet so great was that fleet that as many yet remained, a force still greater than all the vanguard. And their crews were driven men.

So shattering a breach in nature might have daunted the bravest warrior, the more so when they had seen it lay waste their own forces. Not these. Olvar, sorely stricken himself, wondered how much more terrible their lords and masters could be, to inspire more fear than this. Even as he watched he could see them regaining command more swiftly than the sothrans, of their ships and of themselves, like scuttling ants indeed. Even on half-sunken hulks the black-clad crews were swarming about, hewing down broken masts, baling furiously with kegs and helms, reeving torn ropes, ignoring the imminent hazards of shoal and shore as they drifted nearer. Readiness for battle was all.

Already black yards swung about on surviving masts, sheets tautened, torn black square-sails bulged through their stiffening webs of cordage. On dismasted vessels the sharp-bladed sweeps extended like the limbs of insects. Their fallen fellows they ignored, and rammed aside the unready. The wind was in their favour, and even in the swath of the storm, their numbers, both in hulls and in crew.

His own men, weary with longer struggles, groaned at the sight. The ploughshare had passed. The scuttling had been to a purpose. The ants were free now to swarm out, and sting.

The *Orrin* was one of the few ships left in fighting order, the Powers knew how. The *Javelin* lay still in irons, but *Sea Eagle* was raising new canvas and gathering way, and a few others along the line. The criss-crossing signals sounded weak and ragged, as if there were fewer trumpeters, but Ervalien climbed high upon the stern, and waved to each ship. Olvar found it easy enough to understand; there was little enough choice, the Powers knew. He looked to Kalve.

'He wants us to cut across their tack. Give the rescue ships a little extra time.'

Kalve closed his salt-reddened eyes. 'Maybe ram a few of the bastards, aye. Hold 'em off this end of the isles, at least.'

'That's the spirit!' said Olvar fiercely. 'Who knows? Might even discourage them enough to quit the hunt!' He did not believe it; but a curious peace descended on him, nonetheless. The *Sea Eagle* was already making way, moving up astern, fetching across the wind as best she could towards the open sea. Black sails were converging on her as swiftly, time-drums pounding, shaggy-clad shamans even cavorting on a few bows. Others slipped like sharks indeed towards the sothrans that limped astern, enough to overwhelm them many times over, as it seemed. That still left more than enough heading for the islands, the channel and what lay beyond. The breeze was cool now, and they ran before it with the deadly grace of arrows.

'Aye,' said Olvar drily. 'Scent the hare, do you, my hunter laddies? Well, be sure there isn't a daggertooth in the road first!'

'*Hands to stations!*' yelled Kalve. '*Make sail!*' His voice cracked with weariness. The men moved to obey, but slowly, looking up at the quarterdeck.

It was the hardest thing of all, to have faced one's doom with a will, and against all hope found oneself reprieved, and then to have that doom arise before one again. It came to Olvar then how many times men must face that in war, to survive against all odds, only to face them again and perish unthanked, unsung, forgotten. At best he and his might escape that; but it was comfort too cold to give them.

'Look alive, lads!' he called with careless ease. 'Looks like we'll still send these man-eaters home with a flea in their ear!'

The cheer that went up was feeble; but at least it was a cheer. Then the *Orrin* was sliding through the bobbing wreckage on as clear a tack as Kalve could find, bouncing across the wakes of the warships, out of the bay. They would clear the west point of the bay on this reach, before the black ships came upon them; just. And be well set to come about, then, and strike into them from the flank. That was something, every little gain was something. A swift strike might even demoralise them enough— No. That straw was too thin to grasp. As the point approached, and they moved out into the heavier swell of the open sea at last, Olvar spent one precious moment longing for his quiet old forge. Then, as he drew breath to give Kalve his orders, trumpets blasted from the *Sea Eagle* to port, and a warning hail.

It was as if a corpse stirred upon the battlefield, and sprang to sudden and vicious life. Among the wreckage there was movement. Like a rising skeleton, one of the black hulls that drifted in the sea beyond the bay's mouth was in crazy, jerking motion. Its rigging and its sail were gone, its mast uprooted, its gunwales sunk to sea level and awash. But what must be the remnant of many crews manned it, and paddlers filled its benches, under water as they were. With sheer brute force they drove it into motion, while others bailed swiftly. Listing, lurching, they had nothing to lose. They were about to ram.

Olvar yelled. The men on the yards left the sails and swung frantically for the ratlines. The deckmen ran with the sheets, and the mainsail billowed about, just enough to take the *Orrin* across the wind a little – too little. The weight of water in the black vessel slowed it, but gave that slender hull a terrible impact.

The blow caught the *Orrin* amidships, and shook her from stem to stern, rattling the mast in its step. The sail billowed wide. All way was lost. *Orrin* heeled violently, away from its assailant and then back towards it. As it swung back, the sharp-edged sweeps hacked at the rail and sheared sheet and halyard, boarding pikes thumped home; and then someone opened a chest and spilled out a hoard of screaming madmen.

Their ship, its bow split open like a green stick, was already foundering beneath them. Their fellows would not stay to rescue them. This was their last desperate grasp for life. Armed or unarmed, they swarmed over the decks, slashing and striking insanely at any in their path. Olvar was already at the after-rail. One of the paddles lunged at him, shaving a great curl from the carven wood, and a vast unreasoning anger welled up in him. He ducked down, seized the paddle by the shaft and with all his great strength hauled up, lifting its rower half out of the boat, then drove it down with main force. The sweep smashed the man down into the water-filled hull, and Olvar had the fearsome weapon in his hands. He heaved it up, batting one leather-clad warrior screaming from the rail, hefted it in his huge fists, shoulder-high, swung it once. The inrush to the quarterdeck was stemmed in a single struggling heap. Blood sprayed across the rail and ran in the scuppers, and the ravening boarders, brought up short by the sight of what awaited them, checked, slipped and fell back. Olvar, grinning fixedly, took two short steps to the taffrail and chopped the paddle down like a poleaxe into the screaming mêlée below. Back and forth he swung it, a deadly pendulum that struck bodies this way and that, clearing a space in which he could spring down among them.

The narrow deck boomed and groaned. His heavy feet skidded in steaming blood and filth, he stumbled over twitching, groaning bodies, but he pressed forward, scything about him with the deadly blade, left to right and back again till he heard his back muscles crack, and foe and friend alike dove from his path in terror.

A warrior found the speed to duck beneath that terrible stroke and strike at him. The bright burst of pain seemed almost exhilarating as the broad-edged spear slashed along his ribs, and the movement that brought the paddle down was easy and sure, and dashed out the spearman's brains. Olvar heaved the paddle up to parry another blow and swung the handle to catch this man under his lantern jaw and spill him backwards on to the hold tarpaulins. Pain bit at his arm, another blade caught in his jerkin and with an animal roar he flailed loose and rammed the paddle straight into the spearman's midriff, then jerked it free for an upward slash across the sword-wielder's throat. The sword dropped to the deck. He stood panting, facing the snarling faces as they gave back, as if their bite had infected him with their fury. He was barely aware of the pain or the sickly stickiness of the blood that mingled with the sweat in his clothes, or of the writhing bodies at his feet. But one thing came to him; all the faces were foes. And they did not give back far.

Then, somewhere in meaningless distance, the trumpets sounded again; but this time they were not merely weaker, they ended in startled discord. The faces in the ring did not change, but froze, uncertain. Another sound was growing, a feeling almost, heard in the air, felt in the hull, climbing the legs like a shivering presage of weakness. Olvar's fury drained out of him, and he too stood, blinking uncertainly at the lights before his eyes, and what seemed to be prickles of white fire all over him. He stepped back, hoping for support, found the quarterdeck ladder behind him and backed up it, the dripping war-paddle a living menace before him. The ring of faces did not brave it; but they closed in around the stairfoot.

Something snagged against the rail and stopped him, there was a burst of pain in his shoulder that almost made him drop the paddle; then a snapping sound, and he was free again. The broken haft of an arrow fell to one side, and he realised dully that somebody, at some point, must have shot him in the muscle between neck and shoulder. Not very deeply, a glancing hit; but the head was still in, he could feel the barbs prickle at every movement. Another of those would wear him down; and there might be venom.

He stopped on the last step, nonetheless, forgetting the blood, the pain, the faces; for the trumpets sounded again, and he looked out over the sea. He did not even notice the stabbing spear that touched his stomach; touched, and no more, for the blow faltered. The bold warrior who had deemed Olvar distracted, and risked springing up on the first step, saw then what Olvar saw, and his blow also slackened. He paid no heed to the harsh cries of his fellows below. Both weapons hung suspended, as if time itself ran down to a halt, and the coil of the world unwound.

And suddenly both were hurled from their feet, the warrior downward, Olvar on to his back on the quarterdeck, staring stupidly up at the mild sky. An impact; and another, a series of impacts that boomed through the hull and made the deck buck and toppled men like straws. Olvar feared another ramming; but no mast loomed over the decks. There was no new onrush; only more impacts, glancing blows to either flank that felt unnatural, displaced, like nothing that should happen at sea. They were curiously, idiotically familiar, the feeling of a springless farm cart on a bouncy road. Trying not to giggle, he sought to scramble up, fell and crawled to the vibrating rail. The scene was as he had seen it. The wind was light, the sun yet shone, there was no hint either of storm or calm or any change at all; but from end to end under the skies even the waves were gone.

Their infinite ranks were broken, their endless advance shattered, their very pattern dispersed. The hand of the wind was feeble against the forces that came spewing up from beneath, and set the very face of the Ocean itself bubbling and churning like an overheated cauldron. Wrecks and debris danced crazily among the whirling, foaming ferment, the great ships rocked and jolted this way and that, their sails shivering. The whole hull throbbed to the growing music, and more; shrilling, chittering, rumbles, groans, inhuman moans like the complaint of stressed timbers. Dizzy, helpless, shaken by the crashing blows, Olvar felt the seams spring beneath him, the deck lurch violently, and thought he heard, far below, the hull begin to give way.

Gille was almost beyond thought, crouching on the rock in the posture of a child unborn. The thunders of sea and fire above his head had brought him low, and those veins of glaring light, silvery and fast-flickering as the lightning that sports among clouds. His own mind ached with it, the tiny portion of that force that was his, yet that he had never properly learned to use; and with the shame. Whom it was had come in answer to his call he knew full well, whose the voice of earthfire that had claimed him for its own. Every fibre of his being ached with the truth of that claim, like a billet of firewood slowly kindling. He could only wait to be consumed.

Only gradually, therefore, did he become aware that silence had settled again, real silence, with not even the watery rush around him, or the hissing menace of the flame. The rock felt warm and dry beneath his face, the air mild and balmy. He had a brief vast rush of relief, that he had been dreaming, on the beach somewhere, and outslept the dawn. Then he became aware that he was hearing footsteps.

They were hard, heavy, crisp and intentional, and they echoed altogether too loudly, and too close. Shuddering, he risked a glance up; and wished most fervently he had not. He was looking into another face. In the madness that had enveloped him, the shifting, shapeless domain of Powers, he might have been glad to see another human face; but not this.

All too human it was in its aspect, more so even than Saithana's, for the pale skin bore the insignia of age and experience, graven lines of deep suffering and deeper wrath. The hair was bristling, grizzled white; the beard also, though shot with black. It could have been a handsome face; had been, perhaps, long ago, before a lifetime of frustration and fury, of constant struggle and strange searches for stranger knowledge had chiselled it so profoundly without and within, and so harshly. The eyes were brown, flashing, frighteningly alive; their gaze seemed to spear down into his own, and contemplate the miserable remnant of craft that crawled within as an eagle might a worm. From such a height they seemed to look, indeed; for this was a huge man, wrapped in a black mantle which made him huger yet. That great height was more daunting to Gille, in its way, than all Niarad's monstrosity; for it was in truer proportion to his own.

Yet for all of that, the countenance might not have seemed so terrible, in such a time and such a place, had it not been one that Gille knew. From coins; from old books; from the carven walls of mighty Ker Bryhaine he had seen some fifteen years since, and never forgotten, he recognised that face; but not from life, for in life it had no place. Those carvings had been made some two centuries past. And even then this face was but a memory, of a life like none before or after, and a death. He could almost laugh at those images; he had thought them a little grotesque, the eyes especially. Now, though, he understood well what likeness it was the artists sought to capture, the cast of the features, the piercing, commanding glitter of the glance, as if deep within it there lurked still gems of red fire.

He ducked his head down, and sobbed.

'Get up, little smith who is also a master!' said a deep voice, clear and cultivated, but with a rough-edged accent he had never before heard. 'Sit up, man. I want to look at you properly.'

Gille's limbs obeyed that voice before his mind took it in. At his side the kantel swung and bounced, the strings sounding. The old man made an exclamation almost of surprise, reached out and took it in hands that were huge, hard-skinned, knob-knuckled and yet strangely graceful. He tapped the silver plate and bridge with tapering fingertips that conveyed immense delicacy amid such strength, and listened, head to one side. Then with a swirl of his cloak he sat down beside Gille, still towering over him. He contemplated the instrument an instant with a sudden, melting half-smile. Then, unexpectedly, he passed his hands over the softly gleaming wood, and began to play.

The notes cascaded down that silence like rain in a drought, like tears of sudden joy. The melody seemed instantly familiar to Gille, like one he had known and loved since childhood, and yet full of surprises with every phrase. For that brief moment or two the cavern of water became the happiest place he could wish to be; and beside him he was vaguely aware of Saithana raising her head. Then the tune broke off and he was desolate, lost; and yet still happier for having heard it, even once.

'A middling mastersmith,' said the old man. That quiet voice hinted more at contained power than all Niarad's rolling thunders. 'Not much of a man, to begin with. But a better one than began this voyage. You do not have greatness in you, Gille; but that is the common lot of men, and one to be thankful for. Nonetheless, you have brought about great things.'

Gille found some part of his voice. 'I - thank you, Lord Vayde. But how have you - who was it came—' He could not put sensible words together.

'*I* came.' The voice grew sombre once more.

'Vayde is long dead, and a part of me died with him. His bones lie blackening somewhere in the morasses of the Marshlands. But he could not wholly perish; and this is still the most ready form in which I may talk with men.'

Gille struggled to form a question, but even as his lips moved the shaggy head nodded, slowly. 'Has no man ever guessed? Yes, I was Vayde.'

Gille's wits, strained enough already, came close to deserting him. He felt as if he was caught up in somebody else's song, and the singer were mad. But through all the fear and the confusion a great stem of wonder swelled and blossomed, and the white fire leaped high in every thread of his being.

'Aye,' said the voice. 'What is it you call me? Patron of smiths. The image you've seen in their every Guildhall, the length and breadth of your land. I, the Mountain-Smith, as the duergar name me, I, the Lord of Flame. Even I, Ilmarinen. I was he. As I have been others, and will be yet. Though never, I hope, such a disaster as he!'

The old man laughed, softly, staring into infinite distances; and the kantel rang in sympathy. 'You must never again get too deeply involved with the Powers, Gille; not even if any of them seem to wish it. It is not good for any human. Do you not feel that, in the madness that has surrounded you here? And that began as the Sea-Daughter's attempt to make a sufficiently familiar place for you, a point of contact!'

He laughed again, not unkindly. 'Another disaster! Our places and tasks in this our world are different, our vision and our minds very distinct. Yet we are forever drawn to humans, in jealousy and enmity like the Powers of the Ice, or in compassion and a desire to help. A good thing in itself. We were the steerers of this world when it was young, and of all upon it. Like all fond parents, we find it hard to let our children depart and grow. Sometimes too fond, and so too constricting, unwilling to let them break out of the cocoon we make them, and fly free. An all too human failing! But that charge we must finally relinquish one day, and follow the paths of our final destinies.'

Those glittering eyes looked sidelong at Gille. 'Can you guess what those may be? I believe you have seen them in action here, today. You represent a parting of the ways to us, you and your kind. On the one hand, if we cling to the old mastery of the elements that are ours, we must as the long years pass become ever more dispersed within them, and at the end all but lost. So it will be with Tapiau, the Forest-Lord, I think; no more than a sleeping shred of mind, a dream shared among a world of trees. And perhaps with Niarad also. But there is another path: to do as I do, to wear the shapes and the lives of men, and share their new mastery. In that, though, lies casting off and forgetting all that once we were, until at last we change no more.'

He gave a short-breathed chuckle, a very human sound. Yet to Gille's ear there was an echo in blackness behind it, a mighty laughter out of the void.

'Saithana, now, she is drawn to humans. Indeed! One day she may become a very good one. But not yet; it would serve neither her nor you. To don the mantle of humanity, Gille! You who wear it so lightly, you cannot guess how hard it is for a Power to assume, what it does to us. Imagine cramping all that you are, all that you know and can do, into the form and spirit of an ant or a woodlouse. And then acting like one! Of course we make errors. Grave, stupid, bitter, damnable errors! Damnable, damning and eternally damned!' The voice became an inhuman snarl that bristled the hairs on Gille's neck. The old man swept to his feet and stamped, and the rock splintered beneath his heel.

'The perfect man, Gille! Can you conceive the stubborn pride of me? I had lived many lives before, I felt I could understand what men needed better than they themselves. I thought to make myself at last the perfect man – smith, swordsman, artist, musician, sorcerer, warrior chieftain, support and mentor of kings with no wish for kingship himself. And what did this man of men, this master of masters become? A tower of loneliness; of bitterness, of half-remembered hopes and fears. A giant who stalked in shadows and shied at the sun. Who found love, yet hardly knew it. Who sired children, yet had never been a child himself. Who could not raise them properly or protect them, so little he understood them. And in the end ... Too much craft I gave him. Too many duties for it. Too much memory of what he had been, too many lifetimes to live. It was more than human heart and mind can hold. One day I may become another man, Gille; but it will be a better, simpler one, one capable of much, but also of much error, who must learn, who must live as men do.' He laughed again, differently, and the sound filled Gille with a warmth that sent tears to his eyes. 'Maybe he will resemble you, little singer. Then the women will like him, at least!'

'Lord, I – I would have him taller,' stammered Gille. 'Not too tall. Of middle stature and over. Small men have a harder time, not least as children.'

The shaggy brows raised in polite interest. 'Do they indeed? Yes, I see; and it explains some things about you. Very well, I shall remember that. For the counsel I thank you; and for looking after my poor old kantel so well. I now reclaim it; for though Vayde left it as a device of power against a day of great need, I see more clearly than he. It partakes too much of our existence to be a healthy influence in yours.'

Gille looked up sharply. Till then he had had

no thought of the future, of his own existence beyond that point, even; but at the thought of losing that glorious music, beyond caution or reason, his heart rebelled.

'Be still!' said the old man sharply, before he could speak. 'I cannot undo what is done. You will always yearn. But I will pay you for it, fairly enough; and for all else. Only remember without bitterness, and the consolation of music will always be with you. But go no more whoring after the ideal, boy, in struck strings – or,' he added with a wry smile, 'any thing else. Even if you find perfection, it is not in you, or any man, to live with it! Imperfect as you are, strive to amend your own imperfections before seeking better; for that is how you learn and grow. And in the end, perhaps, approach an ideal more truly your own.'

Swinging the kantel, he strode over to Saithana, and stooping, laid a hand upon her head. She sprang up and shrank back in the same motion, shivering like a hunted beast. 'Have no fear!' said the old man. 'Your father returns to his element, as should you. The voice that called you is stilled; but Gille remains. Take him back now to his own; but then you must leave him utterly.'

'I shall not!' she snapped defiantly, though her long fingers clenched to keep from shaking.

The old man shook his head slowly. 'Girl, even beneath your father's deeps my fires burn, unquenchable and bright. By the boiling waters of my sulphur springs life came into the waters. Upon the forge of Ilmarinen the whole world floats, like dross on steel.'

'I cannot leave him!' she hissed. 'I love him, I have pledged to protect him!'

'That you may continue to do, when he is near water. And his descendants, if you wish. But no more; and no jealousy. Your love would waste his life, and make him a shoreside dreamer, happy in some measure, but drained and worthless in the world. Has it not been thus and thus before?'

She looked past him, past Gille, and her eyes sank to the rock.

'Well then,' said the old man. 'Go. Look to his safety, for great events are afoot. Go now! Go!'

Saithana sprang, cat-lithe, caught Gille's hand and tugged him away. Her own felt chill and cold in his, dead almost; and he reached out his other hand to warm it. But as they padded down the rock like frightened children, they looked back a moment, and saw the old man, his back to them, raise a commanding hand.

> *Hear me, Sea-King! Take up once again your true sceptre. Assume once more your infinite throne!*
> *And what your folly has brought about, undo!*

Then Gille heard, for the last time in his life, the song of Vayde's kantel, richer by far and fuller than he had ever been able to command, a surging, complex chant of wonder and rejoicing. Its themes became textures weaving and twining like the borders on some ancient text, fronds of gilt that wind around images of fantastical birds and beasts and heroes of old, blossoming into leaves at every turn and finally flowering into some enormous and ornate character that embodies the words they frame. Somewhere among those textures, if only as ornament to a more heroic theme, he heard the ancient melody he had sung that night upon the shore.

Then the sound was suddenly lost, drowned in the devouring hiss of fire, and the inrushing roar of the sea. The vast grey figure slumped, losing its humanity, and fell back, or subsided, or melted into the wall; something of all of these, too swift to be seen. Beyond the waters of the dome streams of shadows swung about. For a moment, across its circumference, there formed two swirling pools of glittering greenish blue, vortices that faded at their hearts to infinite, icy darkness, forever beyond the reach of the sun.

For that moment the eyes of the Ocean were turned upon him, and he cowered. Then the earth shook, and in the darkness great bubbling streams of white steam awoke. Their stern gaze lifted, high above his head, and the water-wall grew for the first time green-glass clear and bright, opening the whole surrounding expanse of the sea to his view, the rough landscape of the seabed stretching away into dim distance. Save on his right hand, where like distant mountains or a valley wall it sloped up towards the ceiling of light; and on his left, where it fell sharply away into blackness, the steep slopes of the true depths, the primeval abyss.

Far out across that hidden land, things were stirring. It was as if hands lifted from the floor, hands so natural that their size came to him only slowly, and with shock. Up towards the light they arose, opening fingers long and sinuous, fingers any one of which might have scooped out this whole vast amphitheatre, as a child plays with pebbles. As they opened they seemed to release great rising streams, and themselves dissolved to join them. All that, in one instant of seeing. Then Gille flinched, as above his head the waters cracked like thunder, and a deluge poured down upon his head.

'It is fulfilled!' cried Saithana. 'Niarad mounts his throne once more!'

A green wall rushed in at them from all sides. In it the great shadows moved, curving inward, rising. Gille was borne up after them, by the cool hand in his. Again he yelled as the clamps of pressure snapped close about his chest, and violently squeezed the very air from his mouth. In that agonised moment the first of the shadows surged past him, so close he rode an instant on its swirling wake. A grey flank, mottled, vast, rising in a serpentine curve of slow power; and in it, dwarfed, an eye that fixed him without expression he could interpret, and yet had something familiar. Past him it twisted, and a hundred shadows with it, beyond it, beneath him, great beating bulks arcing upwards to the light, the wash of their passage bouncing him this way and that like a trailing leaf. Bubbles streamed past him, an explosion of them. He fought to breathe, could not help himself, and again his lungs flooded with cold fire, and the pressure eased.

Another vast shadow shot up, not steadily like the rest, but in an arrowing, pulsing thrust that brought it beyond him, hanging there, fixing him with an eye of a kind he had seen before. As high as a door indeed, but now he could see the body behind it. Long as a boat, pointed and vaned like an arrowhead, with a fletch of those long boneless arms trailing behind it, there in the green deep it glowed still, rippling with scarlet fire. The two longest arms, tipped with diamond-shaped graspers, poised to lash out. Gille, forgetting himself, tried to shout. Others darted out of the deep to join it, eyes glittering and blank, yet still with some awareness he knew.

But a voice spoke in his ear, as before. 'Fear not! Niarad is enthroned!'

Against the lights moved Saithana's silhouette, across the many stares, and the scarlet pulse shifted suddenly to pallid white, then green-mottled gold; and with a thrust that twisted him violently about in the water, these creatures also were gone, spurting high above, lost in the light. Behind them rose other shadows, cloud upon cloud in the

churning dimness, great and small. Some were
familiar, among them the great whales he saw in
season from the cliffs in passage south or north,
blunt of head and long of jaw, or broader-bodied
with winglike fins. Some were smaller, high-finned,
black-backed, rising swiftly in groups in a heavily
sportive spiral. Yet in the rush and confusion of the
waters he was never sure what he saw, how much
was real, how much the phantasms of his overtaxed
mind and senses.

Once or twice, amid the confusion and the
turmoil, shadows still smaller flashed and darted
about, shapes all the more imposssible for being
familiar. Once one darted past so close he reached
out instinctively, mistaking it for Saithana, only to
feel her grip still firm about his wrist. A powerful
pulse exploded the water into opaque billows
bubbling with a ringing, silvery laughter, and the
indistinct shape arrowed away with an otterlike
flip. More than that he never knew; but the face
among that billowing hair was human.

Others, more distant, he saw clearly enough,
yet were wholly and terribly strange. There were
shapes long-bodied and sleek that wriggled upward
like monstrous otters. There were silhouettes truly
serpentine, yet with long heads and wide predatory
jaws, driven by lashing tails and small fins that beat
not far behind the head. And some there were,
longest of all, swan-necked, small-headed, that
floated easily out of the abyss with no more than
the lazy flick of limbs flattened like a penguin's
wing. And as it came to him how great these must
be, and he remembered the old tales of the Sea
Devourer and his kin, he was glad indeed that they
swam no closer.

Around him they rose, the shadows, and deep
among the waters ever more, in hordes he could not
conceive of counting. Many bore the tall back fins

that chilled his heart with memories of the raft. Coursing grey-white hunters, three times his length, circled upward with calm, relentless intensity, fixed him with a beadily blank gaze and then twisted intently on their way. Yet still vaster beasts of the same shape, with broad mottled backs and heavy chiselled heads, sculled along in harmless ease, sheer bulk their only menace. They ignored the clouds of lesser fish, merely man-size, great glittering shoals that darted this way and that with flicks of their sickle tails, buffeting him in their wash. Even their glassy eyes, it seemed, fixed him with a shred of understanding. He understood, then; and great wonder fell upon him.

'It is so!' Saithana answered, though he had spoken no word, and could not. 'For though all the waters are his domain, he reigns from all the minds that they contain, the lowest to the highest. All the life of the sea is the regal seat of Niarad, the endless chains of being in perpetual circulation his body and limbs, the cycle of life and death and regeneration mightier and more noble than any palace or fane of men. You behold the Sea-King's manifold throne!'

Mighty indeed; for high above Gille's head, as far as he could see, the innumerable host of swimming shapes reached the rippled window that opened on to his own half-forgotten world of air. And even as he watched, it crazed in many places as they touched it, and shattered like the thinnest glass.

'The highest it is that hold the most of him,' said Saithana's voice. 'And that most readily work his will. But their way is not ours, Gille! For you and I must part for ever now, and of the song between us, though it was passing sweet, an end must come. Cleave to me now, at the last!'

The *Orrin's* hull juddered and moaned. Like a cart indeed, Olvar thought crazily, as an old forgotten memory awoke. The planks squealed, the seams popped; caulking rose up, and it seemed only a moment before the first fountains spurted up from the hold, or the rudder miscarried. The shapes that surged past, jarring the hull so violently, might have been more upturned ships, for the size they were. But they did not slash the water aside, but rose and fell in serpentine curves, or swam with leisurely sculling. Some had high fins at back and tail; some glistened with scaly armour, and made the air acrid and stinking with blasting spouts of spray. But they moved as one flow, one purpose, a mighty driven herd.

It came back to him all too clearly – a dumb fisher lad with a talent to foster, setting out to find a master, hitching a ride on a haycart; and the flock of cattle passing, the first he'd seen. Huge beasts of the ancient breed with horns spanning wider than his arms, white-flanked, red-eared; lowing monsters, yet guided and goaded by two small boys alone. They had brushed the cart casually, scratched themselves alarmingly against its timbers, or snatched trailing mouthfuls of its sweet hay, and almost his boots with them. Daunting, damaging, yet unmalicious, unconcerned; and so were these, or the ship and all about it would be overset by now, or shaken to matchwood. The merest few could have devastated them all, for there was *Sea Eagle*, even, bouncing ungainly under the thudding impacts, heaving like a child's toy in the surf.

The battles on the deck stilled, as crew and boarder alike stared in horror at the sea. Such a seething Olvar had seen when the trawl closed in upon a great shoal, leaping and thrashing. This, though, stretched almost to the far horizon; and the bodies that lashed and leaped and twisted clear of the foaming water were little smaller than the hull beneath him. They made the very ocean boil; and yet, impossible as it seemed, he guessed they must mean no harm. So Olvar thought; and then they came to the black ships.

Before the first of them a glistening back arched up, and the bow juddered. The shaman who swayed there in the hoglike guise staggered, over-balanced by his gore-tusked mask, but fell to his knees and clung. Then the back plunged, and a vast flattened tail burst up, and slapped at the snarling face beneath him. The shaman was flung up and out, to plummet screaming into the creamy cauldron. The painted bow cracked away like a rotten nutshell, and spilled out the meats within. Another tail arose, and another, among the men who struggled in the foaming water, and the flukes smacked down with an ear-rending crack. Foam fountained, and blotted them from sight. A frenzy it seemed, a rage in nature itself beneath the smiling sun; and no less terrifying as it became clear its fury was focused upon the black fleet alone.

The sleek spear-hulls bucked, twisted, tipped as the broad backs heaved them high in the water. Masts rocked, stays snapped, lookouts and archers spilled from their stations. Tails stove in planking or smashed steering oars, jaws snapped at paddles and plucked their wielders overside. Chieftains in their robes and tall hats shouted and gestured, and men with spears and pikes ran hither and yon to strike at their assailants, only to be themselves spilled into the appalling cauldron. The tall fins knifed through it, this way and that, and the cream was shot with scarlet. Olvar knew their kind and dreaded it, as any seaman did; but their size chilled his heart's blood, something from tall tales and legends beyond crediting. He gave thanks that at least poor Gille with his squeamish nature was not here to see this.

But these hunters were no cowards, even as

prey. One bold warrior clambered out upon a heaving prow, clinging fast with one hand and both feet, striking out with a harpoon at the thing that played with his ship as a daggertooth its prey. And the thing rolled over, half out of the water; and Olvar gasped at the expanse of the jaws as it yawned wide and snapped, almost lazily. Warrior, bowsprit and bow themselves vanished into that maw, and then the shark bit down. The black ship tilted and went nose down as the water flooded in, and the warriors struggled up the narrow stern, scrabbling over one another for a handhold, an iron-clad boot in a comrade's face to delay, even a heartbeat longer, the slide into that monstrous cauldron below.

Even in their extremity they were hunted. Out of the water, here and there, white trails arose and closed in, faster than aught else that swam. The sea seemed to sprout whips to punish the black raiders, lashing about their rigging, their paddles, anything, sweeping their low-lying decks. One serpentine form reared up high as a proud masthead, curled back and struck, slapping the lookout from his post. Another trailed its diamond-shaped spearhead tip across one of the greater ship's sterns, where a robed and hatted chieftain slashed at it with a sword. It reared sharply, then darted home. With sluggish, irresistible ease he was lifted up and over the transom, kicking and screaming, and swallowed from sight in the pallid mass of slime alongside.

Still greater arms entwined the rigging of a lesser longship, and with the slow impossibility of a dream, it began to tilt. Whether by panic or design its crew rushed to the rising side; it heeled back momentarily, drawing its assailant half out of the foam, uncovering so monstrous a bulk that many men on board *Orrin* and the sothran ships alike fell to their knees and called upon the friendly Powers.

The thing flushed pale, then obscenely brilliant red, and foul yellow ichor bubbled up to coat the hull. Then, as its weight told, the stays snapped, the timbers creaked and split, and among the slime and the screams of men it filled and foundered in that intolerable embrace.

Then, at last, many of those in the rear of the fleet sought to flee, coming clumsily about with paddles flailing and baggy sails bulging, as close-hauled as they dared. They made little way. Some, too eager, caught in the ocean's churn, heeled too far, flooded and went over. Some struck hidden obstacles that heaved them aside, and the end was the same. The warriors who fell from them seldom surfaced even once; and there were those among the watchers who claimed that when a stray head did bob up, they saw it drawn swiftly down in the clasp of all too human arms.

Then the raiders that remained, the dark fleet's heart, seeing escape cut off, gathered defiantly. One ship lashed to another by bows and stern, and those to their neighbours, pulling together all the while with the ant-like precision of long drill to make great floating fortresses that no single sinking could shatter, nor any bulk pull down. They massed their archers and moved their heavy deck-bows to unleash volleys of darts at the sleek backs that rampaged about their perimeters, while at their hearts the few remaining shamans danced and drummed up whatever shreds of war-luck might serve them against the wrathful waters.

It was not enough. For now, as if great hands slapped it skyward, the very ocean erupted. Sweeping walls of water lifted the hastily gathered islands, and hurled them against the mastheads of their fellows. Others were snared with a force not even the great beasts of the maelstrom could match, and drawn below as inexorably as a child would snatch down a toy. Among the fortresses of the servants of the Ice a ruin general raced.

Olvar, stunned, thought then that the sea itself had risen in revolt against the men who defiled its surface with war. Hurled this way and that about his bucking deck, more helpless even than in the storm, he believed himself already lost, to be assailed at any moment, drawn down or devoured. It no longer concerned him greatly, he found, when a moment left him still enough to think. At least he had seen his forefathers' foes brought low, and the power of the Ice their masters humbled. His chief regret was for Telqua; and that never now would he tell Kunrad and his lady Alais what became of so great a venture. Gille also; but then he guessed he might be meeting him, soon enough.

Gille had no such thoughts. Cold crashed about him, he gasped and drew in only icy water. In panic, choking, he reached out to Saithana, and felt her body in his arms, smaller somehow than before, as if she was diminished now by circumstance. Her breasts crushed against him, her thighs against his, her lips on his, in a kiss that seemed eternal, an embrace of rushing waters. Her green eyes gazed deep into his, and grew wider and more luminous, lighter and deeper, as if they were becoming the whole world.

He grasped at her, and his fingers grated through fine wet sand. He tried to call her name, and salt water half filled his mouth. Then it washed back and air took its place. Weight dragged him down, and there was nothing beneath him save damp sand. He struggled to raise himself, to look about, and it welled bright water beneath the weight of his arms. Another wave slapped back and soaked into his breeches, almost teasingly; and another, foaming about his head. He coughed, and elbowed himself further up the sand, effortfully as a turtle, and weeping the same salt tears. The water left him and fell back, and he slumped down in the sand, and sank into sleep.

He woke quite suddenly, wide awake, alert, as if out of some refreshing dream. He looked around, and clutched at himself. He was sun-dry now; his clothes were stiff and salty, but then they had been since he set off on this insane venture. Sunlight dazzled him, and sound rushed in upon him. Waves, yes; but thundering across a beach. There was another rushing in his ears, almost as loud. He blinked uncertainly up. Green leaves stooped over him, long low boughs waving in the wind and creaking, tall green ground-growing things with bright flowers. Small birds in unlikely, glowing shades of blue and rose and vermilion bounced from twig to twig, and peered astonished at him, cocking their orange and yellow beaks, before bounding off again, twittering. And above them, a still more impossible, dazzling blue, stretched the open sky.

Gille sank back, helpless. Wherever he was, this was nowhere that he could call home. It looked much like the islands, or others very similar.

Had he been cast adrift then, only to fetch up here? And in delirium dreamed all that had passed?

Quite a dream, if so; for it was still clear in his mind, from the irruption of that dreadful, statuesque figure to the shadows mounting from the deep. And to Saithana's kiss. He reached around urgently, then sank back again, hollowed out with loss. Whatever the truth of it all, the kantel was gone. When that sickening realisation wore off, though, and he began to care again, he saw how that might have happened, easily enough. What he could not imagine was drifting far enough to reach land, wherever it might be. Not even if he had still been on those planks; and though there seemed to be wreckage aplenty nearby, he could not see them. He felt surely dry enough. He licked his lips nervously, tasted his mouth caked with sand and salt, and was instantly, murderously thirsty.

With that prompting, his ear separated another sound from the searush, a different song of water – a bubbling, splashing flow. He sat up and stared around. Barely twenty paces away a small creek flowed out across the beach through a channel in the sand, a few yards to the sea. Its origin was a crevice in the slope above, under the shade of an overhanging tree; and on its leaves he could see the rippling light of a pool. He clambered up. It was wide, shallow, sandy; and it was fed by a chuckling flow that fell through verdant vegetation across a grey cool face of rock. It looked fresh, and when he staggered forward and almost collapsed into it, he found it was, unbelieveably, delightfully fresh and cool. Not the islands, then, he thought dazedly, as he stripped off his clothes and tumbled headlong in, drinking and swimming as one.

The water washed him and slaked him, cleared his salt-choked skin and left him fresh as one reborn. After a moment he pulled his clothes in after him, wrung them out and draped them from the branch to dry. He rolled over lazily in the cool embrace, bubbling out his breath, and let the sweetness clear his bleary eyes, thinking of nothing, as if to wash out his thoughts also. That was why he did not hear the voices at first, through waterlogged ears, or react fast enough.

By the side of the pool a woman stood, lean, tall; but her skin was dark. He stared.

'T... *Telqua?*'

Her round eyebrows arched high. '*Gille?*' she yelped. '*Gille-chekew'ya?*'

He yelped still louder. She threw a chattering

stream of words at him as he snatched up his breeches, clearly questions, clearly incomprehensible. He spread his hands helplessly. She spun round impatiently, put hands to mouth and let out an ululating call that scattered the little birds from their twigs. A loud call, unafraid and free; and as others answered it from the near distance, a new hope and excitement began to swell in him.

Within moments there were running footsteps in the sand, and he was suddenly surrounded by a crowd of copper-skinned folk, young for the most part. They bore spears and swords, but let them drop in the sand as they clustered around him, standing there helplessly in his tattered, dripping breeches. They poked and prodded and patted as if he was some kind of prodigy, and chattered away even faster than Telqua. Running and puffing up behind them came another dark-skinned young man, but in the grubby garb of a Nordeney sailor. And when he saw Gille he stopped so short he almost dived into the sand, eyes bulging with sheer fright.

'I know you!' barked Gille. 'Hoi, stand still! You're from the village, aren't you? Ingor, that's it! Hella's tits, man, I hired you for this damnfool trip! *I* ought to be running away from you!'

The burly young fisherman unstuck his tongue. 'B ... boss? I mean, Mastersmith ... I mean, skipper? It is you, isn't it? Oh my sweet Saithana, it is - but they said you was lost overside! How'd you ever get here?' He squeaked suddenly as Telqua seized him by the ear and spat a few emphatic words into it. 'She wants to know too!'

'Walked!' snapped Gille; and then regretted it, as the sailor's eyes bulged even wider. 'No, idiot! What d'you think? Just drifted, probably; a bit delirious - wait a minute! *They* said? Who said?'

Ingor gabbled his translation for Telqua before

he answered. 'Ore, boss! And Dall! The *Rannvi*! Nils brought her in a few hours back.'

Gille closed his eyes, and the fisherman babbled encouragingly. 'In a bad way, baked white, but the stragglers from the fleet sighted 'em! They picked up the bosun and Ore, an' they said you'd slipped off the raft to save 'em!'

Mentally Gille tried on heroism, and found to his deep regret that it was a poor fit. 'I just slipped, more like. The fleet? Then our word did get through?' He looked to Telqua. 'You and Olvar?'

Her face was a bronze mask at the mention of the name, and the others of her tribe fell abruptly silent. 'Gone,' she said tonelessly, finding the words. 'Out. To fight.'

'The other fleet got here too!' amplified Ingor. 'The hunter bastards. He and the sothran fighting ships went out to hold 'em off, while the princess took me off with her to get her folk away. Then – well, first there's yon storm, like all Hella's harpies broke loose. And we couldn't get aboard, all of us. And then – oh, Powers among us, skipper, you just would not bloody believe what cut loose next!'

'I might,' said Gille grimly. 'And Olvar and the sothrans ... they were in the middle of it?'

The sailor's face twitched, and he looked at his feet. 'It was the whole earth shakin' like, skipper! Yon fire-mounts just blew their tops, whole hills jumpin', and the sea, now, the sea – it went bloody mad! There were waves as high's a house, just run on run of 'em – honest, you should have seen't! Even the ships at anchor in the bay here took a pounding. And them maneaters' skiffs, it just spattered 'em from one end of the sky to t'other. Gone – buggered up – finish! The sothrans, they were chucked all over the place, battered, scattered, past handling, all along the archipelago. They've been limping back in these last hours, one by one. One went down on the way, but they got everyone off, Powers only guess how. There's another aground out in the bay, but she'll refloat. But, well, skipper, these were big sothran warcraft. Twice *Orrin*'s tonnage the least of 'em, and...' His eyes flickered sidewise to Telqua. 'Well, they barely made it. *Orrin*'s not been seen since.'

Gille read the bitter thought in her impassive face. *Why him, why this one? Why not...* Her man. That was obvious. Well, well. Not a pleasant thing to think, not an ideal thing; but a very human and natural one. Why me, indeed? Olvar deserved to get out, more than he did.

Gille swore, and then shook his head. He stumbled out of the shallows and seized Telqua's hands. 'Tell her I'm not giving up. Look, this is a strange place, a strange time ... There may be higher forces at play here. If the sothrans survived – if I can survive! Aye, survive and come back all that way! And wash up conveniently right next to—' He broke off in sudden amazement, as his mind swung about on his own words. 'I thought you said there wasn't any water in the islands!'

He was startled when she replied stiffly, but in his own tongue, 'There is not!' She looked to Ingor to say more.

He shrugged. 'Can't be. All the water we've got's what the fleet brought, and it's barely enough. These folk have been sniffing ... round ... every...' He looked hard at the stream, and at Gille, and at the pool again.

'Does look fresh, don't it?' he admitted, with a slight nervous giggle. He began sidling away a little. Telqua too was staring, and so were all the others, looking down at the pool and sniffing. A young girl stooped down; her long black tresses touched the water, and she recoiled, shivering a little. Then she dabbled her fingers in it, and put them to her lips. She gaped, wide-eyed, and plunged her face in it. A young man scooped some to his mouth, screamed aloud and hurled himself bodily into the pool.

'Hey, steady on!' said Gille, as the others splashed after them, Telqua among them. He felt strangely possessive. One of the young men, his hard-planed face split by an unbelieving grin, seized Gille in a bear-hug and chattered faster than Ingor could translate.

'He says this is a new thing. That if it had been here before they'd've found it.'

'What? That's bloody daft!' Gille's tone evidently needed no translation. 'Springs and waterfalls don't just pop out of nowhere! Couldn't it have been the quake, or the storm, or something—'

He stopped. The sand was being kicked up now, the water turning cloudy; but he saw something within it gleam an instant, green and pale. He stooped as if to taste it again, and saw beneath his face, half hidden among the sand, a gem. Cautiously he scooped it up, and dabbled it clean. It was set upon a ring, golden and simple, yet so fair in its simplicity that his smith's instincts marvelled; and within it, though they were not strong, coursed qualities that were subtle and hard to define.

Nobody else seemed to notice; they were too busy splashing about and ducking one another. The young man gestured like a windmill, leaving Ingor shaking his head in bewilderment.

'Says he's walked this beach many times, that they all have. He says ask anybody, they feared they'd not have enough water for the voyage home, and that now - it's a, a something like a miracle, a ... a ...'

'A gift of life,' said Telqua slowly, and nodded. 'He speaks truth. Again you come down as if a Power, bearing our lives in your two hands. This - to this water-place - I think we put your name to it.'

Gille sighed, relishing its last cool embrace, and trying to be philosophical about the happy young bodies that capered and glistened in the pool. He slid the ring on one finger, and then another. It fitted his fourth finger, after a fashion, but felt curiously uncomfortable there. All the same, he decided, he'd starve in the gutter before he let it go. 'No, Princess. Call it for the one who gave it, who loves all men who ride the sea. Call it Saithanaborn, or whatever that would be in your tongue, the Sea-Daughter's Gift; and use it well. You lot! Show a bit more bloody respect, you hear?'

They didn't understand him, most of them; but there was no mistaking his gesture. They fell silent at once, and trooped out of the pool; for clearly this was a shaman whose word was best heeded. He felt a little ashamed of himself, and looked away out across the sea.

He did not feel like a shaman. The waves were still tossing sodden debris about the beaches, drawing it back, thrusting it on, as a child tosses a ball. 'I'm just another piece of it,' he muttered. 'One that's sunk deeper than most, and more sea-sodden.' He noticed there was a body among it, broken, bloated. It could have been hunter or prey, a man of his land or a sothran; death had blurred all distinction. At least he was better off than that. He sat down, and contemplated the calm rhythm of the swell. It came to him that he might offer his thanks, but he did not feel comfortable with that.

He twirled the ring on his finger, and watched the sea.

A hand touched his shoulder. 'You hunger? You come, find your crew, eat?'

'Thanks, Telqua, I'm not hungry. But you're right, the lads...'

He levered himself painfully to his feet, surprisingly weak. But he stopped, lost his balance, sat down in the sand; and then he shaded his gaze, stared, and positively sprang to his feet.

'Telqua! There – d'you see?'

It was only a small pale patch, visible beyond the point of the island opposite; but it was growing by the minute.

'I see!' she said tautly. 'Not black! Not white, like these red-haired men's!'

'Cream colour,' said Gille. 'Northern weave, well weathered. And you say the *Rannvi*'s in harbour already.'

They did not dare look at one another, or anywhere but that swelling expanse of sail. It looked strange, to Gille, and he realised it was sorely askew, hung on a sagging jury-rig cruder than he could have imagined. As it came about, the ship was listing under its pull, as if it had sprung a seam or two; but it was making good way in the breeze, and coming on to a new tack towards this island. And there was no doubt at all, then, what ship it was.

They watched it grow rapidly, wallowing but secure. Gille realised suddenly that he had the feel of it; he could make a good guess at its best points of sail. He could have handled it, at a pinch. Like it or not, he had become a seaman of a sort.

Telqua still said nothing. She stood tall and taut as a bow, quivering with tension so physical that it filled the air around like the onset of thunder. He did not dare say any word of comfort or encouragement. He did not dare disturb her pride, or she might do anything. Abruptly her long fingers clamped hard around his arm.

'Gille! You see?'

He shook his head.

'Look! One there waves! Wave again!' She waved, with her arm and his. 'Maybe – Gille! See!'

'I can't!' he protested. He'd forgotten these people's eyes.

'Maybe – *it is!* Gille, is him! Is him!' She sprang where she stood with a wild war-whoop, almost dragging him off his feet.

'I'll take your word for it!' he laughed, and managed a shout of his own.

The ship had come about again, was paralleling the shore, heading for the main anchorage. Telqua sent her people running with a shout, and dragged him after her, still waving wildly. Gille could make it out now, the bulky figure high on the lurching quarterdeck, waving as best he could while hanging out over the rail, to help the balance.

Gille waved too; but it was only in part to his friend. 'Thanks!' he shouted, as he ran. Now, at long last, he felt he could say it, and mean it. 'For everything! My lady, thank you! My lords, my masters, thank you all! Thank you! Thank you!' He leaped and came down capering, kicking sand. 'Hella and Powers and glory, damn you all! *Thank you!*'

CHAPTER 10
The New Song

The days that followed burned away with great haste and great labour. There were the people to gather, the warriors from the farthest islands who had been decoying the hunters, the weak and the old who had had to be left in dangerous places. To abandon them now would be intolerable. So the soundest ships were sent with search parties to every isle, to every corner of the archipelago. They were war parties, too, to flush the remnants of the hunters that yet lingered. To the men of the Eastlands it would have seemed harsh enough to maroon them in these lonely isles; but Telqua and her people had too great a legacy of cruelty and horrors to be so lightly repaid, and they wished to leave no witness of their escape. Prey turned on predator, and blood was again shed beneath the green leaves.

Gille and Olvar were glad enough to occupy themselves with the other demanding task, that of repairing as many of the damaged ships as possible, and salvaging supplies from the rest. It was punishing work, even with the Westerners' eager help, filling every hour under the fierce sun and going on far into the night by the light of flotsam fires. Yet in the midst of all this, incessantly, Gille was pestered for his tale.

It drove him near distraction; and yet he could not resent the interest, for he knew it was a token of affection and respect, even awe. These were things he had long been starved of. For the first time in his adult life he was genuinely a person of consequence, and it went a long way towards healing the inner sadness he felt. Yet not altogether; for he felt that in truth his part had been small and inglorious, to put it mildly, and that it was Saithana who deserved most of the credit. However he tried to tell the tale to himself, he sounded too much the hero. He had always wanted that; but facing it in real life, having to make his own account of it, terrified him. How much of a hero he had already become did not occur to him. The best answer he could give was always 'Later!' And the pestering went on.

He had thoughts of confiding in Olvar, but that presented problems. Olvar was no less busy, and was a woman's man now besides, his time and attention too well spoken for. To Gille the bond between him and Telqua seemed oddly undemonstrative, passionless even; once he would have found it funny. Now, though, he could guess at depths of feeling of which he himself did not seem capable, depths he had only once come near experiencing; and that for somebody not even human. And then, when the captains had a free moment together, while the grounded merchantman was being caulked with pitch boiled from the black ships' wreckage, it was Olvar who asked him.

'Well, lad?' he rumbled. 'When're you going to spill it?'

Gille, in confusion, looked at the pitch his men were stirring.

'Not that, loon! Your story! Your escape!'

And being asked made telling suddenly almost impossible. 'There's not much—'

'Not *much*? Laddie, this is your Uncle Olvar speaking, remember? Who knows a fair amount of what you've been up to since the beginning of this mad jaunt, and can guess more - remember? So spill.

How'd you ever make your way back here from the far south seas at all? Without either drowning, starving or feeding one of those gentlemen with the black fins and big teeth? Let alone do the journey little slower than your own damned ship! There's a tale to tell there, isn't there?'

Gille looked at him, and shook his head. 'Olvar, I hardly know myself.' He touched the ring he wore, turning its great stone inward towards his palm. Olvar did not appear to notice; his eyes, deceptively sleepy as ever, still held Gille's. 'Maybe I'll tell later. When I've had a chance to think it over. It isn't an easy thing to just open your mouth and...'

'Then make a song of it, man! That's what you usually do.'

Gille shrugged unhappily. 'The inspiration's gone. And the kantel.'

'Ah, yes. Remember I mentioned the crews had some music-makers? Well, among them ...'

And he handed over as battered an old box of strings as Gille had ever seen. Its varnish was all but stripped, save for a few flakes around the sides by the seams; and some of those were sprung, by the slow warping of the wood. It was patchy and ringed with old damp stains; the bridge looked loose, and the fingerboard was reduced to a broken shard of base metal. Someone had put newish strings on it, but Gille couldn't think why; they fizzed and buzzed as he strummed a few notes, wincingly out of tune.

'What,' enquired Gille, 'am I supposed to do with this old fishbox?'

Olvar shrugged. 'Oh, nothing. Doesn't belong to anyone; just hung on a nail in the fo'c'sle. I thought you might enjoy fixing it up. Stop you fretting – give you something to do.'

'To *do*?' growled Gille, glaring up at the great-bellied hull. 'Powers, have you seen how much more refitting these craft'll need? They'll be bailing all the way back home as it is, and holding the masts up with their bare hands. We'll surely never make landfall in Nordeney.'

'We can try; though a sothran port will be safe enough, one of the border ones where Kunrad's writ runs. But that wasn't what I meant, exactly. Something to do – later. When your hands might be feeling idle, and you have to have some care where they fall. Well, send the pitch down sternwards when you can. That great merchantman looks to have sprung every second transom plank on the sand.'

'Olvar—'

'Yes?'

'Nothing. Another thought. It can wait.' It could indeed, the other reckoning. Both of their ships were intact. Both still held some saleable cargo. Even if they didn't have to offload it to carry more people, they would not now be able to get it to the far Southlands, where the highest prices were to be had, and the best return cargos. They could still get rid of their goods for something, probably. They might, with luck, still break even upon his investment, once the wages were paid, and the geld for those who had been injured or lost their lives. He sighed, and staved off unhappiness by telling himself that it wasn't really his, that Saithana had given it him simply so a Northern expedition could be launched, one that would turn aside for the fugitives. She knew that a sothran one might not. It was unlikely he would be able to launch another; so what then?

Olvar would go back to his forge, happily enough; or join Telqua and the others in clearing their new settlements. That rough life wasn't to Gille's taste; and he was no more ready than before to bury himself neck-deep on Utte's farm, however

easy that might be. Assuming Utte still had any use
for him; and it was a mark of his anguish that he
was able to doubt that so deeply. But about the farm
he was sure and certain. At perhaps the worst point
of his life, his ultimate desperation, he had proclaimed what he was in the face of the very Powers
incarnate; and a mastersmith, however inadequate,
he had to be.

'Hey! Master Gille!' Some of Telqua's young
men were passing the work-site, trailing back from
an expedition with their warrior friends, and
trophies hanging from their belts that he didn't
want to look at. 'When you tell us wha' happen, uh?'

'Later!' he shouted back. 'When you can ap-
preciate my polished verses!'

They laughed. They could probably understand them already; the younger folk were picking
up Nordeney speech swiftly. Telqua was becoming
almost fluent; but then she had the best kind of
schooling. Fine, bright folk; but scarred and hardened, through no fault of their own. He wanted to
live among more civilised neighbours. He watched
a group of sothran captains strolling along the
beach, smiling around with a languidly superior air
that made him want to line them up and kick them.
They were civilised, to be sure. It was all right for
Kunrad, married into their aristocracy and no
longer a smith; but among the sothrans Gille would
just be a superior sort of tradesman. Just then the
pitch did spill, among clouds of smoke and coughing and oaths; and he gave up his fretting for that
time.

When it was done for the night, and they
turned wearily to their beds, he came across the old
kantel on the sand, and almost left it there. Then he
shrugged, picked it up and sat tinkering with it a
little while before he slept. Compared to Vayde's
marvellous instrument it sounded ridiculous, but he

was almost grateful to it for that. He went for a drink at Saithana's spring, and slept, somehow, much more happily.

At last the fleet was ready once again, and though most of the ships were as crowded as cattle-boats, the fugitives had no trouble obeying the stern discipline that kept them habitable. Compared to the voyage here, they said, this was high comfort. They insisted, too, that Gille and Olvar should keep their cargoes rather than give them more space, and this was easier because they made up the depleted crews with fugitives. The weather was mild, the sea was kind, and though their rations were scanty enough, their waterbarrels were well filled and sweet. Trumpets rang across the ships, and a great cheer arose as the *Sea Eagle* spread her well-patched sails, hoisted her anchors and lumbered about the point out of the channel into the east-ward ocean. And though the *Rannvi* and *Orrin* followed her with less pomp, it was to them, with a brassy salute, that she ceded the passage.

'And a bloody long while you'll wait,' grinned Nils, 'before you see a sothran do as much for a Nordeney ship again!'

Gille only grunted. As soon as they were under way he took a comfortable seat against the rail, and a piece of fine sharkskin, and began trying to rub down the kantel's miserable remnants of varnish.

Throughout most of the return voyage it was the sailing masters who commanded the merchant-men, for Olvar was much occupied with Telqua, and Gille with such materials as he could find on board, glues and pitches and pots of the coarse varnish kept for proofing the planking and spars, scraps of steel and patching plates for the hull's coppering against sea-worms and such. He even took to hammering out scraps of metal by the galley fire, cursing the cook because it could not be made hotter. The crewmen, feeling themselves privileged by their common adventures, went on pestering him. Now, though, he took his cue from Kalve, and answered that he was saving any sea-tales till he was safe in port. The sailors, inclined to be superstitious, were suitably impressed at this example of their captain's canniness. They were even inclined to credit him for the reasonably calm weather they enjoyed, and winds as fair as one could expect for the season. And, which impressed them more, the vast fleet of ice-islands, which even now could still have come in their way, were gone without trace; as if, one said, the sun had sent down some great flame and melted them all to nothing.

Their first landfall should be off the northern marches of Bryhaine. From there the commanders could decide whether to head for Ilyan or some other sothran port, or take the fugitives on to their new home in the North. Much would depend on the speed they made, the level of their supplies and the conditions on board, and these were anxiously watched, by the sothrans especially, as the days passed. But although the fleet was held back to the speed of its slowest craft, it was within little more than a fortnight that the dawn showed them the pinnacles of the Shieldrange once more.

'The second time lately!' said Olvar cheerfully, from the deck of the *Rannvi*, where he was sharing a sparse celebration breakfast with Gille. 'It was to somewhere around here those black-garbed bastards chased us – and fell foul of the *Sea Eagle*!'

'I wonder if any still swim around!' said Telqua, making as if to look over the side. She made spear-jabbing gestures. 'We go fishing, yes? Throw the little ones back!'

'You're a bloodthirsty young menace,' said Olvar amiably. 'You'll have to learn to live in peace now, you hear? Take up embroidery, or at least hunting or something!'

She grinned, and settled back, stretching languidly. Evidently this was a usual exchange. 'Long as you are nice. If not, I hunt you!'

'Run me down and eat me alive, that's right,' grinned Olvar.

Gille watched them embrace, with tolerant enjoyment. Olvar seemed to be making up for lost time. He continued to fiddle absently with the corroded tuning keys of the decrepit kantel, and a thought struck him. Could this be what Olvar had meant? Something to fill his mind, while Olvar had a woman and he didn't?

It could be. Gille had to admit that normally he might have been getting restless by now, maybe chasing some of the copper-skinned fugitive girls. True, they frightened him a bit, but none as badly as Telqua. There were certainly some fine lookers among them, all smooth lithe limbs and big dark eyes and lean slender bodies, sweet little tip-tilted breasts outlined through their ragged clothes. Very enticing if you liked the type; and Gille normally liked all types, so long as they were of the female persuasion. So Olvar had expected; and had been dropping him a hint, no doubt, because in such a crowded situation Gille's old tricks might have caused some trouble. But things were different now, just how different Gille himself hadn't realised, till then. He had hardly noticed the women, as women. He felt a slow sense of horror creeping over him. Had Saithana done this to him, stolen away his manhood? Or worse – was it just old age?

Tentatively he summoned up visions of those coppery breasts again, and relaxed in warm reassurance. The old smile spread across his face. Nothing wrong with his reactions, there. And yet somehow...

Not every man or woman finds their ideal. He had. And now she was lost to him. Nobody else seemed to compare. He could hardly imagine anyone else, any one woman. Except, more faintly…

The tuning key gave suddenly, with a tormented squeak. Telqua and Olvar looked up sharply from their clinch. 'It's just the sound of progress,' said Gille apologetically.

The next day the fleet commanders met to decide on their best course. With the wind still mostly in their favour, and no worse than a few mild rainsqualls, even the sothran captains were happy enough to turn northward. 'Could be they don't want to show up in their home ports with such a raggle-taggle cargo,' grunted Olvar under his breath, and Gille agreed.

'Don't entirely blame them. Remember how the sothran soldiers reacted to you, back when? As if you were some kind of talking animal. What would the common folk of Ilyan or Armen think of a couple of thousand copper-skins suddenly sailing in?'

Olvar shrugged. 'They got used to me, soon enough. And they must know why their ships are away. But I agree, they might fear it was some sort of Northern trick, whatever Master Kunrad might say. It's decided, then,' he added, more loudly, for the meeting's benefit. 'My sailing master will give you the course for Saldenborg, and the directions and marks. It's a tidal harbour, so you deep-draught vessels will needs watch out for the mudflats; but the channels should be wide enough for us all.'

With the coast already in their eye, the sail back to Saldenborg seemed slow; but Gille was in no particular hurry. He had emerged from his daze enough to pay some mild attentions to the women of the fleet, and found them quite happily returned, for he was a hero and a chieftain in their eyes. It surprised him, though, how easily he could keep matters casual, and feelings unhurt. He had never taken the trouble to, before. Light of heart himself, he had assumed everyone else must also be as easy, whatever they said, and that they came to little lasting harm. But now he too had found himself out of his depth, in every sense, treading water above a dark abyss. He would not leave anyone else so gravely adrift, not now.

'That's wisdom,' said Olvar, surprised. 'There's enough generous dames in the world who think as you do, to keep you busy.'

'Well, it was mostly that sort who took to me,' said Gille. He ran a caressing finger along the length of spare string he was threading across the kantel. 'But somehow they don't interest me so much any more.'

'You'll get over it,' chuckled Olvar; but though his thoughts ran slow, they had their depths, and his eyes were keen over more than distances. He wondered at his friend.

When they passed the first Northern villages, Olvar sent word ashore, lest somebody decide they were a sothran warfleet. But the tale of the fugitives had reached the North by now, and of the merchants who had turned aside to save them, and the largely sothran fleet sent to their aid. Gille suspected Kunrad, always eager to improve relations with his old home, had made sure of that. All along the coast ships came out to cheer them on their way, and offer fresh supplies, usually in return for tales; and it came to Gille just how much of a hero he was in his own land also, and how little peace he could expect. Still, his answer was the same.

And one red dawn, when the wind seemed unduly brisk, the shape of the peaks upon the horizon was suddenly more familiar, and the concept of home came rushing in upon Gille - the street, the forge, the inns, the shadow of the castle, the old familiar pavements. And with them, all the other baggage of his life, and the choices he would have to make.

The weather was keen as the fleet drove in towards Saldenborg, with its vast fortress crouching lionlike atop the crags, overlooking the rooftops that rolled away below it, across the hills on every side, but most of all down the wide river vale in the cliffs to the harbour below, and the saltpans which gave the city its name.

It was not an auspicious day for a home-coming. Rain had been, and plainly rain would be again ere long. Grey clouds scudded behind the crags, and the waters beneath were choppy and dark, as if they too partook of the city's stony strength. Ervalien, who had come aboard to consult Nils, whistled in reluctant admiration. 'No wonder our great-grandsires got so little change here! What a grand grim place, and that stronghold most of all. I never guessed Nordeney towns could be so strong, I'd heard of them as rustic places.'

'Vayde's work,' said Gille, and shivered a little. 'But it's not so grim, once you're inside. Good inns and taverns, solid food, sothran wines and the best of Northern ale. Pretty women, too, running to the pale-skinned kind if that's your preference. And as to the old wars, they're remembered here also; but nobody much minds. The folk are well disposed to sothrans, so long as they're fairly behaved – saving your grace!'

Ervalien, a younger son of the Ardhren lordship, grinned. 'A timely warning, Master Gille; I'll make sure my crews are suitably admonished. We don't want another war started in the taverns!'

'Oh, they're used to sailors here, and they'll make much of your lads, after all this. Warn 'em they won't find the great stews and brothels of your sothran ports, though. Our girls are more the independent sort!'

Ervalien chuckled, but drily. 'Like all Northerners, eh? Well, I must go see us to our proper stations. Be sure you leave us plenty of sea-room when you take the lead!'

Gille was looking up to the trees along the cliffs, thinking deeply. 'What?'

'You hadn't heard? But of course, we only settled it with Master Kalve and Master Nils just now. Your ships are to lead the fleet in. You know the channels, of course, being local. But that's not the chiefest reason. Not at all! And, while we're on the subject, if you don't mind my asking, Master Gille, we've all grown rather curious as to—'

Thus it was that, in the early even of that day, trumpets blared high on the walls of Saldenborg's citadel, and the town's banner ran up the flagpoles, bursting free into the breeze. Word passed along the streets and alleys of the town, and out beyond it even into the rough and lawless quarters that crouched beneath the wall; for this was a moment long awaited, and prepared for days past. Bells rang, and men ran; and every coign or quarter that had a view of the great bay known as the Saldenborg Roads was crammed with jostling watchers. The sinking sun, striking through the passing rainclouds, turned the waters to a sheet of silvered steel; and across it, singly or in pairs, filed the greatest procession of ships that had been seen in these parts, in both their numbers and their size, since the old wars with the South. But at these massive mastheads there fluttered not the flag of the Southlands, but the green emblem of a castle above waves. This was the flag of Ker an Aruel, ensign of the Marchwarden Kunrad whom the Northerners trusted. And leading the giant ships came two much smaller merchantmen of familiar Nordeney shape.

One flew the Saldenborg flag; but the other, black in background but worked in gold, carried the image of Raven stealing the sun for men. This was the Marchwarden's personal banner, emblem of the royal line to which he now belonged, by marriage and adoption, and which only his chiefest commanders flew; and into it, as if in homage, the sun struck living fire.

The folk on cliff and roof and quayside cheered, a thunderous roar of welcome, as the leading craft came through the channel at the sea wall. Even in that moment Gille spared a brief look at the rocky point, wondering if there still might be any gold he'd missed the first time; and concluded there probably wasn't. Behind their sterns, ponderously dipping as it entered the sheltered water, came the massive prow of the *Sea Eagle*. The ragged figures that thronged the sides of every ship waved back, a little tentatively at first and then, as the feeling of the moment came through to them, every bit as wildly.

More than three fourth parts of the townsfolk shared some Eastern blood, and many had the same colouring, from Telqua's pale copper to Olvar's polished mahogany. For them, it was as if they looked upon their ancestors coming to land. They gave them loud greetings, and crowded the quays so thickly that it proved hard to get the first of them ashore. Olvar had urged that it should be Telqua, but she refused to touch ground before the last of her folk.

So it was that the *Rannvi* and *Orrin* held back till the first of the great sothran ships had docked; and, whatever the later songs said, the first of the fugitives ashore was some anonymous man with a mooring line who clambered from the tall decks on to the iron tide-ladder of the main quay. The rungs had virtues in them against rust and barnacles, but none to repel slime. As he reached the quay he slipped; but eager hands helped him over the top. He stood wondering only an instant before he stooped to help his fellows, and became lost in a grinning, dazed crowd.

Telqua nodded sternly as her orders were obeyed, but her eyes shone. 'So many!' she said. 'And so great place! And truth they give room for us in this your fatted land?'

For perhaps the twentieth time Olvar nodded. 'There's land for the taking and the working, along the cliffs northward, or inland, or in many other places further afield. Few already settled are desperate enough now to meet the hazards and the hard labour, or risk their children's upbringing; but that won't daunt your folk. Soon you'll be as strong as any of us. And by the look of this you won't want for help.'

Nils piloted the *Rannvi* to her place alongside the quay. As she was made fast she rocked a little with the jolt as Kalve brought the *Orrin* alongside her in turn, for with such crowding in the harbour they had to share their mooring. Ropes were wound around bollards, and the gangplank sent crashing and rattling against the stones. But before anyone had even the chance to disembark, a broad red-headed figure in a rain-cloak of oiled cotton trimmed with sleek otter-fur came stumping and strutting aboard, stamping with his silver-headed staff and roaring out Gille's name and Olvar's. A train of no less costly robes trailed unsteadily after him, and among them Altor the goldsmith and the merchants Vangar and, more surprisingly perhaps, Stulte. They looked remarkably cheerful.

'*Tanle!*' laughed Gille, leaping down the deck-ladder. 'You old pirate, what brings you here?'

Tanle pounded him on the back, and waved a wine-flask at Olvar, who was heaving himself over the rail. 'Money, laddie! Money and trade – what else? That, and the pleasure of seeing you returned!'

He glanced around as old Erkel the Guild-master fell off the gangplank into the water, to the loud cheers of the onlookers. 'Never mind him, he floats! The merrymaking's started, as you see! Have a drink, both of you! By Saithana's little pink tits, it's good to see you alive and uneaten in this pack of – *and who's the lovely lady, then?*' he added with smoothly diplomatic haste, as Telqua at her most regal came striding up.

Even unbecomingly clad in tattered breeches and one of Olvar's shirts, hastily altered, she was an arresting figure. Her long hair was combed straight down around her face, framing her fine cheek-bones, and fell in a sleek waterfall to the level of her lean haunches. But beneath her new-trimmed fringe her eyes shone still brighter black, and she gave not the slightest sign of being daunted by the louring power of the citadel, or the noisy enthu-siasm of the crowds, or the evident wealth and authority of these newcomers. Only Olvar knew her well enough to say otherwise; and he had more sense. When she heard Tanle was the merchant who had helped them, she lost a lot of her hauteur, and even accepted an injudicious swig of his fiery twice-distilled wine, which made her cough violently.

'And listen, you!' he added, while Olvar rubbed her back. 'We have got to have a little wee talk, my buckos, and seriously, soon as all this nonsense blows over. That stuff I took off you went at top prices even in Ilyan, with all this fuss about the fleet and all.'

Gille stared. 'You've sold it? Already?'

Tanle made a loud sucking sound. 'Practically took my hand off. A clean sweep, best rates this season. Got it all redded up and locked away back on the *Ker Dorfyn*, but even after my commission there's a tidy little sum for you. And have you got any still left? You have? Then I want it, I don't want to hear you're offering it up and down the quay, I want the lot, you hear! The lot - I'll even stand the cost of shipping it down to Ker Bryhaine. 'Cause by the time I get back there the story's going to be everywhere, and they will go half mad, I'm tellin' you! Furs that've been all the way an' back—' He seized Gille by the shirt. 'Have still got the furs, haven't you?'

'We found a use for those leathers,' sighed Gille abstractedly, anxiously scanning the milling throng. His men had to keep them back off the plank, lest they all try to swarm aboard. 'And we shipped a bit of water now and again, and got very hot. There's going to be some damages. But the furs are all right, I think.'

'Fine! Wonderful! Know how much I shifted my lot for in Ilyan? You don't want to know, it'd bring tears to your eyes, those poor people! Have another! You still mightn't get quite as much as you would have otherwise,' he admitted. 'Can't be helped. Made your choice, and it was the right one, fine, fine! But with the proceeds, why, you could fit out another little flotilla, next spring. Make it all the way south, this time. Take this lovely lady along. They'll all have heard about you by that time. And then, ah, then! Have another, go on!' He rubbed his hands gleefully. 'Then you'll clean 'em out! I'll help! With a hook like that - they'll be slaverin' to hear it, the whole tale from the horse's mouth, hah! Have 'em ready to pay any price—'

'Haven't heard it all ourselves yet,' observed Olvar, as Tanle tilted his flask yet again; and he looked directly at Gille. 'Horse isn't too talkative.'

'Then now's the time!' proclaimed Tanle. 'Feast gettin' goin', ox-roasts and all, right down here on the quay. Proclaimed by the Guilds, just this hour as you came in. Free for every man an' woman, your newcomersh an' all, for the glory you've brought on the town.'

'And to persuade Telqua's folk to stay?' suggested Gille, still anxiously eyeing the crowd.

Tanle laid a finger to his nose. 'No fools, like I alw's say, these Northern laddies! Right, Master Vangar?'

'S'right!' chuckled Vangar, a great deal drunker. 'Up goes our population in a stroke! More land cleared, more corn grown, more livestock kept, more ale brewed - you do drink ale, don't you? More ale - lo'sh more! Volume of trade swells, reserve of cheap labour—'

'Strong soldiery, if they're as tough as they look!' grinned Stulte, with a kind of chilly glee. 'Strong arms for the warehouses, stout backs for'a fieldsh! And then there'sh the salt panning, an' the fisheries—'

'There y'are, see?' demanded Tanle. 'Why, give it ten years and a bit of well-run foreign trade, and this town'll redouble its fortunes. An' yours with it. And mine, even, 'cos now I'm hon'rary Guildman of th' town. And I can broker a reg'lar trade run, every season. And we'll all be filthy stinking rich!'

The merchants staggered on in a sort of chaindance around the deck, to general cheering. Few sights are so festive as one's august elders making utter fools of themselves.

Gille looked after them a little sourly. 'So now we know why we ventured it all. To make our master merchant friends even richer. To bring home some cheap labour. Sound principles of commerce.'

'Can't get away from them,' said Olvar, wryly, and smiled at Telqua, too happy to care very much. 'Even the best deeds can have odd roots and odder flowerings - eh, my lady? But I wouldn't worry about our friends. Let Stulte dream about how he's going to exploit them. He'll be laying himself up a nasty shock. And as to riches, well, you were after a little gain yourself, Gille, weren't you? In among the freedom and adventure and all else. Now you've made it, and done a lot of good along the way. And if it happens to benefit others too, good luck to 'em, say I!'

Tanle, reeling back across the deck, wrapped iron-heavy arms about their shoulders. 'Ach, that's only life! That's all for later, that's *work*!' He swung his flask high, and his staff boomed upon the sun-bleached deck timbers. 'For now – and seein' as his worshipfulness the Guildmaster is being wrung out an' hung out t'dry–'

He spread his arms out wide to the crowd, who greeted the prospect of a speech with an ironic cheer. 'Honoured merchants and master-smiths! Stout-hearted seamen of my own dear Southland and worthy Northland! Our new friends, brave warriors and beautiful ladies, and by the look of it many of you one an' the same–'

He drew a deep breath. 'From the Guild-masters, masters, journeymen and good people of the free town of Saldenborg, and from my own folk of the Southlands I give you a toast. *Welcome home!*'

There was a deafening hubbub as the toast was simultaneously returned, translated, and drunk. The crush on the quay grew, and many more people spilled into the harbour. Others started jumping in to join them. Along the castle walls flares burst out in the dusk. Tanle sank another mighty swig, and waved his staff vaguely.

'And for now, we entertain your good selves – and you entertain us!'

In the end, sitting on the *Rannvi*'s after-rail, surrounded by an admiring and more than merry crowd on deck and quay, it was Olvar who told the story. He did not tell it very skilfully, rambling this way and that; but his very clumsiness made the truth of what he said more impressive, and his blunt language brought home the desperation they had faced, and the horror in his voice at the dark visions of the jungle and the crater. But for the quest among the ice-islands and many other such moments he kept trying to pull in Gille, who was prowling restless about behind him.

Gille's answers, though, were short and nervous; and he seemed to grow more discontented the more they cheered him. But at last, as Olvar told of that strange day of storm and havoc, and the final eerie rout of the black fleet, and of Gille's curious reappearance, the cries grew too great to resist. It was plain from his unhappy demeanour that Gille wanted out of this; and no less plain that nobody would let him go.

'*Give us the tale, Gille! Give us the word, Mastersmith! What happened, Gille?*'

The roar redoubled when they saw him reappear, and the kantel that swung from a cord at his shoulder. '*A song, my master! Going to sing us a song, are you, Gille?*'

He held up the instrument, but it was a while before the row subsided. He waited patiently, and his voice was clear and carried on the evening breeze.

'Yes. One song. And listen well, because this is one ditty I'm not going to sing ever again, in public anyhow. Yes, something did happen, out there on the sea; something that had been brewing ever since this whole adventure began. And mark my words, because, upon my honour as a player, every word is true!' And he turned aside to sneeze loudly.

Then the crowd roared; for that, as every man knew, was the sign that the speaker was speaking the absolute truth. Evidently a very tall story was to follow.

Then he struck the strings, and even the most drunken voices fell instantly silent. They had never heard a tone like that from such an instrument, so rich and full, and so compelling. Olvar swore softly; and the sailors who had heard Gille play the mysterious kantel whispered among themselves. This was not so commanding a sound; but it echoed the other too closely to be accidental.

At first all Gille did was play, a swirling little melody like the lap of waves on a sunny beach, and the crowd, caught up, swayed to the lilt. When he shifted suddenly to an old tune they all knew, a familiar dancing rhythm with a refrain in praise of the Powers, they were humming along with him, all along the sea wall. Even the flares and torches seemed to ripple in the sea breeze; and when Gille suddenly began to sing, they streamed out sidewise, like flickering pennants.

> *Out there by the sea I wandered,*
> *Singing lonely songs of sadness,*
> *Sea-King's mighty daughter heard—*
> *Sweetest singing won her heart!*
> *Hail to her! Praise to her!*

> *Golden fishes she found for me,*
> *And a mighty ship she gave me,*
> *Sent me sailing southward swift—*
> *Sent me into Ice and strife!*
> *Hail to her! Praise to her!*

The crowd, intrigued and delighted, echoed the familiar refrain. Gille launched into the second half of the melody, jolly, jaunty, anything but serious, with rhymes deliberately cockeyed for a more comic effect.

Then down to the lonely waves I fell, ah,
And instead of sinking down to Hella,
When life and hope damn near forsook me
Down to her father's halls she took me,
As minstrel to the mighty Sea-King!
To turn his wrath I made shift to sing,
Played till I thought my head would turn,
Played till my hands began to burn!

And fair Saithana began to dance,
Made the Sea-King turn his glance!
He in his turn, he started prancing,
Through the mighty Ocean dancing!
Like a soup-pot stirred the water
Skipping faster than his lovely daughter,
Mighty waves began to form—
Stirred the oceans to a storm!

The kantel thrummed and rumbled, and the
audience thrilled to the crash of the waves.

Then I called for the help of an ancient name,
He heard the song of a smith, and came—
Made the Sea-King cease to batter,
The marauding fleet to shatter!
Hail to him! Praise to him!

Seaking's Child and Master's Master,
They have saved us from disaster!
Saithana and Ilmarinen!
Praise to the Powers that love us men!
Hail to them! Praise to them!

And you who don't believe my story—
Don't deny those Two their glory!
If you think my tale's too strong—
Sing yourself a better song!
Hail to them! Praise to them!

Gille bowed, with an impudent grin, while the crowd roared out the refrain, and with it their cheers. And he knew, looking over their laughing faces, that probably not a one of them believed him, and none at all cared. And that was exactly what he intended.

He had taken the nightmare he had lived through, and lifted it from his heart. He had not lied; for he would have had to live that lie for the rest of his days, and besides, he had heard that lying about such deep and eerie matters could be very dangerous. He was only too inclined to believe that, now. But the burden of the truth, with its endless doubts and explanations that would make too much of him, or too little, he had managed to throw off.

He had turned it all into cheerful doggerel, a boast, a brag, too outrageous to believe. He had cracked a fine joke, one that fitted the mood of the crowd, one that even seemed modest, coming from a man who had already achieved much. 'Just like Gille!' they'd say, and laugh. They might even sing the song again; but hardly a man among them would ever give it another serious thought. So, now, nor need he. And among all the laughter he had given honour where honour was due.

He bowed again, while the sailors clustered around him, roaring with laughter, throwing their arms about his shoulders, and thrusting flasks and tankards into his hand, to his lips even. 'You're a one, you are, Master Gille!' boomed Dall the bosun, face beaming wide, and Gille guessed that he too had had something of the horrors of the raft lifted from him. 'Thought Saithana'd be coming for me myself! Might've known you'd got in there first, eh?'

Gille slapped him on the shoulder, and stepped down, with the crowd still cheering and whistling and toasting his health and Olvar's. They would let him alone now, for a little; and he meant to make use of his time. He slipped off to the far rail, as many did in the course of their drinking; but a hand caught him by the arm. A huge hand, Olvar's.

'Some display, my lad!' said the big man quietly. 'Is it that you've been being so secretive about, these last weeks? And is that the kantel I gave you, that clapped-out fishbox, as you named it? I won't say I've never heard better, because I have – as we both know. But this one reminds me of the other; and that's almost more of a miracle than aught else so far!'

Gille wriggled, in both body and mind. 'No, no. It's just that, well, I know now how a good instrument *can* sound – how it feels, everything. So I just started tinkering with this one, with the sound of the other in my head – tinkering, trying this or that, anything that made it more right. And...' He shrugged. 'I had some of the string left, her string; but not enough. I thought at first that would make the difference, but the sound's just the same without it. It was the varnish, layers of it rubbed well down. And paring down the wood around the soundbox. Most of all the metal, the soundboard. Getting the copper to just the right thickness and shape for the resonance, because the wood had so little – and the steel plate for the bridge, shaping and angling that... A thousand little things.'

'If you can do that,' said Olvar slowly, 'then I don't think you need worry any more about your livelihood, Gille. You've found your niche in smithcraft. A small one, maybe, and of modest powers; but then maybe you were simply given all you needed. Go on back to the forge and make more such kantels, Gille. Study the making of musical things. Leave the mundane work to me for now. You'll repay me soon enough, I know.'

Gille nodded, hardly able to speak. 'I'll repay you. As He said he'd repay me...'

'Who said?' demanded Olvar, his keen eyes glittering in the flarelight. 'I know you, Gille. You won't blind me with a song, however merry. There was some truth in that, wasn't there? However you disguised it, there was some, wasn't there?'

'No,' answered Gille.

Olvar squinted, thinking with an almost visible effort. 'No? But I... No. You said just, no - meaning no, there isn't *some* truth... Powers alive, man - you're not trying to tell me it was *all* true, are you? Literally true?'

Gille was silent.

'*Whew!*' exploded his friend, and ran his fingers through his hair. 'What one little smith can start, with an ounce of discontent and a nice clear tenor - and a few other attributes, also. Well, it seems I'm just one of the many who have you to thank for a new life. And I do, my friend.' He clapped Gille on the shoulder. 'And what of you, yourself? I guess I understand you a little better now. And that ring you keep trying to hide. A mortal girl must seem a poor substitute for the love of a Power.'

'I was wondering if Utte would be here,' said Gille.

'Haven't seen her. But I made out one of her brothers over on the quay there - yes, see? Porre, or whatever his name is.'

'Bure,' said Gille. The two friends looked at one another, in the growing dark; but it was not with eyes they saw.

'Thanks for your dream, my lad,' said Olvar. 'Thanks for letting me share it. If we'd listened to me—'

'It could have gone wrong a hundred ways,' said Gille. 'Ruin, confusion, death for us both. It nearly did.'

'You were right, though. The risk was worth it. Well worth it. I thank you; and Telqua thanks you.

And a few thousand others. I hope that'll count for much – as and when.'

Gille nodded; and they clasped hands briefly, and took their leave without more words.

Utte's eldest brother, thought Gille, was a jolly, kindly man; but he needed only the snout of a tankard over his nose to complete his resemblance to one of his own pigs. How he could share Utte's blood was hard to imagine. He spluttered as he saw Gille, tried to lever himself off the bale of clothes he was sitting on, and failed. He slapped his thigh, which made a soggy noise.

'Laddie! Good t'see yer back! That was a song and a half, har! Laughed so much I went arse over tip into the harbour, har!'

'So I see,' said Gille. 'Where are Thjave and Ulfr?'

Landholder Bure grinned and pointed downward, at the bale.

'I see,' said Gille again. 'And Utte? Has she not…'

'Didn't feel like, she said. Women! Washday, an' too much doin'. Wash, wash, scrub, shwash…' The farmer grinned fixedly, spewed ale down his smock, wet himself and slid slowly down to join his brethren. Gille commanded his crew to haul them into a more comfortable spot aboard. Then he faded away once more into the rainy night, and let the sound of the celebrations die away behind him.

So it is that the Mastersmith Gille enters into the Chronicles, and the legends that surround them, as lover of women, adventurer, singer, merchant, smith of strong music, but above all as a teller of the tallest tales, something of a figure of fun. It did him no harm. When he and Olvar did indeed launch a new trading venture, men flocked to invest in his cargo, and to serve on his ship; for though he never became that much of a seaman, sea-luck was something that could not be learned, and his was known to be remarkable. In the Southlands, too, as their trading prospered and grew, he became a well-known figure, a merry swashbuckling mountebank, a popular and lively guest who leavened Olvar's solid gravity and lent an air of romance to the goods he sold, his marvellous musical instruments above all.

Together they came almost to represent their country there, and to raise it in popular esteem. And it was Gille and Olvar, in the height of their prosperity, who took up for the North the building of the Great Causeway across the terrible Marshes, that their old master Kunrad had begun, and saw long stretches of it made complete. Such bold journeys and weighty enterprises were bound to bring them adventures of all kinds; but never again, as they thankfully agreed, one so dark and perilous, and so significant in the history of the North.

From the Westlands over the Ocean little more was heard. The bleak grasp of the Ice had tightened upon those lands, beyond the power of men to lift. Only once in a lifetime might a lonely fugitive or two escape, but never again any number. Most perished in the attempt. It was long centuries, none-theless, and a sadder, less vigilant time, before the black fleets ever again dared penetrate the Western sea.

And meanwhile, those fugitives whom the smiths had gone through so much to rescue settled throughout the Northlands, to wide welcome and acclaim; but chiefly indeed in the Saldenborg region. The copper-skinned folk swelled its pros-perity even more swiftly than the merchants predicted, and with it their own, becoming masters of rich homesteads which were in time to grow into villages and even small towns. And in every one of these, alongside their chieftain Telqua, the names of

Gille and Olvar were honoured as lords, their most casual visit a cause for high rejoicing, and their names bestowed upon the firstborn in the land. It is said of Olvar and Telqua that they had many children of their own, and in the process the one grew fuller and the other leaner, leading Gille to claim that theirs was clearly a balanced match. She went with them on their journeys when she could, and much is told of her in the Chronicles, and their long and happy life.

Of Gille and his life thereafter, though, less is said. It is known that he had offspring, for many of his line carved out names of their own in the Chronicles; but his immediate family are made to seem no more than shadows at his back. Only from chance accounts do we learn how slight was the truth of that, and how little understood was the change in his life, from the moment he fled the festivities.

There was no getting through the town tonight, not for him. He knew he would have to stop, and talk, and accept so many drinks he'd be blind drunk before he reached the gate; and the guards would probably be somewhere else, and drunk too. There were no horses to be had around here. He thought of taking one of the boats, but by now the tide was out, and he did not trust himself in the channels. In the end he simply took a staff for safety, and clambered down the far face of the sea wall to the beach. He walked along the narrow sand-strip as far as he could, and thence across the edge of the mudflats towards the rift in the cliffs where the little fishing village lay. It was not so long a walk, and close to the shore there was small chance of quicksand, the more so as he could try with his staff. Nonetheless it was slippery and slidey walking, with great stretches of rank-smelling weed. The sand clung and squeaked beneath his feet, and now and then a shell crunched, or driftwood snapped with a soggy pop. Every so often he looked out to the starlit breakers that boomed across the distant sands.

The wind was rising, telling them its own gloomy and lawless tales of the North, singing runes of such dark potency that the spray seemed to leap for sheer joy. So he saw it; for his view of the world was changed, and of the sea most of all.

He fell down several times, and it was a mud-caked apparition who slowly climbed the track to the summit, and the open fields that lay beyond. The moon came out from behind the clouds now, and eased his way; but nonetheless it was past midnight when he came to the old manor, and he saw not a light behind the heavy shutters.

He swore, and struggled up over the wall, very effortfully. He had done this before, but usually standing on his saddle, and without a coating of slippery mud and sand all over his breeches. He was still at the top when the rain started again, heavily, and he had to pull up his hood like some ancient wanderer. He slid down into the yard and landed awkwardly on one ankle, which hurt. He had never felt less like a hero of romance in his life.

He was about to find a pebble to rattle off Utte's shutters, when he heard the familiar creak of the kitchen pump, inside the house as it often was in wealthy households. He hobbled hastily around the back, leaning on his staff, and saw between the heavy wind-slats the glimmer of a single lamp. One of the farm-girls, probably; but he was past caring. He rapped his staff on the heavy door.

'*Who's there?*' demanded a voice, sharp, a little alarmed, even; but very familiar. On the other side of the yard a dog started barking, and he hoped devoutly that it was tied up as usual.

He drew breath. 'Utte! It's me!'

There was silence behind the door, a silence that grew and lingered while the wind whined and blew about Gille's soaking neck. The light flickered behind the shutter, but there was no sign of movement. At last he heard the scrape of the great bolt being drawn back, very slowly, and the two others snapping back. A golden crack split the shadowy rim of the door, widening a little; and he saw that the steel loop-latch was still engaged, that he himself had forged. A narrow beam of light spilled down across the step from the raised lamp. Then the door closed softly, and some feeling he could not name gripped Gille; until he heard the snick of the loop being put back, and the door opened wider than before.

It was not Utte; it was one of the farm-girls, in her long nightdress topped by a heavy woollen shawl, and she allowed Gille in, unsmiling. The air smelt of steam and woodsmoke. At the far end of the long manor kitchen, Utte, also in her nightdress, dark hair loose about her shoulders, was stretching out strips of amorphous laundry on a great hanging frame of wood by the tall chimney. As his boots clumped on the worn flagstones, she did not so much as look around.

'Thank you, Ylla. You can go to bed now.' The girl drifted away to the inner door, looking back doubtfully. Utte waited till the latch closed, but still did not turn.

'Well, Mastersmith? A late hour to be calling?'

'I saw the light. I took you at your word.'

'Well, welcome.' She still scarcely turned to him. 'I heard you were coming. You might have sent word.'

'I hadn't much chance, Utte. I'm here now. You were slow to open up.'

'I thought it might be someone else.' She folded another piece of linen on the rack.

'Someone—' Gille tried to speak calmly. She still would not look straight at him, but she was smiling, a little archly.

'Maybe. I've had offers. One before your ship was even out of sight of the quay. From your friend Master Vangar.'

Gill winced. 'That vulture? Powers, no—'

'He's handsome, in his way. And no swagbelly; a keen rider, very hard. And he's very, very rich.'

'I had his last penny in my hand! And his - I should have taken the lot! You didn't accept. Naturally.'

She chuckled. 'Not altogether. But he started something, when folk saw me on his arm. There've been a few more sniffing around, too. Landholder Hend of Uffesley, for one. I took to him more.'

'He's young enough, at least,' said Gille grudgingly. 'And decent enough. And well landed.'

'And fun,' she said, with a demure little smile that made Gille's heart sink. 'A fine dancer. I haven't said no to either.'

'But you were slow to open the door,' said Gille.

Utte made no comment, but picked up more linen. 'And you? You've met somebody?'

Gille shuddered. 'I met somebody all right!' he said savagely. 'I met myself!'

She almost turned around, with a faint chuckle. 'Did you, indeed? Well, they say you travel to meet strangers. And have you found your dreams?'

'They met me!' he snarled, and subsided. 'Never look for perfection, Utte. You may find it, and what then? It's *your* perfection! It's only you yourself.'

She turned sharply, about to speak; but instead she stared. 'Ach, you're soaked! More of a mudpie than a man, and dripping all over the flags! The girls'll take on fits! Come, off with your cloak. And those great sea-boots now – no, fool,' she exclaimed as Gille hopped on one leg. 'Put your bum down here on the settle, and I'll pull them off, see? And your britches – yes, come on. Leave the kantel there. Now go sit you down in the inglenook and I'll brew you some herb tea with burnt spirits in it. Did your horse throw you or something?'

'No. I walked from the harbour.'

'Across the sands? At this hour? You must be daft. Even the Powers might catch a cold on such a night.'

Gille felt ridiculous in only his shirt, but the warmth caught him. He stretched luxuriously, and put his numbed and wrinkled toes up on the hot bricks around the hearth. It all seemed unbelievably secure and warm and still. 'I was in haste.'

'Were you now?' She peered at him more closely. 'Stars and Powers, that's not all mud, is it? You're burnt brown as a penny biscuit, even your toes!'

'You should see the rest of me.'

She ignored that, and went to make the tea, filling a blackened iron kettle at the pump. 'All the sun down in those sothran parts, they say. How they're supposed to be so pale-skinned, I'll never know.'

'I was a lot further south,' he said, and there was that in his voice that made her look sharply around, kettle in hand.

'Gille – where have you been? Somewhere terrible, awful – I can see that.'

'Terrible, yes. Awful – yes. Filled with awe.'

She sniffed, tilting her nose in the air. 'Let me guess. There you met your perfect woman – which I am not, we'll agree? Fine, fine, no need to splutter so. And then it all went astray?'

'Yes,' he said sullenly, both rebelling at her gloating, and conceding her the right. 'But the more she was perfect - the less she was a woman. She was ... a ... thing, a creation. A mould into which I pressed myself. Nothing more!'

'She must have been something of herself,' objected Utte. 'Every woman's a human being, though little some men believe it.'

'She wasn't human!'

There was a long silence, broken only by the bubbling of the kettle. At last Utte took herbs from packets and jars, and unstoppered a small stone jar of distilled corn liquor. 'Well, well, indeed. A living dream, it seems. You must have felt honoured.'

Gill could only shake his head. 'Not that. Her feelings were real enough, perhaps. For men. I was only the one of the moment. Everything she showed me was what I chose for myself. What she read in me, she modelled there. Her look, her manner, her allure ...'

'She saw the wings in the night, and made them a nest,' said Utte. 'How strange!'

'Not a nest,' shivered Gille. 'A fiercer wind. It was what I thought - you're mocking me!'

'Oh, I believe you,' she said simply. 'I meant, how strange that you saw through it. That you did not accept it, that you didn't fly to the wind with all your heart's desire.'

The kettle was squealing for attention. Utte rose and took it from its hook, a cloth wrapped around her hands. Gille admired the way the flames set her pale face and neck glowing with crimson highlights. She poured water on the herbs in clouds of scented steam; then she added a large splash of sticky brown sugar spirits. 'There, get that down you!'

He gave her heartfelt thanks as he took the mug; and as he sipped the scalding liquid, there was a clink at the rough pottery. The ring had turned again on his finger, loose and insistent. It seemed like a bad joke now, his own glittering arrogance made solid. Carefully he slid it off, fingering it uncertainly, wondering whether he could reach a pocket to slip it away without her seeing.

'Anyhow, that wasn't what I meant,' she said, seating herself on the other side of the fireplace. 'About your dreams. Your way in life, was what I intended. Your thoughts of profit, of opening up the trade routes again, of making a fat merchant of yourself?'

'Not wholly,' he admitted. 'We got turned aside.'

'I heard. You did very well there, Gille.'

Gille noticed how the firelight made her eyes glitter. 'Maybe. It's not what a true merchant would do. The ones who stay at home and take no risks, they're the ones that grow fattest. It cost us the best of our profits; but we've enough to try again. And there's something more.'

He reached over to the settle, and drew his fingers across the strings of the kantel. Melody seemed to ripple through the room, curling like the heady steam of his drink. Utte leapt up, half laughing.

'Enough! Will you rouse the whole household upon us, like this?' But her eyes were dancing. 'It's a lovely sound, though. You made that?'

'I made it sound like that. And I can make more, I think. Maybe better ones.'

'Then you'll never want for a living,' she said quietly.

The hot spirit was loose in his stomach now, running like fire past his heart; and suddenly he felt a great, an overwhelming wave of understanding, and gratitude. The pump dripped, and she turned away a moment to stem it. He made no move, said nothing, sipped the infusion. The fire hissed and spat at him, and he realised suddenly that his soles were growing far too hot. He sprang to his feet on the hearth, so violently she dodged behind the pump.

'Look – why I came ... I came to tell you that ... That I've, I've learnt the error of my ways!' he finished in a rush, half shouting the embarrassing phrase.

Utte clapped hand to mouth, almost shaking with laughter. '*What?*'

'I mean it!' Gille insisted, drawing himself up with what dignity he could, which only made the front of his inadequate shirt ride up. He tugged it down. 'Look, I brought you back something,' he said, and thrust the ring awkwardly at her. 'I've ... I've played around enough. I was a fool. I didn't value ... what I had in you, not enough, not nearly. I'm not going to chase girls – women – ever, ever, ever again. I want to, to make it up to you – to, to wed you and settle down and, and ...'

'Bore the bum off me?' she enquired sweetly.

Gille's mouth hung open.

'Idiot!' she said sweetly. 'Wantwit, lack-brain, numbskull, ass! Booby, buffoon, dick-noddle, clown! Why should I wish to change what I like so well already?'

Gille closed his mouth. 'You like ...'

The ring slid off his palm. She caught it, held it to the firelight, clicked her tongue in wonder. 'Gille, it's lovely, it looks ancient, and it must be so costly, fit for a great lady of the Southlands!' Then she stopped, considered the jewel, tossed it in the air and caught it deftly, closing her chubby palm about it. 'She gave you this, didn't she? She knew what she was doing. But Gille – it's not what I want.'

He still could scarcely speak.

'Not if it's to be a fetter, to keep you stifling and growing stale. Why should I ask such a stupid thing, now that I know you at last for what you are? When I heard what you did,' she went on, more quietly, 'I thought: that's the Gille I always think I see. The complete Gille, neither the clever dreamer, nor the kind, eager boy, nor the eternal skirtchaser. That's him all together, the foolish with the splendid, and more than either. I thought, there now! He's found what he sought. That's him behaving like himself at last.'

Gille said nothing. His eyes had gazed on immortal fires, but now he lowered them. Utte's voice was rich in laughter still.

'I don't want to shape you a cage. It would break you, or you it. And it would cage me, also. Did I not say it was the romance I loved, the game we played? Your freedom, that also sets me free. I've no wish to wander; but I love a wanderer. And think you, shall I not be proud to be the one such a man as you always comes home to?'

She smiled. 'But you had to have the roots in yourself, to set them down in me. To be the father of our children. And now you have. Go where you will, now, and how you will – so long as you return, and bring colour and laughter and adventure and songs to light up our lives. So long as you always come home!'

She opened her palm. The ring was about her finger, and it settled there as if made to fit, sparkling merrily in the firelight with the green of distant sun-warmed seas.

Gille seized her hand, and her touch was a spark among kindling. The wind roared in the chimney, the fire blazed, and a great tide of love and tenderness and lust billowed up in him. He caught her to him, and she flung her arms about his neck, pressed his lips to him, and her breast and thighs as tightly. Clutching at one another, shirt and night-dress yielded, and their hands ran and played over all the warmth they uncovered. He lifted her, solid as she was, so that her plump legs slid about his thighs, and laid her very gently back on the well-scrubbed timber of the masive table.

'*No!*' she protested, in a determined whisper. 'What're you about? Ylla's probably listening just behind the door!'

'Let her!' laughed Gille. 'She'll have to get used to it. I'll always come home to you, thus!'

'And you'll find the hearth just as warm!' she breathed.

He kissed the laughter on her lips. 'For what is a rover, after all,' he whispered, 'lacking the point from which he roves, the fixed place and pivot of his heart? Naught but ragged wings, whirled upon the blast. Let the world think what it likes – your song and mine shall always be sung together!'

Their breath mingled, fast and hot and shallow, like a furnace-draught. As if in answer the fire billowed, throwing their blended shadows huge about the walls and ceiling; and the pump gurgled faintly, musically, trickling out a thread of fine clear water.

Appendix

Of such matters in the tale as are not there made plain; of the nature of Hunter and Hunted, and of the forces that worked for and against them

The authors of the Winter Chronicles were writing, as men must, for their own times. They left much unexplained that we no longer know, and explained many things we would now take for granted. Much that is relevant to the tales of Gille and Olvar has been said already in earlier books, and need not be repeated here; most notably the story of the lands of Nordeney and Ker Bryhaine, Northland and Southland, their tragic ancestry, savage beginnings and tangled history.

More is there also of the menace of the Ice which at this time sought to engulf the world, throwing into the balance the fates of humanity and all things living, and of the contention of the Powers of the World which lay behind it.

Some matters central to that time play only a lesser role here, such as the strange and potent art of smithcraft. This was not only the art of the shaping of metals; though that lay at its heart, and though, in the greatest of the mastersmiths, it grew to a pitch modern knowledge and device has not yet exceeded. But beyond that, even the least of them could imbue the works of their hands with virtues, forces that enhanced the nature and utility of the thing they made, and in extreme cases could endow it with arcane and formidable potency. In doing this they tapped a force which flowed within themselves, and could be perceived within their works and even within their eyes by others who possessed it, as a glinting, glancing flux of light. It is a belief often stated in the Chronicles that this potency was given to men, and to their Elder Race the *duergar*, by the benign Powers, to help them survive the travails of the Winter of the World. Yet by many that power was rejected, as by the sothrans of Ker Bryhaine, who, officially at least, considered it a superstition. And there were others who sought to exploit it in different, and often darker, ways; as is later laid out here.

OF THE WESTLANDS, THEIR NATURE, CONDITION AND PEOPLES

The great pursuit that is central to this tale had its roots in the lands across the Western ocean; but they are only glimpsed from afar, through the eyes and the actions of those who fled them. In truth, although more is known of them and their realms of men in later centuries (Appendix, *The Hammer of the Sun*), far less can be said with any certainty of this era. No chronicles were kept there, save by word of mouth; or none, at any rate, survived. Only legends remained; but the picture they drew was bleak.

In extent this was a country greater even than the continent of Brasayhal, one immense landmass that stretched out from the deep vales and wide plains bordering the Seas of the Sunset. To the west this land extended so far that a traveller might wander at last around the curve of the world to the subcontinent of Kerys, if he lived so long. To the south and southwest the land stretched into strange country that the coming of the Ice, compressing and disrupting climes, had turned to hot jungles and wastes. But to the northward all this great country was the domain of the Ice; and it drove its chill hand forever deeper, towards their heart.

That heart was vast, nonetheless, an expanse of forest and hill and rolling plainland, wide enough for many realms; and it was here that most men yet lived, many races of them. Whether or not they had once had high civilisations of their own, the Chronicles do not agree. Only a few ancient ruins survived, and tiny relics such as Telqua carried, tokens of vanished crafts and skills. Some chroniclers held that these were most

likely the legacy of the *duergar*, those strange endur-
ing shoots of an ancestral line; or, at best, of brief
spasmodic blossomings of civilisation, brought about
with their help. Such thinkers were unwilling, perhaps, to concede that men could fall so far from their
civilised state towards the savage and desperate condition as had the men of the Westlands. Or, it may be,
they wished to believe that no folk save their own
could be the cradle of such civilisation, especially folk
with darker skins. That was a common view among
historians of the Southlands.

The evidence, however, is against them. Even the
legends tell of the remains of cities so great that the
rustic folk who wandered in their shadow thought
them the work of giants. In fact, like the ruins of
Zimbabwe, or Bath, these were built by their own
ancestors; but they had long forgotten, or ceased to
believe. It may be that the tribes and clans that ran like
veins through the lands, maintained even across vast
distances and wholly altered ways of life, were some
survival of those vanished realms; but, if so, their significance was utterly forgotten.

Every so often some little kingdom would spring
up once again among the remains of the old, often
harsh and greedy as such young realms are, yet
bearing within it a seed of greatness. It would re-
discover the secrets of agriculture and animal hus-
bandry, and the storing of surpluses that allowed men
to live for more than the food in their mouths. But it,
too, would fall, and pass back into the dust at the feet
of those ancient ruins. Its folk would be reduced to
subsistence farmers, and generally within a genera-
tion they would be the lowest of nomadic hunter-
gatherers once again. Sometimes the fall came from
within, in treachery and warring kin; but just as often
it came from without, from constant assault and
harassment. To many such a fall came to seem in-
evitable; but behind it, always, lay the cold hand of
the Ice.

Often, though, the blow was not direct; and the Ice
did not even have to lift another finger. Its coming, and
the desolation its chilling weather spread before it, had

stripped once fertile lands to a country of stones and dry earth. Its winters froze the soil as hard as steel, its summers dried it to powder, its winds scoured it away. The great rivers, swollen and driven by its meltwater, no longer laid down much of the rich sediments they carried from the mountains, but swept the greater part away to the deltas of the coast, which became marshlands and stinking swamps as fearful as those across the ocean. The icy winds spawned by the Ice flayed the flesh from the land and laid bare its bones.

In these harsh conditions kingdoms would grow to a certain point, at which they could just, by constant labour, feed their folk; and then a run of harsh summers, or the exhaustion of their land, would tear them apart. Other lands they had overrun would rebel, neighbours they had threatened would destroy them, and often ruin themselves in the process. Such hatreds and jealousies the Ice had had long practice at fomenting; and when it could not induce war, it had its own warriors to unleash.

Of the Hosts of the Ice

Sometimes, as in other lands, these seem to have been extraordinary creatures, wholly supernatural, or fearsome beasts preserved from an earlier time, and often monstrously changed. Against these, though, men often fought more successfully than might have been expected; and so the weapon the Ice increasingly chose to wield against men was other men. These were the tribes known by many names, but in their own tongue as the Hunters, *Aika'iya-wahsa*, that became Ekwesh in the tongue of Gille's folk.

Where they came from is doubly uncertain. Probably they were never truly a distinct people in themselves, but were ensnared by the Ice over many generations from the various races of the lands, and nurtured in the inhabitable regions around the Ice's borders, under the eyes of its ruling Powers. Here, as a number of loose and quarrelsome tribes, they scratched out a crude and primitive existence, one which seems to have been enforced to harden their hearts and breed distrust of all other men. They maintained the ancient clan system among themselves, although unlike all other folk they acknowledged no kinship with clan members outside their own people. Nor did clan kinship stand in the way of bloody rivalries over matters such as land, or water, or simply status. The Ice imposed this, as it sought to impose all else about them. Once, it is said, it had tried to breed men as it did its monsters, and with some success; but the creatures it bred turned out, once again, to be a poorer match for men. So for now it left them to live and breed in their own fashion, but within a fearful culture based upon ruthless cruelty, constant aggression and grim, self-tormenting discipline.

The Ice had learned, perhaps, that many men would be susceptible to this, and enter into it wholeheartedly, not least for the hold it gave them over others. It cemented their obedience by creating a cult of its own worship, a dark creed of constant war and bloodshed, with atrocities at its heart. Its adherents vied with one another for superiority and standing, which would bring them the domination of others and the rewards of power. This was achieved by success in war and the perpetual harrying and raiding they carried out, or otherwise carrying out the commands of the Ice; by the accumulation of wealth this allowed; and by the practices of the cult, including the sacrifice of prisoners.

Thus becoming a chieftain among the Ekwesh was a process designed to extinguish any shred of pity or human feeling, and to foster a spirit of ruthless rivalry. It also demanded the gathering of wealth in various forms, and its distribution or purposeless destruction for mere display. Many relics of the past probably perished in that fashion; indeed there is evidence that they were especially prized and sought after for it, because that pleased the Ice. Maintaining that position, or rising higher among one's fellow chieftains, went still further. It was an escalating process of acts from which ordinary men would recoil, but which fostered both their sense of separateness and their contempt for all others, even their own. In later years the rulers of the Ice extended this to create the elite of the Hidden Clan, a more subtle attempt at selective breeding of men to override the disunity it had itself created, and one that, had it lasted longer, might well have succeeded.

The word 'men' is accurate. In Ekwesh societies, though they varied widely, women were barely one stage above slaves, sometimes even denied names of their own. At times some unusual women overcame even this barrier, usually by earning the special favour of some Power of the Ice; but almost always it was at the cost of becoming even more fearsome and cruel than the men.

In the centuries after the events of this tale, when there remained no more free tribes of any significance to enslave, and the Ekwesh achieved some semblance of unity, they became a nomadic elite, dominating great settlements of slaves. Yet even then they continually vied and fought among themselves for ownership of those settlements, often to the frustration of the Ice. It had shaped its thralls too successfully, and consistently failed to weld them into a coherent force until the Mastersmith Mylio, through Elof, found a way.

Of the Escape and the Pursuit

Why the Ekwesh sought so fiercely to arrest or to destroy the escape led by Telqua's people is not immediately apparent from the Chronicle narrative. Even if they had succeeded, the cost would have been terrible. As matters turned out, it was a disaster which curbed their power for generations to follow, and seems to have driven the Ice to wrath. It would have been far simpler to let the refugee fleet vanish into the mists of the ocean, from which no word returned, and bend their efforts to make sure no further fleets were built. That, though, was a failure the Ekwesh neither could nor dared tolerate.

In part their need stemmed from their ethos of superiority and the need to dominate which was instilled in them at every level. The escape was the achievement of free men and independent minds, the existence of which was abhorrent to them. They saw, and they hated, with a hate that ran deep as the foundations of their lives. Ekwesh chieftains could not believe such a venture could arise among the down-trodden peasants, savages and slaves they were harrowing; it had to be some malign plot by a rival power, and as such stopped at once.

But it also presented them with a genuine threat. For a century or more the various tribes had enjoyed such success across the lands that they had become complacent. This massive act of defiance challenged them in every quarter. Left to succeed, it would have spawned a hundred more such attempts, and they could not prevent them all. That would further diminish the terror in which the Ekwesh were held. It might even give heart and purpose to the petty kingdoms they were extinguishing, and win those kingdoms belief and support from the rustic tribes. Bringing a few back in chains, to tell of the destruction of the rest, would strengthen everything they had threatened, and discourage all future such attempts. They had little choice but to try.

It seems that one powerful tribe among them, dwelling near the coast and specialising in sea-raiding, may have taken the initiative, but managed to co-opt the help of others. It may be, given the racial dif-ferences Gille noticed in his raft companions, that the seamen and warriors aboard the ships stemmed from different tribes, which may not have helped their efficiency. They were, however, united in their deter-mination; for behind them was the Ice. It too had reasons to fear.

Men could not fight glaciers with swords and spears. If left to develop civilisation, though, they could in time learn to manipulate nature, enough to make weapons that would fight the Ice, or move their dwellings beyond its reach. The Ice knew that better than they. Its first weapons were darkness, division, ignorance and fear, and only when their work was done could the obliterating weight of the glaciers follow. The flight of a few fugitives was nothing to them; but its masters had their cold eyes fixed on a further future, and their attempt to dominate those lands. An influx of refugees would both strengthen their folk, and make them more aware of their ancient enemy; it might even inflame men enough to raise an invasion.

It was with that thought that the minds of the Ice unleashed their hunters on the trail; and with some success. For though the hunters did not prevent the escape, and lost an immense fleet, they created such an impression of overwhelming power and danger that few men of the East would dare dream of challenging it. Yet, in the long term, the escapers did indeed bring both new strengths and new awareness to the lands, and a less partisan and more unifying spirit, since both North and South had come to their aid; and that was no small victory.

OF THE POWERS, AND THEIR ROLES

One unusual feature of Gille's tale is how closely he came into contact with Powers in their non-human guises, and even penetrated the outer borders of their realm. This was very rare; even Elof Valantor at the summit of his craft only ever attained glimpses. Few others did; and fewer still survived the experience, at any rate with their minds intact. It was undoubtedly for this reason that Niarad and his followers strove to take some semblance of human form, however remote, the moment they encountered Gille. They knew well that their mere presence, and the fluid, chaotic world they inhabited, could be literally crushing to mere humanity, physically and mentally. This may account for much of their overbearing quality; from their points of view they were already making a considerable concession to him, and probably an uncomfortable one.

As Vayde told him, only the lesser powers could comfortably remain in human form; even Saithana would have found it difficult, and Gille was right to suspect he was only seeing a minor aspect of her. The real being was undoubtedly much vaster and more complex. She could be compared to modern naturalists who 'live' their subjects, such as the one who learned to imitate and communicate with a particular variety of snail so perfectly that despite vast disparities of size and nature, they accepted him as one of their own; or the other who learned to perform the mating rituals of endangered cranes convincingly enough to help them breed.

Another aspect of the Powers is touched on, their relative authority. Niarad and Saithana appear to take orders from Ilmarinen, as if subservient to him; but their relationship was in no way so simple. As far as can be determined from the Chronicles – and as far as this can be expressed in human terms – the Powers, friendly and hostile, were largely independent of one another. They certainly differed greatly in strength, and this could be a factor; few stood willingly against Ilmarinen, ancient master of the world's fabric and its inner fires – hence Saithana's terror. But some could and did, most notably the Powers of the Ice; and Niarad himself was powerful enough to have risen in wrath against Ilmarinen, if he chose. But this would have been incredibly destructive of everything around them, sea, air and land alike; and that was something even the least concerned and committed Powers strove to avoid – all, again, save those of the Ice. The more the Powers understood of the world as a whole, and not merely their segment of it, the less ready they were to intervene directly. The figure known as Raven, though his strengths were great and his intentions benign, seems to have preferred to manipulate matters as little as possible, and even then only by the lightest of touches, often veiled in rather disturbing trickery.

The true source of authority here seems to have been moral. Each of the Powers had originally had some specific task to perform, vast portions of a still vaster whole. In these spheres of responsibility they found both their power-base and their identity; but how well they performed their tasks seems to have varied greatly. Nonetheless it was a matter of pride. When one could be shown that he had deviated from his charge, the offender's authority over others would be greatly reduced, his own lesser followers especially, inducing feelings that in a human would correspond to shame. Since the Powers seem to have been too intelligent to take refuge in exculpatory self-deceptions, though, shame was direct and devastating to them, and it would give another great authority over them, as Ilmarinen assumed. There is only one record of such a direct moral humiliation inflicted upon a Power of the Ice, and that was, strangely enough, by a human.

OF MUSIC

Music, in one form or another, plays a great part in the stories of Gille, and of many others in the Chronicles, because it was so important in the lives of the peoples of that age. Much of it was what we would call folk music, the direct expression and entertainment of people for themselves and their neighbours. But in the high cultures of that time – ancient Kerys, its offshoot the realm of Morvan, crushed by the Ice, and the refugee lands of Nordeney and Ker Bryhaine – it became highly sophisticated. At the time of these events everyone, at every social level, was expected to have some interest in music, even lords and ladies, soldiers and men of affairs. In both Nordeney and Ker Bryhaine, whether at the farmhand's bench or the tables of great lords, the man or woman who could not at least sing a song was considered deficient, and those who could play and sing even reasonably well were esteemed. They used, on the whole, very similar forms of music and instruments, part of their common heritage; but in rather different ways.

And both there and in other cultures of the time music could take on a still greater significance, more mysterious and more potent, and often darker.

Of Music in Nordeney

In the North, music remained largely a personal thing. Singing was the entertainment of the ordinary man, from worksongs in the fields and at sea to the lively country dances enjoyed by people of every level, especially at fairs and festivals. Some of these were fiercely athletic, contests of skill and energy in which both men and women competed at tricks like whirling one another off the ground, kicking rafters, leaping fires or hopping and squatting in the manner we associate with Russia. The music would be provided by singers or a couple of simple instruments. Northern songs tended to be strong and rhythmical, reflecting the vigour of their folk origins.

Instruments were rarely used to accompany solo singing, except for declamatory strokes in ballads; other voices might supply a backing or chorus of 'mouth music', like Gaelic *puirt'a beul*, for a solo narrator. It seems they might also mime the action of a ballad, swaying with the waves of a sea or whirling sword and spear. Some singers would even act out individual roles and characters, for example in dialogue ballads. Ballads were sometimes also sung competitively, by two singers seated at either end of a bench, flinging alternate lines at one another; if one forgot a line, he would often invent one to toss back, and the best ones would be remembered and incorporated.

A prosperous village might maintain a couple of semi-professional players, but almost always they held other jobs, or were too old for other work. There were also strolling musicians, but in the country these, like player companies and other entertainments, were fairly rare. Many came from the South, and so disappeared in time of strife.

As in many societies, from China to Renaissance Italy or Elizabethan England, music was considered as essential an accomplishment as reading and writing in more urban and sophisticated circles. Any man or woman with the least pretence to education was supposed to know songs and be able to play an instrument, at least a little. Smiths, the best-educated class in the land, were expected to pick up some essentials of music, and not only because it served them in their labours. Mastersmiths were expected to achieve a high level, and those who couldn't – it seems Olvar was one – were thought to be inferior in craft generally and better suited to less skilful tasks; which was unfair, but often true. People would play together in informal groups for their own pleasure, but seldom in anything resembling a band or orchestra. Choral singing was more popular, and often, it seems, very complex, like madrigals or West African chants.

In part this was because there was so little organised entertainment. In the towns professional musicians were more common, but these were generally like the medieval *jongleurs*, minstrels with other skills, from tumbling to conjuring or acting, often in the semi-religious dramas of high festivals. They were in demand for larger formal celebrations like Guild banquets, and weddings, and only performed regularly in the wealthier private houses and inns, on one or two nights a week, perhaps. It was just as usual, therefore, for guests in an inn or eating-house to entertain the others, as Gille did, usually with no more reward than applause or a drink on the house. Such performers would become locally well known, though, which made it useful advertising for tradesmen. Gille was considered skilful but not exceptional, until his return from his adventures, which he always said put the music into his hands; but more probably they simply drew out what was there already.

The music played by the educated classes was very often the same mix of ballads and songs as the ordinary people, for there was no great social gulf between them; but the ballads had generally more historical interest, the songs were more consciously poetic, and subtler erotic allusion took the place of bawdry. Their dances also tended to be more formal versions of country styles, often substituting skilful footwork for country athletisicm.

The Guilds had their own bodies and styles of music, such as forging songs for the smiths, sea-songs for the mariners, hunting choruses for the foresters, and songs in praise of the Powers who were their patrons, as near as the North came to hymns; these would often be sung in chorus at Guild dinners.

Towns also maintained musicians, and sometimes too the wealthier Guilds. These, though, would be semi-military, often bodies of trumpeters and drummers backed up with other instruments such as pipes and woodwind. They would sometimes be part of the town guards, generally marching with them, and would also serve the town as signallers, or simply to attract attention for gatherings and proclamations; but sometimes they would also play for entertainment. Along with the *jongleurs*, they were the nearest equivalent to modern bands. The music they played apparently had a style of its own, vigorous and percussion-heavy, with memorable, highly rhythmic tunes, often more associated with recruiting songs than marches.

Of Music in the Southlands

In Ker Bryhaine the peasantry had their songs and played musical instruments for their own pleasure, but these were little regarded or written down. Music was considered to be a matter understood only by the state and its governing classes, the hereditary lords, the official classes, the military and the merchants. This was more democratic than it suggests, since the lowest clerk or petty functionary was encouraged to extend and cultivate his education, but it left music still a minority interest.

Children would be taught to play and sing, but allowed to neglect it as they grew older, for supposedly more practical concerns. Wealthy households might have beautiful instruments as part of their furnishings, but never play them. Women, especially ladies of fashion, often played, but their incompetence was a standing joke. As in the North, an educated man was expected to have some appreciation of music, but only as a social accomplishment, rarely to play or even sing. That was the job of professionals.

They came largely from the lower classes. Wealthy music-lovers might organise a chorus or band from the most talented peasants on their estate, though this was not always of a modern kind. One or two even raised strange ensembles not unlike the serf bands of feudal Russia, in which each man had an instrument, usually a horn, capable of only one note which he played by rote, individually or in groups according to a conductor's rhythm, to create an effect that is hard to imagine, but was probably something like a vast organ. Such activities often offered an escape for the base-born from the back-breaking labour on the land and the near-serfdom that dominated the South at that time. A talented player might be sent off to the cities for training, or even sponsored through a full education, and this could take him further – into the anonymity of a company of players, or into one of the military bands that accompanied the South's armies and ships.

These played not only the drums and trumpets of the North, but a wide range of instruments to raise morale, ease the burden of marching and entertain their officers; they were often very well trained and educated in military colleges. A few of the best musicians were often recruited from these to serve in city bands, or even as minstrels in great households. Well-educated musicians would frequently mix with their masters on the familiar terms of valued servants. The social divide, nonetheless, remained wide.

Large choruses were also a popular spare-time activity for the lower and middle orders, often sponsored by a wealthier man, such as an employer or superior. They would rehearse and perform either for this pleasure, or on the rare religious festivities in honour of the benign Powers. These were largely massive public celebrations of social solidarity, more than direct worship, and as such were state-sponsored.

Even the actual music varied greatly between social classes. Folk songs and dances not unlike the North's remained popular among the peasantry. This only confirmed the South's opinion of the North as rough and uncultured. In fact, the Northern songs were more polished and imaginative, written down and revised by poets, whereas the Southern ones were generally passed on as purely oral tradition among unlearned men, often losing much of their original meaning.

The upper classes had their own styles of song. Epic ballads on historical subjects were favoured, especially glorifying the family of the lord for whom they were performed, often at appalling length. Other ballads had romantic or even erotic subjects, generally very stylised. Some appear to have romanticised officially unacceptable subjects such as adultery, incest or homosexuality in very veiled terms. Shorter songs on amorous themes were also popular, especially sung as serenades; the custom of serenading admired women under their windows in the dead of night was common, often at great and elaborate expense, with a whole band of musicians. It was pursued even for other men's wives, either to suggest an affair or as an insult to the husband, or simply as a general nuisance, and led to brawls and street duels. This custom is often satirised in Northern plays, though gallants such as Gille occasionally imitated it - generally at their peril. The Northern response to an unwelcome serenade was liable to be a robust shower of water, or worse.

Sothran melodies tended to be slow and declamatory or languishing, to suit the subject, with very broad rhythms. Likewise, upper-class dances tended to be slow and formal, though their intricate exchanges called for considerable skill and elegant deportment, and left plenty of opportunity for flirting and courting, and body contact. Sometimes stylised versions of Northern dances became popular, and sometimes the North adopted a sothran dance with added vigour.

Of Musical Instruments

As one might expect from their common heritage and musical language, the musical instruments of both North and Southlands were very similar. Most of them were quite close to today's, fitting into the same broad families, so it is easy enough to find equivalents in the narrative. Whether they sounded the same is another matter. Music is not a universal language, and though their notation survives in the Chronicles it is not possible to translate it accurately. What one can say is that the intervals suggest traditional music was mostly pentatonic in style, not unlike Celtic folk song, for example, but that most sophisticated music used a more advanced and flexible scale. It may have sounded not unlike Western music of today, or it may have taken an equally advanced and stylised direction, as with the divergent scales of Chinese music. The most refined instruments were evidently capable of something like chromatic scales.

It may be indicative that the type and style of instruments was highly flexible. The distinction between brass and woodwind was less firm, for example. Similar instruments might be made in a variety of forms, materials and mouthpieces, depending on local fashion and the maker's whim, so that what started as a simple trumpet pattern might evolve with time and distance into a double-reed instrument like a Chinese battle-horn, yet still be called by the same or a similar name. Pipes came in a bewildering variety, from a peasant's cut reed to complex silver forms and endless types of bagpipe, some with multiple chanters. Techniques like the keying of wind instruments and the tuning of drums had been invented, but were used for only the most expensive versions; older and simpler ones existed alongside, from the skin-tipped log drums of sothran peasants to the timpani-like horse-drums of their lord's military band.

String instruments were mostly smaller, more portable varieties, plucked or hammered; bowed instruments, curiously, were fairly rare, and keyboard systems like piano or harpsichord unknown. The

commonest forms were the lyre, the harp, and
varieties of dulcimer. The lyre, resembling the ancient
Anglo-Saxon kind or the Ethiopian *krar*, was a very
common instrument among simple folk, easy to play,
and mostly used to strike a few impressive chords
during a song or poetry declamation. Harps ranged
from the small kind, like a Scottish *clarsach* carried by
minstrels, to the large floor-standing models of rich
households in both North and South, some of which
were fitted with key-change mechanisms not unlike
the Erard mechanism today. Gille is often said to have
invented these, but he may simply have copied them
from Vayde's design. Commonest of all, however, in
both North and South were the stringed soundbox
instruments we call dulcimers (used for the sothran
name). Like today, these came in all shapes and sizes,
but the small portable kinds had the same universal
status as guitars, lutes and the like have had in our
culture; and Gille's own instrument was of this kind.

The illustration shows a typical example. The basic
design was always the same, though the number of
strings, the depth of the body, the size of the soundboard, soundhole, and so on, varied widely. The hooked
end at the top, shaped here like a bird's head, may
have been used to hang the instrument up, or secure it

against the player's arm. (There is a hint that Gille's had a different kind of carving, but what is hard to say.) It was in fact more convenient than a guitar, compact, solid and lacking the delicate outstretched neck, and even ordinary ones were capable of volumes surprising for their size. The disadvantage was the high tension of the shorter strings, which made breaks fairly common. From its looks, and the accounts of its sound, it was very close to traditional North European instruments such as the Russian *gusle* and Finnish *kantele*, their clear silvery sound somewhere between a harp and a guitar, and that is how its name has been translated.

The soundbox might be left as wood, or, as in Gille's, made more resonant with an inserted metal plate, which would also provide a solid anchor for the bridges and tuning pegs. Such models were often richly decorated, because metal inlays in the wooden body could be used to modify the sound still further. The whole would be covered by some solid varnish, usually the maker's well-kept secret.

Some larger models might be played with hammers, like a modern cimbalom; but the smaller ones were plucked or strummed with the fingers, usually of the right hand. This allowed them to be played at various angles, cradled in one arm, flat across the knees or supported against the body by the strap, like a tray. A skilful player would use both hands, 'walking' them across the strings, sometimes using the fingers of the left to deaden strings, and this seems to have been how Gille did it – though how well, to begin with, is not said. At the lower end is a key-change lever like the one Gille found, a carved plate of wood worked by the elbow, which essentially stretched the strings over a secondary bridge, changing their tension and greatly increasing the instrument's range and expressiveness.

Of Music as a Force

It is worth noting that in no culture of the time was music thought of as merely music. It always took on other significances, often strange to us, in their lives and beliefs; and in the unique abilities they wielded.

Of Music and Smithcraft

In the North, as is established throughout the Chronicles, the Mastersmiths made great use of chants and songs in their labours, 'singing' the virtues into their creations as they toiled over them. Many claimed that this was simply a way of concentrating the thought and personality of the maker into the work under his hands, a means of directing the power that had been set within him. That was probably true, as far as it went. But to deeper and more perceptive thinkers among them the music itself took on a greater significance, not just a ritual cantrip but a subcreation in its own right, which became a part of the final more solid creation. Perhaps it even set the paths in which the smith's power coursed within the metal, the veins along which flowed the blazing power that Ilmarinen had given to mankind.

Of War-music in the South

The people of Ker Bryhaine made a point of disbelieving and disparaging any hint of forces beyond the everyday and mundane, and Northern smithcraft most of all. They bought Northern work (they said) for its skill and craftsmanship, and not for any 'mystical' qualities; that was all Northern superstition and salesmanship. Yet they themselves found a strange use for music, and one not wholly untainted by such beliefs, little as they would credit it.

This was in their unique knightly order, to some extent a legacy from Morvan and ancestral Kerys itself, but brought to its highest (and most exclusive) peak in

Ker Bryhaine. Its members were recruited from the young children of the highest orders, the aristocracy and the upper levels of the official classes, and indoctrinated with its extraordinary skills. For the centre of their teaching, they were taught to dance.

This included ordinary formal dances, but also a more secret and startling form, vigorous and demanding martial rituals based on the movements of weaponplay. Even as children they would perform these in full armour, specially made, and increasingly with weapons, sometimes sharp and dangerous. Injuries were not rare. Throughout their active career they would continue these ritual dances at special gatherings, even when out on campaign, until they entered late middle age, when they would often train the younger men. These gatherings were more than training sessions, more like fraternal and mystical rites to reconfirm brotherhood and mutual dependence. Even deadly enemies would still acknowledge their fraternal bond in these gatherings, though ready enough to slay each other outside them. To ordinary men a fight between two such initiates appeared almost superhuman, more like a slashing conflict of great predatory cats than humans.

From the descriptions of the time this training, more in keeping with the martial arts of legendary northern India than the better-known ones of the Far East, made the knights of Ker Bryhaine as fit and lithe as any professional dancer of today, and probably much stronger. The use of dance seems to have created the startlingly fluent fighting style that marked them out, and may have influenced other factors, such as their preference for mail armour over plate. Had they extended even a part of this training to their common soldiers it would have made their armies devastating; but it was considered to be a knightly mystery of which only the high-born were capable, and surrounded with secrecy, ritual and frightening punishments for prying. Even the music for their dances was secret, played only by older members, and only oral accounts of it have survived; it was apparently stark and hypnotic, fierce drumming and shrilling eerie flutes which no doubt reinforced the frightening aura. More ordinary marches based on it sometimes led men into battle.

Probably this aura was maintained deliberately to overawe the ordinary men and emphasise the might of the rulers, supposedly bestowed by the Powers. They were certainly concerned that if the common man gained any special military ability he might become less docile, or even rebellious in imitation of the less feudal North. More enlightened lords such as the Marchwarden Kunrad - not himself of the order, but with followers who were, such as his admiral Ervalien - would subvert this as far as they dared, and often gained considerable power thereby; but it was not until the return to power of the Kermorvan monarchy, in the desperate times of a thousand years later, that any semblance of knightly training was opened to a wider class of suitable candidates. And even Keryn Kermorvan maintained the inner circle to which he himself belonged, and its secrets.

None of them would ever have admitted that there was anything supernatural about the dancing, or its effects. And yet it did bear more than a passing resemblance to another ritual use of music, and that by their deadliest enemies; and in that outside forces certainly came into play.

Of Music and the Ice

This was the ritual magic of the Aika'iya-wahsa, the Ekwesh. To some extent it was the form of magic common to all the peoples of the Western lands beyond the ocean. Whatever higher culture they had once had, it was now largely tribal, and their higher arts reduced to forms of shamanism. They saw the world as surrounded by a host of largely invisible but highly active forces, both without and within the self, forces which could be tapped and directed. But they relied for their contact with these on visionary priest-figures, at once oracles, counsellors and healers, who would enter this other realm through the medium of trance and concentration; and these were generally invoked by music and dance, often with the aid of images, costumes and masks.

It appears, from such fragmentary tales as have come down to us, that this was no mere superstition. The tribal shamans were legendary figures, regarded with something of the same awe as the folk of Nordeney regarded their smiths. Like the smiths, even the least of them could help maintain prosperity and health, while the more powerful could perform extraordinary and often heroic deeds. It may well be that the power within them was much the same, the gift of Ilmarinen and his fellow Powers, for the descendants of great shamans often became great smiths in Nordeney.

But among those peoples who fell under the spell of the Ice, and were bred and schooled and turned by its rulers against their own kin, this benign shamanry took on another and deeply sinister form. It became the medium by which the warriors of the Ice took communion with their inhuman lords, and were themselves indoctrinated with the inhuman savagery which characterised their culture. For the ordinary warrior it would usually take place *en masse*, at gigantic festivals filled with martial and savage ritual, in which the warriors would dance and chant themselves into frenzy and exhaustion, punctuated with participation in carefully contrived and systematic acts of torture, human sacrifice and ritual cannibalism. This was intended both to set them apart from ordinary humanity and to bond them all the more strongly to one another. Smaller rites would be held to celebrate a success or purge a defeat.

The elite, however - the chieftains and shamans and senior warriors - would have rites of their own, extended chants and dances which became tests of vicious asceticism often involving flagellation, self-mutilation and similar practices. The shadowy Ice cult that infiltrated Ker Bryhaine also pursued these, with the object of both venerating the majesty of the Ice and tapping its strength. These were all kept secret even from the rank and file of the Ekwesh, save for the battle-rites which are many times recorded in the

Chronicles, when costumed fanatics danced in the vanguard of an army or on the flat prows of ships, risking the first arrow or spear to call upon their force's totem spirits. This was no mere morale exercise; they could, with good fortune, bend weather and winds to their advantage, and many other natural powers. Some renegade smiths, such as the Mastersmith Mylio, also became adept in such shamanry, and were often among the most powerful of all. Their music was frequently only that of the drum or the squalling reed and bone flutes and whistles, for the Ekwesh were allowed little pleasure in anything more advanced; but its resemblance to the drumming of the Ker Bryhaine warrior cult was remarked upon at times, and it is known that some of its knights were among the leading Ice-worshippers.

OF THE SEA

In these tales the Chronicles include a wealth of detail, relevant and irrelevant, about various aspects of the sea. Most significant is what they reveal about the chain of islands that was the refugees' first landfall and the central stage for their rescue.

Of the Islands

The chain of islands appears to have had at that time no name. It is mentioned elsewhere in the Chronicles, but only in casual sightings by seafarers. Their charts gave it names enough to show that the tale was well known, though the isles are never described in great detail. Northern names included Njvatneyjar (probably a reference to the lack of water), Hjaleyar (refuge or healing), and Saithanneyjar, which is self-explanatory. The tall volcanic island was apparently known as Gillejokke, which meant Gille's Peak or Volcano, but had a definite double meaning. Sothrans sometimes used these names, but also had their own: Bryelainnin; this means something like Isles of Freedom. The original word was highly charged for them, the same as in the name of their own city-state Ker Bryhaine, rather as 'Liberty' once was to Americans.

At that time the oceans, usurped by the Ice, were shallower and narrower, making distances hard to define. Nonetheless, all these references confirm the position of the islands in relation to the coast as it then was, at least eight days to a fortnight's sailing; but there are no islands at all in that region today, or anywhere near. This is no reason not to accept their authenticity. Two factors account for this: the first, their strongly volcanic origin, the second, the great rise in sea-level that has since taken place.

Their descriptions are reminiscent of cratered islands such as Thera in the Mediterranean, or the steep volcanic cones near the Andamans – one of which is evocatively named Narcandam, translatable as 'The Mouth of Hell'. The Saithanneyjar are not, like many volcanoes, right on the edge of a tectonic plate; but they are not far away from one of the most active ones, whose subduction gave rise to the Shield Range mountains on Brasayhal's west coast, its defence against the Ice. In such regions volcanic islands often arise due to activity along stressed areas in the plate, like rifts running back from its margin, especially when one has passed over the fiercely active area of the underlying mantle known as a plume. Beginning as submarine seamounts, their lava outflow, cooling in the ocean, swiftly builds them up into steep peaks, either of basalt or the mineral-rich andesite. Some would close off their particular vent and render it dormant, perhaps increasing the pressure in others, so that they remained open and volcanic, with wide craters and caldera.

This would not prevent them being as fertile as they are described. Volcanic stone and dust is mineral-heavy, and builds up into rich soils surprisingly quickly. Plants and animals establish themselves swiftly, provided there is adequate rainfall, not unlikely in such a region. After the devastating explosion of Krakatau in 1883 the ecosystem reasserted itself within only a couple of years. The Andaman cones, though very active and unstable, are thickly forested; and the Hawaiian islands, probably the nearest isles of this type still surviving, are proverbially rich.

From the description of the crater and the volcanic displays which bedevilled the rescuing fleet it seems that the Saithanneyjar were indeed very active, and that may have been their downfall. It is not hard to imagine one of the geologically frequent earthquakes or other seismic disturbances elsewhere along the margin shaking down the loosely constructed volcanic slopes, and unleashing yet more lava, this time spreading laterally instead of vertically – the more so, as the melting of the Great Ice raised sea-levels that could pour explosively into the new crater. What had been peaks would become a minor ridge, slipping once again below the ocean surface. It is not unlikely, therefore, that the Saithanneyjar were overtaken by eruption, and at last covered by the returning ocean meltwaters as the dominion of the Ice came to its end – for the present. There are several areas of raised seabed and seismic or volcanic activity which could be their remains.

Ships

Designs and patterns of ships were in general similar to those in use of Elof's day, though often smaller and simpler. The square rig, with one or more masts and only simple secondary sails, was almost universal. The huge warships of the South, impressive as they appeared, were relatively slow and ungainly fighting platforms, at their best in a line of war formation such as is described. Northern merchantmen like *Rannvi* and *Orrin* were in fact more seaworthy designs, beamy and stable, although relatively crude in some facilities and equipment, such as unassisted tiller steering. Tanle's ship, it seems, was either Northern-built, or a copy with improved comforts, which would certainly be worthy of his shrewdness.

The longships of the Ekwesh peoples, though much cruder, appear to have changed hardly at all over the same period, save in size. This may partly have been the result of the defeat they suffered, discouraging them from too much interest in the sea; but it is also a testimony to how little the Ice was ready to let its thralls develop and grow. In the thousand years that followed, the lines changed very little, except that larger versions were built - probably to match the great sothran warships, and render them less vulnerable to ramming, though also less swift and lithe. The hull design was the same, except that more decking was added, and the fore and after platforms became more like railed 'castles'; but even so these ships still relied on paddles rather than true oars, a single squaresail, heavy and poorly stiffened, and steered with an oar instead of a true rudder. Lighter versions, for small-scale raiding, reflected these changes, but otherwise remained much the same.

Even so, however, the power of these ships is not to be underestimated. Like Viking longships, they were essentially developed from war canoes, designed to deliver an overwhelming force of men to another ship as swiftly as possible. Comfort and safety were secondary considerations. As such, their sheer speed and manoeuvrability at close quarters often outweighed their primitive qualities. Their very lightness and flexibility made them conform to the sea rather than fight it, and in skilled hands they could handle superbly; as witness the chase they gave to two larger vessels with more complex and adaptable rigs. Some even carried secondary skills like true sailing canoes, light and swift, for even faster scouting and pursuit; and it was one of these that the old chieftains salvaged to make their terrible voyage.

About the ships of the fugitives nothing much is known, save the wrecked hulks that Gille and Olvar saw. They appear to have been big and solid, felled from some of the last great forests along the shores, but very crude. One tale has it that their design came from an oracle, a shaman who spoke with the powers; another, that it was seen on a coin or fragment of

bas-relief. Certainly they were not of the canoe type
one might have expected; their hulls were deep and
beamy, founded on massive keel timbers, and sides
built in clinker fashion (also called lapstrake) with over-
lapping planking, a grossly friction-dragging design for
larger ships. The planks were actually sewn with wires,
sinews and other tough fibres, caulked with bark fibre
and gluey pitch; and they seem to have been much
thicker than they needed to be, and hard to bend. This
made the ships heavy and low-riding, but also rather
beamy and stable, and sheer weight served them well
against the lighter hunters' vessels, though they were
much less manoeuvrable.

Their rigs varied, but squaresails were the
commonest, with others adapted from small fishing
craft, possibly lugsails or lateens; sails were made of
anything from fabric to reed matting. One or two were
said to have used wooden sails, when that ran out -
which might mean beaten bark, or even strips of wood
like a slatted blind. Probably they were not very
manoeuvrable, but that also may have been as well in
the hands of not very skilled sailors, more used to
small fishing craft.

How they navigated is not certain. Both Nordeney
and Ker Bryhaine had compasses of some sort, but
used these in conjunction with instruments of smithcraft such as direction bracelets and devices for star-
and sun-reckoning. The Ekwesh seem to have known
the use of lodestones, but not as complete compasses,
and they used cruder star observations. On the whole
they were coastal sailors, preferring to stay within
sight of shore and next to helpless in fog. Probably the
fugitives were much the same; they certainly had a
legendary star-reckoning of some kind to follow, but
little more.

The courage it took to embark in such uncertain
vessels, and the privations and miseries of an ill-
supplied and poorly guided voyage, can only be
imagined.

Of the Golden Fishes

One other maritime matter, dwelt on at some length by the Chronicles, was the shipwreck from which Gille retrieved his 'fishes'. He seems to have taken some trouble to identify this in later years, in case, it was said, people were suffering for lack of the money that had helped him. This, as it turned out, was also a ship of fugitives, caught up in one of the many power struggles that bedevilled the Southlands. A peripheral cousin of the former royal family, the Kermorvans, had attempted to set up an independent dukedom centred on the port city of Bryhannec, then growing in prosperity and power. Well removed from the succession, he had little legal or moral right. What support he attracted was chiefly due to his charm and apparent courage, and popular discontent with the government of the Syndics after the abortive wars with the North. He proved a petulant and unpredictable governor, however, and no military genius. The Syndics put down his supporters, and then marched their army on Bryhannec, cleverly placing another and more temperate Kermorvan in command. The usurper deserted his followers, plundered exchequer, treasury and mint, and fled northwards in a warship with his close confederates and their families, and few proper seamen. What welcome they would have found is uncertain; but they perished within sight of harbour. Tidings of their fate seem never to have reached the South; but evidently Saithana knew.

Sea Life

Gille's poor seamanship did not prevent him being fairly familiar with the creatures of the sea. Sea life was familiar and written and talked about, especially in a port such as Saldenborg. Most of what he and Olvar saw was well observed, and can readily be identified from the Chronicle's descriptions; but one or two cannot. Some can be identified with the great sea creatures described in other books of the Chronicles. Others suggest the more primitive species which the

Powers are known to have preserved in their own service – the serpentine and armoured whales which Elof was also to encounter, for example, probably of the zeuglodontid line; and the huge deep-sea sharks. The monstrous but harmless whale shark is clearly identifiable; but there are others of a size not known today. These may have been of the species *Carcharodon*, today's Great White Shark, but of a larger variety, as much as twice the maximum length of around twenty feet. This creature is known to have existed around this period, and something of the kind was recorded in other episodes of the Chronicles, including Elof's. Perhaps fortunately, they are known to us only by fossil teeth and jawbone fragments, indicating a mouth a man could sit in, however briefly. If any have been discovered alive, the discoverers have not returned to tell anyone about it.

The same could be said of the creatures that attacked the raft survivors, and took part in the devastation of the fleet. These seem to have been varieties of giant squid, probably the most familiar genus, *Architeuthis*. Enormous as they sound, they are not incompatible with the largest specimens washed ashore, in 19th-century Newfoundland and New Zealand, for example. However, recent research suggests that smaller *Architeuthidae* are relatively weak in the arms; so it may be that the larger specimens are more robust, or that there is another giant genus, which is by no means impossible. The frightening pattern of night attack on swimmers matches the experience of Pacific shipwrecks during World War II. The colour changes observed, in the battle especially, might also point to some varieties of octopus.

One curious reference in the original text has been preserved without explanation: the appearance of human forms Gille saw during his ascent. Given his condition and state of mind these might be ignored as hallucinations, if they did not relate both to the battle account, and curiously to other less certain tales to be found in the Chronicles. If so, the sea was a stranger place during the dominion of the Ice than even Gille ever guessed; and may be still.

THE WINTER OF THE WORLD SERIES

Michael Scott Rohan

The chronicles of The Winter of the World
echo down the ages in half-remembered myth
and song – tales of the mysterious powers of the
Mastersmiths, of the forging of great weapons,
of the subterranean kingdoms of the duergar, of
Gods who walked abroad, and of the Powers
that struggled endlessly for dominion.

Praise for The Winter of the World:

'An exciting adventure ... Rohan creates a
haunting sense of mythology rather than
fantasy ... a gifted writer of stories and pages
turn as if by magic'
Jean M. Auel

'A wonderful story'
Raymond E. Feist

'An outstanding piece of fantasy fiction'
Andre Norton

'A very good and very powerful writer'
Anne McCaffrey

The Winter of the World series
THE ANVIL OF ICE
THE FORGE IN THE FOREST
THE HAMMER OF THE SUN
THE CASTLE OF THE WINDS

Available from Orbit

THE NAVIGATOR KINGS TRILOGY

Garry Kilworth

Book I: THE ROOF OF VOYAGING
Book II: THE PRINCELY FLOWER
Book III: LAND-OF-MISTS

Delighting in the rich and colourful detail and myth of Polynesian life, The Navigator Kings trilogy is a landmark in fantasy fiction.

Praise for The Navigator Kings:

'Kilworth's evocation of Polynesian culture is a triumph of both research and storytelling. It's a sunny book, full of azure skies, white sands, clear seas and vividly depicted characters who you genuinely care about'
SFX

'Fascinating ... Kilworth is a skilled storyteller'
Starburst

'A rich, expansive read'
Interzone

Orbit titles available by post:

❏	The Anvil of Ice	Michael Scott Rohan	£6.99
❏	The Forge in the Forest	Michael Scott Rohan	£6.99
❏	The Hammer of the Sun	Michael Scott Rohan	£6.99
❏	The Castle of the Winds	Michael Scott Rohan	£6.99
❏	The Roof of Voyaging	Garry Kilworth	£6.99
❏	The Princely Flower	Garry Kilworth	£5.99
❏	Land-of-Mists	Garry Kilworth	£6.99

The prices shown above are correct at time of going to press. However, the publishers reserve the right to increase prices on covers from those previously advertised, without further notice.

ORBIT

ORBIT BOOKS
Cash Sales Department, P.O. Box 11, Falmouth, Cornwall, TR10 9EN
Tel +44 (0) 1326 372400, Fax: +44 (0) 1326 374888
Email: books@barni.avel.co.uk

POST AND PACKING:
Payments can be made as follows: cheque, postal order (payable to Orbit Books) or by credit cards. Do not send cash or currency.

U.K. orders under £10	£1.50
U.K. orders over £10	**FREE OF CHARGE**
E.C. & Overseas	25% of order value

Name (Block letters) ....

Address ....

....

Post/zip code: ....

☐ Please keep me in touch with future Orbit publications

☐ I enclose my remittance £ ....

☐ I wish to pay by Visa/Access/Mastercard/Eurocard

Card Expiry Date
